COMPOSING MYSELF

COMPOSING MYSELF

ANDRZEJ PANUFNIK

METHUEN LONDON

First published in Great Britain in 1987
by Methuen London Ltd
11 New Fetter Lane, London EC4P 4EE

Copyright © 1987 Andrzej Panufnik

Made and printed in Great Britain
by Redwood Burn Ltd, Trowbridge, Wiltshire

British Library Cataloguing in Publication Data
Panufnik, Andrzej
    Composing myself.
    1. Panufnik, Andrzej   2. Composers—
    Poland—Biography
    I. Title
    780'.92'4   ML410.P1615

ISBN 0-413-58880-7

TO MY MOST BELOVED TRIO:
CAMILLA, ROXANNA AND JEREMY

CONTENTS

LIST OF ILLUSTRATIONS

The majority of these photographs come from the personal archive of the author and his wife; many of them were smuggled out of Poland after the author's escape in 1954, representing a remarkable story of survival.

8a.   A concert in the presence of Mao Tse Tung.

8b.   Meeting Chairman Mao and Premier Chou En Lai.

between pages 308 and 309

1954–1984 (England)

9a. and 9b.   Delivering statements for Radio Free Europe and the BBC.

9c.   My first appearance at the Royal Festival Hall with the Philharmonia Orchestra.

9d.   My second London concert: at the Royal Albert Hall with the London Symphony Orchestra.

10.   Celebrating my engagement to Camilla Jessel.

11a.   After our wedding at Caxton Hall.

11b.   Our reception at the Dorchester Hotel.

11c   Decorating our house.

11d.   Nadia Boulanger in my studio.

12a.   Leopold Stokowski with his goddaughter, Roxanna.

12b.   Leopold Stokowski helping in the garden.

12c.   Leopold Stokowski recording *Universal Prayer*.

13a.   Rehearsing *Sinfonia di Sfere*.

13b.   Rehearsing our children at home for the recording of *Thames Pageant*.

14a.   Rehearsing my Violin Concerto with Yehudi Menuhin.

14b.   LSO Chairman Anthony Camden and Leader Michael Davis rehearsing *Concerto Festivo*.

14c.   Discussing my *Concertino* with André Previn.

15a.   Rehearsals for the première of *Sinfonia Votiva*.

15b.   With Sir Georg Solti between his rehearsals of *Sinfonia Sacra*.

16a.   Recording *Metasinfonia* with the London Symphony Orchestra at the Royal Albert Hall.

16b.   After my seventieth birthday concert with the London Symphony Orchestra at the Barbican, with Camilla, Roxanna and Jeremy.

ACKNOWLEDGEMENTS

Unlike my great compatriot Joseph Conrad, I never felt any inclination towards literary activity, and my English, even after living more than thirty years in Britain, is still rather precarious.

However, I was strongly persuaded (even bullied) by friends to write this autobiography. Through their questions, I found myself provoked to go back (a somewhat painful experience) over the chain of dramatic incidents which provided a stormy background to the peace of which I had always dreamt as a composer. I am grateful to these friends for their kindly curiosity, for sparking me off and giving me the impetus to carry through my task, spurring me on to write details about my personal life and my creative work, which, without their insistence, I would probably have kept to myself for ever.

My thanks go especially to our family friend, Jenny Pearson, who used to bicycle twice a week from Kew to Twickenham in order to work with me on the newly scrawled pages of my unpolished (all-too-Polished!) English. Through her unbelievable patience, determination and the magic she performed on my grammar and spelling, as well as her splendid typing, my scribble became a manuscript. My warm thanks also to others who have given me practical advice and help; David Drew, Antony Hopkins, Bernard Jacobson, Janis Susskind and my editor Christopher Falkus. Above all, of course, my deepest gratitude goes to my wife Camilla. Without her tireless assistance, and her gentle encouragement, I would never have kept away from my composition long enough to complete this book.

I

ARRANGED BY VIOLIN

At the beginning of this century there lived in Warsaw a young man, an engineer by profession, who earned his living as a specialist in hydro-technology, but whose real passion was the construction of violins.

His days were passed in a city office where he concerned himself with the sinking of wells and the drainage of marshes; but his long and sleepless nights were spent in obsessive efforts to unravel the secrets of the seventeenth-century Italian masters in the craft of violin-making. The studio where he lived and worked was filled with all manner of oddly shaped metal implements and curious small curved saws, as well as sketches, mathematical diagrams, chemical formulae, pieces of carefully chosen mature wood, instruments in various stages of construction, and, in due course, some beautiful finished violins of his own design.

He was a lean, rather aristocratic-looking man of medium height with chestnut hair and a trim moustache, his small grey eyes, somewhat short-sighted, often half-hidden behind a pair of pince-nez. He dressed smartly, with infinite care over the neatness of his appearance, and was thought to be handsome. Yet he avoided social life, never making any contact with his neighbours. As they passed his door, mystified by the strange smells of lacquer and glue, hearing the sound of the saw, seeing his lights burning all night, they cast increasingly suspicious glances in his direction — concluding, maybe, that he was involved in some sort of medieval alchemy.

One morning he was surprised by a visit from an elegant

middle-aged woman, who had been given his address by a famous Warsaw teacher of the violin, Professor Isador Lotto. She had heard that he constructed excellent violins and wondered if he would consider letting her purchase one for her daughter.

The young man was flattered to discover that his instruments were becoming known; but at the same time he was almost hurt that anyone should imagine that his interest was commercial. He answered that he was not a salesman, that he was engaged in serious scientific research, and that he constructed his models for that purpose alone.

However, his visitor was determined, gently replying, 'My daughter is a very talented violinist; she is Professor Lotto's favourite pupil. She plays all the classical concertos from memory. And she desperately needs a good instrument.' Pausing for a few moments, she had an inspiration: 'Why don't you bring one of your instruments along to Professor Lotto's home? Then my daughter could play it and you would hear how it sounds. Then you might reconsider . . .'

A week later at Professor Lotto's home, the young man was introduced to the violinist, a shapely young woman with fair hair, light brown eyes and a fair, delicate skin. Her manner was extremely reserved — a quality which strangers sometimes mistook for arrogance but which the young man found rather interesting. He handed over his instrument for her to play. Professor Lotto sat at the piano and they started to perform the Mendelssohn Violin Concerto.

The violin-maker was overwhelmed, not only by the entrancing appearance of the young performer, but by her masterly performance, and the exquisite warmth of tone she produced from his precious violin, which made his many years of dedicated work seem even more worthwhile. When the concerto was over, he was at a loss for words to express his admiration. Professor Lotto expansively congratulated him on the quality of his craftmanship, but the violinist, maintaining her reserve, was almost silent.

Thereafter, the young man's way of life became noticeably less austere. He received and gladly accepted invitations to the home of the violinist and her mother. Being very proud and very Polish in his attitude, he was never persuaded to sell the violin. But, when the attraction between him and the beautiful violinist resulted in their betrothal, he gave it to her as a symbol of his attachment even more pertinent than a ring. They were married shortly afterwards at the Monastery of Jasna Góra in southern Poland, under the famous Icon of the Black Madonna.

The scientist who made violins was my father and the beautiful violinist my mother. Being fanciful, one could say that my birth was the result of a marriage arranged by a violin! The charming, elegant woman who started this chain of events was my most beloved grandmother, my 'guardian angel', to whom I owed most of the happiness and inspiration of my otherwise lonely and difficult childhood.

My parents were not very young when they married, especially by the standards of 1909. My father at 44 would have been looked upon as an old bachelor, my mother at 27 considered a confirmed spinster. Before they met, they had each taken a firm decision against marriage. My father, despite his liking for good-looking women, had been determined that nothing so distracting should interfere with his commitment to his instruments. My mother, praying eventually to be accepted to study in Berlin with the world-famous teacher, Carl Flesch, had similarly vowed that she would avoid family ties so that music could be her whole life. By yielding to their mutual attraction, both my parents committed themselves to sacrifices which would inevitably put a marriage (and their children) under great stress. Nevertheless it was a true love-match.

For their honeymoon, my father took his bride into the wilds of Siberia, not for the sake of the wide open spaces, but because he had been engaged by the Tsarist Government to survey land and organise the digging of wells. My newly married parents travelled a long way beyond the Volga river across an empty land with almost no population, no roads or trees and only rare clumps of bushes. It was like being in the desert, with green grass instead of sand. They stayed in a remote village inhabited by uneducated, extremely unpredictable people. Every morning, my father would disappear to carry out his surveys, leaving my mother to spend her days alarmingly alone, in dread of bandits or looters. To keep her boredom and fear at bay, she played her violin continuously; and the strains of Bach, Beethoven, Mozart and Mendelssohn soared majestically over the empty Steppes.

It was an unusual start to a marriage. They comforted them selves with the belief that they would save a large sum of money to bring back to Warsaw. But my mother quickly be- came pregnant, and within eight months they were home for the birth of my brother, whom they called Mirek (short for Mirosław).

My father instantly turned back to his consuming passion, eventually succeeding in constructing with his own hands two quartets of string instruments: the first set, the 'Antica' model, was based on old Italian instruments and the second, the 'Polonia' model, was his own original design. He also began to write scientific books describing his techniques.

This peaceful interlude ended abruptly with the outbreak of the First World War in August 1914. The fighting grew in- creasingly intense and zeppelins flew threateningly over War- saw. In these difficult circumstances, on 24 September my mother gave birth to a rather frail, dark-haired, dark-eyed boy: I was said to look like a scrawny gypsy – a total contrast to the energetic, lion-like five-year old Mirek, who was fair-skinned, yellow-haired, with pale blue eyes. My father was not able to stay at home to see me grow through babyhood.

Poland at that time was partitioned between the Russian, Prussian and Austro-Hungarian Empires, and Polish men were drafted into the armies of whichever sector they belonged to, resulting tragically in Poles being forced to fight and kill other Poles. Warsaw was under the rule of the Tsar, and all too soon my father was conscripted as a captain in the Russian army. When he said goodbye to us he had no idea, and nor had my mother, that several years would pass before he could come home again. He kept up his spirits with the belief that the war would soon be over. He survived all manner of dangers at the Front; most memorably, he escaped death by a matter of inches when German planes dropped showers of heavy coiled spears from the air on to his division as they were galloping their horses into action. Whenever possible he wrote to my mother, and he sent us money regularly via the neutral city of Stockholm. However, this arrangement came to an abrupt end in 1917 with the Russian Revolution, after which chaos ensued.

With no more money arriving, we were almost destitute. My mother was forced to sell her valuable inheritance from her grandfather, a well-sited piece of building land in Warsaw for which she received only a pittance from a grasping war-time speculator. Even with money, essential items such as bread, milk and meat had disappeared from the market-place. Saccharine was used instead of sugar; my earliest childhood memory remains my ecstasy at the way a saccharine tablet would hiss as I dropped it into a cup of tea.

When the war ended in 1918, Poland was declared an independent country. However, my father still could not come home. He was trapped in a no-man's land by a reign of lawless terror. In the post-revolutionary turmoil, Russian soldiers, returning tired and demoralised from the War, were committing every sort of atrocity – looting, robbing, raping – killing anyone who got in their way. Death was meted out also by Bolsheviks, who were determined to exterminate the entire intelligentsia: they forced even the poorest-looking people to show their hands, and smooth skin was a capital crime.

Gradually my father was able to make his way into Poland, collecting as he went useful goods left behind by Russian soldiers, such as motor bikes and military weapons, which he patriotically arranged to be transported home for the newly created Polish army. He finally reached Warsaw just after the Christmas of 1919.

Trotting into my mother's room early one morning, I saw a man in her bed. 'Who's that horrible creature?' I asked indignantly. My mother was laughing. 'It's not a creature. It's your father! Your father's come home!'

I was not at all charmed at this news. I stared angrily at the sleeping form, and at the frayed army jacket hung over the chair at the end of the bed.

When the stranger awoke, he made a brief attempt at conversation with me. I looked silently back at the thin, tired face, the worried smile beneath the carefully cut moustache. Sensing my resentment, he fetched a square metallic box full of black cherry jam. Mirek and I attacked this rare luxury with our bare hands. I still remember with indescribable pleasure the sensation of submerging my whole fists into the sticky mass and extracting the heavenly cherries. This gesture of my father's melted the ice, though not completely.

Over the long, grim years of the war, my father's obsession had not faded: he had been dreaming up a patriotic scheme to revitalise the Polish tradition of violin construction, making fullest use of the spruce, silver fir and maple trees of the Polish forests and harnessing the natural talent of Polish craftsmen. He was determined that Poland should no longer depend on imported instruments from Germany or Czechoslavakia which he looked upon as 'trashy cigar boxes'. He resolved to start a factory and not only to supply Poland but to export all over the world. He poured all his savings and his energy into equipping the workshops.

The opening of my father's new enterprise in 1921 was memorable for me because I experienced my first ride in a car. Driven by a supercilious chauffeur in a peaked cap, the brief journey was a deeply sensuous experience: the glistening brass and touch and smell of the leather seated excited me far more than the imposing new buildings with the name PANUFNIK in huge *bas-relief* letters over the roof. Impatiently I watched the priest blessing the factory with a sprinkling of holy water. Momentarily diverted, I witnessed the greatest Polish violinist of the day, Stanisław Barcewicz, his nose purple from long-term abuse of the bottle, playing marvellously the Bach *Chaconne* and other works on one of my father's instruments. (The instrument was not yet finished, having been left unvarnished – a gimmick on my father's part to show the outstanding quality of the sound even before the enhancement of tone through final varnishing.) After the recital, we had to take refreshments, followed by an intolerably lengthy session posing for a formal photograph. The delay was unbearable. All I wanted was to get back into the magnificent limousine.

Regrettably the car-ride was extremely short; as was the life of my father's factory. The company lacked essential working capital, and the financial support pledged by state organisations never materialised. In less than a year, most humiliatingly for my father, the huge letters of PANUFNIK were dismantled and his factory was taken over by a toy manufacturer.

All the money my father had managed to salvage was now invested either in shares or in antiques. Because of Poland's deteriorating financial situation, the shares soon became worthless. The antiques were not much more profitable, and they made our life a misery. Our apartment became ridiculously cluttered. Not only did pictures cover the walls from the ceiling right down to the floor so that the flowery wallpaper could scarcely peep through, but we could hardly move between the ornate tables, the sofas and the clusters of chairs, some with fragile silk covers, upon which Mirek and I were forbidden to sit. Silver salvers lay on hefty mahogany chests. Porcelain figurines, plates, jugs and crystal vases were balanced on every available surface, so that we had to keep our elbows close to our sides to avoid knocking them flying. Our ears were assailed by a dozen or more old clocks, all of them striking more or less upon the hour, but never quite together, so that they sounded as if they were having a frenzied conversation. Once the floor space was fully occupied, my father started hoarding smaller items such as watches and musical boxes. I used to make Mirek laugh saying that, collecting so much rubbish, our father was a dustman.

He was less good at selling antiques than buying them, and we were soon in dire financial straits. He had to take a job with the Department of Agriculture in his old profession of engineering. Of course he could not refrain from constructing violins. His life returned to the pattern of his bachelorhood: his days were spent in the office, his evenings, sometimes nights, in the studio.

By then I was about eight years old. I saw almost nothing of my father, and not much more of my mother, who was, as ever, deeply immersed in her music, practising the violin for hours every day, in the evenings turning to improvise on her piano. The domestic ordering of the house bored her, and she did not enjoy social chit-chat with women friends. She must have been deeply frustrated that her playing was confined to the four walls of her home. The question of her becoming a concert performer could never seriously have been considered, even though the supreme quality of her playing would no doubt have won her the highest recognition. This was not just because of her nervous temperament and tendency to stage fright (a problem she might have overcome) but mainly because of the social snobbery directed against musicians (and all the artistic professions) at that time. Any such ambition would have encountered strong family opposition, despite my grandmother's pride in her talent.

In my early years I never consciously listened to my mother's playing, but it was constantly in my ears, a background music, part of the fabric of my life, so that I knew in my head the concertos of Beethoven, Mozart and Brahms as well as Bach, and contemporary Polish music such as Wieniawski and Karłowicz. This music was an intrinsic part of my existence, like cleaning my teeth, eating my meals, even breathing.

When my mother was not practising, she was always deep in a book. If she took me out, it was usually to the private library in a shop near our house, run by a kindly dark-haired Jewish woman who had a beautiful oval face, reminding me of the Madonna of Jasna Góra whose icon hung over my parents' bed.

I would have been deeply lonely but for my angel-grandmother. It was she who took me to kindergarten early each morning, making sure that I had fruit and biscuits in my satchel for 'second breakfast' at eleven o'clock, and collected me again for *obiad*, the main meal of the day, eaten according to the Polish custom around three o'clock in the afternoon. It was she who took me for walks, usually to the nearby park. We almost always sat on the same bench under a huge tree, talking and sometimes playing word-games. When she grew tired she would start to read and expect me to look at my book too. But I was not very interested in children's stories. I preferred my own thoughts and images. I would sink on to the bench beside her, and look up at the shapes of the leaves and the swinging movements of the branches overhead. The changing patterns fascinated me; they were like improvised choreography in a mysterious ritual dance.

Sometimes another small boy would come up and enquire in the formal manner of the day, 'If you please, would the young master like to play with me?' But I never wanted to play. I was totally happy snuggled against my grandmother, watching the trees and clouds.

My grandmother was always lively and entertaining; she read widely in French and German as well as Polish, and was full of worldly knowledge, wisdom and humour. Everyone in the family adored her; even local shopkeepers gave her a special welcome, appreciating her charm, politeness and dignity. Wherever she went, I would want to go with her, to feel the aura of her presence, the kindness and love that emanated from her. My first experience of church was neither because of curiosity on my part, nor pressure by my parents, but because one afternoon I could not bear to leave my grandmother's side. Though my father was privately religious and morally strict, he was not a churchgoer and had told me nothing about Roman Catholicism. Even my grandmother did not think of explaining that first service I attended, and I found it quite puzzling that the priest turned his back on us, talking to himself in an incomprehensible language, from time to time making interesting shapes with his raised arms. But if my grandmother liked it, so did I.

Though in her sixties, she was still beautiful, taking great care over her appearance. Her silver hair was always twisted into a graceful knot on the top of her head, held in place by a tortoise-shell comb, carved with intricate patterns which showed up against the light. Impervious to the changing fashions of the twenties, she dressed quietly and elegantly, always in black. She wore silky black blouses with long sleeves and high necks, long black skirts, black stockings and black shoes. When she went out she wore a black hat and black gloves, even in summer, as though she had imposed upon herself a state of constant mourning. But her expression was extraordinarily sweet and tranquil. She never seemed sad: she was never nervy or irritated, but always serene and composed — though the tragedies of her early life might have made her very bitter.

When she was only eighteen or nineteen, she had married a young merchant, Jan Thonnes, who was half English, half Polish. They had five children in rapid succession, four daughters (of whom my mother was the youngest) and finally a son. All too soon their family life started to deteriorate. Jan Thonnes began to drink heavily, his business declined and finally his alcoholism took over, so that he often stayed out drinking with his cronies and did not come home at night. Soon my grandmother was without enough money to feed the children.

Her father, Antoni Szuster, a widower living on his own, could not endure seeing her suffer. One day he came and removed her and the children to his handsome home in Mokotów. When Jan Thonnes staggered home after a night's drinking and found the family gone, he took a fatal dose of poison.

A second tragedy followed. Her only son, her youngest child, swallowed a prune stone and died shortly afterwards. (The doctors said it had lodged in his appendix.)

Perhaps because of the loss of her son, I was a special comfort to her, and she was the pinion of my life. This is not to say that my parents were totally unconcerned with my upbringing, which sometimes even became a subject for dispute. Whenever my mother emerged from her preoccupation with music or books, she was loving and protective towards me, and was especially understanding when I fussed over my food.

From my earliest days I was discriminating about what I would eat: I expressed intense delight when the food was good and uninhibited disgust when it was not to my taste. Polish cookery encompasses an exquisitely varied range of soups and some wonderful fish and meat dishes; but there are also some nightmarish specialities, including unchewable tripe, a nauseating sugary fruit soup and a shattering concoction made from goose blood. We never experienced delicate lamb, only greasy mutton. My main dread was our cook's pride: fatty pork cutlets and cabbage with chunks of slimy salted bacon-fat oozing all over the potatoes. (The memory instantly makes me feel sick again!)

My gentle mother, knowing how I felt, would ask our servant to prepare something unfatty for me. However, my father, seeing these separate dishes, would criticise my mother for spoiling me.

One day he attacked me too, asking me angrily, 'Why don't you eat the same as everyone else? Look at me: I eat everything . . .'

To which I replied, 'Only pigs eat everything!'

After a moment's silence when it seemed as if a storm was going to break, there was further silence. For once my father failed to think of a reply.

Often in the evenings my mother would sit improvising at the piano. She would try out different keys for her elaborate lines of melody, at the same time instinctively searching out subtle harmonies. On one occasion, my father, listening with Mirek and me through the wall as she worked away at some particularly attractive fragments, expressed his regret that she did not know how to put her compositions on paper for posterity. He resolved to find her a musical scribe.

Eventually he managed to engage a young pianist and composer, a teacher at the Warsaw Conservatoire, whose visits to our house soon assumed great importance to me. As he sat at the table not far from the piano, I would observe him closely, marvelling at the magical way that he could write down the notes on to the manuscript paper by ear, without even looking at my mother's fingers to see what she had played. I was also deeply impressed by his fountain pen, a very early model. Before using it, he had to remove the cap and screw it on to the blunt end of the pen, whereupon the nib miraculously emerged.

Watching him and listening to my mother's improvisations undoubtedly kindled the first vital spark of my desire to become a composer. When no one else was around, I secretly started to sit at the piano and experiment with tunes and chords.

The young professor of music, whose name was Jerzy Lefeld, was thin and tall with long arms and extraordinarily long fingers, which, I knew from shaking hands with him, were invariably icy. A permanent cold caused him to trumpet frequently into an enormous handkerchief, dislodging his small, silver-rimmed spectacles from his finely chiselled nose. His face was noble and quite handsome, his hair dark brown, chopped almost into a crew-cut. He was always polite, extremely formal in speech, and so very shy that Mirek and I wondered how he would ever marry. How would he find the courage to propose? (We were amazed when we heard eventually of his betrothal.)

Lefeld was so outstandingly gentle and kind that I was puzzled one day to hear him arguing loudly with my father. I later discovered that my father had been insisting on paying him for his work, while he adamantly refused to accept money. He may have been reserved, but his will was stronger than my father's; the only way my parents were allowed to reciprocate his help was to invite him frequently to eat at our home. These meals were always particularly good. I called them 'Lefeldish' dinners, and nothing would ever induce me to miss one.

If anyone asked me in those days what profession I expected to follow when I grew up, I would reply without hesitation, 'I want to be a Lefeld!' I found myself dreaming that not only might I too eventually be able to perform the mysterious act of writing down harmonies and melodies by ear, but also that I might write my own music straight from my imagination like a real composer.

Confiding my new ambition to my grandmother, she immediately made a practical suggestion: 'First you will have to learn the piano. I could help you, if you like.' I agreed with the utmost enthusiasm.

Because our efforts would have disturbed my mother's violin practice, it seemed wiser not to attempt the lessons in our flat, so we looked elsewhere for an instrument. My grandmother eventually found one in the home of a haberdasher, at the back of his small shop, which she arranged to rent for three hours a week. The owner, courteous in the extreme, always addressed me as 'Maestro', which I found very flattering as I was eight years old and just a beginner. His pretty seventeen-year-old daughter also made a great fuss of me, and I always rushed to find her on arrival.

At first the lessons did not go well. Perhaps I was disappointed that I could not immediately play the sort of music I had heard at home; or maybe I was just lazy, and my grandmother was too kind to make heavy demands on me. I almost gave up. She had to bribe me with chocolate cigars to keep me going.

Some time after my ninth birthday, I asked my grandmother for a fountain pen like Professor Lefeld's. She understood without questioning. As soon as it was in my hand, I found some manuscript paper and began to write notes on the stave. First I tried copying printed piano music, especially my favourite simple Mozart piece. Then I tried a new improvisation of my own, and, with a tremendous struggle, somehow I managed to notate it.

My first composition, ambitiously named *Sonatina*, was not of course constructed in the classical form: it was just a simple melody in the right hand with a few chords in the left. However, my clumsy beginning fuelled my confidence in my plan to become a composer. Looking with satisfaction at my spidery crotchets and quavers, I was reminded of the old Polish proverb, 'Not only saints can put a broken pot together'.

As I still did not like to disturb my mother by practising the piano at home, I had to find other occupations for my spare time. Our flat was up on the fourth floor, overlooking our tiny courtyard — a square with a circle of scraggy grass in the middle, a few white flowers in summer and a fountain which never worked. This small open space we shared with the numerous occupants of the neighbouring flats, and children were not encouraged to play there; consequently I spent much of my time in the privacy of our small balcony above the courtyard, looking across at the rooftops and chimneys opposite, to the sky beyond, where on my lucky days I could see military aircraft from the nearby airfield performing the most amazing aerobatics.

Flying machines were a great passion with me — at that stage almost more important to me than music. My greatest dream was to have a model aeroplane of my own. I had virtually no toys because my father thought them unnecessary, just as he refused to buy me clothes, always expecting me to put up with my brother's cast-offs. I would ache with embarrassment when other children wore smart new garments and I had none, or when they asked to see my toys and I had nothing to show them.

However, in retrospect, I think this absence of ready-made toys may have acted as a challenge, forcing my mind towards more creative channels. At any rate, I was never bored. I tried to construct my own planes out of household scraps, but then, to my delight, I heard about a small shop with the Swedish name, Slöjd, which sold craft materials including clay, plasticine and balsa wood, which is ideally light, and transparent parchment, perfect for wings. I would spend hours designing my aircraft, and many more hours cutting and gluing. Eventually I managed to make models which could actually fly, whizzed into the air by taut elastic bands.

Often I sat dreaming on our balcony, waiting for more military planes, entranced meanwhile just watching the shapes of the clouds as they drifted by — they seemed to pile upon each other like moving sculptures in myriad variations of grey. Sometimes they would appear to be skittishly hurtling across a perfect blue sky; at other times they would become dark grey, almost black, heralding rain.

Closer at hand, our balcony served me as a school of life: from my vantage point, I learnt a great deal about our neighbours.

Opposite our flat, also on the fourth floor, lived a cavalry colonel with his wife, their servant girl and, the most interesting member of the household, the colonel's batman — a young manservant of peasant origin dressed in soldier's clothing. I only occasionally saw the colonel striding out in his magnificent uniform with a sabre at his side and his metal spurs clinking. The unfortunate batman came into my view far more frequently as he rushed to and from the courtyard, which he did for three extremely pressing reasons: firstly, to use the outside lavatory, as he was not allowed to use the colonel's; secondly to smoke a cigarette, which was also forbidden in the flat; and thirdly, for hours on end, to clean and polish the colonel's riding boots, at least half a dozen pairs of them, until each one reflected his face like a mirror. Polish cavalry officers were by tradition fanatical about the appearance both of their horses and their magnificent selves; it was a kind of madness which ordinary mortals regarded with a mixture of admiration and sardonic humour.

On the floor below the colonel lived a Jewish family. The daughter played the piano constantly, repeating the same Chopin étude over and over again, with her window open, disturbing my poor mother's violin practice. Then one day much rowdier music and song came from the open window: it was the daughter's wedding party, after which we heard no more of the Étude in C sharp minor. I rather missed it.

Below the Jewish family, on the second floor, I could often see a young student actor gesticulating wildly, practising his rôles at the top of his voice, which could be quite frightening. On occasions his histrionics caught me unawares and I thought that a murder must be taking place. He was unsuccessful in his profession, and one day he committed suicide — also unsuccessfully. He was carried off to hospital, returning home after three months a pale and broken man, uncannily silent. Then followed a second tragedy which upset me dreadfully: his mother committed suicide by hanging herself from the lavatory chain — successfully. I cannot remember how the gossip filtered through to me, but I watched as her coffin was marched through our courtyard.

On the first floor opposite lived an elderly bachelor, a retired office clerk, who also spent much of his day thumping a poor old piano. Curiously he too had only one work in his repertoire: the Paderewski Minuet, which he played with great passion and gross insensitivity. I soon began to hate this piece, despite having been taught at school to admire its composer, the famous pianist and premier-elect of independent Poland.

Eventually his piano was silenced: he was evicted from his flat, having failed to pay the rent. Because he had nowhere else to go, he huddled in the courtyard with all his belongings, which seemed mostly to be books. He spent all his days moving these dusty volumes from shelf to shelf, obsessively trying to put them back into their original order, pausing in his task only occasionally to brew a cup of tea on a primus stove. Since he had neither friends nor family, my mother frequently sent our servant down with some food for him. After several weeks, I looked out to find that he and his books, his primus

15

and his piano had disappeared from the courtyard. I never discovered what became of him.

The ground-floor flat opposite us was occupied by the administrator of our building – a man of humble origin, a builder by trade. He always talked down rudely to our caretaker, who was maddened because the administrator's origins were no better than his own. On the frequent occasions that the administrator yelled at him, trying to treat him as a slave, the caretaker would shout back – but in a rather frightened way, in case he made trouble for himself.

A constant stream of visitors to our courtyard provided interest for me throughout the day. The glaziers, carrying bags of putty and large sheets of glass on their backs, made their presence known with a distinctive street cry, so musical that I tried putting it into my improvisations. Jewish rag merchants cried out '*Handel-handel-handel!*' indicating their desire to buy old clothes, which they would carry away, piled staggeringly high in knapsacks on their backs. Gypsy women in brightly coloured dresses would flounce in, aggressively demanding to tell our fortunes. My favourite was the street musician, who would dance grotesquely, at the same time playing his own accompaniment on the mouth organ, working the drum and cymbals with his elbows, the tiny jingling bells on his legs also forming part of his tawdry costume. Enthralled, I would peep out nervously from a doorway, trying to avoid his glance because I had heard that street musicians kidnapped children to teach them their profession and exploit them for money.

When I was ten, though my parents as ever were struggling financially, they decided to send me to the best private academic secondary school (*gimnazjum*) named after its founder, Lorentz. Each day I left home with a satchel on my back, proudly wearing my new uniform: a dark blue suit with two light blue stripes at the points of the collar, and four-cornered dark blue cap encircled by a light blue band with a stiff leather peak, different only in colour to the traditional Polish army cap. The school was in an apartment building, occupying the whole fourth floor. It was always amazingly clean and shiny: the smell of furniture polish still brings back to me those small individual wooden desks and wooden chairs and the memory of the warm, enthusiastic teachers who managed to make even the dreariest subjects fascinating.

One of the teachers, Father Kaim, was the priest who had blessed my father's ill-starred factory at its opening. I recognised him because of his passion for cigars; he always smoked one after he had taken Sunday Mass at our local church, which all the Lorentz pupils were expected to attend. Church, in our opinion, was a boring occupation, especially the sermon, which we often tried to avoid by slipping out (usually without success). But after Mass, the school cunningly used to arrange a film show for us: comedies such as Laurel and Hardy, Charlie Chaplin or Buster Keaton, all of which I adored. As they were silent films, the older boys often accompanied them at the piano, trying to synchronise their playing with the action on the screen – a skill I longed to emulate.

Quite soon we were being instructed for our First Communion, and I had to start to take religion more seriously. I enjoyed this preparation, but, when the moment came for me to make my first confession, my new ardour suffered a serious set-back. An extremely stern, almost angry priest asked me questions, trying to force me to confess to sins of which I had never heard let alone been tempted towards: whether I had tried to kiss girls, or tried to put my hands under their skirts (for what purpose I was too ignorant and innocent to imagine). I was confused by this disturbing form of bullying and thereafter avoided making confession.

By the time I reached the age of eleven, my grandmother had taught me enough on the piano to be able to play quite advanced duets by classical composers with her. However, practising on my own, I was lazy about my formal studies, spending most of my energy on improvisation, occasionally scribbling down new 'compositions'.

No one in my family, not even my grandmother, encouraged me to consider music as anything more than just part of my general culture and education. The first real inkling that I could study in greater depth came when a schoolfriend invited me to hear him play the violin at a concert of the junior pupils of the

Warsaw Conservatoire. I was overwhelmed by my eleven-year-old friend's acrobatic virtuosity, his almost diabolical power with the instrument. I had not known that anyone so young could attend the Conservatoire, and I immediately asked my mother if I could study there too.

My mother was delighted with my new enthusiasm. My father was not. Music, he said, was not a profession for a gentleman.

My mother pleaded my cause successfully, reminding him how he enjoyed hearing my duets with my grandmother, and realistically pointing out to him that taking weekly music lessons at the Conservatoire at the age of eleven was hardly sealing my fate to become professional.

The next obstacle was an audition. I had never played for anyone outside the immediate family circle. Now I found myself, shaking with fear, waiting my turn amongst a crowd of seemingly confident rivals, their eager parents beside them, in a small concert hall at the Conservatoire. The examining committee sat grim-faced and intent at a table near the platform.

My confidence gradually rose as I listened to the surprisingly poor playing of some of the other children. Then suddenly my name was called. Terror almost overtook me as I walked up on to the platform, but I took a deep breath and plunged into Fibich's *Poem*.

After a few seconds, I heard an indignant, sneering whisper from a jealous parent in the audience: 'Look at him: he uses a pedal!' – someone wanting to upset my confidence by indicating that I was overambitious. I managed to keep going, concentrating my whole being not only on technical accuracy but also on musical feeling. I returned to my seat convinced that I would be admitted. I was right.

My piano teacher at the Conservatoire was Miss Comte-Wilgocka. Her mother was a well-known Polish singer, her father was French. I thought she was magically beautiful with her small delicate features and black hair, and imagined that all French women looked like her. She dressed exquisitely and used a subtle perfume, unlike the Polish sweet flower scents. She always greeted me with a friendly smile, and was encouraging, patient and generous with her time. My two lessons a week with her were a great joy, and I soon began to feel that I was making real progress.

However, as she was not a qualified teacher but just an advanced pupil at the Conservatoire, she was still under supervision from her professor, a particularly unpleasant character, whose bi-monthly presence at our lessons became a nightmare to me.

This Professor Wiktor Chrapowicki, still in his early twenties, was meagrely built and had a black moustache and long flowing hair *à la Paderewski*. His skin was pale and blotchy; I had the impression that, if I were to stick a pin in it, light green blood would come spurting out. He always looked angry, but said little. When he eventually spoke, it was as if a safety valve had failed: he would suddenly burst forth into a stream of fast, furious and often incomprehensible words.

As I played, he would shove my hands off the keyboard with a sudden, sharp slap, and place his own stubby white fingers on the notes to show me the correct position. He would then savagely criticise my poor young teacher in my presence, complaining that she was not demanding enough and that she herself seemed to have forgotten the principles of pianistic technique.

He hated me, he hated her, but I soon realised that he hated everybody else too. He was, I discovered later, an extremely unhappy man. He had shown exceptional promise as a concert pianist, but had on one occasion been so cruelly picked apart by a Warsaw music critic that he instantly abandoned his career as a performer. He thereafter devoted his time to undermining the confidence of his piano pupils.

All the junior Conservatoire pupils also had to attend theory classes, especially in solfeggio: reading lines of melody, singing out the names of the notes (doh, re, me, etc.) and simultaneously conducting ourselves in order to keep our sight-reading rhythmically correct. The only help our teacher gave us was to sound an 'A' on his pitch pipe before each pupil sang.

At first I found these classes difficult, even discouraging, as the teacher would signal any error by banging his pencil loudly on the desk, sharply ordering the pupil to begin again. Gradually I became used to this terrifying exposure, and eventually even enjoyed the exercises.

As I found myself wanting to devote more and more time to my music, my school studies suffered. In trouble with the *gimnazjum*, I then struggled to fit in extra homework to appease my teachers, only to find myself slipping back with my music. I became quite desperate and exhausted.

Just at this unfortunate point, already severely strained, I had to face a crucial test: the annual Conservatoire examination at the end of the academic year, which took the form of a public performance in the main concert hall under the eyes of a jury, in the presence of a large audience of teachers, parents and friends.

As I went nervously into the large hall where my fellow pupils and their families were assembling, I met with a most alarming sight. A huge concert piano stood on a full-sized platform. Beside it stood a long table covered in green baize with two carafes of water and at least a dozen glasses. Behind these glasses sat the examining committee: amongst them I recognised the sweet reassuring face of my teacher and the angry glare of Professor Chrapowicki. The other examiners were unfamiliar, except one whom I recognised from photographs, the composer Karol Szymanowski, who looked tired and deadly bored as he balanced his head gloomily upon his hand.

I was so frightened that I hardly heard the other pupils play. My name was eventually called and I forced myself up on to the platform in front of the vast piano. I sat for a moment, looking questioningly towards the table, expecting a sign for me to start, but all I could see was Chrapowicki looking at me as though he could 'drown me in a spoonful of water'.

I wilted into an appalling attack of stage-fright, suddenly hot, actually pouring sweat, so that my fingers slid all over the keyboard. The notes came out as if detached from me, refusing to sound as I wanted to play them. All too soon I heard a preemptory handbell rung by a member of the examining committee, which meant 'Enough!' I fled back to my seat by my mother.

A few days later I was informed that I could no longer attend the Conservatoire since I had 'no musical talent.' I was devastated.

My mother went straight to Professor Chrapowicki, demanding reasons for my failure, which he refused to give. Much distressed, she asked him, 'What should my son do now?'

He replied in a rude voice, 'Shut the piano for ever!'

2

NO MORE PIANO LESSONS

At home only one person was pleased about my disaster: my
father. Now he could feel confident that music was not my
destiny. He made use of my distress to reinforce his determination that I should have no more piano lessons and that my
general education should come first. My shock at the examination result, together with his attitude, almost succeeded in
making me give up music altogether. Still only twelve years
old, I turned back almost frenetically to my old hobby of
making model aeroplanes, not touching the piano for many a
month, feeling that it was no longer a friend, almost as if it
were a living creature that had let me down.

In the following four years, my life was devoid of music.
This misery was compounded by my father's constant financial
troubles, which caused me to change schools twice.

In the years 1925 and 1926, my father was unable to find
work in his profession as an engineer. His violins had won him
great prestige; even the world-famous violinist, Bronisław
Hubermann, visited our home and arranged some 'blind' trials,
in which my father's instruments won higher praise than any
others, even higher than the old Italian instruments, including a
Stradivarius. However, the violins reaped admiration only – no
financial rewards to save us from disaster. Rich people interested in investment bought old instruments, especially those
which bore the names of great Italian makers, while professional musicians who dreamt of buying one of my father's
instruments could not afford them.

Worse still, my father, through his gullibility and kindness, was plunged by a confidence trickster into the most appalling debts. He was suddenly befriended by a Polish army officer, who professed a flattering interest in his violins, asking searching and interesting questions, so that my father greatly enjoyed his visits. I often saw this Colonel Weintraub, standing in front of the large, glass-fronted shelves in which my father kept his instruments. He was a small, fat man with an expansive stomach which hung over the belt of his uniform. He was mostly bald, and what hair remained was shaved to the skin. He always seemed to be sweating profusely, wiping his brow with his handkerchief and he had a perpetual sweet smile which remained on his face like a mask, regardless of the subject he was discussing. He was always polite – to excess whenever my mother appeared, at which point he would odiously pour forth his exaggerated admiration for her beauty and charm.

One afternoon I answered our front door and he rushed past me, frantically demanding to talk to my father. From the next room where I was trying to do my homework, I heard his voice raised and agitated. The words were not clear, but it seemed that my father was refusing to comply with some desperate supplication. Then suddenly Weintraub was yelling clearly, 'If you don't help me, if you refuse to sign, I will have to shoot myself!' The conversation went very quiet, so that I could discern no more; then the colonel left, my father eyeing him with an anguished, almost frightened expression. Later I saw my mother equally alarmed, reproaching my father, and I gathered that Weintraub had emotionally blackmailed him into signing a financial guarantee against an enormous sum of money which Weintraub was borrowing to pay off his debts.

All too soon, the effects of my father's humane act were to be felt by us all. I found out how bad things were most distressingly, through an incident at my new school, the Lorentz Gimnazjum, where I had just completed an exceptionally happy first year. I had worked hard, and anticipated being moved into a higher form. At the end-of-term assembly, the headmaster was telling each boy which class he would be in the following year, taking us in alphabetical order, at the same time handing out our reports. However, after the names which began with 'O', he went straight to one beginning with 'R'. I was the only pupil he omitted. I thought it must be a mistake, but when I approached the headmaster at the end of the assembly, he said curtly, 'There's no report for you. Your parents will have to come and see me personally.'

I was almost sick with distress, wondering if I had been wrongly accused of some crime or unknowingly broken some rule. That night I could not sleep at all. My new life, my friends and the kindly teachers at that school were of utmost importance to me, and my mind churned agonisedly trying to imagine what awesome sin I had committed to make them turn against me.

Next day my mother naïvely went to ask the headmaster what was wrong. It was nothing to do with my behaviour: he was perfectly satisfied with my progress over the year. However, my fees had not been paid, so that he would not hand over my report, nor would I be admitted to the school the following autumn.

The wicked Colonel Weintraub had disappeared like camphor, probably living in luxury under an assumed name on the money he had borrowed, leaving my father responsible for his enormous debts. We had nothing left for electricity, gas or telephone. Soon a note came from the unpleasant manager saying that if the rent was not paid the police would evict us. A vivid image hit me of the poor old man who had been pushed out into our courtyard. In my imagination I could already see my father arranging and rearranging his instruments in a similar manner, trying to protect them from the rain, while my mother, who had never before had to manage without a maid, and could not even boil an egg, would be struggling to cook our food on a primus.

The injunctions kept arriving with further debts run up by Colonel Weintraub. Because my father was unable to meet them, the executive officer of the court arrived to impound our furniture. Bailiffs wandered arrogantly at will through our rooms. It enraged me to see them, not even bothering to remove their overcoats, lounging about on the fragile antique chairs on which I had never been allowed to sit. Labels were glued on the choicest pieces, and a date for the auction was fixed.

Fortunately, friends of my father had told him an illicit but effective way of halting the sale. The scruffy-looking dealers apparently were an organised mafia so that, on the day of the auction, my father was able to pick out the boss, slipping him what money he had to call off his pack. Thereafter nobody seemed to be bidding for any of the furniture: somehow all the buyers had dispersed. The auction had to be postponed a month or two. Meanwhile my father sold a few trinkets to repeat the bribe. In this way he managed to hold off losing most of his furniture until our financial problems were solved.

He found an engineering job with a fire insurance company, travelling around the countryside, which he appeared to enjoy. To my distress, however, I was not sent back to the Lorentz Gimnazjum, but to the prestigious Szkoła Mazowiecka where my fees were to be covered partly by my father's employers.

This school was much tougher in all ways, especially regarding the colossal load of homework and heavy demands of the excellent but exigent teachers. I particularly disliked the lessons on the Polish language. The teacher was a most unpleasant middle-aged woman, her advanced state of pregnancy emphasising her already ugly figure. She gave us far too many books to read, making us learn whole pages by heart. Polish history was even worse as, depressingly, we had to memorise the innumerable dates and changes in Polish borders in our gruelling national history of endless invasions by ravenous foreign powers. (How different to England or America, protected by the sea!)

However, we had a charming and attractive German teacher who created an enthralling scandal by having an affair with one of the older boys at the school. My belated and hazy knowledge of the facts of life was further assisted by a kindly, rather naïve teacher who took us to the parks of Warsaw to study natural history. Through the interesting behaviour of some insects, he hinted to us the secrets of reproduction, a new mystery which filled me with wonder and curiosity.

The following year, when I was thirteen, one of my closest friends, the son of a famous gynaecologist, most gruesomely conveyed to me all sorts of exciting facts about human birth which he had gleaned from his father's books. Meanwhile I never seemed to meet any girls. My interest remained purely scientific. The worst mischief we perpetrated was to slip off to the parks for smoking sessions, which I worked at furiously, attempting to overcome my giddiness and tendency to cough, so as not to look feeble in the eyes of my friends.

For a while the family's impecunious state did not affect me too badly, except for one further humiliating incident, when I had been sent on a summer holiday to a YMCA camp and was unceremoniously despatched home early because my father had omitted to pay the fees. However, I was not too unhappy about that accident because the camp was painfully Spartan.

In my second year at the Szkoła Mazowiecka, I fell danger-ously ill with typhoid. I pleaded desperately not to be taken to hospital, and my mother, with the help of my paediatrician uncle, somehow managed to nurse me at home, despite the risk of infection to everyone around (except my brother who had survived the disease in his early childhood). I remember for weeks having no visitors at all as I struggled for my life, other than a cousin of whom I was very fond: a medical student, who cheered me greatly with splendid jokes and conversation, though he always kept his distance, standing nervously near the door. I wondered how he was going to be a doctor if he was so afraid of my germs.

As I was recovering, still weak, thin as a stick, my hair all fallen out, I heard to my horror that this bright young cousin was dead, not from typhoid, but from a burst appendix: a stern lesson for the rest of my life not to worry about obvious perils because we can never know from which quarter fate will actually strike. Meanwhile we grieved deeply for him, and for his widowed mother who had no other children.

Our difficulties were suddenly compounded because my father was knocked over by a car, suffering a broken leg and in-ternal injuries so that he too had to be nursed at home. It was months before he could work or earn again.

My education had suffered severely because of my illness. To save money it was decided that I should move to the Muni-cipal Gimnazjum in the next academic year.

Every day, I walked along the same route to my new school, first through the Jewish quarter, where I was intrigued by the exotic appearance of the older generation: bearded men with corkscrew curls, wearing long black caftans, and old women with short, dark wigs covering their own hair. The men and women were all very animated, I noticed, chattering away to one another in Yiddish (which of course I did not understand). Then I went on through St Alexander Square and up a broad avenue towards the Vistula. Near the river bank I would run hurriedly past a pathetic group of ragged drunks, down a flight of stone steps stinking of their urine, then straight to the nearby gate of my school.

Like the Lorentz Gimnazjum, to which I looked back with great nostalgia, the Municipal School occupied the whole top floor of an apartment building, but there the similarity stopped. I now had to become used to smaller, more crowded schoolrooms, shabby and dirty. The windows looked out on a huge viaduct, so that it was easy to be distracted from the uninteresting lessons by an endless procession of passing trams, cars, horses, carts, pedestrians and pedlars. The noise made it difficult to hear the teachers, most of whom were dull and bad-mannered, yelling abuse — words such as 'blockhead', 'fool', 'idiot' — at any pupil who displeased them.

The task of disciplining us was admittedly not easy. With few exceptions, the boys were rough, often virtual hooligans, mostly unwashed and smelly, their clothes grubby. Fists were always at the ready; a fight broke out at the slighest excuse. From them I quickly learnt an expressive new vocabulary of vulgar and rude words (mostly related to the sexual organs), which cropped up in almost every sentence whatever the subject of discussion.

It took me a while to find friends. Though I felt no inhibition that most boys were of working-class origin, they were highly suspicious of me because my parents were members of the intelligentsia. Gradually, however, I found some fellow-spirits. One boy especially, a quiet and sensitive character, the son of a Jewish watchmaker, was delighted to discover my love of music. His passion was jazz, and soon he began to invite me to his home, where he demonstrated his banjo and ukulele, as well as playing me some marvellous Dixieland recordings — a fabulous new experience for me.

The teacher who worked hardest at making my life a misery was the Catholic chaplain. At the age of fifteen I was beginning to feel deeply drawn again towards religion, but, in my genuine interest and enthusiasm, I tackled him over some awkward theological statements which I had found difficult to accept without questioning. He was angry rather than interested, and thereafter seized upon every opportunity to crush me. One day, during break, he strode up to me, and looked me up and down through his blue-tinted glasses, observing with evident disgust my pristine shirt, well-pressed trousers, tidy hair, and even worse, my clean finger nails. 'My dear boy,' he sneered, 'this is very bad, very bad indeed. You care too much about your body, not enough about your soul!'

I felt like answering him back, 'What do you know about my soul, you idiot?' ('Idiot' being the term he favoured when addressing us). But I wisely kept silent, bowing my head in mock humiliation until he wandered off, gloating to himself over his little victory.

The rhythm of our home life went on much as before, my mother still playing the violin all day, my father spending his evenings in his studio constructing more violins. To earn some extra and urgently needed money, he was now also taking in high quality instruments for repair or valuation. As ever he was gullible, accidentally letting slip the value of a violin without being paid for his opinion, or asking far too little money for extensive repairs which had taken him days. He often rashly lent instruments without charge to players who needed them while their own were undergoing repair, only too often to be rewarded for his kindness with an instrument returned after long delay, sometimes badly damaged.

Mirek was now a student at the Maths Department of Warsaw University and I saw little of him, except at weekends when he was deeply absorbed in his passion for constructing radios. He made some magnificent working sets which he himself mounted in wood. Enjoying my admiration, he would call me in for the ceremonial first switching on of each new model, when moments of nervous silent expectation preceded the very first sound.

Mirek absolutely forbade me to touch his precious radio sets, though I confess that I did in his absence. Turning the dials, I heard different languages from different countries, and experienced as an extraordinary revelation the wondrous sound of a full orchestra, new to me because I had never been taken to a symphony concert. For example, I was amazed to hear the Brahms Violin Concerto as it should be instead of just the soloist's part which I knew so well from my mother's playing. Even through the crackling receiver of an amateur radio, I found myself filled with a wild and choking sense of emotion. At that time I had no opportunity to express my aching longing for music; however I could enjoy my secret communion with Mirek's radio sets when no one was around to catch me.

So far as the family could see, my hobby and my obvious passion was flying. Whenever possible I slipped off to the airport, watching the aeroplanes as they landed and took off. I was fascinated by the different types of aircraft: their flight, even their sound and, when I was able to get near enough to them on the ground, the smell of burnt fuel. I also continued to construct quite intricate flying models.

Otherwise I found little in my life to cheer me. Eventually, unable to put up with the unpleasantness and lack of inspiration at my dreary school, I announced to my parents that I wanted to move to the state engineering school to train as an aeronautical engineer, so that I could cease to be a financial burden to them as soon as possible.

My mother deep down knew where my heart lay, but she could not see the way to help me back towards music. My father liked the idea of the engineering school. He had always wanted me to have a good, practical profession. I was enrolled there in the autumn, just after my fifteenth birthday. For a while, the change seemed to suit me very well.

However, by the time I was sixteen, I had recognised that a great number of years of gruelling study lay ahead of me before I would come near to designing even the humblest part of an aeroplane. Reality extinguished any remaining glimpses of glamour or hope. Overworked and undermotivated, I became hopelessly depressed. It was not just having to acknowledge that my choice of the engineering school was a mistake; I felt in a kind of spiritual and emotional vacuum.

Battling with this sense of void, the cause became increasingly clear to me. I had lost touch with music – and yet without music I myself was lost. With this shock I had to recognise that composition was still part of the fabric of my dreams for the future, though at that moment these fantasies seemed so unattainable that I hardly dared to admit the truth. Though I could not rationally hope for a positive outcome, I resolved at least to try.

My mother was not surprised of course, and she instantly took on the difficult task of persuading my father that I must abandon engineering and start to study music seriously; that this was my true vocation. At first she was unsuccessful, despite bravely arguing with him on my behalf through many a sleepless and noisy night.

Perhaps his eventual change of heart was due to the fortuitous timing of the realisation of his own dream. Just at that point, after his years of struggle, the education authorities in Warsaw approached him to create a state school for the construction of musical instruments, appointing him as its first Director. Receiving this invitation, his spirits rose so high that he momentarily softened, and consented to my mother's pleas on my behalf; on one condition – that I should return to the unlovable Municipal Gimnazjum and obtain my *matura* before becoming a full-time music student – a horrible prospect, but for me a price worth paying.

I felt less lucky when I actually found myself at the Gimnazjum, facing the teachers I disliked so much and the bunch of bullies in my class. But the anticipation of recommencing my music studies made anything seem bearable.

It was not so simple as I had imagined to find my way back into the world of music after a four-year gap. To my disappointment, I was not even allowed to take the entrance examination for the Piano Department at the Conservatoire because I was too old (by the age of sixteen professional instrumentalists normally need to be extremely advanced). Moreover, my ignorance of the technicalities of music prevented me from even attempting the entrance examinations for the Faculty of Music Theory and Composition.

The only alternative was to study on my own. Though I had to cope with all my school work for my *matura*, I also read numerous books about basic theory, instruments and composers. At the same time, I trained my fingers at the piano, forcing myself to practise scales and studies as well as exploring some not-too-difficult pieces (still paying inadequate attention to the business of finding the right position for my hands on the keyboard).

With no teacher to guide me, self-discipline was hard. I would soon switch to syncopated distortions of the piece I was trying to play, using it as a springboard for my own ideas, sometimes transforming it into a wild improvisation. This was not altogether time lost. If I had been studying piano more seriously I would not have had time to fool about in this manner, but these inventions quite possibly fulfilled an important transitional function in my formation as a composer. Only I was becoming increasingly frustrated since, despite my struggles, I did not have the musical knowledge to put down on paper my more complicated rhythms and harmonies.

Sometimes my brother used to join in my improvisations on his banjo, especially with jazz — a field in which I was now completely at home, thanks to my friend the watchmaker's son. After a while I began to compose short jazz pieces, influenced by masters such as Ellington and Gershwin.

One day my mother, searching for some particular violin work, went into a small music shop, one of many in the centre of Warsaw, with shelves full of printed material and an upright, usually out-of-tune piano. When requiring pieces of a lighter character, customers would attempt to sing or whistle the melody. The salesman would then produce some sheet music and would check that it was indeed the chosen tune on the piano. In contrast, my mother knew precisely what she wanted. The owner, Mr Altschuller, a middle-aged man dressed with exaggerated elegance, was intrigued by my mother's obvious musical sophistication, his interest heightened no doubt by her charm. He drew her into conversation about the composition she had requested. As their talk drifted on to the subject of family life, my mother casually mentioned that her son was mad about music and had composed some foxtrots.

Mr Altschuller promptly suggested that she should show him some of my music. Possibly he wanted to encourage my mother as a customer, and was using my music as an excuse. However, she took one of my compositions to him, and he, with apparent seriousness, promised to let her know in a week or so if it had any chance of performance or publication.

My nervous anticipation had only to be endured for a few days. He soon telephoned: the well-known poet, Marian Hemar, extremely enthusiastic about my piece, was already writing a lyric, and it would be performed at the next Grand Revue in the Warsaw equivalent of the Casino de Paris!

My family was overjoyed. My friends at school were agog that my music was to be sung in a real theatre, heard by thousands of people, and probably recorded.

On the day of the première, my parents, my brother and I went excitedly to the theatre. Arriving punctually and showing our tickets, to my astonishment, I was not allowed in: the show was for adults only. By law, the theatre could not admit anyone under eighteen. The commissionaire was unmoved that I had come to hear my own composition performed by the great comedian, Adolf Dymsza. Forlornly I trudged home alone and waited to hear my family's impressions.

They came back captivated, and triumphant on my behalf. Dymsza had been superb; the audience had 'shaken their sides' at his hilarious acting and the words he sang to my music. The song was about an uneducated boor of a man: desperately trying to be polite and elegant, he used the French word *pardon* to cover up his lack of culture, manners and education. The words went something like, '*Ach pardon! Ach pardon!* Goodbye Madame! Go to bloody hell!'

Ach Pardon was a hit. The gramophone record sold in thousands: suddenly I had more money than I could have imagined. I was startled – quite bowled over – when I began to hear my tune whistled or sung in the street.

I was asked to compose another foxtrot for the same lyricist and same performer: another big success, but this time with sad overtones. The title and refrain of the song was *I Want No More*. The main verses were a long, humorous list of things that the comedian no longer wanted, concluding with 'I have five children and I don't want any more!' One day, while the song was at the height of its popularity, his own child died – a tragic coincidence. I could not understand how he could bear to go on singing the song or at least why he did not alter the text.

As the months passed these successes began to worry me. Though writing the songs had been both fun and profitable, I did not want to be a composer of light music. I wanted to study seriously and to learn to write the sort of music that I heard at symphony concerts.

Though the family now accepted that music was to be my life, I was still receiving no formal musical education. Understanding my anxiety, my mother plucked up courage to approach the Rector of the Warsaw Conservatoire, Eugeniusz Morawski. He was more than helpful, perhaps influenced by the respect in which my father was held by musicians in Warsaw.

Since I was still not knowledgeable enough to be accepted as a student of music theory, Morawski suggested that I should apply to study percussion. The entrance tests involved only the playing of some easy piano music, the main requirement being a strong natural sense of rhythm and a good ear.

Director Morawski's plan worked perfectly. I passed easily. At last, aged seventeen, in February 1932, I again became a student at the Warsaw Conservatoire, ostensibly to study percussion, but with permission to sit in on classes of music theory, music history and the reading of scores, and to get back to my piano studies as part of my general musical education. I started immediately, part-time, as I still had to fulfil my promise to my father to gain my *matura* at the Gimnazjum.

My teacher was the percussion principal of the Warsaw Opera Orchestra. An elderly man of humble origins, small and stocky, bald with a round face, he was inseparable from his huge, stinking cigars which he habitually chewed with his false teeth. (These cigars presumably lent authority and stature to his much-prized position at the Conservatoire.) He always slightly flattered me, perhaps impressed not only that I was the son of the famous Tomasz Panufnik, but also that I was planning to study composition.

Before touching any real percussion instrument, I had to learn to hold the drumsticks correctly and to practise endlessly on a piece of wood with a tiny cushion in the middle; it was surprisingly hard work, resulting in painful blisters on my hands. But I progressed fast and was soon rewarded by promotion to a proper side drum and later to the timpani, which I found more challenging and exciting.

Eventually, to my great delight, I was allowed to join the student orchestra. I found this an extraordinary new sensation. Instead of the symphonic music coming at me from a distance at a concert, I was surrounded by and part of the live sound of the music I loved and admired: Mozart, Beethoven and Schubert.

That summer I passed my *matura*, and, in the autumn of 1932, became a full-time student at the Conservatoire.

3

THE CONSERVATOIRE

To my great joy I was allowed to enrol immediately in the
Faculty of Theory and Composition. I instantly gave up my
percussion lessons; they had just been an excuse to get me into
the Conservatoire (though the experience undoubtedly paid off
later in many of my compositions). My teacher was devastated.
He begged me to continue, assuring me that I could expect a
highly successful career as a percussionist.

I now plunged into my music studies at top speed. The normal pattern at the Conservatoire was to study basic musical
knowledge for one year, followed by three years for harmony,
three more for counterpoint, then two years for composition –
a timetable which I considered ridiculously staid and slow. I
not only worked energetically at my piano technique every
day, but also attacked my other work so hard that eventually I
found that I had completed the course in theory and composition in half the prescribed amount of time, despite the vast
amount of written work involved. In addition, rapidly bored
with the endless succession of dry academic exercises, I practised both my counterpoint and my harmony by actually composing so that I could introduce some emotional content as well
as technique.

Soon compositions seemed almost to pour too fast from my
pen, including some *Variations* for piano and a *Classical Suite*
for string quartet which was played at a public concert in the
Conservatoire hall by a group of advanced students led by my
old schoolfriend, Stanisław Jarzębski. Fate still seemed unwilling to allow me to hear my own performances: I was stuck

in bed with 'flu, unbearably tantalised to be told by witnesses of their 'superb rendering, received with wild applause'.

My *Variations* and *Classical Suite*, however, were still no more than student works, written as part of my classwork in harmony and counterpoint. When in the spring of 1934, aged nineteen, I composed my Trio for violin, cello and piano, exploiting my newly acquired techniques in the basic musical forms such as sonata, song and rondo, I was becoming confident enough to be much freer with my invention and musical imagination. The piano trio was my first serious achievement in composition. If I had given my works opus numbers, I would have designated it as 'Opus 1'.

My life at the Warsaw Conservatoire was extremely happy. Besides my studies, I luxuriated in the often superb public concerts given in our hall by such international celebrities as the pianist, Józef Hofmann; by the fabulous black American contralto Marian Anderson singing exquisitely a succession of Schubert *Lieder* as well as deeply moving Negro spirituals; and I was thrilled to hear Sergei Prokofiev brilliantly playing his own piano works. On a much lower level, I also indulged in more foolish occupations, such as singing in the chorus wearing make-up and ridiculous costumes in the student production of *Don Giovanni*.

I made a number of close friends, especially amongst fellow students of Jewish origin; particularly with Tadeusz Geisler, a violinist of great talent, highly intelligent with a deliciously wicked sense of humour. We often made music together at his home, or went for long walks together arguing intensely for hours on end about music and the great instrumentalists of our time.

One evening Tadeusz and I happened to meet, each of us seeking some information in the Conservatoire office. All the clerks had gone home and we were about to leave when the telephone rang. Tadeusz could not resist answering, putting on a deep voice and pretending to be one of the office administrators.

I gathered from the conversation that someone was enquiring about engaging two of the best graduates from the Conservatoire to perform at the celebratory dinner of some important institution. Tadeusz instantly made a deal, naming a fee which to my ears sounded astronomical. He then went on – in outrageously flowery language – to recommend the finest violinist, Tadeusz Geisler, and the most outstanding pianist, Andrzej Panufnik.

Our appearance was to be the very next evening. I begged Tadeusz not to choose anything too diabolically fast or difficult; then rushed home to practise all night before our rehearsal together in the morning.

Arriving that evening in a slightly shaky, nervous state, we were effusively greeted by the organiser. He knew all about us from his telephone conversation with the office of the Conservatoire, and accordingly treated us as though we were the likes of Fritz Kreisler and Ignacy Paderewski.

We played mostly classical 'pops': virtuoso recital pieces in which the violinist could show off his technique. Our performance was not too disgraceful, though I had difficulties with the upright piano: its heavy keys were unwilling to respond to my *pianissimo* which meant that some crucial notes did not sound at all. Nevertheless we were warmly applauded after each item. After the concert, our splendid fee was handed to us; fortunately the Conservatoire authorities never discovered our trick.

My friendship with Jewish students annoyed some of the non-Jews at the Conservatoire, especially a small group which was overtly, even militantly anti-Semitic. They collected their allies by means of a test which apparently they found hilarious, rounding on a likely fellow thug, shouting, 'Beat Jews and barbers!' If this drew the indignant reply of 'Why barbers?' they knew they had found another bully-boy for their horrid clique.

One day a friend warned me that this grotesque gang had misguidedly attempted to persuade him to join them in their scheme to pick a fight and beat me up. Scared for his own skin, he surreptitiously pointed out my enemies one by one in the corridors of the Conservatoire.

Mostly from the Teaching Faculty (future professors!), studying general musical knowledge, they were members of an organisation called 'Brotherly Assistance' which had been initiated with the ideal of helping fellow students, rather like a modern union, but which had been taken over by an unpleasant Fascist element. Brotherly Assistance resembled the student society, Korporacja, at Warsaw University; a hearty, beer-swilling fraternity on the German model whose members moved about the streets in groups, identifying themselves by wearing tiny, brightly coloured caps and thin ribbons across their chests over the top of their ties. They often carried thick walking sticks which they used in their cowardly attacks on the minorities of which they did not approve. Fortunately they were only a minority themselves, and most students held them in utter contempt.

The danger of assault from Brotherly Assistance was not to be ignored. I was bursting my brains wondering how to prevent losing any of my teeth or getting any bones broken while at the same time letting them know what I thought of them.

My opportunity came quite suddenly. One day I noticed four of them standing at the tiny Conservatoire canteen. As usual, they were smoking and laughing loudly in their vulgar way, probably at dirty jokes. They all looked remarkably alike, with the same empty expressions on their faces.

Forcing myself to take courage and approach them head on, I controlled my shaking limbs and taut throat and introduced myself, announcing that I knew their cowardly plan to beat me up. I stood there challenging them on the spot to carry out their threat, but, taken aback by my apparent aggression and troubled also no doubt by the somewhat public surroundings, they mumblingly denied any such intention.

I was then able to hold forth with the greatest relish about why I enjoyed having so many Jewish friends, saying that I admired their devotion to work, their greed for knowledge and their love of music which I so ardently shared. The group of Brothers just stared at me silently; so I carried on my attack in, I fear, an overpious manner, criticising the way they could always be seen idling about the corridors of the Conservatoire, cigarettes dangling from their mouths, playing cards in the café, probably drinking in the evenings, never to be seen at concerts. To my amusement (and relief) they seemed unable to defend themselves, and slunk away. For weeks afterwards, I peered rather nervously over my shoulder down the darker corridors of the Conservatoire, but they remained unable to look me in the eye when we met. I do not suppose that in private they changed their ugly attitude, but they did appear to be less aggressive within the Conservatoire area.

Amongst our professors only one, Piotr Rytel, was anti-Semitic. Ironically, one of the subjects he taught at the Conservatoire was harmony (also counterpoint and composition). It became almost a laughing matter amongst us the way that he never missed an opportunity to air his prejudices during his classes. For instance, all he could say about the great Artur Rubinstein's piano-playing was: 'I don't like his Jewish touch'!

Rytel was well known as the very severe music critic on a right-wing newspaper, but he was also a frustrated composer whose works were only rarely performed in Warsaw. Rehearsing his appallingly derivative music, members of the Warsaw Philharmonic Orchestra were heard to joke amongst themselves that when Wagner threw his sketches into the wastepaper basket Rytel must have taken them out, stuck them together and rewritten them as his own composition. (In my view, this suggestion was too flattering to his uninteresting scores.)

Rytel hated Poland's leading composer, Karol Szymanowski, partly because he suspected him of having Jewish origins and knew him to have many Jewish friends, but mostly I think because of the wildest jealousy. Whenever a piece of Szymanowski's music was about to be played in a concert, Rytel would noisily and publicly demonstrate his antipathy, rising with fuss and clatter from his seat and marching out of the concert hall, banging the door loudly behind him.

As with most Poles, Rytel's anti-Semitism was confined to barking. His tailor was Jewish, his wife bought food and other articles from Jewish shops and he even gave private music lessons to Jews. I knew these secrets because he lived in our street, just opposite our home.

Illogically, in contrast, Professor Rytel's closest friend, our Professor of conducting, Walerian Bierdiajeff (a relative of the well-known Russian philosopher), was passionately pro-Jewish. He could always be counted upon to support Jewish people in

argument at the expense of Gentiles. No one could help noticing that, in his classes, when we took turns to conduct while the
music was played by four hands on the piano, our Jewish colleagues were privileged to receive considerably more time and
attention than the rest of us. And one of his hobby-horses was
that an orchestra would not 'sound' unless at least 90 per cent
of the string players were Jewish.

A large proportion of the string section of the Warsaw Philharmonic Orchestra was Jewish, and indeed it could sound
magnificent. Unfortunately it did not sound so wonderful
when Bierdiajeff was conducting. He was only bearable in his
over-emotional but exciting renderings of Tchaikovsky. His
knowledge of classical music was poor, his understanding and
feeling for it non-existent.

Bierdiajeff spoke Polish badly, with a strong Russian accent,
and he often asked his students to help him with grammar or
spelling when writing his letters. He looked like a tall, handsome teddy-bear, but his considerable personal charm was
never directed toward me. He must have sensed that I was
critical of his musicianship and his teaching methods.

At that time I had no ambitions as a conductor, but I conscientiously attended his classes for a year, hoping to learn
more about the orchestra and to grasp some technique in case I
needed to conduct my own works. However, he never seriously discussed music – structure, instrumentation, phrasing, etc;
he obviously did not have much to impart to us on such matters. Instead we would beat a rhythm with our sticks in time to
the piano, and he would praise only those of us who were proficient in imitating his conducting technique. I soon became
bored with these lessons, which I called 'gymnastic exercises'.

Of all the teachers at the Conservatoire, I liked and admired
most my childhood idol, Jerzy Lefeld. Officially his subject
was the reading of orchestral scores at the piano. However,
with me, he far exceeded his brief, taking it upon himself to impart to me his deep interpretative understanding and colossal
general knowledge of music, covering every epoch in great detail from Gregorian chants through to recent composers, of
whom Debussy was probably his favourite. It never worried
him that our lessons went on longer than scheduled. His dedi-

cation to his pupil's needs was total, his kindness and patience beyond description. For me he was a saint.

Our Rector, the composer, Eugeniusz Morawski, taught me instrumentation. He was a good-looking man, always immaculately dressed, tall with flowing grey 'artistic' hair. His unusually mobile face underwent a vast range of transformations, from Beethovenian when he was serious to like a Pekinese dog when he was being frivolous or ironic. He was full of amusing anecdotes about composers, their works and disastrous performances. He gave cogent advice on all aspects of composition: for instance, that a young composer should make a mark a metre high upon a wall and should not try to get any music published until his pile of compositions was tall enough to reach the mark.

I became very fond of Morawski, not only because he had initially eased my path into the Conservatoire, but also because I enjoyed his teaching and benefited from his encyclopaedic familiarity with the orchestral repertoire of the nineteenth and early twentieth century.

To my regret, his knowledge of the newer musical trends in Europe was limited, but this was not altogether his fault: most of the scores were not yet published, let alone recorded, or performed in musically-provincial Warsaw. The Polish conductor Fitelberg occasionally conducted the more acclaimed avant garde works of the time; for example, *The Iron Foundry* by the Russian, Mossolov, *Pacific 231* by Honegger and a dazzling piano concerto by Prokofiev. These performances were major events for me, and I remember my even greater excitement the first time I heard some Stravinsky when Klemperer conducted *Petrushka*. (I remember also that Klemperer was so tall that he dispensed with the podium.) These tantalising visions of the world of new music, however, were excruciatingly rare. Warsaw must have been the only important European capital where there was no pre-war performance of *The Rite of Spring*. Stravinsky was hardly heard; Bartók, Schoenberg and Webern were not played at all. Therefore Morawski could perhaps be forgiven that, in his classes, composition seemed to have come to a halt with Scriabin, Ravel, Dukas, Falla and Respighi.

Though composition had always been part of Morawski's

life, he had also passionately wanted to become a portrait painter. He had studied art in Paris for many years, subsisting in utter poverty. Eventually, his predecessor, Karol Szymanowski, invited him to abandon his painting and return to Poland as a Conservatoire professor, so that he could live in decent conditions with some social standing, and have time to compose again.

According to malicious gossip, he had later plotted with other professors to get rid of Szymanowski, so that he could become Rector instead. I never believed this tale. It seemed far more likely that while Szymanowski was Rector and Professor of Composition he had been too deeply absorbed in his own work to make time for his students; eventually someone had to be appointed in his place who would be available to teach and to direct the artistic policy of the Conservatoire.

Szymanowski had accepted his appointment as Rector some years before purely for financial reasons. So far as his composition was concerned, it was the act of a 'drowning man clutching at a razor', even though, as was pointed out by unkind rivals, he was delighted with his new social standing and liked to hand out his card engraved with all his titles: Professor Doctor Karol Szymanowski, Rector of the Warsaw State Conservatoire of Music. The novelty wore off, however, and he soon found his duties a painful burden on top of his ardent creative endeavour.

I found myself deeply in sympathy with Szymanowski's absolute preoccupation with his work. After all, he had bravely taken on the task of trying single-handed to bring the excessively backward Polish school of composition up to date. This exercise seemed important at the time, even though probably the jump would have been made anyway by the following generations. For him personally, it could not have been an easy task, as it meant striving to match such strong individuals as Bartók and Stravinsky, Schoenberg and Webern, controversial innovators whose works he must have come upon on his journeys through Europe, but who were not necessarily comfortable sounding boards against which to pitch his own luxuriant voice. Absorbed in carrying out his personal and patriotic ambitions, he understandably allowed himself to neglect his academic commitments, perhaps believing that, in the end, everything would be forgiven. I suspect also that he pictured himself as a victim, as an under-appreciated composer, living in desperate poverty.

In fact Szymanowski's financial position was not so extreme as he wanted everyone to believe. He received considerable personal support from industrialists and from the Polish aristocracy, and even the otherwise apathetic state organisation plunged quite substantial sums into his pocket. Yet it was true that he was constantly broke: however many banknotes were poured in to this barrel without bottom, they immediately disappeared without trace, because he indulged in an extremely high standard of living.

He travelled abroad extensively, always in the greatest luxury, staying at the most expensive hotels. For his suits he had a life-size dummy made to his measurements at his tailor in London's Savile Row. He loved to invite guests to the best restaurants, while the costs of his very complex private life were enormous. He was completely impractical, forever in financial straits – particularly in his last years, when, because of his tuberculosis, he needed more and more money to support himself.

The Polish intelligentsia respected Szymanowski's unique stature, and most musicians rightly regarded him as our greatest composer since Chopin. The apparent lack of interest in his music, resulting in empty concert halls whenever it was performed, was not due to popular prejudice against him; it was a manifestation of the lack of musical education of the Polish nation.

Poland has produced in all generations individual musicians of the greatest talent, even genius, so that the rest of the world has the impression that the Poles are inherently a musical nation. However, in those pre-war years, for most of the citizens of Warsaw, including the aristocracy, the professional classes, and even the intellectuals, the only contact with the art of music was in cafés or restaurants: an ensemble of instrumentalists playing light music, gypsy airs or jazz. After a few vodkas, some of the more 'musical' members of the audience would whistle or sing the melodies, or beat time by striking their plates with their forks. Beyond this, most people's musical experiences had extended no further than occasionally hearing brass bands during national celebrations or organ music in church during Mass, weddings or funerals, too often ill-played on out-of-tune instruments.

Recitals, chamber music, even symphony concerts were poorly attended, however 'popular' the repertoire. Unless the soloist was a star with a magnetic name, the Warsaw Philharmonic often performed to empty seats. Sometimes, in consequence, concerts had to be cancelled. The Philharmonic Hall was then transformed into a cinema: members of the orchestra, to avoid starvation, positioned themselves below the huge silver screen, playing 'mood-music' as a background to the silent films.

At one point serious opera had to be abandoned altogether and replaced by light operetta, to save the singers and instrumentalists from poverty and oblivion. I wondered if there was any other nation in Europe whose government and people would allow such a collapse of musical life in the capital. (Marshal Piłsudski was not himself interested in music and his colonels were completely deaf!) The average musician's income was shamefully small, and his social position not much higher than a waiter's. I was beginning to understand my father's concern over my choice of profession!

Like most students in all epochs, becoming more aware of politics, I found myself deeply critical of many aspects of the government in office. As my disillusionment grew, I became interested in the tiny and idealistic Polish Communist Party, wondering if perhaps they had the answers to the issues that worried me. I was attracted by their talk of establishing a new order, in which there would be no racial problems, no exploitation of man by man; in which crime and prostitution would finally cease to exist; in which people would be free of evil and, they fervently declared, would not even swear at each other any more!

My inclination towards the Marxist ideology was fuelled by my consciousness of the appalling poverty endured in our backward country. In some areas, the people were desperate enough to split a single match in half, or to share between families the salted water in which the potatoes were boiled (though salt from our own rich mines was plentiful and cheap). Huge numbers of Polish peasants were driven by poverty to emigrate to North or South America. I often saw them, crowded like sheep almost on top of each other in buses, coming into Warsaw from the country to be herded through the necessary formalities before being shipped away. Among them were beautiful girls, apparently unaware that they would probably end their voyage in the brothels of Buenos Aires or Rio de Janeiro. Though food was plentiful and probably the cheapest in Europe, the poorer members of our population were tragically and unnecessarily undernourished, so mismanaged was our natural agricultural wealth.

I remember a number of discussions with my father in which I took the Communist line; he reacted to my views with deep suspicion, ridiculing me and angrily calling me a 'Bolshevik', not without accuracy at that time. However, I never became active on the political front because music took priority and absorbed almost every waking moment of my time.

At the end of my second year at the Conservatoire, in the summer of 1935, I allowed myself a brief break from my studies at Zakopane in the magnificent Tatra mountains of Poland. Even then, I did not get away from music altogether, since many of my friends were also on holiday there. At a gathering of artists and intellectuals, I was fascinated to meet Szymanowski, who surprisingly recognised my name, possibly having heard about me from his friend, Kazimierz Sikorski, my teacher of composition at the Conservatoire. He seemed interested in my work and asked me if I would visit him at his home. I felt very honoured and immediately though rather shyly suggested the next day.

Szymanowski was living in a simple, rather gloomy villa on the edge of Zakopane. He himself answered my rather timid knock and welcomed me in a most gracious and dignified manner.

We sat in armchairs in his drawing-room, in front of a low circular table on which stood a huge ash-tray full of cigarette ends. The room was sparsely furnished with a primitive couch in one corner, covered with a rough, colourful rug, probably made by a local peasant, and a black, upright piano on which stood a few photographs, the largest of which was of Serge Lifar, the principal dancer and choreographer in Szymanowski's ballet, *Harnasie*, which had just been premièred at the Paris Opéra.

Szymanowski did not talk to me about his current work, as I had hoped and expected; nor did he ask about my studies or what I was writing at the moment. Instead, he immediately burst into a tirade about his former colleagues at the Conservatoire. He angrily attacked them one after the other, using words such as 'brute', 'rascal', 'swine', 'pig'; even 'son of a whore' — the worst words predictably being directed at Professor Rytel.

It was astonishing to hear such crude words pouring from the lips of Poland's greatest composer. I listened to his outburst with mounting embarrassment because I was still studying with these apparent enemies of his at the Conservatoire. Obviously he had been badly hurt by his colleagues and wanted me to know what he thought of them, perhaps in the hope that I would spread some words in his defence. All the time he was talking, he chain-smoked, carefully placing his cigarettes in a slim holder. His flow of words was interrupted only by his frequent, racking, tubercular cough.

Eventually I managed to change the subject, twisting our conversation to his recent work, and questioning him on the secrets of the peasant music of the Tatra region which he loved so much and which had so strongly influenced his compositions. At last I was getting some interesting replies from him. Sitting at the piano, he illustrated his comments, playing some characteristic melodic patterns of this music, starting to explain to me the eccentric but effective manner in which the peasants always performed the fourth note of the major scale slightly sharp, by almost half a tone, because . . .

To my dismay, I never discovered the reason. He suddenly looked at his watch, and stood up, apologising: he had to collect a prescription from the pharmacist before closing time.

We left the villa together, but soon our ways parted. I

turned my head and sadly watched his efforts to make his way to the town. Though not much more than fifty, he appeared at least twenty years older; with his shoulders bent, he limped along slowly with the aid of a walking stick, one leg dragging behind him. I never saw him again. He died two years later.

By happy chance, my brother Mirek was also on holiday at Zakopane. It was one of those rare periods in our lives that we had time together, walking and talking in the mountains. I loved and admired him greatly. He was exceptionally well read, a man of high intelligence with a broad outlook on life.

He introduced me to a beautiful fair-haired, blue-eyed girl, of great warmth and charm, still convalescent after leaving the sanatorium for tuberculosis. I think that they had only just met, but they were obviously in love. The knowledge that TB was then not fully curable did not seem to deter Mirek, and he planned to marry Maria almost immediately.

On our return to Warsaw, we found both our parents deeply depressed. My mother had some mysterious, undiagnosable illness. My father was feeling frustrated, even humiliated, again owing to the lack of public recognition of his work.

That spring, the Polish Government had put up two large cash prizes for an International Competition for violinists, which had been organised to mark the 100th anniversary of Wieniawski's birth. My father had decided to present the winners with two of his best violins made by his own hands: his *Polonia* model violin as first prize, and his *Antica* model as second prize.

His generous gesture seemed highly appreciated by the first-prize winner, Ginette Neveu from Paris. I remember very well how charming she was when she came to visit my father, and what a terrible shock it was to us later when we heard she had been killed in an air crash. The second prize was awarded to the young David Oistrakh from Moscow. He was unable to thank my father in person: even then, Soviet artists were forbidden to visit private homes when they came to Poland. But I learned many years later that he had used the violin extensively.

However, to my father's distress, the Polish press and radio had virtually ignored the gift of these two violins, the fruit of many years' hard work, reporting vaguely that the instruments had come from Panufnik's 'firm' or 'factory' – with the maker's name distorted by wrong spelling. He quoted with bitterness from the Bible: 'A prophet is not without honour, save in his own land.'

In my last academic year at the Conservatoire (1935-6), my composition teacher, Kazimierz Sikorski, gave me two assignments. First I was to compose an orchestral work in the form of symphonic variations, then a large-scale work for solo voices, chorus and orchestra – my diploma work on which my final results would depend.

Sikorski was said to be a 'progressive' and a devoted admirer of Szymanowski's music, so I had imagined that he would be sympathetic towards my more adventurous efforts in composition. Consciously setting out to be somewhat avant garde, I began my *Symphonic Variations* writing in four keys simultaneously, to be free from conventional harmonies. However, when I rather proudly showed him the first few pages, to my dismay, instead of admiring my boldness, his face contracted into deep disapproval. He curtly ordered me to abandon my polytonal technique and to begin again, strictly in the traditional tonal language. I felt as if my wings had been clipped. But he was my teacher: I had to obey him.

Swallowing my frustration, I started again from scratch, composing a theme in F sharp minor with a distinctive element of Polish folk song. From this I built up my *Symphonic Variations*, ending with a passacaglia – variations within my *Variations*.

I have to admit in retrospect that Sikorski was right to force me first to master the craftsmanship of conventional tonality before letting me fly off in an exciting whirlwind of exploration: in this way he helped to instil into me the necessity for unity of style and discipline, which was to stand me in good stead in my future searches for my own musical language and rules.

Another unusual aspect of Professor Sikorski's teaching, of lifelong value to me, was that he required his pupils to think symphonically from the inception and write orchestral music immediately as a full score – contrary to the usual practice, composing first for the piano then orchestrating afterwards.

Otherwise, though appreciative of his musical knowledge, I found him dry, even discouraging. He was stingy both with the time he allowed for my tutorials and with his comments on any work that I brought to him. (He took greater interest in a more conventional student, who later gave up composition to become a musicologist, editing the words of Chopin for the Polish State music publisher, PWM.) While I was still working on my Variations, I also composed for my own satisfaction two short orchestral pieces, *Symphonic Allegro* and *Symphonic Image*. When I showed these during a lesson to Sikorski, he said he had no time to look then. He took them home. After a couple of weeks he returned them with the brief comment that my music was sparse. 'Bare, naked,' he added with distaste. As usual he was in a hurry and had no wish to discuss my attempts in more depth.

Perhaps he took my asceticism as an indirect criticism of his own compositions. His own eclectic works were richly adorned with counterpoints and were very densely orchestrated. Obviously he would react against my pieces because, from my earliest years, I favoured clarity and economy of means of expression, making it my aim never to write a single superfluous note. Recognising that we differed in matters of taste, I settled to learn all the craftmanship I could from him, but determined meanwhile quietly to go my own way.

After finishing my *Symphonic Variations*, I attacked my diploma work, choosing a beautiful Polish translation of one of the Psalms. It took me only two months to compose a work of half an hour's duration, scored for four solo voices, mixed chorus and huge orchestra.

When I showed it to Sikorski, I expected as usual to meet with no more than a curt acknowledgement, but, to my amazement, he appeared to be quite impressed. (Perhaps I had made some compromises by producing more polyphony and a richer sound in the score.) He told me that he had to pass it around to a few of the other professors, since the diploma awards were agreed collectively.

My final examinations were approaching at an alarming

pace, so I accelerated my efforts with my secondary subjects, especially the piano. I practised incessantly, memorising the two works which I had been allowed to select for my assessment: Bach's Prelude and Fugue in C minor from *Das Wohltemperirte Klavier* and Beethoven's Sonata in A flat (Opus 110). In the exam, fear seemed to add some excitement, and I not only got through both works without wrong notes, I found myself playing with genuine enjoyment too. One of the professors in the panel of judges told me afterwards that I had a magnificent future as a concert pianist. (How different from the view of Professor Chrapowicki ten years before!)

Most of my other examinations went smoothly, the one exception being the analysis of musical form. Although, fortunately, I passed, the process was unexpectedly distressing because I accidentally upset my teacher Professor Witold Maliszewski, a charming and highly cultivated man, once a pupil of Rimsky-Korsakov. For the final examinations he allowed us the freedom to choose which work we would analyse. With my passionate interest in contemporary music, I picked a Szymanowski *Mazurek*, difficult to play and extremely dissonant. In the presence of Professor Maliszewski and some fellow students, I first played it right through, then spoke about it for about half an hour, making a thorough analysis and demonstrating musical examples on the piano.

After I finished, Professor Maliszewski stayed silent for some moments. Then he said in his Russian accent, carefully controlling his voice in spite of the agitated expression on his face, 'I accept your analysis – but I did not understand the piece you played. For me it is just a cacophony.' Then he added, 'Thank you, my dear sir' (the way he always addressed his students).

We were all astonished at his comment. I felt perplexed and guilty that I had unintentionally hurt him, not having realised that he was so profoundly conservative in outlook, and probably had some personal prejudice against Szymanowski. I remained at the piano, silent and embarrassed, not knowing how to react. To my relief, Professor Maliszewski called the name of the next person to be examined and I was able quickly to return to my place in the audience.

A few days later, I had a message from the Conservatoire office that Professor Maliszewski was away because of illness, but that he wished me to come to his home to talk about my *Psalm*.

Expecting still to be strongly out of favour, I gathered my courage and called on him next day. He lived in a small flat in a huge, dark house near the Vistula river. He greeted me as always with dignified politeness, and immediately asked me to sit near the piano. He then sat in front of the keyboard himself and opened my score. As he slowly turned the pages, I saw that he had marked in some comments: tiny words, written lightly with a sharp pencil. In the few seconds of silence, I thought, 'Oh God! He's going to destroy me utterly with his criticism!' I took a deep breath and told myself to hold on to the wind (a Warsaw slang expression supposed to give one extra courage).

Then he began to analyse my work, reversing the procedure of our recent encounter, playing some fragments of my score with great fluency, praising with the greatest warmth (to my amazement) my 'serious and excellent achievements with regard to the clarity of the score, the proportions of the whole structure, and the skilled vocal and instrumental writing'.

He must have studied my work for a great many hours, with such thoroughness that he had noticed a number of minuscule mistakes − faulty transposition, lack of some accidentals and even a few wrong notes. I felt most ashamed as he pointed them out. But, noticing my worried face, he reassured me: 'Don't be upset! In creative art, the most important, the most rare thing of all is individuality − and you possess it. So not to worry, my dear sir!'

This was the first time that any of my teachers had given me any such sincere encouragement. I almost choked with surprise and happiness.

A week or so later, I was informed by Professor Sikorski that, with the unanimous agreement of all the professors, I was to be awarded a diploma with distinction, the highest honour for Conservatoire graduates.

This meant that I would be taking part in the gala concert given annually by the Laureates of the Conservatoire, conducting my *Symphonic Variations* with the Warsaw Philharmonic

Orchestra in the city's Philharmonic Hall. Naturally I was elated at this prospect, but also unnerved by the thought of conducting so difficult a work in public; furthermore, I would for the first time be rehearsing and performing with a professional orchestra of high calibre. I had been warned that the orchestra was not too well disposed towards young composers and new music.

However, my worries were groundless. When it came to the test, I amazed myself with my apparent confidence – I don't think anyone could have guessed at the undercurrents of fear that were driving me. Moreover, to my relief, my work sounded just as I had imagined while I was composing it, which was more important to me than the other exhilarating new experience of the evening, my first ever ovation by an audience.

Amongst the other performers in the graduation gala, my two close friends, both Witolds, were destined to become famous: Witold Małcuzyński was playing the Liszt Piano Concerto and Witold Lutosławski, graduating as a pianist rather than a composer, played a concerto by Beethoven.

After the concert, all the performers were invited by our Rector, Morawski, to the well-known restaurant Gastronomia for a celebratory supper. A few of the professors came too – without their wives, as it was a bachelor spree. We ate a lot and drank heavily, talking and joking about our experiences with the Warsaw Philharmonic and our first contact with the real concert-going public.

As we were swallowing our last glasses of vodka, one of the professors of piano, Paweł Lewiecki suggested that we should come to his home to share another artistic experience, to see some interesting and exciting films.

As we were all in highest spirits (in the chemical as well as emotional sense), we accepted his invitation enthusiastically. On the way, we joked amongst ourselves, and to our delight, Professor Bierdiajeff kept teasing his friend Professor Rytel, saying that he must be Jewish, that his real name was 'Rytel-son'; Professor Rytel scowled, being quite incapable of showing even a glimmer of humour.

Professor Lewiecki's home was a spooky ground-floor flat.

He lived alone, and made a hobby of collecting films, which were lying around everywhere on shelves and tables, and which, I imagine, he watched hour after hour through his lonely bachelor evenings.

As soon as we sat down, our host switched off the lights, and the pictures started to flicker on to the screen which had hospitably been awaiting us. The subject of the film was utterly unexpected. It was pornography from beginning to end — hard porn at that!

The first person to react was our Rector Morawski. He suddenly picked up his chair and moved nearer to the screen. After a while, he began to shout at Professor Lewiecki, 'Slower! Slower!', and 'Stop! Stop!' — wanting time to appreciate more fully the peculiar situations which each frame was revealing to us. I was almost as entertained by our dear Rector's performance as by the content of the film.

It was already morning when this spectacle came to an end. The street lamps were switched off. I trudged home slowly with heavy legs and an excruciating headache. But as I walked, the oddity of my night out slipped from my mind and I evoked the whole saga of my studies at the Conservatoire — in reverse order, until I had reached the point ten years back when I had been thrown out. It had taken me just four and a half years to complete the course in theory of music and composition — half the time required and with a distinction. But my puff of self-satisfaction only lasted an instant: I knew only too well that this was still no more than the starting point of a very long musical journey.

4

COMPOSER IN UNIFORM

After the happy conclusion of my studies at the Conservatoire, my immediate intention was to further my education abroad. I passionately wanted to hear the great European orchestras as well as to find out about the newest directions in composition at source.

Most young Polish composers gravitated towards Paris, because of the traditional cultural ties between Poland and France and the possibility of studying with the famous Nadia Boulanger. However, my goal was Vienna, partly because my German was more fluent than my French, but mainly because it was the city of the composers I admired most — Mozart and Haydn, Beethoven and Schubert — as well as the birthplace of exciting new developments in contemporary music: I had been fascinated by the score of Webern's *Five Pieces for Orchestra* which I had recently been shown in Warsaw, but not yet heard. I was aching to experience first-hand the Vienna Philharmonic Orchestra and the Vienna Opera with their famous director, Felix von Weingartner, perhaps the only living conductor to have worked with Liszt, Wagner and Brahms. I had long admired his inspiring recordings of the classical repertoire. Discovering that he taught a handful of pupils each year at the Vienna Academy, I had no doubt in my mind that this was where I must go.

As I had no money, I applied for a grant from the state-run Foundation of National Culture. Knowing that my future depended on it, I was very nervous when I arrived for my interview. However, the Director of the Foundation was friendly and unfrightening, with a noble intelligent face and the long greying moustache of a Polish country gentleman. He asked a succession of penetrating questions, puzzled that I wanted to study conducting rather than composition.

I explained that, though it was still my long-term intention to become a composer, at this point in my life I felt that I could learn more about the orchestra and about music in general through initiation into the secrets of the art of conducting the great classics than I could from any specific teacher of composition. I expressed my gratitude for the help I had received from the Warsaw Conservatoire; but now I felt it would be better for me to struggle alone to find my own musical voice. I was convinced that the most important elements – spirituality, poetry and invention – could not be taught but must spring from within the composer, from inborn creativity (backed by self-discipline and persistence). Indeed I was afraid that a teacher of powerful character such as Nadia Boulanger might stunt my development through his or her strongly held convictions, or a one-sided view on the direction new music should take. If I could discover within myself anything to say, then I must express it in my own natural, individual way, not in a style imposed by someone else. For better for worse, I was determined to be true to myself.

I was duly awarded a grant to go to the Vienna Academy for the year 1936-7, but my elation was short-lived. Only a few days after my grant was confirmed, to my horror, I received an order to present myself in two months' time for National Service at the Military College in Dęblin, about one hundred kilometres outside Warsaw. I was first to join the Infantry, then, after a medical examination, to be transferred to the Air Force.

I had been so absorbed in my musical future that I had completely forgotten about National Service, though this was in fact my second call-up. The first, two years before, to my considerable alarm, had consigned me to the Cavalry. I could not remotely imagine myself on a horse. I admired the magnificent creatures from afar, but had always been afraid of them; perhaps I sensed that they were as nervous and unpredictable as I was myself, and that a partnership between us would be risky! Fortunately my father had managed to deflect that first summons until my studies at the Conservatoire were completed, at the same time getting my assignment changed from the Cavalry to the Air Force in view of my old interest in aeroplanes and flying. However, I felt none of this enthusiasm now – only black despair at the thought of cancelling my plans for Vienna. I imagined my grant withdrawn, my whole future doomed. Unpatriotically, I would have sold my soul at that moment to escape National Service.

Distraughtly seeking a solution, I suddenly thought of Professor Major Śledziński, who had taught me history of music and brass instrumentation at the Conservatoire. At his request I had made a brass version of Fibich's *Poem*, a piano work, and he had conducted it with his best military band.

Major Śledziński always wore uniform – I believe he was responsible for Polish Military Music. He had always been friendly and seemed to have a high opinion of me, so I called at his house for advice. He greeted me warmly, and, seeing the worried expression on my face, asked with evident concern if I needed some help.

I longed to beg him to get me out of my National Service, to suggest that I could do more for my country as a musician than a soldier. However, I looked at his uniform, and realised that he would probably show me the door without another word. I explained my problem with all the calmness I could muster, only asking whether he could help me to get a temporary release from the military authorities so that I could go to Vienna before my National Service.

To my dismay, he said that my duty to my country came first, and, that I would have to ask the Foundation of National Culture to postpone the grant. Crushed, I was turning to leave, when he asked to see my summons. He read it through, made a few notes, then suddenly his expression changed. Looking straight at me, he said, 'You will report to the Infantry as this letter requires. But before you are transferred to the Air Force, you will undergo a medical examination. You don't know the state of your health, do you?' There was a hint of hidden meaning in this question, and I guessed that he was formulating a plan. Then, on the spot, he wrote a letter for the doctor who would be examining me, and gave it to me in a sealed envelope. With gratitude, I knew that he had understood the unspoken words with which I had entered his room.

To my relief, the Foundation of National Culture raised no problem over postponing my grant for a year. I dared not dwell on the momentary promise in Major Śledziński's voice. I waited at home glumly through the summer vacation, wondering how much time I would have to compose in the next twelve months.

The atmosphere at home was even more depressing than usual at this time. My mother's health was always poor. My father was steeped in further financial crises, so serious that again he could not pay his bills. He was constantly angry, often for trivial reasons: because he thought the barber had cut his hair too short, or because a new pair of shoes were uncomfortable. (He tended to buy them too small because he thought that small feet were elegant!) My brother, living on the outskirts of Warsaw, was constantly worried about the poor health of his young, pregnant wife. Unlike most of my student friends, I had no money for summer holidays in the mountains or by the sea. Submerged in gloom, I was almost relieved when the unpleasant moment arrived to report to the Military College.

On arrival in Dęblin we were all subjected to the rough regimentation with which officer cadets were traditionally knocked into shape. Our heads were shaved. Then about a hundred of us were ordered into a large hall, where some non-commissioned officers literally hurled pieces of uniform at us. Boots, belts, trousers, caps and shirts came flying towards us willy-nilly; the items aimed at each cadet bore no relation whatsoever to his size or shape. Our only hope of obtaining clothes that fitted was through barter with neighbours, shouting amongst ourselves details of any exchange we needed to make. It was a grim scene, at moments almost a free fight, since everyone was anxious to be comfortable in the uniform he would have to wear for the whole of the ensuing year.

In spite of our efforts, comfort was out of the question. My jacket was too long, the trousers too short and the heavy boots too big. I also had the greatest difficulty trying to wrap my feet in the long, narrow pieces of cloth which were supplied instead of socks.

The next few days were spent waiting for something to happen, though no one seemed to know what that something would be. We pottered about the huge, ugly building, endlessly smoking cigarettes and chattering in groups. From time to time we saw officers walking briskly by, with an air of tremendous importance.

One of them came up to me as I was casually talking with another cadet, breaking in on our conversation with a sarcastic voice, asking, 'Are you cold?'

Surprised, I answered, 'No.'

Almost shouting at me, he repeated his question, 'I am asking you, are you cold?'

I was baffled, but my companion was quicker off the mark: 'Get your hands out of your pockets,' he whispered. I slapped my fists to my sides and stood to attention. The officer looked me over severely, then stalked off in search of another victim. As he went, I uttered a very rude word from the soldiers' vocabulary which I was fast assimilating.

Each day we had to get up very early and waste time arranging our beds with geometric precision. After a breakfast of bread and lukewarm, watery coffee, we were marched outdoors for physical training, earning many a blister from our ill-fitting boots. Often we returned breathless and exhausted from our exercises, only to find our beds in complete ruin, the non-commissioned officer assailing us with his favourite joke: 'An aeroplane just passed through the room . . .' This was his idea of a punishment if on inspection he found a single bed not up to his standard. Biting back our fury we then had to start bed-making again.

One evening a lieutenant came up to me and said that, as I was a musician, I was to conduct some singing. To my mortification, he named a French popular song, the *Madeleine*, which I did not know at all.

I stammered nervously, 'I'm very sorry, Mr Lieutenant, but I do not know the tune.'

'What?' he shouted. 'You have a diploma from the Warsaw Conservatoire and you don't know the *Madeleine*? What *did* they teach you there?'

In the dead silence which followed, I could hear my heart beating loudly as I tried to formulate an answer. Probably this little bantam-cock of a lieutenant had never heard a string quartet or a symphony orchestra, so any logical response was pointless. I just had to remain silent and humiliated while I waited for his next move.

A fellow cadet mercifully came to my rescue, raising his arm to attract the attention of the furious lieutenant, announcing courageously that he knew the tune and could conduct it. I drew in my breath with relief as I heard the first notes, sung in several keys at once, everyone taking a different speed, but all in the highest spirits. This was my only musical experience in the armed forces.

One afternoon we were strolling aimlessly around the vast corridors of the barracks when another lieutenant came up to me, and addressed me by name: 'Officer Cadet Panufnik?'

'Yes, Mr Lieutenant!' I replied, surprised that he spoke to me, as my hands were out of my pockets.

He told me that I was to go to Warsaw immediately for a medical examination, and that I could spend the night with my parents, then report early next day at the Military Hospital. I was escorted on the train by a middle-aged, non-commissioned officer, who treated me with gentleness and deference as if I were gravely ill. I wondered if Major Śledziński had already acted on my behalf – but then told myself this was wishful thinking.

At home, despite the comfort of my own bed, I did not sleep at all. My mind was pounding over the misery of life in the forces and my interrupted studies. Very early in the morning, still lying wide awake, I stretched out my hand involuntarily – almost as though it was moved by some will other than my own – and put the crystal radio receiver to my ear. Suddenly I heard music of unbelievable beauty: a simple line of melody sung in unison by women's voices. I had never heard it before and it seemed to transport me to another world. It was the first known Polish hymn, the *Bogurodzica*, a Gregorian chant dating from the Middle Ages.

Still almost in a trance, I went to the kitchen and made myself a lot of very strong black coffee, which I sat silently drinking, cup after cup, still borne along by the exquisite simplicity of this divine melody. The music had completely taken over my consciousness, pushing my future, my problems, any sort of reality from my head. No one else in the flat was awake. I was unaware how many cups of coffee I drank or how long I sat there, but suddenly I realised that it was time to go to the hospital. Leaping up in a rush from the table, I could feel my heart hammering from the amount of coffee I had swallowed and I was extremely giddy.

At the hospital, I was shown straight into the presence of the medical officer. He was an elderly man, tall, almost bald, with a mild, kindly face. I gave him the letter from Major Śledziński (wishing I had dared to steam it open to see what it said). He read it, and sat silently considering for a while, saying nothing. Then he asked me to undress and proceeded to examine me, listening to my chest with his stethoscope. It did not take long. His face creased with concern as he asked, 'Does your heart always beat so fast?'

I nodded an affirmative, and said, 'I hope it's nothing serious, Doctor.' He did not answer my question, but told me to dress and return to the Military College.

A few days later I was sent for by a senior officer, who informed me rather pompously, 'I am afraid I have bad news for you: your medical examination was unsatisfactory and you are not accepted for the Air Force. In fact you are released from National Service altogether.' I took from his hand the precious release document, trying to maintain the part of a young man disappointed that he could not serve his country, stifling any expression of glee at the prospect of returning to music, biting my lip not to let out my great whoop of joy until I was safely out of hearing. I was soon on the train to Warsaw in comfortable civilian clothes.

It was too late to take up my grant for Vienna for that academic year, but at least I could think again about some serious composition. Unfortunately, I was penniless, and did not wish to be a further burden to my father, so I had first to earn some money.

My brother Mirek worked as an engineer at the Polish Radio and my cousin's husband, Maksymilian Weronicz, a writer, was Director of the Literary Department. Thanks to their intervention, almost at once I was invited to compose some incidental music for radio plays, which I found quite easy and enjoyable.

However, my next assignment for the radio was disastrous: I was asked to act as music critic. I had to listen to all music broadcasts from early morning to late at night and write my comments. I was assured that my reports would be strictly confidential, to be seen by heads of department only with a view to improving the standard of programmes. I was extremely conscientious, and – frequently disappointed in the quality of performance – uninhibitedly severe in my opinions.

To my horror, I soon discovered that the promise of confidentiality had been broken. Everybody, including the performers of the programmes in question, had access to my reviews. Suddenly I found that I had acquired for myself a nest of enemies. My fellow musicians were saying, 'This impudent puppy has taken too much upon himself.' My efforts had been sincerely directed towards the raising of standards of music on the Polish radio, but the reaction of my fellow musicians persuaded me to leave the job as soon as possible, never again to dabble in music criticism.

My next source of income was film music. It was not my first experience in this field. Two years before, while still a student, I had composed music for *Warsaw Autumn*, a short, very poetic film with fine camera work by an old schoolfriend of mine, Stanisław Wohl. Not only had the fee been generous, the script had presented me with the opportunity to write lyrical music depicting the colours and moods of autumn, but also providing me with invaluable experience through having to engage and conduct nine of the finest players from the Warsaw Philharmonic Orchestra.

With *Warsaw Autumn*, I must have shown more than just musical feeling for film work; now, to my amazement, Wohl and the producer, Cękalski, asked me to be co-author of the script and to help in the final stages of cutting, as well as acting as their musical adviser.

The project was to create a short, rather experimental film, with existing, well-known music. I suggested three Chopin piano études, and, as visualisation, three aspects of dance. The first section, using the Etude in G flat major, 'On the Black Keys', I conceived as an abstract ballet of kinetically changing geometric patterns. For the second, to the dramatic climate of the Etude in C minor, the 'Revolutionary', we filmed branches of trees swinging back and forth tortuously in a strong wind, also to create a kind of dance. We concluded with pure, classical human dance performed by a leading Polish ballerina to the Etude in F major. I found the work on this film fascinating, especially the synchronisation of pictures with music, trying to find the most striking correspondences. At the preview, all three names, Cękalski-Wohl-Panufnik, were on the credits as authors and I felt a real sense of achievement.

I was highly delighted when I heard that our film had been awarded a Gold Medal at the Venice Biennale. However, when I later saw the award document sent from Italy, I was astonished to find that my name had been omitted, with the result that all the credit went to my two colleagues. I had in mind to confront them, but decided to shrug it off and return to my true calling of composition.

A further helpful income was achieved through the first and only attempt in my life to teach theory of music. I was charmed into this by a man from the provinces who wrote an impassioned letter asking for lessons while warmly praising my music, which he had heard on the radio. Thereafter, for several months, he sent me enormous lists of questions, addressing me most flatteringly as 'professor' and, to my even greater pleasure, always enclosing a handsome fee. I reciprocated with lengthy and elaborate answers including musical examples, happy to share what I knew. This unusual method of instruction gave me surprising satisfaction, especially when he wrote and told me how quickly he was progressing. We seemed to develop a real bond of friendship, though I never met him and never knew anything about his family or even what he did for a living.

These attempts to earn money fortunately did not totally obstruct my creative work as a composer. As I had no serious commissions, I was free to choose the kind of music I wanted to write, and I enjoyed being able to return to purely abstract ideas once more, without the constraint of fitting in with the theme of a film or radio play. I explored fresh harmonies and experimented with different orchestral sound colours; I was more intent just then on pleasing my ear than undertaking any search yet for new or complex musical rules.

Although I composed a few pieces for piano, I was already coming to regard the full orchestra as 'my instrument'. One orchestral work which I hurtled on to paper at great speed at this time was my *Little Overture*, which I was lucky enough to hear performed by the Warsaw Philharmonic Orchestra under the baton of Grzegorz Fitelberg.

Fitelberg was without doubt the best Polish conductor of that epoch, though in classical repertoire he could not really compare with visiting conductors such as Bruno Walter or Jascha Horenstein; this was perhaps due to his inherent laziness rather than any lack of talent. He was a dedicated champion of Polish contemporary composers, especially of his closest friend, Karol Szymanowski; but unkind people sometimes questioned his motives for performing so much new music rather than the old favourites, suggesting that he felt that the audience could less easily judge the accuracy of his interpretations in unfamiliar repertoire. Whether the music was old or new, the orchestral players used to complain bitterly at the way he arrived at rehearsals without having adequately bothered to study the scores. While conducting, he never took his eyes off the written notes, using the index finger of his left hand to keep track of the flow of music whilst attempting to maintain the beat with his right. In spite of this precaution he often lost his place, earning the disrespect of his instrumentalists by beating one instead of three or four in the bar as indicated in the score, in order to avoid total catastrophe.

He was uncomfortable to deal with, as it was impossible to know what he really thought or felt. He disliked discussion or argument. When faced with any serious musical question, he would escape reply by parrying with another question: 'Well, since you're such an expert, can you sing me the second subject of the first movement of Mozart's 'Jupiter' Symphony?' He was constantly acting: sometimes he constricted his features into an affectedly severe grimace, his eyes half shut behind his black-rimmed *pince-nez*; other times he demonstrated the warmth of his heart with an artificially benign expression like a badly painted saint.

Aware that the good will of the orchestral players was an important contribution to a successful concert, he always exuded an excess of friendliness in the few minutes before rehearsals. He would unctuously approach individual musicians, addressing them with falsely sweet words, but failing to listen to anything they said in reply.

The orchestra, of course, were never fooled, especially after Fitelberg really betrayed himself: one day, he affectionately patted a player on the shoulder and said, 'Oh, how nice to see you again, my friend. How good to have you playing for me today! Tell me: how are you? How are you?'

The instrumentalist replied in a broken voice, 'A great misfortune has befallen me, Director. My most beloved mother died last Wednesday.'

'Oh wonderful, wonderful!' Fitelberg replied heartily, clapping the poor man on the back, and turning away quickly to dispense his sweetness elsewhere.

But whatever people said about him, as a young composer I was very grateful that he took the trouble to programme my *Little Overture*, and, naïve as I was, he succeeded in giving me the impression that he was genuinely enthusiastic. It was a rather unusual score, without any violins, giving prominence to the wind section. Unfortunately, he had no wish to discuss performance details with me, nor did he invite me to any rehearsals, which I regretted because he took much too fast a tempo so that at one point some instrumentalists got left behind. However, the performance was undoubtedly exciting, the audience called me to the platform and I could see my family amongst them swelling with pride.

As the time approached for my departure to Vienna, I wrote to Felix Weingartner to make sure that he would be teaching at the State Academy in the coming year, and to say how much I looked forward to becoming his pupil. He answered immediately, most politely, on a handwritten postcard, saying that he would most certainly be there and that I should contact the Secretary of the Academy as soon as I reached Vienna.

I could not wait to go, although the actual leave-taking was traumatic: my poor mother wept copiously, sighing that she was 'losing' me. My father, however, said 'goodbye' as casually as if I were off just for a week's holiday.

The station brought back childhood memories of the many times that I played truant from school (not daring to face my teachers because I had been practising the piano instead of doing my homework). I would buy a platform ticket, and touch — almost caress — the magnificent long-distance trains with their exciting placards: 'Warsaw-Berlin-Paris', 'Warsaw-Amsterdam' or 'Warsaw-Geneva-Rome', dreaming that one day I might join the bustling passengers and be borne out of the station into new and exciting lands.

Now my dreams were becoming reality. I almost sang with happiness as I climbed aboard the Warsaw-Vienna express. The journey was uneventful, except that I struck up a new acquaintance in the restaurant car; not anyone who could tell me about Vienna or the rest of Europe, but, by curious coincidence, a distant cousin, Jerzy Preiss, whom I had never previously met.

I was glad enough of Jerzy's companionship when I arrived in Vienna, because he suggested that we might just be in time to get to the opera that evening. To hear the Vienna Philharmonic at last! Though I was extremely tired, I dumped my luggage at my small hotel and rushed to rejoin him. The opera that night was *Don Giovanni* which I knew so well and had enjoyed so much in our student production at the Conservatoire. We sat in the balcony, and when I heard the first few bars played by that magnificent orchestra, and then the glorious voices of the soloists, I felt that I had arrived in heaven.

But the beautiful decor and costumes, the brilliance of the opera house, and above all, the superb performance of Mozart's divine music proved too much to be absorbed all at once by the wide-eyed youth from provincial Warsaw. I had a strange sensation that I was becoming airborne. The music was getting further and further away, my view of the stage becoming blurred. I felt cold drops of sweat on my face and realised that I was likely to faint. Sliding out from my seat, I made for the fresh air, and wobbled back to my hotel like a drunk. Somehow I found my way and collapsed on to my bed into a deep sleep. I suppose in a way I was indeed drunk: intoxicated almost to the point of extinction by my first musical experience in Vienna.

5

STUDYING WITH WEINGARTNER

Presenting myself at the State Academy next morning, I was startled to discover that the Registrar had heard nothing from Weingartner about my arrival. I asked anyway to register my name and complete any necessary formalities. To my amazement, I was told that I would have to undergo an entrance examination on musical theory and keyboard skills in two weeks' time. In vain I explained about my diploma with distinction, my experience conducting Beethoven and Brahms with the Conservatoire Orchestra, and conducting my own *Symphonic Variations* with the Warsaw Philharmonic. The Registrar did not seem particularly impressed. He said that about a hundred applicants would be competing for very few places, and that no exceptions could be made.

Suddenly I felt alarmed, imagining failure, an ignominious return to Poland, my grant cancelled, my future in ruins. I pulled myself together, put my name down for the exam, and, while walking back to my hotel, started to plan how to prepare myself. I would find a room where I could live and practise and would take daily lessons in German so that I would be more fluent in answering questions. I plunged into action at once, finding a beautiful room with a piano in a large flat in central Vienna, the home of a prosperous shopkeeper. The attractive daughter of the house, plump, blonde and blue-eyed, seemed only too willing to give me some lessons in German and perhaps something more, to judge from her provocative manner – though at that time I was so obsessed with my work for the impending exam that I was living a monk-like existence.

On examination day I found myself in a crowded room, my heart thumping furiously. I watched a Japanese student, his face greenish grey-white instead of amber, walk trembling into the examination room. My turn was next. Standing by the door, I tried to hear as much as possible of the procedure.

First the jury asked him to play the piano. I heard him attack Bach's Prelude and Fugue in C major. After ten to fifteen seconds, he came to a stop. He tried to carry on from where he had stumbled, but could not, so he began again, breaking down at exactly the same place as before. Two more disastrous attempts were followed by a long silence. I guessed that the examining board had taken pity on him and moved on to the next stage of questions. Feeling worse than ever, I moved a few steps away from the door to try to calm myself.

After a short while, the Japanese man emerged, looking quite confident, his face restored to its normal colour. I took this as a good sign on his behalf and felt more confident myself.

On entering the room I walked over to the examiners' table and handed them three of my scores, which I had brought at the Registrar's suggestion. Amongst the small group of un-known, stern faces, I recognised Weingartner from his photo-graphs. He hardly looked at me: he grabbed my manuscripts and started to read them. Meanwhile, another of the examiners chose excerpts from the two piano works I offered: the Bach Prelude and Fugue and the Beethoven Sonata which I had played for my final exam at the Conservatoire. Thanks to my two weeks of hard practice they seemd to go well.

I was then given a score and asked its title and composer. I was terrified it would be Bruckner or someone else whose scores were not yet available in Warsaw. Fortunately in an in-stant I recognised Dvořák's 'New World' Symphony. I was questioned about the structure and instrumentation of the work, and, asked to analyse some passages and then to play a few pages straight from the orchestral score on the piano.

I glanced anxiously at Weingartner several times during these proceedings, and each time found him glued to my scores, apparently oblivious to my efforts to deal with the questions. My compositions were holding his attention; perhaps he was intrigued by the graphic appearance of the notation, as I had invented a new way of clarifying the score, by leaving blank spaces instead of writing rests in the staves where an instrument or groups of instrument were silent.

Weingartner asked to keep the scores longer. I left the room feeling relieved and quite optimistic about the outcome. Two days later I called to collect my music from the Registrar and was told that I had been selected; that my studies would begin next week. I paid my fees for the term and left the office happy as a new-born child.

Weingartner made an impressive entry at our first class. Already about seventy-five, tall, and upright, a man of great dignity and elegance, he was wearing a smart navy-blue suit, a light blue shirt with a dark silver bow tie and dark brown, well-polished shoes. His expression was friendly and yet reserved. We greeted him, *'Grüss Gott, Herr Professor!'* He shook hands with each of us, then explained the form that his classes would take. The Academy owned an extensive collection of eight-hand piano arrangements of orchestral scores. So four of us would play the two pianos and try to follow the beat while a fellow student practised conducting us. In this way we would study a large part of the classical repertoire.

During these lessons, Weingartner would sit in the corner of the room, using his ears rather than his eyes. Musical interpretation was more important to him than the purely technical aspects of conducting. Understanding and respect for the composer's intentions was paramount. After listening to each of our efforts to conduct, he would comment incisively on tempo, dynamics and particularly on details of phrasing. Woe betide any of us who had made insufficient preparation before a lesson. He expected us always to have precise and thorough knowledge of each score, his favourite line of attack being a tirade against any conductor with 'his head in the score rather than the score in his head'.

On the technical side he insisted on economy of gesture. Here again he had a favourite catchphrase: 'What is the point', he would say, 'in spending pounds on something you can get for a few pence?'

Weingartner intensely disliked conductors who 'danced and

clowned' on the rostrum. He found these affectations unnecessary, disturbing to the audience, as well as ridiculous in the eyes
of orchestral players who, he said, prefer serious, untheatrical
guidance with a controlled, clear beat.

Therefore what mattered most was precision of movement
at the tip of the baton. To achieve absolute control, we had to
practise keeping the lower part of the right arm firmly resting
on a desk or piano, so that we moved our hands strictly from
the wrist while indicating the different beats.

He taught us that during a performance the conductor's
body should be almost motionless; the right hand should maintain the beat and the left hand should be free to indicate phrasing, dynamics, or to bring individual instruments into prominence in certain passages when the need arose.

Weingartner's vast performing experience, as well as his intimate knowledge of each of the works he unravelled and eluci-
dated for us, was the most musically enriching privilege for his
pupils. I was always particularly moved when he passed on to
us some comment the composer had made to him personally.
Once when I was conducting *Tristan und Isolde* in class, he
interrupted me saying, 'Wagner told me that this phrase should
be started mezzoforte rather than forte as indicated in the score,
and then to make a slight crescendo'. I felt that such advice was
being delivered to me almost straight from the composer.

I again had this sense of almost direct contact with the composer another time when I was conducting Brahms's
Symphony No. 2. On that occasion, for some reason, only four
of us students were at the class. Weingartner himself therefore
sat at one of the pianos with the other three, and asked me to
conduct.

It was most interesting to see him at the piano, watching me
closely with his alert eyes, performing strictly in accordance
with my conducting, so that if I made any mistake, he played it
– even exaggerated it. He stopped me a few times with valuable suggestions, to which I listened with the greatest rever-
ence, knowing that he had conducted this symphony in the presence of the composer, who had kissed him publicly afterwards
as an expression of gratitude and admiration. (I could not help
wondering if anybody at home would believe me that Wein-

gartner, the friend of Liszt, Wagner and Brahms, had played Brahms's Symphony No. 2 under my baton!)

Amongst my fellow students, my closest friend was the Japanese Hisatada Otaka. (He later became a highly respected conductor in Japan and a founder of the Tokyo NHK Symphony Orchestra; tragically he died young from overwork.) He and his enchanting wife, Misao, often invited me to their flat so that we could work together. Misao was a fine pianist, so she and I would play together from a piano reduction while Hisatada conducted us; then it would be my turn to conduct them. After our 'homework', Misao would cook a delicious dinner as a reward for our hard work, using exquisite Japanese vegetables, fish and other special ingredients sent by their parents direct from Tokyo. I enjoyed their company enormously and admired Hisatada's talent, industriousness and complete devotion to music. Though he wanted to be a conductor, he was also a gifted composer, and had a wide-ranging general knowledge. We would talk together for hours about everything on earth. The three of us had very happy times together.

Of course I also supplemented my studies by attending concerts or operas almost every night, sometimes to hear classical works new to me, more often to study different interpretations of familiar works.

The conductor who impressed me most was Wilhelm Furtwängler, even more than Arturo Toscanini or Bruno Walter. I think his performances of Beethoven remain the finest that I have ever heard. I shall never forget, for example, his inspired interpretation of the 'Pastoral' Symphony. He started almost in a casual way, in an amazingly slow tempo, his seemingly relaxed beginning building up into a performance of incredible poetry, intensity and power. I would ponder endlessly: 'What is his secret?'

I realised that this question could just as easily be applied to Beethoven himself or to the other great composers; that it was the privilege of only an extreme minority to discover within themselves the special, mysterious key to absolute communication with their listeners, to reach and to stir their hearts and their souls. The conductor's art was almost as evasive as the composer's, I concluded. Though many conductors could be technically proficient enough to produce electrifying and accurate performances, few could be said to possess the ultimate perception of what lies behind the notes, the ability to transmit through the orchestra to the audience the true magic of the composer. Furtwängler was definitely one of those endowed by nature with that power; Weingartner too.

Curiously enough, though their interpretative powers were extraordinary, they were both startlingly less perceptive when it came to their own compositions. Both were ambitious but frustrated composers, a tragedy which has struck many other significant conductors. Weingartner's musical output was enormous, comprising operas, symphonies and chamber music. I never heard his music played, but the general opinion was that his works lacked an individual voice. I imagine that the dearth of performances caused him untold pain, probably accounting in part for his withdrawn personality.

Though primarily absorbed with my conducting studies, I did not lose sight of my other quest while in Vienna: to hear new music unavailable in Warsaw, especially the works of Schoenberg, Berg and Webern. Frustratingly, it proved just as impossible to hear them in their native city. My constant enquiries and careful reading of concert announcements were in vain. Determined to explore their ideas, I was limited to reading their scores in the well-stocked library of the Academy.

It was an exciting experience to come to grips at last with this strange and fascinating development in musical language. With passion and enthusiasm I read virtually all the printed scores, played them on the piano, analysed them in detail and contemplated them long and deeply. The composer to whom I felt closest was Webern. He seemed to me the most original of the three, and I was attracted towards the exquisite crystal-like structures he built with such precision. I saw his music as puzzling, mystical shorthand sketches; as if he were offering an intriguing outline plan without mapping the inner pathways to his musical thought and language; he must also be expressing some profound and poetic human feelings, but in esoteric form, as though they were so secret that he could not bring himself to share them.

Berg's music came through to me as more direct, more communicative, partly because his language was more readily accessible than the pointillism of Webern, and partly because his compositions were strongly imbued with a dramatic element, even a romantic one in such works as his *Lyric Suite* for string quartet.

The nut which I found hardest to crack was Schoenberg. Being myself a so-called progressive composer, I came to his music with a wide-open mind and an eagerness to assimilate even his most difficult and complex scores. However, for all my enthusiasm and determination to come to terms with his ideas, I could not overcome my instinctive reservations. I was after all steeped just then in the study of classical music at the Academy and in the concert hall, especially with Mozart, my God Number One. I found that, despite the gap of two centuries between Mozart and Schoenberg, comparisons irresistibly crept into my thoughts.

Someone once perceptively observed that the notes in Mozart's music love one another. I had the impression that Schoenberg's notes hated each other. Listening to Mozart seemed to me like drinking the dew from an exquisite geometric pattern of leaves and flowers — or tasting the pure transparent water of a mountain stream. But with Schoenberg I felt as if I were sipping the stagnant contents of an artificial lake made by a speculative human hand rather than by nature.

Nevertheless I remained intrigued by the intellectual challenge of Schoenberg's theory; and considered studying with Webern once my year with Weingartner was completed. Meanwhile I tried out the serial method on my own: at first I thoroughly enjoyed these mental gymnastics, but soon recognised that for me its limitations outweighed its advantages. I could see what Schoenberg was attempting. I agreed with the principle of a self-imposed discipline, a limitation to achieve unity. However, judged from the standpoint of my own purposes, his method seemed to achieve unity only at the cost of the equally desirable goal of variety. The 'democratization' of the twelve notes of the chromatic scale seemed to block the way to essential expressive elements: the prohibition against note-repetition meant that, even if the composer succeeded

73

momentarily in creating a certain expressive character by emphasising particular notes, he was immediately compelled to neutralize it by letting the others have their say.

I threw my dodecaphonic sketches into my waste paper basket, and concluded that I should never again try to borrow methods from other composers. My instinct told me, however ambitious or pretentious it might seem in those early student days, that I must search unremittingly for my very own new means of expression, my own new language, at any cost, to remain independent and true to myself. I knew that I would require some discipline, some framework within which to build my own works, but it would have to be constructed by myself. It would have to meet my need for emotional content as well as structural cohesion. I realised even then that my life would be one of ceaseless search; that I would be taking great risks — that I might never reach my goal.

My studies with Weingartner, meanwhile, were going well and I found myself contentedly absorbed into the *Gemütlichkeit* — the cosy and peaceful life of Vienna — until, within an incredibly short space of time, the whole atmosphere was shattered and wrecked by a drastic political change.

As we entered 1938, I began to notice a sense of unrest, of unease, undermining the normal quiet bustle of the city.

Most of the Viennese belonged to the governing national movement, the Austrian Vaterländisches Front, the men often wearing badges in their lapels to proclaim their loyalties. Suddenly, especially amongst the student population, more and more lapel badges appeared with a bold *Hackenkreuz*, the swastika of the Nazi movement. Young men in the streets, total strangers, on seeing another swastika wearer, would now greet each other with a sharply raised arm and a loud '*Heil Hitler!*' In the evenings, workers marched with spades over their shoulders in the manner of soldiers with rifles. Some of them carried burning torchlights which dramatically lit their fierce, angry faces.

As I drifted out from a performance at the Opera House one cold evening in the middle of February, my continuing absorption in the music was suddenly shattered by angry shouting and violent scuffles. Around me, members of the audience wearing the Vaterländisches Front insignia were being grabbed, their badges savagely rent from their jackets by furious-looking youths wearing huge swastikas.

Innocently caught up in the opera performance, none of the audience had been aware — till this rough awakening — of the collapse of Chancellor Schuschnigg's Government. This was the moment of the *Anschluss*, when Austria suddenly found itself a part of Nazi Germany. In the days that followed, I witnessed many noisy demonstrations initiated by Hitler's followers, always accompanied by the continuous rhythmical shouting of the slogan '*Ein Volk, ein Reich, ein Führer!* One nation, one state, one leader!'

The Viennese police tried to maintain some order, to allow the busy traffic to flow reasonably, but gave precedence to the demonstrators, greeting them with the Nazi salute, toadying to them in every possible way to manifest their devoted support.

I neither saw nor heard of any bloodshed at that point. The Austrian people, with few exceptions, seemed to accept the new situation readily. With or without cynicism, almost overnight, virtually every Austrian seemed to have replaced the old government badge in his lapel with the swastika. Indeed, I believe this was compulsory for state employees.

The appearance of the streets altered: as well as a great number of motor cycles, lorries, vans and buses carrying soldiers in German army uniform, huge propaganda posters were strung up at every vantage point frowning down upon us with ugly Nazi slogans.

Before long, Adolf Hitler himself arrived in Vienna to accept the homage of its citizens. Jubilant crowds jammed the streets. My curiosity prevailed: I wandered out, amazed by the huge ripples of enthusiasm rolling towards the fount of what to me seemed the deepest of misfortunes for the people of Austria.

Suddenly a cavalcade of motorbikes was spluttering by at a slow and stately pace, followed by Hitler's open car. Hitler stood in the front, next to the driver, proud and upright as a monument. The expression of his eyes was hidden by the deep peak of his (probably) bullet-proof cap, but his mouth was stern, grimly unsmiling; he hardly acknowledged the joy and adulation around him, except, at intervals, when he raised his arm in a salute, slowly and coldly, almost like a robot.

As he passed, only a few metres from where I stood, I remember shuddering with a terrible premonition of fear for the future of Europe, suddenly understanding that the Nazi movement could have the strength and power to spread, that other countries, including my own Poland, might also see such grim processions featuring this icy, angry-looking Führer, though in Poland I felt sure that he would meet a very different reception.

A fervent admirer behind me in the crowd threw a huge bunch of flowers in his direction, accidentally striking his head. He showed no reaction whatsoever — neither fear nor appreciation — but continued on his way as if nothing had happened. He was supremely confident, aloof, afraid of nothing.

In the days that followed, I saw Vienna rapidly lose its remaining charm. Its handsome buildings were plastered over with huge, hideous slogans. Groups of young zealots began painting big Stars of David or the word '*Jude*' on the windows of shops owned by Jews; not just the smaller businesses but almost all the elegant stores of the Kärntnerstrasse were brutally disfigured in this manner. In the eyes of some Nazi fanatics even Christianity was officially tainted by association; to my amazement, I observed one church with '*Jüdisches Geschäft*, Jewish business' painted in vast letters on its wall.

The unpleasantness manifested itself in every area. The State Academy of Music was temporarily commandeered as living quarters for German soldiers. Teaching was suspended and all concerts were cancelled.

Despite promises that the Academy would almost immediately reopen, I could stand the atmosphere no longer. I fled, taking a tourist steamer up the Danube, and at last I found some respite and peace through the glorious scenery. My spirits further revived on arrival in Budapest, when I saw the breathtaking silhouettes of suspension bridges against the night sky, the splendour of the brightly illuminated Parliament building, and experienced the different smell of the air and the exotic sound of the Hungarian language.

I spent a marvellous few days there. By good fortune I

found a warm, friendly family who took me as a paying guest and introduced me to some delightful, most hospitable people, proving to me the centuries-old saying, 'Pole and Hungarian are two brothers'.

Naturally I went to concerts, including a most moving choral work, the *Te Deum* by Zoltán Kodály, performed at the Liszt Academy. I was filled with admiration for the way that he wrote for voices and I was thrilled to be able to congratulate the composer personally after the concert, and to be invited to his home.

The prospect of going back to the sad, sullied city of Vienna was unappealing; however, the thought of discontinuing my studies with Weingartner was even more depressing. I steeled myself therefore to return to the State Academy.

It had indeed reopened, but the first lesson I attended was not reassuring. Coming into the room, we found Weingartner looking very pale, nervously pacing up and down like a lion in a cage. Suddenly, the two Austrian students in our group marched in, stood to attention like soldiers in front of Weingartner, clicked their heels noisily, and raised their right arms in the Nazi salute, shouting, '*Heil Hitler!*'

Weingartner momentarily froze with fear before realising that this was just a 'normal' friendly greeting. Blushing visibly, eyes to the ground with shame, he lifted his right hand slightly without moving his arm one inch and answered almost inaudibly with just one word, '*Heil*'. Then, with a deep ache as I understood his predicament as a state employee at the Conservatoire, I noticed a minute silver swastika, so small that it was hardly visible, in the lapel of his favourite navy blue suit. In contrast, the two zealous Nazis in our class were ostentatiously wearing, like most people in the city, large round badges with heavy black swastikas on a background of white encircled by red.

The anti-Semitic campaign in Vienna was intensifying and the Jewish population becoming more and more frightened. To my horror, I heard about appalling physical violence against them, which the general population seemed simply to ignore. The Polish Jews, permanent residents of Vienna, with long beards and caftans just like the more orthodox Jews in some parts of Warsaw, sought to protect themselves by wearing on their chests large emblems of Poland – a crowned white eagle on a red background – to identify them as foreigners, and therefore untouchable. I saw a great number of them queueing in front of the Polish Consulate for documents to enable them to return to Poland.

Concerts with Jewish performers were called off. The famous leader of the Vienna Philharmonic, Professor Arnold Rosé, was dismissed to be replaced by a Gentile. I never could find out what happened to the other Jewish players.

Though other concerts were once more permitted, I preferred now to limit my horizons to my studies at the Academy and at home. My only outings were to study (and eat) with my delightful Japanese friends. I continued to make the most of my lessons with Weingartner in order to acquire as large a repertoire of classical works as I could in the time, in case in future I might find it necessary or desirable to make a living from conducting. I excluded everything else from my mind during this period. I even stopped composing.

Towards the end of the academic year, we were suddenly informed that Professor Felix Weingartner was to be replaced by a teacher sent from Germany. It was a terrible blow. I tried to contact Weingartner, but in vain. There seemed no alternative for the moment but to continue my conducting lessons with this totally unknown newcomer.

I don't think I ever bothered to discover his name. I remember him as a strongly built man, about forty, with light blue eyes and blonde hair, a prototype Aryan. When he took his place in Weingartner's chair, he was plainly aware that it might be difficult to gain our respect. He tried to cover his embarrassment and sense of inadequacy with forced politeness and false good humour, but his teaching method was non-existent, and he was totally at a loss when attempting to comment on our work. I suspected that he had never in his life wielded a conductor's baton in front of a real orchestra; possibly he was not even a professionally trained musician of any sort. One thing was certain, that he was a good loyal Nazi; otherwise he could not have been appointed as a professor at the Viennese Academy of Music.

I realised that I would henceforth be wasting my time in Vienna, and decided to return earlier than planned to Warsaw. By lucky chance I met Weingartner in the corridors of the Academy on his way to see the authorities. I told him how unhappy I was not to be working with him any more, and that I was therefore going home.

Weingartner looked distressed, almost guilty. He urged me to stay long enough to take the final examination so that I would have the diploma of the Academy. I replied that I did not care to have a piece of paper stamped with the Nazi swastika. Such a document would hardly inspire me to be a better composer or conductor, or help my musical career in any circles which I might care about. Without the possibility of continuing as his student, I could find neither purpose nor pleasure in staying on.

Then I plucked up courage to ask him a favour, to write a note for the records of the Foundation of National Culture in Warsaw confirming my work with him. I also asked if he would let me have his photograph to keep as a memento.

I was longing also to ask whether he had resigned from his post at the Academy of his own will or whether he had been dismissed. But though Weingartner always had the most perfect manners and had shown me exceptional kindness and encouragement, he kept his real personality hidden behind an impenetrable curtain of reserve; any such enquiry would have seemed an intrusion. So we just shook hands warmly and parted. As promised, he immediately sent me a handwritten certificate for Warsaw together with his photograph, inscribed with a most flattering and warm dedication.

I was very moved when these documents arrived. I took them as a full stop to my Viennese chapter, and caught the first possible train back to Warsaw.

6

EXPANDING HORIZONS:
PARIS AND LONDON

Back home my family situation was much the same, my mother still unwell, my father dividing his time as ever between constructing violins and trying to make enough money to live. However, I now had an adorable baby niece, Ewa: at least in my brother's household everyone was happy.

In Warsaw I found that the storm-clouds over Europe were watched merely with detached disapproval; no one seemed seriously to imagine that Poland might be directly affected. The Colonels who governed our country indulged in occasional bouts of sabre-rattling to demonstrate our unconquerable might, and the general public apparently were fully reassured by these hollow gestures. Certainly I was not. After witnessing the demagogic power of Hitler in Vienna and the almost complete devotion of the German-speaking nations to their Führer — one of the greatest crowd-hypnotisers that mankind has ever known — I was convinced that he would not be easily satisfied with ideological victories, and I fretted that my fellow-countrymen seemed so unaware of the threat to the rest of Europe posed by his dangerous expansionism.

However, I did not allow these anxieties to deter me from making my plans for my own life, which meant, as ever, for my music. I wanted to continue my studies abroad. Though Weingartner had passed on to me so much of his great knowledge of classical music, he had never touched on the music of the early twentieth century. For him, Bruckner was almost too modern; Richard Strauss was never discussed (they were said to have quarrelled); and Debussy, in his eyes, was an avant garde 'experimentalist', an adventurer not to be considered. I still longed to experience in live performance the music of Schoenberg, Berg and Webern; also other composers with fresh ideas, such as Stravinsky, Bartók, the French *Groupe de Six*, and a great many others who were still just names to me. Of course I also urgently wanted to tackle some serious composition of my own, my creative impulses having temporarily dried up in the painfully disturbing atmosphere of Vienna.

My greatest desire was to spend several months in Paris then London, if only I could find enough money – a painful dilemma which was suddenly resolved when out of the blue I received a request to compose music for a large-scale film, again from Wohl and Cękalski. How glad I was that I had been too lazy to quarrel with them when they had deleted my name from the titles of *Three Chopin Studies* for the Venice Biennale! Meanwhile, the memory of their treachery eased my conscience over extracting from them the maximum fee. They were in a magnificently bad bargaining position as their film was due for release very shortly. I rather enjoyed playing an extended game of 'hard-to-get', thus winning myself enough money to live modestly for a whole year abroad.

My jubilation almost turned to dust as I contemplated the vast quantity of music I had agreed to write within a few weeks. The title of the film was *Ghosts*. It was about a pretty young girl seduced by an evil character and finally driven to suicide, which made for a really cheerful summer of composition. I had to write original music for various vocal and instrumental groups as well as full orchestra. Somehow, working night and day, I fulfilled my obligation in the allotted time, realising that I had done much more work than I had expected, so that the princely fee was more than justified, especially by the time I had engaged all the players and directed the recording.

If anyone had asked me what inspiration had enabled me to compose so much music so fast, I would have answered without hesitation with a single word: 'Money!' I was suddenly – by my standards – rich, and ready to rush off to France. It was only heartbreaking to leave my mother in poor health, though she understood how much I needed to go and bravely insisted on my departure, reminding me that she had my father as well as my brother close to her.

My first impression of Paris was dire. It was a cold autumn of unceasing rain. Unlike Vienna, the streets were dirty and noisy with the unbearable hooting of impatient drivers. From the Gare du Nord, I took a taxi to the hotel enthusiastically recommended by one of my colleagues from the recent film.

The hotel was small and shabby, in a street off the Boulevard Montparnasse. The porter showed me into a tiny room on the first floor. Tired after my journey (perhaps I had enjoyed slightly too much wine on the train) I went straight to bed, but could not get a wink of sleep. Strange, sinister noises kept coming through the thin wall of my room. It sounded as if a murder was being committed: deep moans, terrifying groans, a violent shout and then a long rasping exhalation, like the last sigh of a tortured human being before death, followed by an almost more alarming silence. I lay very still, listening for some sign of life, wondering if I should call the hotel management, but eventually the door slammed a couple of times, and I heard different voices, different gasps and different groans. More door sounds ensued, bringing yet another set of voices. I finally understood that the neighbouring room was rented, not by the week nor even for the whole night, but for hours, if not minutes at a time. My friend who so warmly recommended this source of hospitality must have misconstrued my motives for visiting Paris.

Next day through friends I found myself a quieter hotel in the same *quartier*, where the sympathetic proprietor not only offered a peaceful corner room, but agreed that I might bring in a hired piano.

Ready now to pursue one of my main aims in Paris, to study French music, I energetically set about finding a conductor of real authority with whom I could immediately start work. The name which came up most frequently in my enquiries was Philippe Gaubert. He had begun his career as a flautist, but had achieved fame as a conductor, especially for his interpretations of Debussy and Ravel, in whom I was particularly interested.

I went to the Paris Opéra to hear him conduct *L'Après-midi d'un Faune*, coincidentally with Serge Lifar dancing the principle rôle. I was curious to see Lifar, remembering his photograph on Szymanowski's piano a few years back. Though small, and not especially handsome, he was indeed impressive, musically sensitive, possessing great technical skill and poise. But I was even more struck on that occasion by the beauty of the orchestral sound, due to Gaubert's masterly direction.

I called on the maestro at his home, and asked him if he would give me private lessons, especially in conducting Debussy. Gaubert, very French-looking with his black moustache twirled up at the ends, expressed pleasure that I should choose to come to him after my studies of the classics with the great Weingartner. By good fortune, he had a certain amount of time over the next few weeks and he gladly agreed to help me. As I felt comparatively rich at the time, I did not ask how much I would have to pay for his teaching. I simply asked when I could start.

These lessons always took place at the piano, with Gaubert effortlessly playing Debussy's music from the orchestral score as he explained his interpretation. We discussed everything, not just the general structure of the work in hand and his secrets in shaping it during performance, but also all the subtle nuances of tempo and dynamics. He went into immense detail over the varying shades of sound colour, and even such small details as the precise bowings of the string instruments or where the wind players should breathe. Through him I found that Debussy's melodic element was stronger than I had realised before, his rhythm more marked. Gaubert poured out with absolute generosity all the riches of his knowledge and experience, teaching me how to bring out the profundity, the sensuality and warmth in the scores, and helping me to discover yet more poetry and exquisite new facets in the music. Working with him reinforced strongly my conviction that Debussy was the greatest poet among the composers of the early twentieth century.

When these few but incomparably valuable lessons came to an end, it only remained for me to pay him. I suddenly took fright, in case the fee might be so huge that I would be forced to cancel my trip to London; or even worse, find myself without enough money to buy a train ticket back to Warsaw. I steadied my voice at last and managed to ask quite casually how much I owed him.

Gaubert, with his usual charming smile, replied 'Rien, Nothing!'

I was more than amazed, and said, 'That's impossible. You have given me so much of your time. I MUST pay you!'

But he insisted gently, 'Nothing. You owe me nothing.' However much I argued, he firmly rejected any payment, saying modestly, 'It was real pleasure to be of some assistance to you.' Eventually he cut short my persistence, saying, 'I wish you every success with your work. *Au revoir, monsieur!*'

I was overwhelmed by his kindness, and felt my letter of thanks could in no way be enough to express the gratitude I felt to him, although I was helped to couch it in the most elegant terms of gratitude by my language teacher, Madame Cotte.

Madame Cotte, who was well over seventy years of age, was tall and incredibly thin with cropped white hair. She lived in the garret on the sixth floor of my hotel. She was highly intelligent with a broad knowledge of almost everything on earth. Our lessons would start out with her firmly speaking French to me, but before long we would get into deep and exciting discussions, and I would soon break into German which she understood perfectly. The more interesting the conversation, the less my French progressed.

Politically we both belonged to the Left. One day Madame Cotte invited me to accompany her to a meeting of the Communist Party. The secretary, a Pole, urged me to attend further meetings. But, while agreeing with many of the intellectual ideas, I could not sympathise with the French Communists' passion for everything which emanated from Moscow, and I intensely disliked the atmosphere of fanatical belief in the New Faith. (I never had been very good at being holy about anything.) Besides, my time was precious.

I had decided that I was more than ready to focus my view back on to my own composition. Obviously I was making fullest use of my presence in Paris to attend concerts and hear as much new music as possible, as well as enjoying the museums and other magnificent tourist features of the city. Otherwise, I tried to organise my life with some discipline and avoided succumbing too much to the temptations of the French capital. I devoted each morning now to contemplating and planning my new work, which I had decided was to be a symphony — my first.

Before writing a single note, I had to search for the symphony's 'architecture' and its musical material. Not surprisingly, my approach was deeply influenced by my recent studies; from Vienna the domination of my mind for a year by the perfect proportion of form in the German classics, particularly Mozart, then the recent voluptuous weeks bathed in the sensuality as well as the clarity of the French composers, especially Debussy. With the confidence of youth, I intended to try to fuse these two elements together. I was not yet especially seeking a new language, nor trying to invent new rules, but striving to arrive at an equilibrium between craftsmanship and emotion, attempting in a small way to emulate (though not imitate) my idols, Mozart, Beethoven, Chopin and Debussy, all of whom I felt in their different ways had achieved this near impossible balance.

Going to numerous concerts and listening to a great many works of contemporary composers (especially the bad ones) was both instructive and useful in my search for my musical self. Programming in Paris then was rich and interesting as regards twentieth century music, with no fanaticism, no particular school of thought predominating. Stravinsky, Poulenc, Honegger and Milhaud were probably the most celebrated figures of the moment, and the very promising young Igor Markevitch, who later sadly deserted composition for the podium. At last also I could hear Schoenberg, Berg and Webern: my opinions formed in reading their music so intensely in Vienna did not alter much, except that Berg's *Lyric Suite* sounded even more attractive than I had expected, perhaps because of the superb performance by the Kolisch String Quartet, who played it from memory with stunning precision and great warmth of feeling. (The brilliance of their playing was all the more sensational to me as their first violinist played with his bow in his left hand.)

The opportunity of hearing such a variety of new works at first was fascinating, but after a while grew slightly depressing.

85

All too many of the pieces, by greater or lesser names, though often cleverly constructed, seemed to me to have little profound musical substance; rather, they fell into the category described by the great Polish pianist, Paderewski, who complained that, 'Most modern music is like soda water: you can enjoy drinking it, but it doesn't satisfy your thirst.'

The work which impressed me most was Bela Bartók's Sonata for two pianos and percussion. Hearing this masterpiece supremely performed by the composer, with his wife at the second piano, I found myself placing him in my score chart as the greatest living composer. I found his music uniquely satisfying spiritually, emotionally and aesthetically. Unlike so much new music, his compositions were rich with rhythmical vitality, harmonic ingenuity and a stunning feeling for tone colour.

At this time, the French capital was a Mecca for young Polish musicians. Most of them had state grants (like mine to Vienna) and stayed at the inexpensive Polish House in rue Lamande. Deciding to look up some of my former associates from the Warsaw Conservatoire, I set foot there for the first time, only to be practically torn to pieces by a tigress of a Polish manageress. Questioning all who entered, discovering my independence, she attacked me as if I were a naughty schoolboy, proclaiming that I was 'unpatriotic' to be staying elsewhere. Having got past this grim middle-aged dragon, I found my reunion with my old friends was not particularly satisfactory either. It was amusing to meet up again with one student, a great character, with a fabulous memory for jokes. He was a born tease, always taking the other side in any discussion, especially on music or politics. His music was provocative too: I remember hearing a piano work of his which seemed in argument with the listeners, sounding like an orgy of wild cats jumping about on the piano keys. But he was not a particularly comfortable friend or companion in Paris.

Soon after our reunion, he arrived at my hotel in a sorry state just as I was sipping my morning coffee. He was desperate to use my room to sleep off a night of card-playing and drinking: the severe manageress of the Polish House would have made his life a misery if she had caught him sleeping instead of working during the day. His miserable face softened my objections. he collapsed into my bed, while I went over to my table and started trying to work. A few minutes later, the hotel manager came in to collect my breakfast tray. Catching sight of my sleeping compatriot, he looked at me with deep suspicion and left the room quickly with lowered eyes.

I was amused at this little incident, though my reputation with the hotelier was obviously shattered. But at the same time, it gave me an insight into the way my 'patriotic' fellow-Poles from the Polish House spent their time (and their grants) in Paris. As I was single-minded about the use of my time for my music, I rather avoided them after this.

My solitude paid off, not just because I could work undisturbed in the hotel on my symphony, but also because I could better absorb the atmosphere of Paris as I strolled alone and without particular direction through different parts of the city. With the utmost satisfaction, I discovered the characterful small back streets as well as the famous avenues, becoming totally bewitched by the subtle charms and fascination of the more ancient *quartiers*. Every evening, being less puritanical about my eating habits than I was over my social life, I took great care in my choice of bistro, exploring with enthusiasm the delights of the French culinary art. I was never bored alone, and found constant entertainment in observing the Parisians as they studied the menu, arguing over what should be ordered so seriously that it seemed a matter of life and death.

After six months, I was totally at home, almost in love with Paris, and could have stayed for ever. On the other hand I still wanted to visit England, the country of my mother's ancestors. I crossed the Channel early in March 1939, carrying in my suitcase the first twenty pages of my Symphony No. 1, which I hoped to finish during my planned four-month stay in London.

The British boat was very clean, with a curious mixture of smells: white paint combined with Virginia cigarettes, pipe tobacco, and bacon fried in heavy fat. I did not yet feel equal to an English breakfast, but attempted the strangely pale brown coffee, which, by my continental standards, tasted like mud. Almost all my fellow passengers were British. I suppose I may have seemed rather exotic with my excruciating English and strong accent, my high cheekbones and slanting slavonic eyes; I suddenly felt that people were looking at me askance, that perhaps being 'foreign' was less acceptable to the islanders of Britain than in the cosmopolitan atmosphere of Paris.

My visit to England began unexpectedly with an argument in immigration. Since I planned to stay for a matter of months I had to fill in a form with my biographical details. The immigration officer then prepared my identity card, but for my place of birth, he wrote, 'Warsaw, Russia' instead of 'Warsaw, Poland'.

I showed him my Polish passport, pointing out that Warsaw was in Poland not Russia. But he refused to alter my card. I argued in vain. My English was not strong enough to pursue the discussion successfully, and I felt myself up against a British brick wall. True, in 1914, the year of my birth, Poland did not exist as a state, being partitioned then between the three empires of Russia, Germany and Austro-Hungary. But I was not at all sure that the customs man even knew these historic subtleties.

I felt even more foreign as I was driven from Victoria station in an upright, box-like British taxi, eventually having to pay my fare in the perversely complicated English currency: twelve pence to a shilling, twenty shillings to a pound – it took me days to master this extraordinary monetary procedure.

The taxi delivered me to my so-called residential hotel, a huge old house, recommended by two of its regular residents who had befriended me the previous Christmas on a brief visit to Cannes. My large room was heated by a gas fire, but only if I put shillings in a meter – an extraordinary invention I had never met elsewhere.

My friends, who were retired music teachers, greeted me warmly and soon introduced me to everyone else in the hotel. To my surprise, all the occupants were booked in indefinitely, and almost all were between the ages of about 70 and 100.

Their elderly waitress was plainly unused to foreigners. My first morning at breakfast, she reeled off a huge list of menu items at great speed in a strong cockney accent. I timidly asked her to repeat herself, which she did in an excessively loud voice, apparently convinced that my lack of understanding was due to deafness. It was inconceivable to her, as indeed it was to a great number of the English people I met on that first visit, that anyone might not understand her native language.

Not wanting to starve, I gave an order in accordance with sounds I was able to copy during her recitation. Each day I made the effort to contort my tongue round some different con-glomeration of her incomprehensible syllables, waiting then with amused anticipation to see what would arrive. In this way, one morning I received kippers, another morning sausage, another bacon with eggs, another, to my amazement, prunes.

Breakfast was not so bad from the culinary point of view. At lunch or dinner I was frequently confronted with greasy lamb, overboiled vegetables, and a sweet, heavy pudding, smelling of perfumed soap, sometimes decorated with a kind of shaving cream. To my astonishment, all the residents seemed delighted with our diet, frequently saying that the food was 'lovely'.

Everyone arrived for meals with extreme punctuality as if catching a train. While waiting, they would talk about the weather with incredible intensity, looking towards the dining-room doors in the hope that they would soon be opened, with expressions on their faces like hungry but well-trained dogs.

Although all the residents of the hotel were more than three times my age they were always friendly and undemanding. If they talked to me, the subject would invariably be the vagaries of the English weather, which I felt was a sort of coded intro-duction to find out in a subtle way whether I was willing to have a longer chat.

I noticed that, if I ever used the normal polite formula, 'How are you?' without exception, the answer was 'Very well, thank you'. This was a complete contrast to the answer I would expect from a fellow Pole, who would be more likely to reply in a gloomy voice, 'Terrible, awful! I have a horrible toothache, my wife has been in hospital for several days, my son is doing very badly at school, my mother-in-law is coming to us tomor-row for a fortnight, etc.' Perhaps these catalogues of misfortune were revealed on the principle that the listener's own disasters might in comparison seem less bad than they'd imagined.

I liked and admired the British respect for privacy, the lack of curiosity or self-indulgent complaint. In this way I was happy to anglicise myself, and quickly adopted the 'Very well, thank you' response to any enquiry after my health.

Only occasionally, if one of Hitler's speeches was being relayed on the radio, the residents would drop their reserve, and call me urgently to translate the German in more detail than the announcer's summary. In the spring and summer of 1939, the British seemed to be watching events in Europe with considerable foreboding and fear; yet I could detect no sign of urgency, nor positive attempts from the politicians to prevent disaster. People listened to the speeches of Adolf Hitler with a sort of alarmed helplessness, watching his every move passively, as if he alone had the power to decide between war and peace – as if no one but he had a hand on the steering wheel of history. My alarming impressions from Vienna had imprinted into me a sense of desperation at the lack of positive action about or restraint of Hitler's ambitions. But, whatever I felt, there was nothing I could do, other than concentrate on my work, trying not to think too much about what might come next.

My hotel room was peaceful and perfect for composition, except that I had to contribute to the quietness myself, and was not allowed to bring in a piano. I was allowed to use the antiquated upright in the dining-room only for an hour or so before lunch, half an hour before tea and before the evening meal – moments at which the room was empty of diners or domestics. Fortunately, the piano was not essential to me while composing. I was happy to have just a few minutes a day touching the keyboard, trying out my melodic and harmonic thoughts.

As well as seeking out the few performances of contemporary British music, I also spent time at the British Museum studying in depth the manuscripts of some wonderful early English composers: Avison, Boyce and Arne. But I enjoyed most the non-musical aspects of London. I was overwhelmed by the richness of the English heritage. I particularly sought out the splendour of the architecture, so often hidden away and difficult to find, and I tremendously appreciated the great variety of magnificent works of art scattered through the numerous museums and galleries.

I began also to take pleasure in the mildness of the climate and the stability of the English way of life; it was so different from Paris where people seemed always irritated and impatient. Among the great British virtues, I was impressed by the political tolerance, which contrasted strikingly to the approach of many of my countrymen who were inclined to think of a person with different views to themselves as an enemy, or uneducated, or just stupid. Visiting Speaker's Corner in Hyde Park, I was amazed to hear so many strong conflicting opinions expressed and listened to in one place – without bloodshed!

I was particularly taken with the character and atmosphere of the London parks and gardens because of their areas of wilderness, giving at least a feeling of some slight communion with nature – so unlike the tidy and neatly cultivated continental parks. And I found the affection for animals most touching; for dogs, it seemed, the British Isles must be the happiest place in the world!

My stay in England thus turned into a serene epilogue to my musical studies abroad. The calm atmosphere of London brought me some peace of mind and put me into a meditative mood, so that I was able to digest my recent studies in Paris and Vienna, and give serious thought as to how, politics permitting, my future career might develop on my return to Poland. In the mood to write music rather than listen, and disappointed that the rather dull and conservative programmes of the London season included hardly any contemporary British works, I found myself going to fewer and fewer concerts. Even the performance of Beethoven's Choral Symphony, conducted by the famous Arturo Toscanini in the superb acoustics of the Queen's Hall, did not deeply stir me. Though I appreciated the high standard of musical performance in London, it was a moment in my life to look inward rather than outward. I was funnelling my mind, building up a far more intense concentration on my composition than I had managed before, with the result that my Symphony No. 1 was progressing fast.

The time passed swiftly and peacefully. For me the only really memorable musical event was when Felix Weingartner came to conduct Wagner at Covent Garden. His performances were magnificent, as always. He seemed very pleased to see me again. Now at last he was able to tell me how, though not a Jew himself, because of his deep anti-Nazi principles he had been ruthlessly dismissed from the State Academy: 'My seventy-fifth birthday present,' he said with some bitterness.

With his customary reserve, however, he did not want to talk more about himself, but asked me whether I had plans to try to establish myself as a conductor in England. When I replied that I was about to return to Warsaw, he reacted as if I had said something horrifying. Whispering in my ear with the greatest agitation, as though he were telling me a very important secret, he said, 'Don't go back to Poland. Stay here. Don't you realise what is going on in Europe?'

I replied, 'Yes, I do realise, and for this reason I feel it to be my duty to go back to my country, and, if necessary take part in its defence. I also have family duties: my old parents, my sick mother – they may need me.'

I found myself speaking almost apologetically. Weingartner however continued to urge me with considerable emotion, 'Stay here! I will help you. I have many friends who would certainly come to your assistance. You could have so many opportunities here – opera, ballet, concerts. In Poland you may not have the chance to develop your musical talents. Even worse, your life could be in jeopardy. Stay here! Stay!' he insisted urgently – and I saw tears in his eyes.

I could only be silent, and Weingartner, seeing my unrelenting expression, seemed to understand my determination.

This was my last encounter with him. He returned to his new home in Switzerland, and I was soon on my way back to Poland. I thought him a great man and one of the few truly great conductors.

7

OUTBREAK OF WAR

In France and England, I had noticed, despite the curious apathy, at least a vague awareness of the dangers of the deteriorating situation in Central Europe. Back in Poland, I found my countrymen completely out of touch with reality.

A few days after my return to Warsaw, I met an old school-friend and our conversation soon turned to politics. I told him gloomily of the scenes I had witnessed in Austria the previous year, voicing my dread that Hitler's expansionist aims could lead to tragedy and annihilation.

'Hitler?' my friend said, and burst into laughter, as though I had told him a good joke. 'You have just come back from abroad, so you don't know what we think in Poland?' His tone became suddenly harsh and aggressive: 'Hitler?' he repeated. 'We all shit on him with loose bowels!' (a charming expression he had coined from Marshal Piłsudski).

He plainly expected to shock me. I replied quietly, 'Of course, but don't you realise that he's capable of invading us. He's power mad! And the German army is said to be extremely well organised, disciplined, very strong . . .'

I was interrupted, 'The German army? They don't know how to fight!' It was a firm declaration of faith, based on the widely held belief that only Poles had military prowess.

'But they have incredibly tough, lethal tanks,' I argued. 'I saw them in Vienna. What is more, they can produce them with great speed, in great numbers.'

'German tanks?' My friend laughed with total assurance. 'They are made of paper. Everybody knows that. If they dare to attack us, our boys from the cavalry will finish them off in a flash!'

His naïve views on the invincibility of Poland were shared by practically everybody I met. For the time being I had to keep quiet about my fears. However, as the situation in Europe worsened, the Government gradually began to admit to the general public the possibility of military conflict in the not-too-distant future. These hints soon turned to positive defiance. An optimistic slogan, borrowed from Marshal Rydz-Smigły, the Minister of Defence, was trumpeted forth by press and radio so many times a day that eventually it became sickening: 'Incursion by force will be repelled by force!'

In the second half of August, Ribbentrop and Molotov signed the Nazi-Soviet Pact, which anybody with the remotest political awareness could see would be leading towards another partition of Poland. But neither our press nor our public took much notice; the only dissent emanated from a small group of Polish Communists who were puzzled and distressed by the concept of partnership between Fascist Nazi Germany and Communist Russia. Even when the Government suddenly issued gas masks and imposed a blackout after dark, life in Warsaw continued apparently carefree: the streets were full of happy, strolling people, the cafés were bursting with life as never before – we were like the passengers on the *Titanic* just before it sank.

On 1 September 1939, I switched on the radio; a voice calmly announced: 'This morning the enemy began military action.'

With a sort of numbness, almost beyond fear, distress or horror, I instantly translated that casually uttered phrase into one most tragic word – WAR!

Not much later, the same day, the detonation of exploding bombs dropped by German aeroplanes and the smaller explosions from our anti-aircraft artillery starkly confirmed the radio announcer's words.

In our courtyard, two innovations appeared for our protection. The first was a warning bell, installed in case of gas attacks. The next day, the alarm sounded and we all put on our gas masks, though a few minutes later we were given the all-clear. Was the alarm a mistake? Sabotage? Nobody knew. Now fear was rife; the false calm had switched to over-rapid panic. The second innovation, also for our protection, was a large crucifix which was certainly no less effective than the warning bell. Elderly women sang religious songs in front of it and prayed on their knees to God for deliverance.

During the days that followed, however, I obtained the strong impression that God was on the other side: not one protective concealing cloud marred the clear blue skies. Vision was perfect, ideal for the evil purposes of the German pilots. Bombs rained from the wide open heavens.

My brother Mirek spent day and night at the Polish Radio in central Warsaw. Although only thirty, he was director of the technical department, and was in charge of the emission of a constant barrage of fiery patriotic messages from the Mayor. My mother spent her days amongst the frantic crowds who were panic-buying every last morsel of food from the almost barren shops. But my father remained calm, telling us with total conviction that he 'dwelt in the grace of God', so that the situation concerned him little. He displayed anxiety only over the preservation of his precious stringed instruments. He spent hours packing them carefully into boxes so that he would be able to carry them to safety in case of fire.

Lacking my father's absolute faith in God, I was depressed and frightened, not so much by the thought that I might be killed within the next few hours — even minutes — but by the overall recognition of the likely consequences of war, the huge loss of life and destruction of our national heritage. I could not suppress my pessimism about the outcome — a pessimism contrary to the belief of the majority of the Polish nation — that the enemy would be quickly and easily repelled and that total victory for Poland was as beyond question as two plus two equalling four.

Our defending army was now strongly in evidence in the streets in Warsaw. The traffic consisted entirely of army vehicles, except for one private car I saw parked near our home — a highly polished limousine into which an army officer was loading large, elegant suitcases. A few moments later I saw him drive off rapidly in the company of a beautiful woman. It did not look to me as if he was going to the front line . . .

Three days after the outbreak of war, great news came through on the radio; that England and France were coming to the defence of Poland. Our joy was indescribable.

We also were told of the heroic resistance our soldiers were putting up in the face of the German invasion. My pessimism suddenly turned into hope. I found myself in high spirits as I began to dream about a Polish victory, and these emotions translated themselves into an idea for a new composition. For at least a small part of each day I forced out of my consciousness the terrifying bombings, and the hazards and frustrations of our current existence, and started to write my *Heroic Overture* to celebrate the courage of our Polish defenders.

The basis of my overture was some notes from the powerful and popular patriotic song, *Warszawianka*, though I did not quote the actual melody. My idea was to reflect its rousing spirit, yet also introduce an element of optimism, leading to a triumphant conclusion.

This creative activity helped me to combat my sense of uselessness and helplessness as a non-soldier, allowing me at least some outlet for the patriotic feelings which I needed to express tangibly. However, it was not easy to compose with so many problems in our day-to-day lives.

Shortages of almost everything became a dominant theme. One morning I heard shouting down in the courtyard; an appeal for help for our wounded soldiers arriving from the front. Civilian volunteers were urgently collecting bandages, cotton-wool and linen, all desperately needed for the hospitals. I went straight to my bedroom, pulled the sheets off my bed and threw them down from the balcony. My mother, weeping, also gave much more than we could spare. Tragically the Government had made no preparations for such emergencies. There was a lack of medicine and disinfectant, and the soldiers were dying in their thousands. Among them no doubt were those valiant cavalrymen who, on their galloping horses, had indeed attacked the German tanks and found that they were not made of paper.

Another day I heard someone shouting that poisoned sweets had been dropped in the streets throughout Warsaw from German aeroplanes, and that children must be warned not to pick them up. A more promising piece of news, also spread by word of mouth, was that English soldiers had landed on our Baltic coast and were advancing towards Toruń (a town in northern Poland). Both these rumours were false. The English ships had made no move to leave their ports, and the German aircraft were dropping not poisoned sweets but bombs.

As street after street was demolished, I volunteered for the Anti-Aircraft Defence. I was armed to fight off the invaders with just a spade and two buckets of sand. My duty was to climb out on to the narrow platform in the centre of the sloping tin roof of our own apartment building, and watch for incendiary bombs, which were falling in great quantity all over Warsaw. I was to pile sand on any bomb that landed – a task for which I was ill-equipped, as I had neither a fireproof suit, nor a helmet, nor even gloves.

Each day on the roof, I had an astonishing view of the explosions all around us, flames from burning houses in our neighbourhood and feathers from burst cushions and pillows, fluttering densely on currents of air like snowflakes. It would have been a magnificent sight, but for the human suffering and loss.

Inevitably the dreaded moment came: an incendiary bomb fell just a few metres from my feet. Looking like a small fat brandy bottle, it burst on impact, with sparks flying in all directions, reminding me of innocent childhood fireworks called 'cold flames' (sparklers). But this was no toy. The sparks were deadly dangerous, far from cold; they could penetrate the flesh through to the bone in an instant. Fear gave me courage. Hurling sand at the blazing canister, I battled for ten gruelling minutes to extinguish the continuing outbursts of sparks as they jumped all over the sloping roof. It was a miracle that no spark reached me and that, with all my rushing about, I didn't fall four floors into our courtyard. The inhabitants of our building remained oblivious, its fabric and their belongings unharmed.

In spite of perpetual hunger and the increasing activity of the German dive-bombers, I carried on with my watch. After a few more days the Polish Anti-Aircraft Defence collapsed, enabling the bomber pilots to fly extremely low without fear of reprisal, diving over our houses in broad daylight with their penetrating howl, killing innocent men, women and children. The wings of the planes were so close to my rooftop that I sometimes imagined that they would slice me in two. The real danger was that they now sprayed the rooftops with bullets as well as dropping their quota of bombs.

My parents and I now had to face the fact that we had finished our modest store of food. We were painfully hungry, but all the shops had been either destroyed or looted. I went out to hunt for something to put in our empty stomachs, and fortunately encountered a peasant offering a live chicken at an astronomical price. I emptied my pockets, and brought it home proudly to my parents — but the problem of satisfying our hunger was still not solved. None of us had the courage to kill the pathetic, still clucking creature!

My father finally volunteered. He took the bird to the kitchen and stood over it with an axe in his hand for several seconds before conceding that he was incapable of committing murder. We didn't know what to do. Eventually we had to beg the co-operation of a tougher neighbour, though we had to exchange some of our precious meat for his help.

Throughout this time of hunger, fear and tumbling bombs, the Mayor of Warsaw continued to harangue us with fiery patriotic speeches, exhorting us to defend our capital ener-getically. The Supreme Commander also kept chivvying us along on the grounds that 'Our defence is inseparable from the honour of the Polish people'; that 'Victory is certain'; that 'Time is on our side'; that 'We must never lose heart', etc. No one explained how we were to achieve these noble aims with-out any anti-aircraft defence and without our superb cavalry regiments which had already been decimated.

Tragedy struck on 17 September: in addition to an ex-ceptionally heavy bombardment, the destruction amongst numerous other buildings of the magnificent Royal Castle and the Cathedral of St John, and as well as the death of a huge number of people, came the news that the Soviet Army had begun its occupation of eastern Poland. The Russians had stabbed our beleaguered, battered country in the back.

The Soviet excuse was that their action was to protect the

minorities in those areas; the Ukrainians, Byelorussians and Lithuanians. The truth was that the fourth partition in Poland's history had neatly been completed on the basis of the Hitler-Stalin Pact.

Some Polish forces had stood their ground bravely in sporadic but fierce resistance to the Russians, but the final outcome was disastrous. Many hundreds were killed, thousands more arrested and deported to the depths of Russia. The unending martyrdom of the Poles had now entered a new phase.

Together with the bombs that were raining down came the propaganda leaflets that cleverly exposed our own fears: 'resistance is pointless, without hope, because the English and French, your so-called allies, are doing nothing for you'; 'the Russian Army has crossed the whole length of the Polish frontier, and is now invading Poland'; and 'the Polish Government has run away to Romania'.

Almost everyone gritted themselves to ignore these leaflets, determined to defend Warsaw to the last drop of their blood. I half agreed, yet could not help questioning this extreme stoicism, which, in such dire circumstances, could only cause further horrendous loss of life without hope of regaining our freedom.

A tragic outcome now inevitable, my plans for the *Heroic Overture* with its victorious conclusion disintegrated. I could not even bring myself to look at my sketches. Creative work and the very idea of committing notes to paper or imagining the foregathering of a symphony orchestra was unreal, unattainable. It was better not to think about music at all.

Anyway, what time I had free from my rooftop watch was taken up either comforting my sick mother (for whom medicine and painkillers were no longer available), or else searching for food. Once our hunger was so intense that I followed our neighbours' advice, and went out, kitchen knife in hand, to find a dead horse. (There were plenty of horses in Warsaw, from *dorożki* taxis, the peasants' carts, as well as the army.)

Amidst the smoke and dust from burning and ruined buildings, I threaded my way between the human corpses that were rotting on the pavements. Retching in vain – for my stomach was empty – I turned a corner and saw a few people fighting over the body of a dead horse, and hacking chunks of flesh from it. I closed my eyes, trying to gather the will and the strength to join them, but without success. I returned to my hungry parents empty-handed.

Towards the end of September, the bombardment had become continuous; the Germans were fiercely determined to crush the last remnants of resistance. The beautiful seventeenth- and eighteenth-century houses of the old town were flattened. The nightmare was intensified by the failure of all water, gas, and electricity supplies. In the large mirror in my parents' bedroom, I hardly recognised the filthy, starving creature who looked back at me. My dust-stained face was very thin, with black circles under my eyes and several days' stubbly growth of beard. My body was in constant motion, caused by the plague of parasites that was afflicting the entire city.

My anger was directed not only against the enemy but also against the craven dishonesty of those leading members of the Polish Government who never desisted in their rash assurances of our military might, yet left our people defenceless against the invincible enemy. They were still exhorting us to 'fight to the last man' even after the Soviet invasion and their own escape to Romania. However, my indignation could only be shared amongst close friends: most of our suicidally courageous compatriots would have written off such an attitude as treason.

The bombardment continued without pause for many more days. But then suddenly there was silence — no explosions, no screams. Amazed, I hurried out into the street, and heard one word being shouted — '*Kapitulcja!* Surrender!'

This was 1 October 1939. Within hours, German soldiers were driving through the streets in their open cars, admiring the ruins of my Warsaw, ignoring the inhabitants of the city, who mostly hid despondently indoors.

Over the next few days, emerging like rats from their holes, the Polish population summoned their remaining energy to bury their dead and seek out the bodies hidden beneath the rubble of houses, some of which were still smouldering. The city looked like an immense graveyard, marked all over with hundreds of crosses. Corpses were interred in the streets, the squares, everywhere.

Gradually, people's eyes began to open as they recollected the assurances and promises of the Polish leaders, now safely abroad. Their bitterness was beyond expression.

With no choice but to try to subsist under occupation, the city began very slowly to move again, like a wounded man staggering to his feet, tottering blindly, not knowing if he was struggling towards some sort of survival or a further agony of pain and death.

As the Germans were commandeering the dwindling produce from the farms, the food crisis continued. A few restaurants opened, offering no more than a bowl of watery soup. All we could legally buy was a tasteless and nutritionally valueless *ersatz* bread. The sale of real bread or meat or vegetables was illegal. But after some weeks, a black market gradually emerged for those who could find a lot of money, usually by selling jewellery or antiques. In order to raise cash, extraordinary risks were taken by the peasant girls, who transported meat for sale by concealing it about their persons. Large joints were smuggled into Warsaw by train and hidden in lavatories during the searches. Sometimes we could also buy the lethal *Bimber*, a vodka, I suppose, made of potatoes. It tasted as revolting as it smelt, but conferred a supremely comforting warmth and fairly rapid oblivion. We never knew when we might be shot in a round-up on the streets, or sent off to a labour camp, so death by burning our guts held no particular fear; we drank the liquid eagerly whenever we could lay hands on it.

As winter set in, the Germans tried to work upon our minds with the publication of a daily newspaper, *Nowy Kurier Warszawski*. Even the dimmest amongst us could see that this was no more than cheap propaganda and no one took the contents seriously. Yet we bought it sometimes: reading between the lines was for the moment our only hope of gathering any hint of what might have been going on anywhere else in Europe.

As well as building on our despair and attempting to crush any dream of resistance, this paper immediately set about pouring out a torrent of anti-Semitic invective, ascribing to the Jews the responsibility for our national catastrophe. They even tried to make us believe that the Jews had instigated the war and had provoked Hitler to attack Poland; that they had done this by the manipulation of press, radio and films, which (according to this newspaper) 'had all been under Jewish control'!

An order was issued that all Jews must wear a white arm-band with a blue Star of David whenever they left their houses. In this way the invaders could spot a Jew at sight. Thus the relentless Nazi persecution of the Polish Jews began. The invaders began to grab the wearers of arm-bands at will for any extra work, rounding them up on sight from the street, forcing them to mend roads and drains, to load and unload trucks: slavery at pistol-point.

My brother Mirek, who, on the day of the invasion, as a radio engineer had broadcast defiance against the Nazis till the last moment, had escaped with seconds to spare from the radio buildings. Now obviously there was no work for him and he was penniless with a three-year-old child and an alarmingly frail wife. I suggested that, to save money, they should abandon their house in a village outside Warsaw and join us in our flat.

Only days after they moved, a German soldier was killed near their old home. In revenge, all the houses in their district were raided at night and a hundred young men were dragged from their beds and cold-bloodedly shot. My brother would surely have suffered the same fate.

Christmas 1939 had a special poignancy. We were still together as a family; by some miracle we were all still alive. My mother insisted that we must celebrate. So that we could afford to eat more than *ersatz* bread and water, she sold some jewellery and sent me out to find what the black market could offer. After hours of searching, I came home with just a few bits and pieces, which at the time seemed the greatest luxuries, including a small bag of coal for our kitchen stove, a pre-war imported bottle of Vermouth, two pickled herrings, and a wonderful-smelling white loaf, bought from a brave girl standing with her merchandise against a wall in the street, right under a German poster announcing the death penalty for anyone caught selling real bread.

At dusk on Christmas Eve, the Polish tradition is to break

communion wafers and wish each other happiness. This year individual happiness had ceased to be a rational concept; our wishes were for the end of war, for Poland to regain her freedom.

There were no more bombs dropping from the sky. The immediate dangers now were encountered at ground level. In the new year of 1940, the Germans began to organise manhunts on a large scale; not only Jews, but any physically active-looking males became prime targets. Soldiers would arrive unexpectedly in some part of Warsaw, and, after sealing off a few streets, would arrest all the men they had trapped, searching them for arms or illegal literature; then shoot any who resisted or seemed suspect, and load the rest on to lorries.

The destinations of these lorries were forced labour camps in Germany or the new concentration camps the Germans were hastily building within Poland. These we learnt about first by word of mouth, then through the *Gazetka*, an illegal newspaper in tiny format circulated by the Polish Underground.

The possession of a radio set was as serious a crime as being caught with a gun: the penalty was death or a concentration camp. But since the radio was the only source of international news, we decided to take the risk. My brother, with his engineering skills, was able cleverly to conceal his installation in the cellar. Almost every evening we listened intently to the BBC's broadcasts in Polish from London. Even though they often brought bad tidings, the friendly voices cheered us because we knew at least we still had allies. Afterwards we would spread the news we heard amongst our friends and family.

In spite of the terror in which we lived, or perhaps because of it, I felt that I should turn back to my music. I had an idea to compose something very close to my native soil. One day, confined to the house to avoid unnecessary danger on the streets, rifling idly through our bookshelves, I opened a small collection of Polish peasant songs which somehow I had not looked at closely before.

I was spellbound by the beauty of the folk melodies, together with the innocent charm of the words. I chose five of the songs, using boys' or soprano voices in unison, weaving a background for them like a rustic tapestry with two flutes, two clarinets and a bass clarinet, evoking the sounds of shepherds' pipes to emphasise the pastoral setting. Though almost absurdly in contrast to the horror around us, somehow this tribute to the land expressed my faith in the future of my captive country.

As I was making the fair copy of these *Five Polish Peasant Songs*, I was suddenly interrupted by the loud sound of heavy boots kicking angrily on our door. Three German officers thrust past me as I cautiously opened it, demanding to see my father, going straight to a glass case where some of his violins were back on show. My father, sitting at his desk deeply absorbed in some scientific description of violin construction for his new book, was upset at being disturbed by these rough intruders. One of the officers shouted at him, 'All your instruments are confiscated! Pack them carefully and bring them at once downstairs to our van.'

My father spoke no German. As I translated, his face turned white as paper. My mother, overhearing my words from the next room, fainted cold on the floor. I did not know who to help first, my indignant father or my unconscious mother.

My father objected furiously, and so uncontrollably that I had to beg him to calm down in case he physically attacked the officers. They were armed and we were defenceless. We could not tell whether they were army or police; the only reason they gave us for confiscating the instruments was that they were acting 'on higher authority'. Allowing my father just half-an-hour for packing his sixty instruments, they shuffled their feet noisily as they waited. My father was handling each instrument as lovingly as if it were his child, and when the officers left with their spoils, his expression was that of a man bereaved.

Having witnessed my father's agony, I told myself that the Germans cared more for art than for human life, and that since I was in any case unlikely to survive the current situation in Warsaw, I could risk going to the Gestapo and trying to get my father's violins back for him. My plan was to brazen my way through and to complain that my father's life's work had been 'stolen' by individual soldiers for their own gain.

I approached the Gestapo building in trepidation, but forced myself to walk in with a confident air. The man at the desk addressed me in Polish — he was probably one of the Volksdeutsche, Polish citizens of German origin, many of whom collaborated with the enemy. He enquired arrogantly, 'So what are you going to sing out to me? Is this a *donos*, denouncement?'

'It is,' I replied firmly, and I briefly described the 'theft'. Without letting me finish my story, he interrupted angrily, 'This is not a *donos*! *Raus*! Scram!'

Having put my foot into the lion's den, however, I was not going to give up so easily. I worked my way round from the exit, taking a long corridor in the opposite direction, until I found myself face to face with a Gestapo officer, the front of his cap decorated with the miniature silver skull. Again summoning false confidence, I told him of the 'theft' and 'injustice' perpetrated on my father. His untypically sensitive, intelligent face was thoughtful for a few seconds, then he gave me the room number of a very senior officer on the floor above.

I hurried up the stairs, knocked on the door, and strode in on the command '*Herein*!', knowing that my only hope of survival was to maintain my air of calm authority and indignation. The high-ranking Gestapo officer, seeing an unexpected visitor in civilian clothes, seemed puzzled and just a little frightened. He was plainly unused to strangers walking into his office unannounced, but he asked me what I wanted quite calmly.

This third time of telling my story, I added to my act of righteous indignation, and tried to flatter his ego by making out that I was talking to a great and just man, with the power and good conscience to resolve this 'mysterious crime'.

To my amazement, he listened seriously, asked me to describe the men and their uniforms, suggesting that they came from the police rather than the army, and, as he dismissed me, promised to investigate further.

For a fortnight nothing happened. Then another police officer arrived at our house on a motorcycle. This time he did not bang the front door with his boots, but rang the bell. He handed me a letter from a certain Governor Fischer authorising the return of the instruments, which I was to collect from the Governor General's office at the Palais Brühl (the former site of the Ministry of Foreign Affairs). My father's face immediately lit up with joy.

Next day with rather less joy and considerable disquiet, trying to imagine my father's rapture at the sight of his instruments rather than myself under arrest, I arrived at the Palais Brühl and handed my letter to a particularly grim-looking SS man. For some uncomfortable moments he stood there scrutinising me from the top of my carefully tidied hair to the soles of my extremely worn-out shoes. At last he gave the order to follow him.

He led me through doors, locking them behind us, through lengthy corridors, down dark stairs into a cellar — by which time I was terrified, convinced that my last hour had struck and that, at any moment, he would take his pistol out from the huge holster at his hips.

We came to a large, dusty, cobwebbed room, stacked from corner to corner with magnificent antique furniture, paintings by Old Masters, Persian carpets, crystal, silver — a treasure trove of loot amassed probably not for the Nazi rulers in Germany, but for the petty governors and SS chiefs in Poland to distribute amongst themselves.

Amongst the more carefully stacked treasures, my eyes fell on my father's violins. They were scattered on the stone floor, in a terrible state, some deprived only of their strings and bridges, others with their necks broken, some of them with their carefully hand-carved bodies smashed beyond repair. I was dazed with dismay as I silently stared at them. The voice of the SS man rasped behind me: 'How are you going to carry them?'

My reply matched his for arrogance, and was even louder, for I was furious beyond fear. 'The same way that they were taken from us. You will arrange a van and pack them very carefully for the journey!'

He was so surprised that he didn't know how to react. He left me without a word and returned a few moments later with two men, who proceeded to pack the instruments and load them into an army van.

When I arrived home with them, my father couldn't believe his eyes. He was so happy to see his violins again that he would not allow the occasion to be spoilt by the fact that one third of the collection, some of the best ones, were missing, and others

were badly damaged. That evening we had a very special supper, and even managed to find some vodka for our celebration.

Two weeks later, I received another letter summoning me
back to the Palais Brühl. Arriving there, I was led straight to
an elegant *salon*, the office of Governor Fischer himself, who
was actually living in the Palais. He was standing by the window, surveying the scene, and ignored me as I entered. Ac-
customed as I was to my half-starved countrymen, I found his
healthily pink complexion and heavy frame repellent.

Suddenly he turned on me in fury: 'When you collected
your father's instruments, you also took some of mine; I want
them back immediately!' (I learnt later that he liked to play
cello in a string quartet; probably he ordered the confiscation
of my father's instruments so that he could get together some
additional chamber players from amongst his fellow officers.)

I answered in the greatest amazement, 'I most certainly
didn't touch any instruments of yours. On the contrary, we
have back fewer than were taken from us, only two-thirds of
my father's collection. The others, according to your officer,
were "lost on the way"!'

' "Lost on the way"?' he repeated, pausing for a few
moments' contemplation. Then he said curtly, 'You can go.' I
went away feeling, just at that moment, that it was almost safer
to be a helpless Pole than a corrupt SS man on the staff of the
equally corrupt Governor Fischer.

Soon after I got home, two Germans in plain clothes arrived
with an inspection order from Governor Fischer. They were
quite polite, but examined all my father's instruments one by
one, then thoroughly searched every room, even looking in the
lavatory. Of course they could not make his non-existent instruments materialise, so eventually they left, and to our relief we
heard no more of this incident.

8

OCCUPATION

Over the next few months, Warsaw slowly resumed a semblance of life. Shops selling necessities gradually reopened. A few cafés and restaurants were also permitted to trade, some of them newly built; they displayed a brave façade of elegance, with society ladies working as cooks and cashiers; the waitresses were beautiful girls, also often from aristocratic families.

The city's transport system had changed its appearance drastically. Without petrol, cars and taxis had disappeared. However, the red electric trams started to trundle again through the streets, the front seats reserved for the Germans. The tram conductors would pocket our money, usually without issuing tickets, intending later to share out their profits with the driver and controllers; cheating the occupying forces was a patriotic duty so we did not demur. Away from the tram routes, it was sometimes possible to find a *dorożki*, a shabby old carriage drawn by a painfully undernourished horse. The only other form of taxi was a home-made rickety rickshaw. Desperate for some sort of a living, people had converted old bikes into tricycles; the passengers were hunched uncomfortably in a cramped double seat over two front wheels. The driver, provided pedal-power from behind. Only once, when late for an appointment, did I ride in a rickshaw. It was distressing to hear the driver gasping for breath behind my neck. I felt sure that he must be damaging his health, so I gave him the full fare we had agreed, but finished the journey with my own foot-power.

The ways that people earned their living in Warsaw at this time often bore no relation to the profession for which they had originally trained. Highly qualified engineers, doctors, artists, schoolteachers and university lecturers became door-to-door salesmen, touting sausages, tobacco, underwear, or anything else they could find to sell for a modest profit.

Professional musicians of high calibre were to be heard playing in the streets for a pittance. Sometimes they gathered together in ensemble. Once I heard a whole orchestra, so excellent that I stopped to investigate. The conductor was none other than my teacher from the Warsaw Conservatoire, Professor Major Śledziński, who had shown me kindness and understanding when I was struggling in the grips of National Service.

The black market flourished. The rich, mostly the aristocracy, entered into eager partnership with the black market speculators, usually of humble origin. Fresh meat, the best French cognac, English or American cigarettes – all were available to wealthy folk. For the rest of us, a little fresh farm produce was the greatest treat to be indulged in only rarely, at the cost of selling some household valuable. We were constantly hungry, subsisting on our daily diet of rationed *ersatz* bread and jam made from beetroots. Our clothes were tattered and our shoes worn, as they could be replaced only at black-market prices.

Nevertheless, we had a better life than one section of the population. In the summer of 1940, the Jews began to be herded into one part of Warsaw where many had previously lived but which had now been specially allocated to them: the ghetto. It became an isolated island within the city of Warsaw, its borders heavily guarded by soldiers. Many of these soldiers, though in German uniform, were actually Ukrainian, Latvian or Lithuanian, being used remorselessly by the Nazis for their dirtiest work.

Day after day we would see little family groups, wearing white arm-bands marked with the blue six-pointed Star of David, being marched by armed escorts along the middle of the road, each person carrying one small piece of hand luggage containing all they were allowed to bring from their old homes. Once, in such a group, I caught sight of a familiar face, our dear tailor. Unable to control myself, I rushed up to him under the angry eyes of his guard. Marching alongside him, I whispered urgently, 'Mr Milis, I am so sorry this is happening to you. We all wish that we could help you, but what can we do against these armed soldiers?'

However, he beamed at me from under his drooping peasant-style moustache with his usual kindly smile and said, 'Don't worry, Mr Andrzej. As I see it, it's a change for the better. We shall have better accommodation, our lives will be better organised, we shall have more food — everything is for the best.'

At this point the soldier marching nearest to us gesticulated in my direction with his rifle, indicating that I should curtail my conversation. But it was in any case useless to burden Mr Milis with my pessimism and fear on his behalf. I was pounding with rage and frustration that there was nothing I could do for him that would not be suicidal for us both. The trustful attitude of my tailor was shared by other Jewish friends of mine, who had not seen the true face of Nazism as I had in Vienna and seemed to attribute to all Germans the civilised values they associated with Beethoven and Goethe.

Being a non-Jew and living outside the ghetto also had its dangers. The Nazi policy was to keep us all in a state of terror and suspense, so they carried out spasmodic raids, occasionally even rounding people up at random and shooting them in cold blood on the streets. One moment it would seem possible to move freely about the city; the next we were again at gunpoint — like the day I was on a tram when it suddenly shuddered to a screeching halt. A cluster of SS men swarmed aboard and ordered all the men to show their *Kennkarte* — an identity document giving details of profession and place of work. (Anyone out of work could not obtain a *Kennkarte*, except with the help of a skilful forger.)

Neither I nor anyone else present possessed one; we were all therefore ordered out of the tram and into a huge waiting lorry. There could be little doubt about the possible fate awaiting us: a long ride to an unknown destination, a concentration camp or a labour camp in Germany, or immediate death against some lonely wall. I decided that escape was less risky. Climbing down from the tram, I turned as instructed towards the lorry, but did

not stop when I reached it. With studied calm and slow, pur-
poseful steps, I walked straight on. I was already beyond the
front wheels when I heard a loud voice shouting '*Halt! Halt!*'
In one agonising second, I had to decide whether to turn back,
or to behave as if I did not know these words were directed at
me. I continued my slow walk, and to my amazement nothing
happened. After two or three minutes I reckoned the gamble
had paid off. But then another horde of SS men approached
from further down the street, again demanding a *Kennkarte*. In
my fluent German, to which I added a slight Viennese accent, I
told them that just a few moments before I had shown my
documents to their colleagues. Fortunately they were taken in
by my confident air; I escaped again, but I remained haunted
by the likely fate of the other men on the tram.

After this episode, I reluctantly concluded that the *Kennkarte*
afforded at least partial protection against the haphazard death
or deportation being meted out at whim by our oppressors
against any able-bodied-looking Pole. But it was impossible to
find work as a composer or conductor. The German administration did not allow us to carry on any sort of musical life in
the concert halls of Warsaw; in any case the Philharmonic Hall
and Opera had been bombed and the Conservatoire had been
forcibly closed. Some musicians earned their keep by forming a
small symphony orchestra for the entertainment of Germans
only: it was repugnant but perhaps excusable work for those
that had large families of children to feed; other weaker souls
(despised by the rest of us as collaborators), saw no prospect of
an end to German occupation, and persuaded themselves that
playing for our enemy was unharmful to the Polish cause. But
most Poles, even in the darkest, seemingly endless years of occupation, retained a thread of pride and optimism and an un-
broken spirit of resistance.

The musicians and music-hungry audiences of Warsaw
meanwhile had discovered a cunning solution to the ban on assembled audiences. Some imaginative entrepreneurs created
'artistic cafés', featuring leading performers of both classical
and light music. Instead of buying tickets, the public, sitting
casually at tables, paid for their entertainment by ordering cups
of coffee or tea.

Thus a new sort of musical life was born. Our oppressors did not intervene, except that the music of Jewish or Polish composers was banned, especially Chopin. The Germans understood very well the words of their own great composer Schumann, that 'Beneath the flowers in Chopin's work are hidden cannons!'

Without any *Kennkarte*, I had for some time been raising a little money for the family by appearing at one of the artistic cafés. To my joy I had discovered that my old friend from the Conservatoire, the Jewish violinist Tadeusz Geisler, was not in the ghetto, but was still somehow living with his parents in a flat not far from our home. For a while we had been performing as a duo. To emerge and play in public was a mortal risk — for him and everyone else involved — but any such act of defiance helped us to feel less crushed. This particular artistic café was suddenly closed, because, according to rumour, its Jewish owner had committed some anti-Nazi acts for which he was shot. So Tadeusz and I were jobless again. His parents anyway were worrying about his safety, and he disappeared quite suddenly out of my life. Probably the whole family left Warsaw and hid in the country.

Not eager to be a solo pianist, I looked around for a new partner, with whom I could establish a working situation and obtain the essential *Kennkarte*. Another good friend from Conservatoire days, Witold Lutosɫawski, was at that time earning his living by accompanying a popular group of male singers performing tangos, waltzes and foxtrots. I suggested that we might try something artistically more rewarding, that together we should set up a two-piano duo.

Witold agreed warmly, and our three-and-a-half year partnership was rapidly established. It was impossible to buy any sort of printed music so we immediately began creating our own arrangements of classics, writing down our parts by mutual suggestion, then rehearsing them together. We would debate together with great intensity and enjoyment, working out the problems of piano technique in arranging pieces originally written for wide variety of instrumentation, including huge orchestral forces. Both of us being almost obsessive perfectionists, it was time-consuming but fascinating.

The Café SIM, where we first played, had before the war been a gallery for the sale of modern art, its spacious salon lit by a huge glass window in the ceiling. (The recitals always took place in the late afternoon because of curfew at dusk.) Our two pianos stood at the end of the salon on a raised podium. The audience, scattered around us at their tables, was drawn from a wide spectrum of the population. From time to time we rejoiced to see amongst them our Jewish friends, even those with strongly Semitic features, such as the brilliant painter Marcin Szancer and the poet, Zbigniew Brzechwa. With no radios possible, they were so starved for music that they would risk emerging from hiding with their brave non-Jewish wives.

Our constantly expanding repertoire soon encompassed works from Bach and Mozart, through to Schubert, Beethoven, Brahms, Debussy and Ravel, then to more complex twentieth-century music such as Szymanowski and Stravinsky. Szymanowski, being Polish, was blacklisted, but this encouraged rather than prevented us from performing our version of his ballet, *Harnasie*, and one of his violin concertos. We would have performed Chopin, even though the music could so easily be recognised, but it was impossible to transform such perfect piano solo music into anything bearable on two pianos.

Sometimes, for fun, we performed jazz, particularly Duke Ellington and the best of the Americans, dangerously including the music of blacklisted Jewish composers such as Gershwin. Sometimes, to avoid boredom as we performed day after day, we would throw away caution in a different way and improvise our own jazz pieces, totally unrehearsed. Before starting, we would draw a diagram indicating tempo and harmonic progression in a given number of bars. From this tiny scrap of paper, we would spontaneously invent melodies, counterpoints and rhythmic patterns, taking staggering risks, terrifying each other by tearing away in flights of wild imagination, yet never giving away the secret to our audiences that we were improvising rather than performing carefully written and rehearsed music.

We soon found that we had a great many admirers, including some beautiful young women who brought us bouquets of flowers. What a way for two young composers, both so serious and ambitious, first to find their fame!

On the whole, our concerts were without incident. There was, however, one formidable exception.

One afternoon, Witold and I had just launched into yet another duet – I think it was a Brahms waltz – gentle, soft music anyway, and our audience were quiet with concentration, when our hearts almost stopped at the sound of gunshot and screams from the entrance hall. A troop of SS men burst in, their pistols still hot, yelling a command for all the women to go to one side of the salon, all men to the other. Panic ensued with mothers, wives, sisters and girlfriends weeping aloud as they embraced their menfolk, convinced that they would never see them again. The Gestapo forcibly separated them. '*Schnell! SCHNELL!* Hurry! Hurry!'

We had to stand, our backs to the wall, our hands above our heads. The sobbing women were sent home. Once they had gone, the SS men set about intimidating us with threats and swearing at us. One of them waved a pistol, still reeking of gunpowder, right close to my nose, and snarled 'Now you'll see what'll happen to you!'

We all expected to be shot instantly. However, after standing with our hands above our heads for a seemingly interminable time, instead of feeling bullets in our flesh, we were ordered out into waiting lorries. As Witold and I started with everyone else to trudge despairingly towards the exit, the manager of the café intervened, persuading the SS commander that we were not members of the public but professional musicians on his staff. Miraculously, we were allowed to stay.

It was essential not to falter under the daily terror in which we lived. The next day we turned up to play again. We had to tell ourselves that we were not just earning our living, or supporting our families, but that our continuing concerts helped to boost morale. Life had to go on, however unbearable the circumstances. More and more of our contemporaries were being sent to Germany to concentration camps. An agonised letter from my brilliant young doctor cousin, Antoni Panufnik, was smuggled out from Auschwitz; we read it with horror and a sense that our turn might come next.

So we lived from day to day, and went on playing the

piano. As well as our café performances, Witold and I took part in a number of illegal concerts organised by the Polish Underground; fund-raising events for people in dire financial need, such as marked men from the Resistance living in hiding or Jewish artists equally under pressure. At the same time these concerts enabled music-lovers to hear music banned by the Nazis.

They took place in private houses in the centre of Warsaw. For two to three hours before a concert was due to begin, people would drift in gradually, singly or in pairs, taking the greatest care not to show the enemy that a crowd was assembling. And again, after the concert was over, the audience could not disperse all at once for fear of arousing the suspicions of patrolling Germans.

Despite the danger involved, these were always very happy and moving occasions. Almost always we would share out copies of a new edition of the *Gazetka* with the latest news garnered from the BBC and from other Underground sources. People would seize the opportunity to pool their worries and fears, chatting freely amongst themselves and sharing in an atmosphere of friendship and united patriotism.

Another of my Underground activities was to meet secretly with a poet to plan a series of patriotic songs to help bolster the spirit of resistance. These encounters were organised by the AK, the Home Army, the largest and most effective of the Polish Underground movements. (Since 1941 when Hitler had invaded Russia there was also a Moscow-activated Communist Underground movement, the AL, which had only a tiny membership compared with the Home Army.)

For strict security reasons, the poet and I were not allowed to know each other's real names – only pseudonyms. In our clandestine encounters, in a tiny flat in central Warsaw, we would discuss themes that would convey the emotions we felt people needed to express as they sang together to build up their courage and defiance. Then I would sketch rhythms which musically could bring out the intended spirit and subject-matter. The poet would return with fiery texts for which I provided the melodies. Our songs were then printed on hidden presses, and widely distributed by the Home Army, to be sung at illicit meetings and at home amongst the family (sometimes even sung by daring young boys under the noses of the Nazis, who could not understand the Polish language). Some of the songs became extremely popular. Our greatest success of all, *Warszawskie dzieci* (Warsaw Children) spread wildly across Poland.

Because everything around us was sombre and grim, the occasional good moments of normal life shone with a special brightness. The companionship, the conversation, the exchanges of ideas with Witold and our other friends were unforgettable. For some time I had a room in the home of my childhood friend from the Szkoła Mazowiecka, the brilliant writer, Stanisław Dygat. (After my brother's family moved to our flat, there was not enough space or peace for me to work, though of course I continued to help support them, since my brother, fully engaged with his Underground activities, was unable to earn.)

I introduced Dygat's charming sister, Danusia, to Witold. (Later she became his wife.) I myself became deeply involved with a very beautiful war widow, Staszka Litewska, whose distinguished and brave husband, a cavalry colonel, had been killed in action. Staszka was as kind as she was attractive, very feminine, somehow retaining her beautiful full contours when the rest of us were scraggy from near starvation. She was an extremely gifted cook, able to create miracles with the miserable scraps of food we could obtain. Before long, I moved in with her and her two young daughters, helping her in her financial difficulties by sharing costs; benefiting also from her quiet spare room with a piano. We could not think of a future together in such impossible times when no future at all seemed the only rational prospect, but we found real comfort, even joy together; an escape from the blackness of our surroundings.

My mother's health, meanwhile, was a constant problem. Her condition seemed almost as much due to tension as to her clinical symptoms, so medicine was useless, though she drew great consolation from the occasional visits of her Jewish doctor, who, at that point of the war, was still allowed to leave the ghetto under guard to attend longstanding patients. In spite of constant alarms and moments of danger as well as hunger and physical hardship, I managed somehow to find time in the winter of 1941 to finish my Symphony No. 2.

Composition was necessarily sealed off from any thoughts of performance. I could only look critically at my efforts to date, and try to have enough faith in the future to start to contemplate what I would do next. Whereas my first symphony, finished some time before, against a background of man-hunts and terror, was of lyrical character with delicate, almost fragile scoring, and was written in one continuous movement, the second was composed in three movements, more classical in form, more heavily orchestrated. In both works I felt that I had, to a certain extent, broken free from the musical language of the past, but perhaps the first symphony belonged overmuch with the Romantics in character, while the second leant too far towards the classical mould. In my subsequent compositions, I decided, I must strive to combine these two elements in absolute balance, without emphasising one or the other. I would also attempt to impose an even stricter economy of means of expression; not write so much as one note too many.

By the beginning of 1942 it was almost impossible to find peace of mind to compose, even for a few minutes at a time. In daytime, I lived in constant fear of arrest as the German round-ups were intensified. When I walked in the street I had to behave like a hunted animal, keeping my ears and eyes sharpened to pick up any hint of lurking danger.

At night we faced a new danger from our apparent allies as now the Russian aeroplanes attacked Warsaw. When the first planes flew over at high altitude, they illuminated the city for the bombers by dropping bright, sparkling flares like gigantic candelabra, which drifted slowly down towards us, changing darkness almost into day. It would have been beautiful except for the bombardment that followed.

The noise of exploding bombs, mingled with the German anti-aircraft artillery, was ear-splitting. The horrors we had endured during the German siege of Warsaw three years earlier had to be experienced again. To my knowledge no German military targets were hit. The Soviets were in fact killing the innocent people of Warsaw, adding to the misery and despair we were already suffering under German occupation.

Meanwhile Witold and I somehow carried on with our café

recitals, by now at another venue, *U Aktorek* (The Actors' Café), situated in a charming, miniature nineteenth-century stately home. All the theatres having closed, the acting profession, in order to feed their families and obtain the essential *Kennkarte*, had drifted into the business of running and staffing the Artistic Cafés, particularly *U Aktorek*. Famous actors and actresses performed new rôles as waiters, doormen, even kitchen-maids; it was hardly pure acting, as they found themselves involved in hard physical work. Though the majority of our audiences were genuine music lovers, we were amused to realise that a considerable proportion of them were theatre-enthusiasts hoping to see their idols, perhaps so that they could boast afterwards that the Polish equivalent of Greta Garbo had brought them a cup of coffee, or that Poland's Gary Cooper had helped them into their coats with the most polite (and perfectly acted) words.

Our two-piano versions of the general musical literature had by now reached sizeable proportions. But we never discussed whether we would ever want the music published. It would have been pointless to dwell on the distant future or life after the war: we hardly expected tomorrow to arrive.

It seemed impossible that the situation could deteriorate further. But in April 1943, the Germans started their destruction of the ghetto. Day after day, week after week we heard the hammer of machine guns. From my window in Staszka's flat, in anguish, I saw smoke from the burning houses, and sometimes low-flying German aircraft spewing out their bombs in broad daylight.

My brother Mirek and his fellow members of the Polish Home Army smuggled in the few weapons they could get hold of, by way of narrow tunnels hand-dug under the barricades from neighbouring houses, through which they also helped as many inhabitants as possible to escape. Mirek's first-hand accounts of the brave but hopeless defence of the ghetto made me envious of his active rôle. The music of resistance was all that I could offer.

Though many inhabitants of the ghetto were rescued, a total exodus was impossible under the eyes of the occupying army. Eventually about 15,000 Jews were in hiding in the homes of non-Jews in Warsaw despite the dangers involved. I greatly admired my friends who risked concealing refugees. When caught, sometimes whole houses were burned by the Germans, the host families with their babies and children locked in to perish alongside their illicit visitors. Because refugees had often to change hiding places to keep ahead of searches, altogether tens of thousands of Warsaw inhabitants demonstrated their readiness to help. Whenever practicable, new identities were created. Priests falsified church records and provided christening documents. The Home Army punished by death any Pole who betrayed a Jew to the Germans. Of course it was not enough — nothing could have been enough — but our own situation was desperate. Arrests and terror did not let up for those outside the ghetto. A pessimistic catch-phrase was heard on many lips: 'Them today, us tomorrow.'

Somehow Witold and I managed to carry on with our attempts to cheer people with music in the cafés. I hadn't composed any new music for a year. I would sit in my little room in Staszka's flat, turning away in horror from its rooftop view of yet another pillar of black smoke from the ghetto, yet another salvo of gunfire. My helplessness and forcible inactivity were more painful than action: I would sometimes imagine myself crowding in with a group of friends to batter against the barricades with our bare fists, only able to demonstrate, not able to bring relief to those inside the ghetto, but at last to feel peace as the machine-gun bullets flattened us all. In order to hold in check the emotions which I felt were threatening my sanity, I decided to write a *Tragic Overture*, and began with the firm intention that it should be totally abstract, with no literary implications. I returned to my plans of a year before to search for a new musical language, rooting in the ideal of a stringent economy of means of expression, and chose a sequence of just four notes which would run from the beginning of the overture right through to the end. It was my intention to explore this four-note cell to the very limit. It might be transposed, augmented, sometimes inverted, but I must strictly guard throughout the entire work the same intervals between the notes (minor third, major second and minor second), always within a framework of repeated rhythmic patterns.

Once the work was finished, however, I could not help sardonically smiling at myself; though ostensibly I had kept to my rules, I realised that my intellectual disciplines had failed to control my unconscious, that the overture was interspersed with startlingly onomatopoeic passages — for example, the sound of a falling bomb (percussion); the soft engine noise of an aeroplane disappearing in the distance (trombones' glissando); a volley of machine guns (the burst of percussion in the final bars); the final chord shrieked out by the full orchestra, an agonising wail of despair.

Despite these surprises, which could be described perhaps as accidents of war, I think this was the first work in which I began to achieve my artistic endeavour to find a balance between emotion and structure — the fusion of dramatic power with a strictly disciplined economy in musical material. Although it was written at a moment when death seemed inevitable, in fact it marked for me an important musical beginning.

Meanwhile it appeared that *Tragic Overture* not only reflected the horror of the moment, but also heralded a succession of further tragedies, for Poland and within my own family. Even before I had put the last bars of this work on to paper, I received the appalling news that my cousin, Antoni Panufnik, had died in Auschwitz, leaving a widow and three small children.

We almost lost Mirek at that point, too. Not long after one of his dangerous missions into the ghetto, he was rounded up in a manhunt and taken to the notorious Warsaw prison, the *Pawiak*. He was caught by sheer chance; fortunately the Gestapo were unaware of his part in the arms-smuggling operation. After a thorough interrogation and examination of his (forged) *Kennkarte* amazingly he was released, perhaps helped by his Germanic looks – light blue eyes and blond hair – and his extremely nonchalant manner under arrest. (I was alarmed to learn from him that the secret of his confidence in captivity was a lethal poison kept hidden in his mouth, which, if the Gestapo used torture, he could instantly bite and die, so that he would never betray his fellow fighters or the tactical secrets of the Home Army.)

Mirek's problems and responsibilities were not, alas, limited to his patriotic activities. In 1943, his wife Maria's tuberculosis recurred. To pay for doctors, medicine and strengthening food, we had to sell my beloved Bechstein (it had to be the piano, as nobody seemed to want my father's violins). But effective medicine was no longer available, and the sanatorium in the Tatra Mountains which had seemingly cured her before had been taken over for use by Germans only.

The only hope was the delapidated hospital in Warsaw. I fetched a *dorożki*, and helped my brother carry Maria down from our flat. Her face was grey, and she coughed continuously as we carried her. After three months, she died at the age of twenty-four, when little Ewa was only six. It was a heart-breaking blow for my brother, but strangely enough, his agony strengthened him spiritually, making him even more fanatical and fearless in his struggle for Poland's freedom and independence.

9

LAST PHASES OF GERMAN OCCUPATION

After the destruction of the ghetto and the continuing oppression of the remaining Warsaw population, in our state of despair and weakening defiance, it would have seemed that nothing could shock us any further.

But then the Germans informed us, through their Polish-language press, that their army had discovered the bodies of many thousands of Polish prisoners buried side by side in Katyń Forest in Soviet Russia. These young men, the cream of the Polish intelligentsia, who had been trying to defend us against our enemies, had been interned by the Soviet Army. They had been forced to dig their own huge long trench of a grave before being shot one by one in the neck so that they fell into it. Many of the corpses also showed the marks of bestial torture.

The German finger of blame was pointed at the Russians. We were told that this appalling murder had taken place in 1940, over a year before the Germans had invaded Soviet Russia – a fact confirmed, they said, by documents and letters found in the uniforms of the dead Polish officers.

It was hard to know whether to believe in Russian guilt, or whether the story was a German lie to cover up their own crime. At that time we knew the Nazis as merciless mass-killers but had yet to experience directly the similar propensities in the Russians.

The Germans, in need now of more manpower, exploited the Katyń discovery as part of their sudden campaign to tempt us to work with them against the Russians. They also tried to find Poles with some German antecedents to collaborate with them in administration, or even to be sent to the Eastern front. I myself was once summoned and told by the *Kommandant* that I was 'partly German' and could have the 'privilege' of working for them! Fortunately it was only guesswork on their part, and I was able to talk my way out of the situation, laying heavy emphasis on my English antecedents, without giving away the fact that one great-grandmother, Henrietta Mey, came from Hanover.

The Nazis' increasingly urgent requirement for human resources was underlined by the daily sight of German soldiers back from the front. In contrast to their gleaming, ferocious appearance as they had marched through these same streets before attacking Soviet Russia in 1941, the returning soldiers now shuffled miserably past us in small groups, without weapons, heads and limbs bandaged, limping on home-made crutches, faces reflecting the pain of festering wounds and lingering frostbite. They looked more like prisoners of war than an army. Their wretched appearance pleased the citizens of Warsaw enormously.

Plainly the German 'successes' in Russia, as described in their propaganda, were a lie: we could assume that they had suffered huge losses and might at last be coming close to disaster.

At this time I followed with greater interest the events on the Eastern Front, in contrast to most of my fellow countrymen who concentrated their attention on the military activities in Western Europe, clinging to their conviction that the English and American forces would inevitably defeat Hitler and carry on through to liberate Poland. While nearly everyone in Poland, obtaining information through the BBC, studied their maps moving their fingers over Africa and Norway, I found my finger pointing to troop movements in Soviet Russia. My conviction that this was the direction from which the Germans would be chased out was shared by only very few people, most of them the small band of Polish Communists. But whereas the Communists believed in the inevitable victory of their political system, I was just being realistic, taking into consideration not only Poland's geographical position, but also the reputed readiness of the Russian soldiers to make sacrifices far beyond any that the Western Allies were willing or able to make.

A Warsaw joke of that moment illustrated widespread disillusion about the Allies. Churchill arrives in Warsaw to visit an army cemetery. He stands in front of a huge monument and reads, 'Here lie buried 2 million Poles.' On a second monument he reads, 'Here lie 500,000 Germans' and on a third, 'Here lie 10 million Russians.' Finally he stands in front of a tiny monument on which he reads, 'Here lie 14 Englishmen.' Extremely irritated, he shouts at the monument: 'I told you stupid puppies not to push so hard!'

Although the Germans did not renounce their terror-tactics, some slight relaxation of pressure was noticeable by the start of 1944. For example, the organisers of the Polish charity, RGO (*Rada Główna Opiekuńcza* – Central Council for Care) were now able to extend their activities, even obtaining permission to raise funds through charity symphony concerts.

I was invited to conduct the first of these concerts in March 1944, with my own choice of programme, to include one of my own works. The orchestra was to be made up from surviving members of the Warsaw Philharmonic, together with some distinguished soloists and professors from the non-functioning Conservatoire. I decided to perform the Mozart Piano Concerto in D minor, my *Tragic Overture* and my own instrumentation of Bach's Prelude and Fugue in D major for organ (which I had arranged for orchestra during the lonely Christmas of 1938 in Cannes at the time of my studies in France).

With no publisher, nor money to pay a copyist, I undertook the huge task of writing out all the orchestral parts myself, a daunting quantity of work to accomplish in the few weeks before the concert. Apart from the physical effort, it was extremely tedious to write six copies of the first violin part, five of the second, and so on through the whole string section, the brass, the woodwinds and percussion. Somehow I completed the work just in time, arriving at the first rehearsal with all the orchestral material tucked under my arm.

At the start of the rehearsal, for a moment I could hardly summon the courage to lift the baton. Doubts suddenly assailed me about my ability as a conductor. The hall, ominously, was the one where I had failed my exam and been disgraced at the age of twelve. Worse still, eight whole years had passed since I had last stood in front of a full professional orchestra, when, as a newly fledged laureate in 1936, I had conducted my composition with the Warsaw Philharmonic. Orchestras, of course, are far more critical of conductors than audiences. I was suddenly unsure whether they would be able to follow my gestures; how my own composition was going to sound; even whether some of my experimental passages would be technically possible for the instruments.

The orchestra were waiting. There was no escape. Summoning all my willpower, I stroked rather than tapped the desk with my baton to silence the tuning of the instruments, and announced my *Tragic Overture* as the first item for rehearsal. Feeling like a non-swimmer about to leap from the highest diving board, I thrust my arms forward, breathed deeply and gave a strong up-beat with my baton.

The orchestral sound of my overture, heard previously in my imagination only, was suddenly all about me, responsively and richly brought to life by these superb instrumentalists. As they played I gradually felt a return of self-confidence. At the end of the piece, to my amazement, they were wreathed in smiles and warmly applauding me!

The concert itself was far less alarming than that first rehearsal. I knew that the audience had come full of eagerness to participate in a longed-for symphony concert, that they would listen sympathetically to the first performance of a work, however new and difficult, not least because its title implied a close connection with our everyday grim reality. Indeed, the concert was a happy island in a sea of unhappy events and circumstances. The orchestra were generous and responsive to me. The public, crowding into the hall far beyond its capacity, gave us all a huge ovation.

My brother Mirek was there. Afterwards he came up to me and told me that he loved my *Tragic Overture* and that never in his life had a piece of contemporary music moved him so much. In his enthusiasm, he suggested that we should go and have a celebratory drink together. But I refused his invitation, as I had a prior arrangement with Staszka. Later I was to regret this refusal most bitterly.

The RGO organisers, delighted with the success of the concert, invited me to conduct another in two months' time. Again they asked me to include one of my own works. This time I chose my Symphony No. 2 – another first performance, involving me in another frantic bout of hand-copying an even larger quantity of orchestral parts. But I was no longer worried about facing the musicians in the orchestra: I knew now that I could depend on their skill and their friendship. The concert was again like a mountain peak high above the clouds of our wretched everyday life. The response from both orchestra and audience was headier for me than the finest vodka, and my eyes filled with tears of exhilaration and amazement as, at the end of the concert, I heard a tremendous ovation and many voices shouting in chorus, 'We have a conductor! We have a director for the Warsaw Philharmonic when the war is over!'

Mirek was unable to attend the second concert, due to his activities with the Home Army, but my father came in spite of the serious preoccupations which usually kept him at home. Finally he admitted that he had been deeply moved by my music, and praised me highly as a composer and conductor. It was the first occasion that he rescinded his overt disapproval of my chosen profession.

A few weeks after this concert, life in Warsaw underwent another drastic change. Suddenly the streets were filled with German supply columns rapidly on the move. The non-military traffic also increased, and the trams became so crowded that passengers clung on to the outside like clusters of grapes. The mood of the city was feverish and the air felt heavy, as if a storm were about to break.

Meanwhile, we had a new family worry. My mother, probably weakened by concern over Mirek's dangerous occupation, was now too ill to leave her bed. No medicine seemed to help her. The only hope was to take her away from the nightmare conditions of the city for a while. I tracked down an elderly couple willing to rent half their small villa set in a large garden in the rural outskirts of Warsaw.

My father stayed at home to look after his violins — it was unthinkable that he should ever be parted from them. I had not seen Mirek since the performance of my *Tragic Overture*. He was constantly on the move, involved in an intensification of Underground activities. Some time before he had taken little Ewa to stay with another younger family somewhere in the country.

Leaving all my music in my room at Staszka's flat, expecting to be absent for no more than a month, I took with me just a few books and a little manuscript paper. However, I could write no music in this brief break. All my energy went into the loving care of my mother. With long, peaceful chats about my work, about Ewa, about anything else but Mirek and the war, after a couple of weeks she seemed less wracked by anxiety and tension. Her health visibly started to improve.

Her progress, however, was interrupted by the alarming news that the Soviet Army was approaching Warsaw and that our capital could soon become a battlefield. As the warm sunny days of July drew to an end, Moscow Radio appealed to the inhabitants of Warsaw to rise against the occupying Germans, promising support from its own army, which indeed was already advancing into Praga, the eastern suburb of Warsaw, across the Vistula river from the main part of the city.

On 1 August 1944, we heard the news '*Powstanie! Uprising!*'

10

WARSAW UPRISING AND THE AFTERMATH

Isolated outside Warsaw and unable to tell what was happening to the family, my mother was again prey to acute anxiety, and I was little better. We had no way of knowing whether the Russians, now just the other side of the Vistula river, would keep their promise and come to the rescue of the courageous inhabitants of Warsaw. How otherwise could they stand up to more than a few days of hand-to-hand fighting against the well-armed Germans?

Whatever the difficulties of deserting my poor mother, I was frantic to return somehow to fight a last stand against the Nazis alongside my countrymen. But the problem of getting back into Warsaw turned out to be insuperable. German patrols were energetically hunting out wounded insurgents. Anyone with a *Kennkarte* showing that he came from Warsaw was a dead man. Anyone without a *Kennkarte* was also instantly shot. False papers were unobtainable. Without knowledge of the Underground safe houses along the way, there was no hope of arriving alive in the city.

It was hard enough to stay alive where I was. The Germans conducted almost daily searches. Our good, ancient hosts set up an early-warning system to save me; indeed they themselves were at deadly risk of being shot for harbouring me. Constant watch was kept. Whenever a patrol came near, I leapt out of a back window and clambered into the disused garden well, pulling a wooden lid over my head. Waiting for the patrol to move on, I had to balance across the deep shaft, my hands and feet struggling to keep their grip on the narrow, slimy ridges. I performed this operation dozens of times; just one slip and I would have drowned in the brackish black water deep below. I could not have shouted for help, for fear of betraying not only myself but my hosts.

Unpleasant as these episodes were, they were nothing compared with the apprehension and distress we felt as we watched huge clouds of smoke gathering every day over central Warsaw and the bright glow of burning houses at night, our ears constantly assailed by the crash and splutter of heavy artillery, the sharp counterpoint of machine guns, and the thunder of the aerial bombardment.

This nightmare lasted not for two days, not for two weeks, but for two whole months. I spent the interminable days divided between my anger and pain at being unable to join the insurgents, and anxiety both for my city and my family. As I watched over my mother, I thought she would die of despair; but the need for news seemed to keep the pulse of her life just ticking along. The fate of young Ewa and my father was worrying enough, but what about my brother who, without doubt, was in the thick of the action? What was happening to Staszka and her two daughters? When my mind had churned more than I could bear over the fates of those I loved, I wondered also sometimes about my other 'children': my own compositions, left carelessly in Staszka's flat; also the piano duos left with Witold – if only both he and they were safe!

The little news that came our way had been passed by word of mouth from street to street. We would listen to these garbled accounts, never receiving word of anyone we knew, only hearing of incredible heroism; death, death, death, by the hundred thousand of men, women, children; houses flattened; the city littered with corpses. Finally, our hearts sinking even further, we heard the despairing cry of *'Kapitulcja!'* The Uprising had collapsed. Still no word of any of the family, still German patrols everywhere offering certain death if I went out to search.

We hunched together in our tiny house. A few days later we suddenly heard a soft knocking at our door. Fearing a German patrol, I crept to the door and peered through the keyhole. I could see only part of a ragged civilian suit, no sign of uniform. Hearing no warning from our neighbours, I risked opening the door.

There on the step was a very old man. Half his head was covered with a white bandage, soaked in blood. His tattered suit was dirty and bloodstained too. As he stood before me, trembling, unable to speak, I suddenly recognised him and shouted, 'Father!'

As soon as I had brought him in, I forced myself to ask the question 'Where is Mirek?'

There was a moment of silence before my father choked out his answer: 'Mirek is dead. I will tell you the whole story later. But say nothing to your mother.'

My mother was so overwhelmed with joy at seeing my father that even his appearance did not seem to upset her too much. She only wanted to question him. He was able to reassure her that Ewa was with Mirek's friends in the south of Poland. He let her think that Mirek himself was a prisoner, in due course to be released. He had to admit to her the news that our house, along with so many others, had been bombed, that we had lost everything. He portrayed the Uprising as a kind of inferno, yet was also able to describe feelings of radiant triumph while, for a brief, delusory period, the people of Warsaw had experienced the ecstasy of freedom – short-lived as the Germans fought back and regained lost ground.

Finally, on the day the Home Army surrendered, the Germans had rounded up not just the insurgents, but all the inhabitants of Warsaw. They had immediately begun deporting everyone from the capital. My father had been herded like everyone else into a goods train with an unknown destination. About ten miles out from Warsaw, the packed train had stopped for a moment. He had realised that he was roughly in the direction of where we were living and, with some of his companions, had spilled out of the train, staggering away as fast as possible, German guards in furious pursuit. Weak from two months' semi-starvation, he kept stumbling as he ran, which possibly saved his life: somehow he must have fallen out of sight. All he could remember was that he had crashed into a sharp wooden fence, breaking his glasses. Glass splinters had penetrated his left eyelid, his nose and face had suffered jagged cuts. But he had got away. After receiving first aid from a local pharmacist he had used the last of his energy to reach us.

Later, when my mother was resting, my father brokenly told me how Mirek had lost his life. On 16 September at about 11 am, about six weeks after the uprising had begun, my father, on some inexplicable premonition, had taken his violins down to the cellar for safety. He had stayed there, arranging them carefully. An hour later, a bomb had fallen on the house, destroying all the living accommodation, right through to the ground floor. Struggling free from the debris, he was filled with foreboding, for Mirek had promised to visit our flat at midday to bring him fresh drinking water. There was nobody about. Desperate with anxiety, he found his way to the secret Home Army headquarters where Mirek ran the illicit radio communications. Mirek had not returned there as planned. His fellow freedom-fighters searched the ruins of our home. Mirek's body was lying beneath the rubble.

He was buried in the only possible way at the time, under the pavement outside the gate of our house. The funeral was held with full military honours.

My father interrupted his story at this point. In the long pause that followed, I shared with him the extra pain he felt that his valiant son, who had risked so much for so many in five years of Resistance fighting, had died by chance on a domestic errand, coming to help him. If only he had taken Mirek's advice, agreed to leave his instruments and join us at the villa, Mirek might still have been alive.

In the days that followed, my father told us many tales of the Great Uprising, and the brave self-sacrifice of men, women and children as they pitted their meagre resources against the might of the Germans. The more I listened to him, the more I became convinced that the Uprising had been an appalling mistake based on the false hope that the Russians would come to the rescue. According to my father's first-hand report, though Russia had encouraged the patriotic Poles to rise against their German oppressors, the Soviet Army had stood by passively in the eastern suburbs of Warsaw throughout the Uprising; they had not fired a single shot nor sent one aeroplane to help the insurgents during the whole of the two months that the city and its inhabitants were dying. (The Western Allies gave no help either, except for a few insanely brave, individual Polish RAF pilots who made kamikazi flights to drop ammunition and food; however, their heroic gestures had only a symbolic value, offering no real assistance beyond heart-lifting moral support.)

With the loss of quarter of a million men, women and children during the two months of heroic resistance, the Uprising was crushed, our 'brother Slavs' still watching impassively from across the Vistula while the Germans took further savage revenge, flattening the city street by street. The wickedness of the Russians had been given full rein by the madness of the Polish politicians. Tens of thousands of insurgents, true heroes like my brother, who had fought passionately and with greatest self-sacrifice in the name of Free Poland, had died, only to make it easier for the Russians to take us over. The Russians, knowing that the Germans would themselves soon be on the run, obviously welcomed the thought of occupying a defeated city, emptied of the intransigent Home Army. Most conveniently, there would be no resistance left by the time our Soviet 'liberators' were ready to sweep across the country.

At a time when the future seemed as dark as the past, I felt an instinctive need to get the family together. Mirek's only child Ewa belonged with us now that she was an orphan; I proposed to track her down and bring her back to the villa. But my father insisted that he would go, as the patrols were less likely to arrest an old man. He set off as soon as he was strong enough and returned with Ewa. It was a great joy to us all to have her with us again, a trusting, sensitive little fair-haired girl with huge blue eyes, playing with a worn old doll as if tragedy belonged to some other world than hers.

My brother's death was a devastating blow to my father: for a while nothing else was of any significance to him. But as he began to settle into the villa with us, I noticed that something else was distracting him. He was of course missing his violins. Seeing him again broken and grieving like a child, I rashly promised to attempt to recover them. It was a challenge. Warsaw was now empty, except for German soldiers systematically destroying all the houses, one by one. No Poles were allowed back: to venture there illegally and smuggle out the instruments was impossible, especially since I would need transport.

Someone told me that the RGO (Central Council for Care) had permission from the Germans to recover works of art from the ruins of Warsaw. I journeyed the ten dangerous miles to their office on foot, perilously dodging several German patrols, only to be told by my fellow countryman in charge of the operation, with a condescending smile, 'But violins are not works of art. I could help you over antique furniture, paintings, Persian carpets, but not musical instruments.' I told him that the instruments had been played by some of the world's greatest violinists, that they had been awarded medals and diplomas in Poland and abroad, that they were the fruits of forty years of my father's dedicated craftmanship. This guardian of Poland's surviving heritage remained unmoved, abandoning even his artificial smile of helpfulness.

I was furious. I left the RGO office without another word, not even staying to remind him of the charity concerts I had conducted to raise money for his cause. On the long trudge home, again dodging manhunts, I was 'bursting my brain' to find another solution. I realised that the only person who could help was a German. If Governor Fischer was still here in Poland, perhaps his appreciation of the arts could again be usefully tapped.

After careful and rather dangerous enquiries, I discovered that his office was not too far from where we lived. Early one morning I set forth, taking care to choose a country route, and keeping close to trees and bushes so that I could hide from patrols. On arrival, peering from behind some shrubs I saw armed guards stationed at the entrance. Assuming once again an air of confidence which I was far from feeling, and exploiting my fluent German, I thrust my card at one of the guards and told him to take it immediately to Governor Fischer, adding that he would be sure to want to see me. I expected a bullet in my neck any minute, or an almost equally fatal request for my *Kennkarte*, but to my amazement I was taken to the Governor, who asked me with courtesy why I was there. I was so surprised I hardly knew how to begin, but launched out with flattery.

'I hope you remember how helpful you were to us four years ago in finding and returning my father's violins?'

He seemed pleased at the recollection. I decided to play on his pride as well as his love of music and his undoubted sense of power: he had not become a Nazi Governor because he was a benevolent old man – his reputation was far from gentle. I explained how the instruments were once more in danger of destruction as Warsaw was finally flattened, and how they were like children to my father who had devoted his whole life to them. 'I know that you are a music lover, and an art lover' – saying this I almost choked on my own sycophancy – 'so you will understand his inconsolable despair. It is not just his happiness, nor the material value of the instruments: you will be helping to save works of art!'

'Yes,' he observed thoughtfully, 'They *are* works of art.' (Ironic how a German murderer could appreciate that point, while our own RGO cultural rescue operation could not!) He went next door, made a few telephone calls, then directed me to a van driven by a *Volksdeutsche* man in civilian clothes, who was told to follow the Governor's limousine straight into Warsaw. We drove at great speed along wet roads, often perilously close to the ditch. After crossing the city border, the Governor sent the van ahead, telling me to point out the way to my house. But I was quite lost: although I had known almost every lamp-post and every stone in this city where I had been born and lived for thirty years, I was unable to recognise a single street. The view on every side was the same – heaps of rubble, half houses hanging above the roadways, a bed or a bath, a patch of wallpaper, the charred remains of a kitchen stove, the only reminders that these piles of plaster and brick had until recently been human habitations. Anywhere that paving stones could be lifted or the soil dug, little wretched crosses marked the makeshift graves of many thousands of dead – those that were actually buried – for on every street, around each corner, thousands more corpses lay where they had dropped, mown down by bullets: men, women, tiny children.

Trying for the sake of sanity to cling to the image of my

father's sad face, his precious violins and the purpose of my nightmare ride in the van, I wanted only to cry out like some child, 'I'm lost!'

But there was no one to tell me the way, and no map for such a wilderness, so I followed my instincts and gave directions to the driver until at last I was able to recognise some faint landmarks — surviving fragments of houses I had known well, a small turret on a house only partially destroyed. Eventually, I found the way to the street and the house where we had lived.

As we got out of the van, the first sight that met my eyes almost stopped my heart beating. In front of the gate, over an improvised grave — the paving stones lifted, the already greening soil exposed — was a wooden cross with the words, 'Mirosław Panufnik ... Died a Soldier's Death'. Nearby a few Germans were enjoying themselves burning what remained of the houses in the street. My dazed state of existing in a nightmare was interrupted by a shout from Governor Fischer: 'Where are the violins?'

I looked towards the cellars of our building. Flames and smoke were billowing out — we were almost too late. Fortunately the cellar we used on the other side of the house still seemed smoke-free. I rushed in. The heat was unbearable. I kept groping my way as fast as I could down the long, dark corridor, steadying myself against the hot walls so that I did not fall. Amazingly, Governor Fischer plunged into this oven-like situation after me. At last we reached the door of our cellar. By the faint light penetrating through the tiny ground-level windows, I saw my father's instruments, all forty of them packed neatly in their cases, just as he had left them. Governor Fischer, standing by my side, looked at them for a few seconds with great relief and gave the order for them to be loaded as quickly as possible into the van. The flames held off long enough for them all to be rescued, whereupon we were ordered to leave. I had only a second to look back at Mirek's grave. I would have liked to take with me the white and red arm-band that was still hanging on the cross, for my brother had worn it throughout the Uprising.

The Governor jumped into his own car, and we drove off

behind him. The van driver asked me for my father's address, and how to get there. 'But should we not be following the Governor's car?' I asked.

'No,' he replied. 'The Governor has gone back to his office. I am to take you and the instruments to your current home.'

From this casual explanation I realised that the Governor did not want to see or talk to me again – perhaps to spare me the embarrassment of thanking him. Perhaps he also wanted no one else in his department to know of his sudden, extraordinary quixotic action.

We drove straight to the villa with the instruments, and once again my father could not believe his eyes (or rather his one eye, as the other was still in bandages). The sight of the van packed with his precious violins was almost too much for him.

He and our elderly neighbours boasted about my exploit at first to my embarrassment; but then I realised that this was a good idea, and willingly told the whole incredible story to anyone who asked – otherwise suspicious minds could have accused me of some sort of shady collaboration with the Germans.

As for Governor Fischer, he used this one curious act of grace as part of his defence when he was later tried as a war criminal; but his other crimes were gross and he was hanged along with his colleagues.

II

'LIBERATED' BY THE SOVIETS

A few weeks after my adventure with the violins, the Soviet Army found themselves ready to move in and 'liberate' the ruins of Warsaw.

The thunder of heavy artillery grew more distinct each day, so that I feared that even our quiet suburb might become a battlefield. How was I going to save my frail old parents, my little niece (and of course my father's violins)? Casting around for ways of escape, I was able to bribe a Polish railwayman to smuggle us into an empty wagon on a freight train to Zakopane in the Tatra Mountains. The journey lasted six days in the freezing cold of December. Most of the time we were locked into our draughty wagon in railway sidings, with no knowledge of when or if we'd move again, with almost no food or drinking water, nor any kind of lavatory.

Somehow we tumbled out alive in Zakopane, and were lucky enough to find a villa to rent immediately. It was far harder to track down fuel or food. I trod through the snow for hours, driven on by the image of little Ewa in our new home crying with hunger.

I learnt that bread was only available if I were to join a huge queue at five in the morning waiting for the baker to open at nine. Even after hours in the darkness and snow, I could not be sure of obtaining a tiny loaf.

Milk, butter, eggs and a taste of meat were things to dream of. To make such dreams come true, I would trudge for miles through the surrounding countryside in search of a peasant farmer who could be induced to part with such commodities.

My first expedition was unsuccessful because the knowing peasants would only accept US dollars. However, one farmer indicated that he would barter food for jewellery, even for clothes. I returned next day with a comparatively unworn shirt, which he exchanged for a small sack of flour. As I wearily dragged this precious cargo back to Zakopane on a toboggan, I realised how weakened I was by hunger. Back in town I bartered some of the flour for a few eggs, a bottle of milk and a small piece of sausage. The hunt for food became my only occupation while my father stayed at home looking after my mother and little Ewa. (At least there were no complaints of hunger from the forty violins.)

Henceforth there would be an indelible association in my mind between the beauty of mountain scenery – snowy slopes, azure skies, green pines – and the agony of starvation. Even today the innocent sight of a Swiss alp brings on nightmares, thrusting my memory back to those interminable trudges through heavy snow: snow that glistened so brilliantly in the exquisite sunlight that to my fevered, reddened eyes, it sent off sparks which burnt into my vision and almost made me faint.

One January afternoon about six weeks after our arrival in Zakopane, the German army vehicles suddenly seemed to take fright; they roared off into the snowy mountains. The distant rumble of their engines mingled with short explosions as road bridges over the mountain streams were methodically destroyed. At last the Germans were in retreat.

Without policing of any sort, Zakopane became a no-man's land. The frantic and hungry populace looted every remaining article from the German offices, down to the last spittoon.

Two or three days later, we were 'liberated' by rifle-carrying Russian partisan youth in plain clothes. The local people strung together some white and red Polish flags, and we all thronged into the streets to await the Soviet army. Eventually there came into sight a long and slow-moving column of supply carts, pulled with great effort by undernourished and diminutive horses.

As I gazed in wonder at this motley procession, a hand fell on my shoulder. It seemed that I had been arrested by a Russian soldier in tattered uniform. Together with several dozen compatriots, I was hauled off to a nearby square, and then marched out of town at gunpoint. After half an hour we reached a heavy snow block in the road. Spades were handed out to us from a waiting lorry, and we began to dig, not for hours but for days.

No sooner was I back with the family, than our lives were again interrupted. Early one morning three Soviet officers knocked loudly on the door, strode in without a word, and began to inspect the villa room by room. We imagined they were searching for hidden Germans until one of them announced curtly that we had three hours in which to move out. I pleaded with them, knowing that the influx of refugees had left no room in Zakopane unoccupied. The Russians looked at my mother, thin as a bone, now racked with pleurisy, and were unmoved. Their gallant leader turned towards me and repeated his order, 'Three hours and – wheeet!', pointing derisively towards the door as he whistled.

While my father laid his violins neatly outside the villa, I ran from house to house begging for a room. Precisely three hours later, the Russian officer and his colleagues moved in, and my mother was carried outside to wait in the snow.

At last I found a room. As there was no heating, I went in search of a paraffin radiator and fuel, and found both – at a price.

Food was even harder to come by than fuel. The Soviet army confiscated everything, even *eau de cologne* (apparently as a vodka substitute), and ordered the bakers to produce bread for Russian consumption only. Consoled at least by the thought that we no longer ought to have to queue, we could starve peacefully at home.

The Russian soldiers were soon diverting themselves with drinking and looting. They manifested a special passion for wristwatches, which they openly stole from any Pole out on the streets, strapping their loot all the way up their arms, ready to be proudly displayed at the flick of a sleeve. (My own watch had long since been exchanged for food.) What with robbery, violence and rape, the inhabitants of Zakopane became even more frightened to leave their homes than before the 'liberation'. Asking themselves whether Poland was really free, they took down their white and red flags.

It was clear to me that the Russians had decided they now owned our country. I don't even remember exactly when the war was officially over for us. Perhaps it was February 1945, perhaps it was March. There were no celebrations, no joyous thanksgivings in the churches, no peals of bells or victory parades.

With the coming of spring, I struggled to free myself from the state of numbed shock in which we all existed and began to contemplate how to arrange a future for my parents and Ewa. I had discovered that Staszka was alive and settled safely elsewhere; our paths, it seemed, were unlikely to cross again. I started looking for signs that some kind of musical life would emerge from the wreckage, and began to steel myself to the question of whether my compositions (and much else) had survived. But first came a solemn duty to my dead brother.

At the beginning of May I joined the many thousands of former inhabitants of Warsaw who made the grim pilgrimage back to the ruins to seek out the remains of their lost relatives. There were still no passenger trains. We travelled shoulder to shoulder, on our feet for ten hours, in an open truck.

My purpose was to find my brother's temporary grave and take his body to be buried beside his wife's in the family tomb which my great grandfather Antoni Szuster had erected in the Powązki Cemetery the end of the last century.

Exhumation had become an industry, and it was not hard to find two young men with pick axe and spade to help me. Unlike so many of my desperate compatriots, at least I knew where to look.

As my helpers dug, and the sheets that wrapped Mirek's remains came into sight, I noticed a corked bottle containing a scrap of paper which was his identification in my father's handwriting: 'Lieutenant Mirosław Panufnik, pseudonym Witel. Killed 16 September 1944 aged 36.'

I reached down and with my bare hands lifted my brother out from the broken soil. My two assistants helped me lay him in the wooden coffin I had brought, and place it on a hired peasant cart, with a broken-down horse and a drunken driver.

As I was about to drive off, I was hailed by a young man

with long blond hair, a thin, strangely-red face and a deeply receding chin: my longtime friend, a philosopher with Communist leanings, Piotr Chojnowski, whose home had been almost next to ours. Piotr wanted to share my cart to transport the body of his grandmother.

The two coffins were laid side by side. We both sat up front with the driver, tautly gripping the wooden bench so as not to be thrown to the ground as the springless vehicle lurched violently over the ruined road-surfaces. Almost at once the grandmother's coffin burst open. Hastily we fastened the lid down again, but ten, twenty times it defied us. We did not even have to look round; our nostrils told us all. And each time Piotr burst into wild insane laughter. It was a scene from Goya.

At the cemetery, Piotr disappeared with his grandmother and the recalcitrant coffin. With regard to my own problems, the clerk in charge of burials was brusquely unhelpful. After some cursory enquiries, he announced that there was no room for another coffin in my family tomb. Astonished and appalled I begged him to help. He told me I could hire some cemetery workers to re-arrange the coffins to make space for my brother. 'But it will be a huge job,' he said. 'It will cost you a lot of money.' I gave him everything I could, and later discovered that I had been the victim of a trick frequently practised at the time, when bereaved relatives were too distraught to question or protest.

I spent that evening alone in the ruined city of my childhood, drinking vodka in quantities unknown to me before. Who knows where I eventually slept. Next morning, through the grey haze and throbbing pain of my awakening, a second dreaded task confronted me: it was time to enquire whether I still owned a past as a composer, or whether all that I'd written in my first thirty years was now dust and ashes like everything else around me.

I set off to look for Staszka's flat, but again got lost amongst the rubble. Eventually I reached my destination and was amazed to see the house standing on its own like a blackened tooth in an empty jaw.

Finding in hope an unexpected strength, I ran up the four flights of stairs and knocked impatiently at the door that had once been Staszka's. It was opened by a stranger, a middle-aged woman. Puzzled and alarmed by my presence, she asked rather roughly what I wanted.

I answered that I had come to see the state of the flat, that I had lived here previously, and would like to collect some of my property from my room. Reluctantly, with some embarrassment, she waved me in. The piano was missing. I asked her where it was.

'Oh, the piano? It's not here!' she said blandly. 'This is a small room and I have a lot of things. I had to get rid of it.'

'But it was *my* piano,' I said. 'What have you done with it?'

'You think I sold it?' she asked indignantly. 'I gave it to the Polish Army!' She was plainly proud of her generosity. It was pointless to pursue the matter; anyway I had not come for the piano.

With dread, my eyes were searching every cranny of the room, especially the corner where I had left my manuscripts. My vocal chords so taut that they almost choked me, I rasped out: 'Please, where are my compositions?'

'Compositions?' she asked with obvious incomprehension. 'What compositions?' (She answered all queries with further questions.)

'My musical works,' I explained, realising that she was of humble origin, and unlikely ever to have heard the word 'compositions'. 'I left all my manuscripts on that small, low table.' Her face was a mask of indifference. Controlling my impatience, I continued, 'Please, madam, listen very carefully. I am a musician, a composer. I write music. On this table I left a number of works of mine, all the music I have written since I was nine years old. There were piano pieces, vocal and chamber works, and several symphonic pieces.'

'What did they look like?'

By now I was desperate. 'They looked like long exercise books. The pages had rows of printed staves – five lines in groups, all the way down the page. On the staves were musical notes, some in pencil, some in ink.'

The woman grimaced, as though the act of thinking was a rare effort. 'Ah yes,' she said slowly. 'I think I remember . . .' She continued in a flat tone, almost like a medium at a séance:

'Now I *do* remember, and I will tell you.' Pause. 'I will tell you,' she repeated. 'When I first arrived, the mess was terrible – broken glass and furniture everywhere, and yes, papers all over the floor. They did look rather as you described . . .'

'What did you do with them? Where are they now?' I could hardly breathe, remembering the heavy bundle of my first symphony, and the heavier one of the second, the *Psalm* which had won me such praise as a student, the *Tragic Overture*, everything. 'I threw them away,' she said quite brightly, as if congratulating herself on her housewifely tidiness.

'Well, I chucked them out because they looked like rubbish,' She glowed with confident good-wifeliness, as if her behaviour had been nothing more than natural.

'As rubbish?' I shouted.

'Of course,' she said, calmly and reasonably, as if trying to soothe my nerves, 'I had to clean, wash and tidy the flat, didn't I?'

'Where did you throw them?' I yelled, and something of my anguish seemed to have got through to her, for her voice quavered a little as she replied: 'On the rubbish dump in the courtyard.' At that I dashed down the stairs two at a time, leaping on to the stinking pile of rubbish. I began flinging empty tins, rotting food, burnt curtains, broken glass and blackened metal in every direction. With my bleeding hands, I examined every scrap of paper – but hope slowly dwindled into despair as I began to find little heaps of scorched paper, with the tracing of a crotchet or a minim, black on black, hardly visible. Someone had made a magnificent bonfire from the work of twenty years. My manuscripts were gone for ever, victims of the Warsaw Uprising as surely as if they had been burnt by a Nazi firebomb rather than, by grimmest irony, incinerated at the hands of my uneducated, uninterested compatriot.

I felt as crushed and broken as the buildings of Warsaw around me. However, it was not possible to crumble or falter: I had to get back to look after my parents and Ewa.

12

STARTING LIFE AGAIN – KRAKÓW

The ancient university city of Kraków had been the Polish capital until the seventeenth century. Miraculously, the war had left it unscathed. Though strategically less significant than Warsaw, it probably also owed its survival to the fact that, in the nineteenth century, it had belonged to the Austro-Hungarian empire. Perhaps the Nazi commanders felt protective towards it on that account. Whatever the reason for its survival, it now became the Mecca for anyone who wished to be involved in the rebirth of cultural life, while Warsaw remained the seat of the puppet government of Polish Communists (most of whom who had spent the war in Russia).

To arrive in Kraków was like returning from Hades. Seeing streets whole with undamaged houses on each side, I felt a surge of optimism. Within minutes, I met old friends: suddenly I was hailed from across a street by Antoni Bohdziewicz, a brilliant radio drama producer for whom I had written incidental music before the war, and Stanisław Wohl, now in army uniform.

Major Wohl clapped his hand on my shoulder, and with a broad grin said, 'You're under arrest!'

'Thank God you're still alive – you're just the person we need!' he continued. 'We're attached to the Polish Army Film Unit, and, from this minute, you have begun your new appointment as our Music Director. We *must* have a composer! Now! Yesterday!' I became his grateful captive.

In no time, Stanisław Wohl had arranged for me to receive a month's pay in advance so that I could stop selling my last shirts and socks in exchange for food. While I searched for accommodation for the family, he found me a temporary room in a large house belonging to the Film Unit. It was already occupied by some of Poland's leading actors and writers, including Czesław Miłosz, then still quite unknown, and Jerzy Andrzejewski, about to try to film his *Ashes and Diamonds*.

Kraków appeared entrancingly beautiful that spring; the budding trees symbolised hope for a new Polish summer. I would stroll for hours admiring the mellow, ancient Palace of Wawel nearby and the glorious buildings of the University, founded in the thirteenth century only 100 years later than Oxford. The survival of the city was a constant source of rejoicing. Yet the local population was unsympathetic towards Warsaw refugees who admitted nostalgia for their beloved capital. 'You wanted an Uprising,' they would say unfeelingly, 'so you had one!'

Even more disconcerting were the propaganda posters that marred the walls of the city's elegant buildings. One particularly outrageous example bore the caption 'LET US CLEAR POLAND OF FASCISM' and showed men with brooms sweeping away scraps of paper inscribed with the initials: SS, SA *and* AK: our new masters had bracketed together Hitler's SS and SA with our own noble and courageous *Armia Krajowa*, the Home Army! Did they really believe that the Polish people would accept such a slight against either the dead or still surviving patriots of the Polish Underground?

Another affront to sense was the use of the word *Wolność* (freedom) to convince the Poles that they should appreciate and enjoy their new 'freedom' under the People's Government. The authorities bountifully applied this magical tag to a great many objects: the square near which I lived was Freedom Place. There was a Freedom cinema, as well as Freedom cigarettes, Freedom chocolates (*ersatz* and flavourless), Freedom soap and so on. But no Freedom lavatory paper – it was unobtainable under any name.

My efforts to move the family to Kraków ran into difficulties because accommodation was only allotted to people who held paid jobs in the city. The Army Film Unit was based at Łódź, so I was entitled to housing there, but it was essential for me to work in Kraków in order to keep in touch with Polish musical life as it started up again.

Indeed, I was soon approached by the newly formed Ministry of Culture to become Conductor of the Kraków Philharmonic Orchestra, probably as a result of my orchestral charity concerts during the war. Though it was a flattering invitation as I was still only thirty-one, I almost refused. While I longed to conduct occasionally, I was hesitant to take on such a heavy responsibility, because I needed time to rebuild my output as a serious composer, as well as fulfilling my commitments to the Army Film Unit. Eventually I was tempted into accepting the post, partly because I would have the right to obtain accommodation for the family in Kraków; also because I would be working with the best symphony orchestra in Poland, and at last would be able to put into practice all that I had learnt about the classical repertoire with Weingartner in Vienna.

The orchestra had not existed before the war. It had been formed by the Germans, who forcibly enrolled the best Polish instrumentalists, in many cases using threats against their families to secure their obedience. Other orchestra members, however, had been purely opportunist, and to punish them, after the war, patriotic zealots had dissolved the orchestra on the grounds that *all* the players were traitors. It was impossible not to be angered by the behaviour of those players who had collaborated willingly. But no one was proposing to blow up the bridges built by the Germans in strategic places. Why then should we destroy the splendid orchestra they had formed and thus rob the Polish music public of a joy they deserved after five years of deprivation?

Happily it was possible to re-engage most of the best players. Only the leader and the most overtly cynical collaborators were officially banned for three years from making their living through performance. (In the case of the leader, this punishment fell by the wayside as, before long, he turned up again as leader of the newly formed Katowice Radio Orchestra.)

A Committee of Verification had been formed to pinpoint and punish collaborators in every field, not just music. Unfortunately, they soon became widely known as the Committee of

Fools, because so often they took savage revenge on nonentities who had co-operated with the enemy out of weakness or genuine fear, while ignoring major traitors, including many who had made huge material gains. The more cunning collaborators swiftly whitewashed themselves by joining the United Workers' (Communist) Party, which was very short of willing recruits.

With so many other economic difficulties for the authorities to cope with, we artists were not yet under pressure to join the Communist Party, and were still allowed to get on with our work without political interference. I soon had a viable concert season planned, with the classics I had been longing to try out: Beethoven, Mozart and Brahms, as well as much Polish music, including Moniuszko, Karłowicz, Paderewski, Szymanowski and, of course, Chopin. Initially we were able to engage only soloists resident in Poland; but everything on the musical side seemed encouraging. Whatever else, perhaps the new régime was going to provide a fertile field for the arts.

My attempts to find a flat for the family gave me my first taste of the bureaucracy imposed by the Soviets on their new satellite of 'People's Poland'. Under the banner of 'socialist justice', it was impossible for me to rent a flat privately: I had to apply to the state organisation for the 'allocation of living space'. The almighty Director, the distributor of flats, was unimpressed by my public rôle. Each time I returned to his office, he kept me waiting for hours. Once he gave me a key and an address, but the flat was occupied. When I told him that other people were already there, he replied, 'They're not people: they're Russians.' If my newly allocated flat was in the hands of non-people, I asked, was I supposed to treat them as invisible? The Director muttered dryly that he had given me the wrong key. When I asked him for the right one, he said I would have to wait another few weeks.

Finally, under pressure from the Ministry of Culture and the orchestra's administration, I was allocated a dark, gloomy ground-floor flat. Since my parents were anxious to leave Zakopane, I accepted it.

My mother was alarmingly ill, my father frail and disoriented. Neither was fit to be looking after Ewa. Undomesticated bachelor that I was, and stretched to the full trying to regenerate the orchestra, as well as writing music for the Film Unit, I was hardly the ideal foster-parent for my enchanting but lonely little eight-and-a-half year-old niece. I found a Catholic boarding school in Kraków, part of St Ursula's Convent, which had a good reputation both academically and pastorally. I hoped she could be happy there in the companionship of girls of her own age. But after a few months she was forlorn and wan. The nuns were so strict they insisted that even eight-year-old girls must wear underclothes in the bath for the sake of modesty. Realising that she needed a kinder and healthier environment, I arranged with her mother's brother and his wife that she should live with them in the Silesian countryside. Soon the childless couple made her feel almost like their own daughter.

The truth about my brother's death could no longer be kept from my mother. On learning of it, she lost her will to live, and my father and I saw her gradually slip away. Her death left a great emptiness for us both. Work was the only escape.

My father, without any specialist tools, was unable to continue making violins, but he occupied himself with the dream of creating a school for artist-craftsmen in violin construction, together with a factory to produce the highest quality instruments based on his researches.

I was longing to start composing seriously again, but my duties for the Film Unit involved conducting and booking musicians and dashing off film scores; as well as this I was studying new works and conducting the concert series with the Kraków Philharmonic Orchestra. Every waking hour of every day of the week was occupied and I had no time or energy for anything creative. I had intended to abandon all my lost compositions and rebuild a completely new *oeuvre* without looking backward, but I found my *Tragic Overture* constantly forcing its way into my consciousness; I could not forget Mirek's warm words of praise, nor my regrets at not having found time to drink with him after the performance, on the last occasion I had seen him alive. I decided to reconstruct the *Overture* and dedicate it to him, as a memorial to his great courage and sacrifices.

Rebuilding the *Overture* turned out to be an easier task than I had expected; the four-note 'motif of fear' and the tautly organised construction were still clearly imprinted in my mind. Encouraged by that experience, I used every free moment – mainly in the middle of the night – to resuscitate two more short works: *Five Polish Peasant Songs* and the Piano Trio, again without too much difficulty. I then decided to try to rescue my Symphony No. 1. But here my memory faltered and the results were disappointing. I performed it in one of our symphony concerts, but afterwards destroyed the score. With that I renounced further reconstruction work, and looked ahead, hoping to find time for new compositions.

At about this time, however, someone at the Film Unit discovered my pre-war efforts as a producer and presented me with the irresistible challenge of making my own film on a subject of my own choice. I decided to attempt a poetic interpretation of the devastation of Warsaw. I was fortunate in obtaining the best cameraman in the Unit and a reasonable quantity of black and white film. Balancing on crumbling brickwork, or crouching beneath it, we obtained shots of a very different kind from the straightforward conventions of the time. I tried to keep the images in movement – stark outlines silhouetted against scurrying clouds, fragmented masonry reflected shimmeringly in a puddle, or floating along on the water-surface. I played with distortion and narrowing parallels for claustrophobic effect. The montage and editing was determined by the form and character of my chosen accompaniment, Chopin's Ballade in F minor.

The film was highly praised by the directors of the Film Unit, but it did not reach the public screens of Poland. I was informed that it had been 'accidentally damaged' in the laboratory: strange, since I had sat there watching it in faultless technical condition only a few days before with my employers! The true reason for this censorship was political. If it had been released for public viewing, the audiences would have been emotionally redrawn to the tragedy of Warsaw's destruction, inevitably starting again to discuss amongst themselves, 'Why did this happen? What were the circumstances?' They would have been reminded that the Russians had allowed the Uprising to run its course because it suited them to have the city and its brave leaders destroyed by the Germans.

Soviet control of the Film Unit was becoming increasingly obvious. The uniformed officers of the Soviet NKVD (the future KGB), their hats topped with green baize, marched in and out of our offices in Łódź, without any attempt to remain under cover, expecting to be welcomed as liberators. Aware that film was the most powerful medium for political propaganda they looked at everything we did, generously proffering their 'suggestions' for future productions in ways which could not be ignored.

One subject they forced on to our Unit was *The Electrification of the Villages*, a film designed to show that 'People's Poland', a Socialist country on its 'road to irreversible Communism' would not tolerate a backward, pre-war countryside without electricity.

When a team from the Film Unit was sent out into the countryside to start filming, their enterprise ground to a halt, because they could not find a single cottage without electric power. The director and camera team were obliged to destroy the existing poles and cables in order that they could film them under construction.

Political 'education' was by now spreading fast throughout the towns of Poland. Old people, hardly able to read or write, were ordered to attend classes on Marxist dialectics. I knew of one ancient peasant couple who were herded with the rest of their village into a lecture about Karl Marx, delivered by some bright spark from the Communist Party. The talk was so far above their heads that all they absorbed was a mishearing of Marx's name: the old man was heard to mutter as they left the hall, 'Very interesting . . . is it really possible that there is life on Mars?'

Though run by the Army, ours was the only Film Unit in action in Poland, and, even after the Soviet propagandists took over, we were still occasionally allowed to attempt films of an artistic or literary nature. As Musical Director, I not only supervised, chose and sometimes conducted music for a variety of subjects, but from time to time was expected to produce new scores. One film I selected was Edgar Allan Poe's *The Tell-*

Tale Heart, a macabre story in its own right. At the exact moment in the story when the old man was murdered, the actor playing the part was all too convincing. He had suffered a genuine heart attack, and died shortly afterwards.

Once we had recovered from the shock, we began to record the music which I had composed for a small ensemble of harpsichord, piano, celeste and timpani. The first part seemed to be falling together well enough when suddenly the timpanist shattered everything with a storm of wrong rhythms. I repeated the section and again there was chaos. The same thing happened a third time. I rapped my music stand with the baton, and asked what was wrong. He did not answer. I shouted at him 'Why don't you answer me?' There was another silence, then a crash as he fell to the floor. The recording producer rushed over to him. It was too late. The timpanist was dead. Shortly afterwards the producer too died of heart failure.

Although my own heart kept going, the film did not. At its private screening, everyone involved was highly praised and our work deemed to be of the highest artistic standard. But the censors stepped in again and the public was never allowed to see it, because the occult content was too far removed from the practical ideal of building a 'People's Paradise'.

Back in Kraków, another set of orchestral concerts was underway. At last I had been able to bring in a few foreign guests, including Constant Lambert conducting a whole programme of English music. It was a great event for me personally, not only because of my interest in English music, but also because I was captivated by Constant's wit and charm, as well as admiring his great talent as a musician. He wanted to drink and talk with me every evening. I would listen, fascinated by his integrity on musical questions and his boldness of judgement. Alas he would easily down a bottle of vodka at each sitting and he would still be drunk at rehearsal the following morning. With his 'Constant' cigarette glued to his mouth, he would leave the rostrum every few minutes to relieve his bladder and, until the day wore on a little and the vodka wore off, he would keep losing his place in the score. I had to quell the orchestra's threatened revolt.

The concert itself was a huge success. Constant conducted superbly; and the players gave of their best. We were all particularly impressed by his performance of the powerful Symphony No. 1 by William Walton.

After the concert, the two of us went out for a last supper. Because of the elated state of our conversation, fuelled by a great number of glasses of vodka, we accidentally stayed in the restaurant beyond the limits of the curfew (which, two years after the war, had still not been lifted!). I therefore decided to accompany Constant to his hotel.

Walking in a brisk if rather wobbly manner, we were immediately stopped by mounted militia men. Ignoring me, they addressed their extensive tirade of complaints and questions towards Constant, shouting and gesticulating threateningly. Not knowing a word of Polish he turned to me and drawled between narrow lips, 'I say, old chap, what do these funny fellows want?'

Hearing the English language, the Militia men became even more aggressive. I explained to Constant their growing suspicions that he must be a British or American spy, at which he almost choked with laughter. The more he laughed, the angrier the militia men became. Thinking that he would sleep off his hangover better in a hotel bed than on the floor of the state prison, I used all the powers of diplomacy I could muster, and after extensive examination of our identity documents, we were allowed to weave our way towards the hotel.

I was sad to see him off next day; and was sadder still when, not long afterwards, I heard that he had died.

Our home life in Kraków changed suddenly with the visit of an elderly and disagreeable cousin of my mother's. She and her husband had lost everything in the Uprising, and were anxious to find accommodation so that she could earn some money teaching piano. An official allocation had already been refused and their situation, they said, was hopeless. Despite her sharp tongue and unloving nature, I suggested to my father that we should give them a room in our flat. They moved in at once, along with a disreputable-looking borrowed piano.

I paid dearly for my gesture. I had just begun to compose a new symphonic work and, as I struggled with my new ideas, my aunt's untalented beginners were battering the out-of-tune piano in the next room. It was torture. I stopped composing again and wondered if my creative days were over.

13

NEW RESPONSIBILITIES

The task of helping rebuild musical life in Poland now occupied so much of my time that the prospect of serious composition became even more remote. I had now also been asked to assist in the creation of a State Music Publishers by the newly appointed director, Tadeusz Ochlewski, with whom I had collaborated during the Occupation over the distribution and performance of my anti-Nazi songs. He wanted me to help him find and train music copyists to extract orchestral parts. He also remembered our war-time talks about clarity and precision in the way scores should be printed and was particularly interested in my own pre-war innovation with empty space instead of empty stave-lines where instruments were not playing. The first work to be published this way was my reconstructed *Tragic Overture*. (Some of my Polish colleagues later followed suit, as did Stravinsky and several members of the international avant garde.)

The government's commitment to the regeneration of national culture suited Ochlewski and myself admirably. As non-Party members, we were simply concerned to further the publication of Polish music old and new to the best of our ability. We took to meeting regularly in the stark office allotted to the project by the authorities, a tiny room with just a small table and a few chairs. As a musician in his own right, a violinist, Ochlewski had not been successful, but though quite caustic and harsh in manner, he worked for others with absolute devotion and intensity, often continuing through the day into the night without even pause for food. Once I had tracked down and trained suitable craftsmen, he expected them to equal his own self-sacrifice and dedication.

The results were spectacular. Even the sluggish, bureaucratic government chiefs bowed to his will. The offices of his PWM (*Polskie Wydawnictwo Muzyczne*) expanded rapidly. Musical works were published by the dozen, orchestral parts produced. Gradually, the organisation emerged as perhaps the largest of its kind in the world, with the highest standards. Of course it remained dependent politically and financially on the Ministry of Culture, and all the musical works we selected had then to be approved by a special committee. However, in the first four years of Communist rule, composers were still free virtually to compose as they wished. These were exciting times despite petty restrictions and bureaucracy; I was still optimistic about the future of Polish music in all areas.

In the spring of 1946, to my amazement, I was appointed Director of the Warsaw Philharmonic, traditionally Poland's leading and most prestigious orchestra — but at the time a name only, with no players, no concert hall or administration! Fuelled by enthusiasm and some confidence drawn from my experience in Kraków, I accepted the post.

Though the Film Unit would not totally relinquish me, I had to insist on resigning my conductorship of the Kraków Orchestra, so that I could plunge energetically into my new task. My immodest intention was to create the best orchestra in Poland, with the most varied and exciting concert programmes.

The first stage was the recruitment of instrumentalists, beyond the few who had already returned to the city and were struggling to reinstate themselves in their ruined or half-ruined homes. Travelling through the towns of Poland, I tracked down about a dozen more from the pre-war days who were overjoyed to rejoin their old orchestra. I also found some excellent young players eager to come to the capital and work with me. When most of the posts were filled, I approached the Warsaw City President requesting allocation of flats for the players. He acquiesced with apparent readiness, though he said it would take a while to arrange. (Official rebuilding and new construction in the city was only slowly grinding into action.)

Next I looked for a concert hall, and found the old Palladium Cinema still standing. The auditorium was large, the acoustics reasonable. As my bosses at the Army Film Unit were responsible for all cinemas, I pleaded with them and they agreed to put it at our disposal.

Orchestral material for classical and romantic music could be hired from Kraków and contemporary Polish music was available in the handsome publications of the new PWM. Modern French music, including the works of Debussy which I was longing to conduct, proved to be unobtainable.

Awaiting accommodation for the players, I decided to try to get to Paris to purchase some essential repertoire. It was normally impossible to obtain passports or travel abroad, but I managed to obtain special dispensation for my cultural mission from the office of the Premier himself. I felt almost embarrassingly fortunate to be taking time away from the graveyard of Warsaw, to breathe some different air, especially to revisit Paris, which I yearned for deeply after seven years of absence.

At the border, there was a horrible moment when the Polish customs officer searched my suitcase, and I feared he might also go through the pockets of my suit. In one of them was an uncensored letter describing our fettered lives from my composer friend, Zygmunt Mycielski to his revered teacher, the famous Nadia Boulanger whom I was longing to meet. Zygmunt had often described to me her spiritual and intellectual qualities as well as her profound humanity.

Because I had been allowed so little foreign currency, I had to stay in the Embassy-controlled Polish House. As soon as I had left my suitcase there, I slipped out, taking care to dodge about and cast off any Embassy employee who might be following me, in case they found out about the letter. At last I felt safe to telephone Nadia, who urged me to come at once. In less than an hour I was standing at the door of her apartment in the rue Ballu.

She opened the door herself, a spry, spinsterly figure in a heavy tweed ankle-length skirt with a rather masculine matching jacket. Her white hair was swept back into a tight knot. Her intelligent searching eyes twinkled out from behind heavy glasses, her immediate warmth and enthusiasm making her far less austere than I had imagined. As to the apartment, every picture, every ornament on every piece of furniture was exactly as Zygmunt had described it — intact even after five years of German Occupation! She read Zygmunt's letter eagerly and plied me with questions about Poland and music. I answered as well as I could, my French creaking with long disuse.

I was invited to hear her that evening accompanying the Swiss tenor, Hugues Cuenod, at a private recital in the home of her friend, the Princesse de Polignac. A few hours later, arriving at the handsome *palais*, I entered a world seemingly untouched by recent history. I was shown into an ornate *salon* to be greeted in a friendly manner by our hostess. A few guests had arrived already: the women were in long, décolleté dresses, glittering with jewels, the men suave and elegant in black ties. I was wearing my only suit, navy blue, shiny with age. I noticed a few stares from the aristocratic French, but my attention was elsewhere. Accepting a brimming glass of champagne from an antique silver tray held out by a richly liveried footman, my war-worn Warsaw eyes blinked in amazement to see his hands clad in immaculate white gloves.

As I listened to the superb performances of Fauré and Debussy songs, sitting in exquisite comfort on a silk-covered sofa with French Impressionist masterpieces staring down at me from every wall, I momentarily wondered if heaven could be something like this. After the recital there was more champagne, and I encountered some more interesting guests including Yehudi Menuhin and his beautiful wife. They were more friendly, and also more sensitive and curious about life in the 'New Poland' than some of the other guests had been. They eventually gave me a lift home to the shabby little Polish House where I was staying.

That night I did not sleep. My mind kept returning to the absurd splendours of the evening, where I had been the only bird of my kind temporarily out of my Polish cage. I had mixed feelings towards the French, whose magnificent capital had survived the war with hardly a scar in spite of German Occupation. My pride in Polish integrity and defiance was tempered with regret for the appalling sacrifices made.

In the morning, the almost-forgotten luxury of real coffee helped to dispel the clouds. I went straight to Durand, the famous music publishers in the Place Madeleine. I was greeted by a sleepy old man with a long beard, a *fin de siècle* type peering at me through tiny black-rimmed spectacles.

I introduced myself as the Director of the Warsaw Philharmonic Orchestra, explaining that I had come on a special trip to Paris in order to purchase scores and orchestral material of Debussy, Ravel, Roussel and Messiaen.

The old man reacted as if he had suddenly been woken up. His eyes blinking rapidly, he stood extremely still and silent for a moment, stunned to find himself confronted by the representative of an indigent, war-devastated Communist country, offering him a fistful of ready cash for the purchase of a substantial quantity of French music. The transaction was soon achieved. He ushered me from the shop with exaggerated politeness, bowing so low that he almost brushed the ground with his bald brow.

My official mission had been all too quickly accomplished. My miserable allowance of French francs was also almost finished after only forty-eight hours. I strolled dreamily up the Champs Elysées. The sun was shining on to the flowering chestnut trees; people were laughing in the cafés; there was not a bombed-out building in sight. I could not possibly return to Warsaw yet.

The Polish section of French Radio came to the rescue. For the sake of some French francs and a few more days in paradise, I forced myself to overcome my extreme dislike of microphones and my allergy to talking about music. I gave a long interview about the revival of musical life in Poland, regretfully forcing myself to be diplomatic as I knew the Embassy would be listening. I then made two more programmes, one on the history of the Warsaw Philharmonic, another of Paderewski, both illustrated by splendid old records I found in the French Radio archives.

Through these talks, I met the Music Director of French Radio, the *mondain* and friendly composer, Henry Barraud. Discovering my interest in French music and my intention to transport it to Warsaw, he issued an invitation to return that very August to conduct the Orchestre National. With this concert in view, it was not so hard to take the return train to the rigours of life in Poland.

On my return I began the task of organising our first season of concerts. I had to reside in a hotel run by the Army Film Unit and usually shared a room with another man (though once I was not unhappy to find that I had been accidentally billeted with a beautiful actress).

At last I found some time to look up old friends. It was good to see Witold Lutosławski and Danusia again, but sad to discover that our piano duets were no more. Witold had left behind in his house some two hundred of our joint works, and all were consumed by fire during the Uprising (except his own *Paganini Variations* which he must have taken with him when he had escaped from Warsaw). Always wiser than me, Witold was not allowing himself to be distracted by organisational commitments and the constant resulting battles with bureaucrats. He was getting on with his serious work as a composer, while writing light music for the radio under a pseudonym in order to earn his living.

My efforts to get the orchestra going entailed too many long waits for petty officials, and too much concentration on necessary but tedious details. Because there was so much to be achieved before the orchestra could start playing, I came near to refusing an invitation to London to conduct my *Five Polish Peasant Songs* for soprano voices and woodwind at the International Festival for Contemporary Music. However, the Ministry of Culture was insistent that I should attend, and although I already sensed that I was being exploited for propaganda purposes, I was of course eager to revisit London. The Festival concerts enabled me to hear much new music that would not have reached me in Warsaw. I made many friends from both sides of the Atlantic, and gained much satisfaction from conducting the well-disciplined ladies of the BBC Chorus in my own piece.

My next trip was a return visit to Paris, but I kept it as short as possible. Working with l'Orchestre National proved to be most rewarding. The players were extremely responsive. Henry

Barraud had insisted that I should conduct a work of my own. I had only one to offer, my *Tragic Overture.* As well as Bach and Mozart, however, I also included works by my talented compatriots, ex-pupils of Nadia Boulanger, Michał Spisak and Antoni Szałowski. I was struck by the irony that, though both resided in Paris, their orchestral works were unperformed and it took a Pole from Warsaw to introduce them to the city where they had been composed.

On my return to Poland, I was struck in another way: I was strongly attacked by the Ministry of Culture for supporting 'Fascist' composers who lived abroad. I returned their attack with equal intensity, unable to tolerate the ludicrous implication that anyone who by choice lived in any country not designated a 'socialist paradise' was automatically a Fascist. For the time being, they bowed to my anger, and their mouths snapped shut.

By now I was caught in a quasi-official rôle as Poland's leading conductor, and was frequently shunted abroad by the Ministry of Culture. Of course it was not too displeasing to escape temporarily the food shortages and drabness of Warsaw and to make music with foreign orchestras. I particularly enjoyed a visit to Zürich, where I conducted the Tonhalle Orchestra, the programme including music by my wartime friend, Konstanty Regamey.

Of Swiss nationality, half-Russian, Konstanty Regamey was deeply attached to the city of Warsaw where he had spent his childhood. He had even passed the war amongst us, courageously taking part with me in illicit Underground charity concerts, which could have lost him his neutral immunity. In the early 1940s, he was the first composer in Poland to write in the twelve-note method. He was now Professor – in Lausanne and Freiberg – not of composition but of oriental languages, of which he knew twenty-nine!

The work I conducted was extremely interesting, although he still insisted on rather slavishly following the dodecaphonic trend. My only problem was that during rehearsals he kept on revising the music and delivering new parts to the players while I was conducting. Several times he actually leant across me and altered the score right beneath my nose as I tried to beat the tempo! We all had to be very patient and tolerant, but fortunately the result was worthwhile.

Back in Warsaw with my orchestra, new obstacles were put into our way. Our few concerts up to this moment had been given by a still incomplete orchestra in various unsatisfactory venues around the city. We tried at least to keep some sort of music going while we waited for accommodation for the rest of our players and our promised hall. Suddenly I learnt that the Film Unit had reneged on their offer of the Palladium. The decision, I was told, had been made by the 'highest authorities': in other words, from now music would have to give way to film, proven by Lenin himself to be the most powerful medium for political propaganda.

Music lovers in all walks of life privately expressed their indignation to me over this betrayal. Only one voice was raised in public dissent; a brave journalist who somehow slipped his sardonic comment through the censorship:

> The Film Unit's decision was right. Who listens to Philharmonic concerts today . . .? In the concert hall does anyone ever smash glass windows, break ribs, or give any other cause for intervention by the Militia? Serious music? It's a bore! . . . After all, each film they make has a little music in the background, which is entirely sufficient for the promotion of musical culture among the masses . . .

On top of the Palladium disaster, I was shocked to discover that some colleagues in the musical world, my ex-teachers as well as my own generation, were busy stirring up mischief. The infamous Professor Rytel published a malicious comment in the press that I had made a 'Napoleonic' career for myself. (Perhaps he'd guessed that when the Philharmonic concerts got into full swing his music might not be my first choice.) More than one of my would-be successors let it be known that they could perform the duties of Director of the Warsaw Philharmonic better than me. Taking advantage of my short stays abroad, all sorts of contrary plans had been set in motion on the future of musical life in our capital. Someone had suggested a national orchestra, someone else a radio orchestra rather than the reassembly of the old Warsaw Philharmonic. Yet another musical sage thought we should just manage with a chamber orchestra for the moment. It was a typical Polish situation: 'ten

Poles with ten points of view!'

These petty intrigues and jealousies were unpleasant but not too important. A greater calamity was about to strike our embryonic orchestra. On yet another visit to lobby the Minister, I was casually informed that the accommodation for the musicians from the provinces, like our concert hall, was not going to materialise. It seemed that the reconstruction of Warsaw was proceeding slower than expected and that there were more urgent priorities than musicians. It was not hard to guess at those priorities in the 'irreversible wheel of history'.

I was appalled at the thought of the ordeal facing the orchestral players, to whom in good faith I'd promised flats as well as work. How was I to tell them that they would have nowhere to live because the authorities had changed their minds? Many of them had resigned from their jobs as teachers or players in the provinces and passed on their homes to their successors. What was going to happen to them – and their families? However hard I tried to get the decision reversed, the authorities would not show any heart.

I could think of only one way to demonstrate my solidarity with my players. I handed in my resignation to the President of the City of Warsaw.

14

BACK TO COMPOSITION

My mind now lit on the Polish proverb, 'Nothing is so bad that it cannot be turned to good!' Suddenly, fate had arranged that I would again have time to compose.

Not counting my film scores, my last new composition had been my *Tragic Overture* in 1942. With a five-year break in my serious creative work, how was I going to find the resources within me to start again?

While abroad I had become conscious of the growing fashion in Europe to compose dodecaphonically. However, this seemed to me too easy a way out; the straight exchange of one convention for another. I had not abandoned my ambition to seek out my own language, my own voice, if only I could achieve it.

Meanwhile, theories apart, I had to know if I could still compose at all. I began tentatively to improvise on the piano, exploring harmonic, melodic and rhythmic ideas, gradually making additional searches to extend some purely pianistic possibilities. Even three years after my daily wartime performances, my fingers were still in good running order, and I was able to juggle with technique without difficulty. Before long, to my great relief, musical ideas, orchestral as well as pianistic, began to surge into my imagination.

I decided to stay for the moment with the piano and to compose a cycle of twelve studies. Each piece would strongly contrast with the previous one in terms of tempo and dynamics; however, to achieve unity, all were based on the same melodic line, rising and falling like a double wave, with a different key for each study. The first was in C sharp (major-minor), the next in F sharp, a fifth lower; the next in B, again a fifth lower, continuing in this manner, descending a fifth each time. After twelve such descents, the circle was completed and I arrived back at C sharp having used every key in the scale. For this reason I named the work *Circle of Fifths* (later it was published as *Twelve Miniature Studies*).

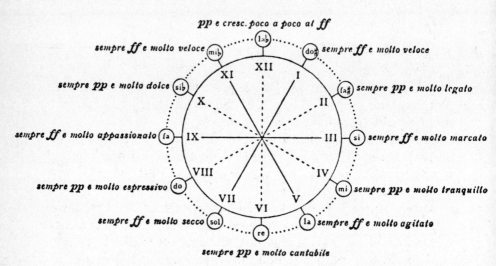

With my *Circle of Fifths* safely written, and my faith in myself as a composer re-emerging, I now felt ready to tackle something more substantial, though my work conditions were not perfect. I still had to travel more than I had imagined, to Łódź to carry out my duties for the Film Unit and to Warsaw for various outstanding commitments. For practical domestic reasons I had returned to live in our dreary apartment in Kraków. My father was frail but, as I had arranged, was well looked after by the caretaker's wife. Our dreadful cousin, enjoying free accommodation, never showed my father the slightest kindness. Irremovably ensconced together with her gloomy husband, she was still demonstrating her genius in finding as pupils the most untalented, unmusical children in Poland. The thumping of wrong notes and fiendish disharmonies in the next room made composition impossible for me at home.

I took to wandering endlessly out of doors, especially at night when the streets were deserted. These peregrinations had a calming influence. As I walked along velvet-dark lanes between the ancient city buildings, musical ideas would start to germinate; without committing a note to paper or touching a piano, I soon realised that I had a complete orchestral work ready in my imagination. Writing it down afterwards was almost a mechanical process.

Through this piece, my *Nocturne*, I was trying to detach myself from the reality of the present as well as the painful memories of the war years. I was weaving for myself a kind of musical night vision, as in a dream; seeing at the beginning cloudy and mysterious images, which gradually were to emerge clearer and clearer, building very slowly and irrevocably up into an orgiastic climax, then transforming little by little back into the misty images of the opening.

While allowing the emotional content of the work fullest rein, I did not abandon my concept of strict discipline in designing the work. I hung my succession of dreamlike images onto a vast arch of sound, the end exactly mirroring the beginning. At the start, silence was broken by the faint rustle of a side drum; gradually more and more instruments were brought in, so that, at the centre, the full orchestra combined to create the maximum possible volume of sound. Then the arch of sound gradually descended again and the volume diminished as the images dissolved into cloud. Finally the side-drum again . . . and silence. I could imagine the whole orchestra and the audience holding their breath for some seconds before the conductor lowered his baton and the players their instruments.

Just after I finished the *Nocturne*, I was invited to take part in another International Festival of Contemporary Music, this time in Copenhagen, where, ignoring my political masters, I conducted another work by the 'rebel' Spisak. Then I went on to England to conduct the London Philharmonic Orchestra at the Dome in Brighton. The all-Beethoven programme with the 'Eroica' as the main work had to be achieved with only one rehearsal.

Just as I was making my way to the rostrum at the start of the concert, the orchestral manager reminded me that the programme was to begin 'as usual' with *God Save the King*. This came as quite a shock. I didn't know a note of it. For several minutes, the orchestra sat waiting, the leader at the ready, the puzzled audience murmuring in complaint, while, backstage amongst the double-bass cases, the manager was humming through the tune and advising me to lift my baton for the roll of the drums, then to pause a few seconds for the audience to stand up before starting to conduct the anthem. After the anthem, the one-rehearsal concert seemed like child's play, and I was able to bask in a warm reception from the full house as well as rather extravagant praises from the Polish ambassador.

Enjoying a short respite in London, I resumed my habit of wandering through deserted streets after the city had gone to sleep. Pausing one night on Waterloo Bridge, I rested my arms on the balustrade, and gazed for many minutes down into the water of the Thames. When I lifted my head, I saw dark clouds drifting slowly across a brilliant full moon.

The river's flow and the night sky over the misty city prompted the idea of music on three planes: a pulsating rhythm of harps to correspond to the gentle, uninterrupted flow of the river; a group of solo string instruments, some moving in quarter tones, for the drifting clouds; and above, like the moon which was also looking down on Poland, the song of a Polish peasant, based almost entirely on the pentatonic scale and played by a succession of solo string instruments: violin, then viola, then cello. The music would thus convey the scene in front of my eyes, the clouds sometimes exposing and sometimes obscuring the full circle of the moon — so that the melodic line would be submerged and then emerge again from time to time.

I swiftly and roughly sketched my *Lullaby* for twenty-nine solo strings and two harps while still in London. The final score was written with great care when I was back in Poland and had found my own new way to notate the quarter tones.

My first ideas for my next work were sharply interrupted by a sudden 'invitation' (handed to me from the clenched fist of the Ministry of Culture) to resume my rôle as an overseas advertisement for Polish Music. At amazingly short notice I was packed off to conduct the Berlin Philharmonic Orchestra. I was not too unhappy with this mission, however. I welcomed the chance of working with one of the greatest orchestras of the world as well as promoting Polish composers unknown in Germany, such as Felix Janiewicz (an eighteenth-century violinist-composer, pupil of Haydn), Mieczysław Karłowicz (highly talented, tragically killed as a young man by an avalanche in the Tatra mountains early in this century) and Tadeusz Kassern (only slightly older than myself) whose lyrical Concerto for soprano and orchestra I enthusiastically included in the programme. I was ordered by the Minister to include my *Tragic Overture* too, as an appropriate reminder to the Germans of their Warsaw crimes.

15

PROPAGANDA TOOL IN BERLIN

I almost failed to reach Berlin in time. Arriving punctually to catch the night train, laden down with bulky scores and orchestral material for my unconventional programme, as well as a hefty suitcase containing my conductor's 'uniform', I waited three hours, the only passenger on a deserted platform, shivering in a temperature several degrees below zero. When the Moscow-Berlin train finally lumbered in, I jumped towards a carriage door with my luggage, but the handle would not budge. I tried several more doors but they were all locked. I ran after the guard, seeing that he was about to blow the whistle for departure. Breathing vodka fumes all over me, he barked that the train was full. Furious, I grabbed his arm just in time to prevent him waving his green flag, and thrust under his nose my ticket and sleeper reservation issued by the Ministry of Culture, ordering him, with what I hoped was the voice of authority, to show me to my place. Suddenly alarmed, he muttered that my booking was indeed valid, and let me into my compartment, where a Soviet army officer was already tucking himself into the lower bunk.

My problems were not over. Longing to warm my frozen limbs under the blankets, I found that my mattress was bare; there was not so much as a pillow or sheet. The Russian officer sent me to the attendant, a tiny Mongolian girl, who was sleeping on an upright seat, her head against the corridor wall. She woke up fast enough at my approach and insisted on payment for the bedclothes in German marks (presumably for black market use), of which I had none. My Russian companion not only saved me from being frozen all night, but was so friendly that he refused repayment. So, I could hardly complain when he consumed a stinking garlic sausage which later would not allow itself to be forgotten. Like most of our fellow passengers, he was *en route* to Berlin on an army posting. Never having been abroad before, he was envious of my wider travels to the rest of Europe. He had a lot to say about his life, his wife and his vodka. Sleep was impossible. His night-long conversation was interspersed at regular intervals by the sounds and fumes provoked by the battle between the garlic sausage and his digestive system. There was also a non-stop programme of would-be Russian folk-music, the same records repeated over and over again, relayed and distorted by a loudspeaker that couldn't be switched off. It was lucky that, on arrival, I had a couple of days' break before rehearsals began.

In Berlin I was billeted at the Polish Military Mission. Surprisingly it was in the British sector, and was, I supposed, a centre for gathering military information rather than for hosting visiting musicians carrying the country's cultural flag. The Commandant was introduced to me as General Prawin, but I was told that his real name was Levin, and that, like many Polish Jews who found refuge during the war in the Soviet Union, he had fought in Russian uniform at Stalingrad. All the other officers in the Mission had also spent the war in Russia. The gimlet-eyed sentry who guarded our entrances and exits from the Mission spoke no Polish at all. He turned out not to be Russian, as I had first imagined, but the son of a Polish miner, a dedicated Communist who had gone into exile in France before the war. The Frenchborn son was chosen as a guard doubtless because he was politically reliable (the more so since he had never lived under the régime and seen his father's idealistic theories in practice!).

The Polish Military Mission was a grisly place to stay, not just because of the awful food in the stark army canteen. The nights were punctuated by loud shrieks and cries coming from the cellar; these, I was told, arose from 'interviews' and 'arguments' with the German war criminals handed over by the Allies to the Polish authorities.

It was a relief to turn from such matters to the challenge of conducting the Berlin Philharmonic, which I had heard only once when they visited Warsaw before the war and gave an unforgettable performance of my favourite Brahms Symphony No. 3 under Wilhelm Furtwängler.

When I arrived for the first rehearsal, the manager of the orchestra came straight up to me, and said, with a quick glance at his watch, '*Guten Morgen, Herr Direktor!* I know we are scheduled to begin our rehearsal in nine minutes' time, but everyone is here. If you wish, we could start early!' Such an attitude I have never met in any other orchestra in the world! From the beginning I experienced a musical delight: wonderful discipline, excellent intonation and precision, and, above all, supreme quality of sound. I had never enjoyed rehearsals more in my life.

The first concert was a gala occasion for invited guests only, including the senior representatives of the American, English, French and Soviet military missions. The entrance was decorated with huge red and white Polish banners. The military men arrived in gaudy uniforms, the women in furs over long dresses. It was a rare festive occasion amidst the rubble and ruins of Berlin.

The Polish singer, Ewa Bandrowska-Turska, performed the Kassern Concerto for soprano and orchestra supremely. Everything went very well. I finished the concert with my *Tragic Overture*. Perhaps the notes in the programme indicating when, where and why this work had been composed contributed to the extraordinarily emotional reaction of the audience. I was overwhelmed by the standing ovation I received.

The other six concerts in the series took place in the other sectors of Berlin. They were all sold out, and again were most warmly received. These successes prompted immediate invitations to conduct in Leipzig and Dresden before my return to Poland. I was told I had to stay in the Military Mission until it was time to fulfil these engagements.

As the moment approached to leave for Leipzig, I suddenly fell ill: I had aching joints, a terrible headache and a very sore throat. Without asking a doctor, I knew that I had 'flu. I reluctantly sent messages to cancel my concerts.

Next day the Adjutant appeared at my bedside, ordering me

to dress and present myself in the Commandant's office. I complied, and Prawin, eyeing me suspiciously as I stood, reeling, in front of him, declared that cancellation of my concert tour was out of the question. I begged for a postponement. 'The dates cannot be changed,' he said, adamantly. 'Too much preparation has already been made. You can't disappoint everybody. You must go.'

To this I replied as firmly as I could, 'I regret it very much, but I do not have the strength to rehearse the orchestras.'

The General's voice became very quiet. He said, slowly and deliberately, 'You have to go. It is an order.' The word 'order' sounded pianissimo but in my imagination it was fortissimo. I realised that further discussion would be useless if not dangerous.

On the day of my departure by car to Leipzig, I felt no better. My head was hot, I was coughing and sneezing, and my eyes were watering. After a wretched night, we started rehearsals on schedule in the morning. To my surprise, the concert-recording was achieved without any obvious disaster.

Next day, only half-conscious, I was packed into another car and taken to Dresden. Somehow the concert was again a great success. The critics who admired the 'economy' of my conducting technique did not realise that I hardly had the strength to lift my arm: 'He does not need exaggerated gestures to be intelligible,' wrote one. 'Disdaining Furtwängler's great gestures of the left hand,' declared another, 'Panufnik is always a master of sound and matter. Such a conductor must possess an enormous discipline of will and temperament!' The only discipline I had needed on that occasion was to remain on my feet at all.

When I arrived back in Berlin, a German doctor diagnosed pneumonia, and pumped injections and medicines into me (antibiotics were not yet in use). For some time apparently I was delirious. There were no visits from General Prawin, despite all his Soviet medals for bravery. When I was just about back on my feet, complications arising from sinusitis necessitated a number of visits to hospital for X-rays and treatment. It was a long time before I was well enough to make the return journey to Kraków.

My father was in a bad state. I had written him several post-cards from Germany, without mentioning my illness, and suggesting that my stay had been extended for professional reasons. But our unspeakable cousin had persuaded him my absence was likely to be permanent. 'He has thrown you off! He will never come back!' she had gloated.

As a result of the critical and public response to my Berlin concerts, the idea of staying on had indeed been put to me by people in the musical world, without political connections so far as I could see. I was told that I 'belonged' culturally in the West, and fervent attempts, backed by generous offers of financial support, were made to convince me that I could more rapidly develop my career in Germany, both in conducting and composition.

My answer had been a definite 'No', partly because of my father, but above all because I wanted to play my part in Polish musical life, which at last was beginning to recover from the devastation of war. Though I had steadfastly refused to join the Communist Party, I was not enamoured of the Western powers either; my resentment was deepened by the realisation that Roosevelt had sold my country to Stalin at the Yalta Conference of 1945, so that we probably would not within a lifetime regain our full freedom as a nation. Despite Russian interference in all aspects of our life, Poland to my mind was still a separate nation, and I was determined to stay loyal to our government even if I regretted its need to bend before political pressures. I admitted to the Germans who tried to woo me with promises of a comfortable life, that existence in Poland was hard and demanded considerable material sacrifices, but for me, poverty was no reason to abandon my country and become an exile.

16

THE RISE AND FALL OF
SINFONIA RUSTICA

For a brief interlude, I found time again for composition. The moment had arrived, I felt, to galvanise myself into tackling a new symphony, of completely different character to the previous ones. Sentiment prevented me from re-using the appellations of my lost Symphonies Nos. 1 and 2. I decided to give my new work — and any future symphonies — names instead of numbers.

My *Sinfonia Rustica* emerged as an expression of my love for the Polish peasant music from the northern part of our country where the songs have exceptional charm. The art of the region is also outstanding, with imaginatively carved woodwork, brilliant folk costumes, and intricate, colourful paper-cuts, either abstract or semi-abstract, often of symmetrical design. I decided that I would reflect these naïve but aesthetically appealing features in my new symphony. The symmetry of the paper-cuts was to enter into all aspects of the composition. Even the orchestral layout was symmetrical, for acoustic reasons as well as for visual effect, with eight wind instruments in the middle of the concert platform and two small string orchestras on either side carrying on a dialogue.

However, I was not left in peace to complete this work. Together with several of my fellow composers, I was chosen by the Minister of Culture to join the governing body of the new Composers' Union. Before I had even a chance to hesitate, I was harangued by a Ministry official to the effect that it would be to my advantage to abandon my 'ivory tower' (a critical label frequently applied to creative artists in the Soviet Union).

In view of all that I had been trying to do for Polish music in general, while others — for understandable reasons — had remained at home composing, it did not seem a fair criticism. Moreover the pressure was unnecessary, because I genuinely wanted to work for the newly created Composers' Union. I realised that with a well-organised Union we should be able to obtain financial subsidies to commission new works, and we could actively encourage conductors and instrumentalists to perform new Polish music. We would also be able to demand that our members receive proper royalties, and stand up for their rights over such vital matters as housing and medical facilities, which otherwise were unattainable.

My colleagues, knowing of my fights on behalf of the Warsaw Philharmonic players, urged me to play a leading part and expressed their particular confidence in my artistic stance. To them, the *Tragic Overture, Nocturne* and *Lullaby* seemed decidedly advanced by comparison with anything else written in Poland at that time. On their insistence I was elected Vice-President of the Union, a position that entailed attending regular meetings in Warsaw, and representing the composers at conferences of other state organisations.

On my frequent journeys to the capital, I stayed at the grandly named House of the Composers' Union, which was in fact a modest, newly-built villa, situated between the former *palais* of my great-grandfather, Antoni Szuster, and the private residence of the most dreaded of all men, the Minister of Public Security. The house had a large room for chamber concerts, lectures or conferences, plus a few guest rooms for visiting members. Most conveniently, I could not only invite my girlfriend to stay (impossible in our tiny Kraków flat) but also I could compose without the background rumpus from my cousin's pupils. Taking fullest advantage of both possibilities, my *Sinfonia Rustica* was quickly completed.

On return visits to Kraków, my father often showed signs of envying my life in his beloved Warsaw. For his sake, I decided to fight for a flat there.

My letters of application to the Ministry of Housing were never answered. Eventually I stormed the fortress. The secretary, recognising me from my concerts, made me an appointment. The Director did not turn up. Twice. On the third appointment at last he granted me the honour of seeing him personally. His name was Gross, German for 'big'. He was indeed Mr Big in terms of power, but in stature he was small and bald as a knee, with a shiny nose and an equally shiny smile. He greeted me in an exaggeratedly friendly manner, his expression suggesting that I was about to say something very amusing.

I explained that it was vital for me to live in the capital, to be readily available to carry out my important commitments at the Composers' Union. I avoided mentioning that I also needed somewhere peaceful for my creative work: he would have cited the official Party line that it was possible to compose anywhere. I also remained silent about my father's longing to return to Warsaw; the unwritten law of our politicians was that old people had nothing left in life except to die. The Housing Director continued to ooze saccharine smiles until I had finished my plea, then laughed nervously as though I had told him a slightly dubious joke. The episode was indeed a joke to him. I heard nothing more in spite of writing many letters to remind him of my request.

My duties at the Composers' Union were occupying an alarming amount of my time, and a situation was developing there which required careful watching.

I had become acutely aware at all our meetings of the permanent presence of the musicologist, Zofia Lissa, a small, plump woman in her thirties. A Jewish refugee, she had spent the war years in the Soviet Union, marrying a Russian composer of no great talent, and leaving him behind when she returned to Poland. After her years of political training, she was an impassioned Marxist, and was well known and respected in Western Marxist circles.

As she was tiny, she always looked at me from below – but with an attitude which clearly indicated that she was seeing me from above. It soon became apparent that the Communist Party was giving us directives through her. We also assumed that she had been assigned to keep officials informed about the political opinions as well as artistic attitudes of each individual Union member.

With time, I developed a cordial relationship with Professor

Lissa; we recognised our political differences but did not discuss them. I respected her considerable musical education and her skill as a writer; I envied her talent and facility in delivering lectures and speeches, which she could improvise brilliantly off the cuff. She correspondingly appeared to respect me as a musician, and seemed to appreciate my willingness to work hard for my colleagues. We always spoke to one another politely, taking care to avoid risky topics. Since she needed my support in order to have influence in musical affairs, and I needed her direct access to 'higher powers' to defend the interests of my fellow composers, we managed to remain on good terms.

However, hers was an uncomfortable presence, and the Union members could never drop their guard, despite her fervent attempts to appear friendly, and her request that we address her by the diminutive of her name, Zosia. I remember one informal social occasion as particularly typical of the way she worked. We all drank quantities of vodka, (except Zosia who always would abstain while generously refilling our glasses in the hope that our tongues would loosen). We wanted to listen to a foreign radio station – Paris or London, I don't remember which – to hear a new work by a contemporary Western composer. Reception was even worse than usual and Zosia provocatively remarked, 'How terrible! Those awful Russians are jamming it!' Despite the vodka, despite our true feelings, fortunately none of us was drawn to agree. Her comment was simply intended to win our confidence and provoke expressions of disloyalty to the régime. It was a favourite ploy of Party members.

My Union activities left me little time for composition. But I managed to complete a work for UNESCO in Paris to commemorate the hundredth anniversary of Chopin's death. This commission was a welcome honour, and all the more so since I was the only Pole amongst several international names chosen to honour Poland's greatest composer. Knowing Chopin's life-long love for Polish folk music, I made use of some melodies and rhythms from the region near Warsaw where he was born. I treated the voice as a purely musical instrument without need for text, and wrote five *vocalises* for soprano and piano, *Suita Polska*[1].

Before this work was finished, I was invited at short notice to conduct three concerts, in Paris, Bordeaux and Marseilles. I greatly enjoyed conducting my *Nocturne* with l'Orchestre Radio Symphonique in Paris. I enjoyed Bordeaux too, both the wine and my reception there going rather to my head.

At the Opéra in Marseilles, there was a wild ovation, not for me but for Borodin. The Director, when planning the concert, had told me that the Marseilles audience were in love with the *Polovtsian Dances*. So long as I finished my concert with this work I could conduct anything else that I liked. He was right: the success was resounding. Afterwards, the delighted Director and his wife invited me to their home, where I ate the first divine oysters in my life. (Honesty forces me to set my gastronomic experiences alongside musical ones — coming from Poland, French food was a sensation close to heaven!)

My only other trip abroad that year was to Holland to conduct my *Lullaby* at the 1948 International Festival of Contemporary Music. The concert was at Scheveningen, a once fashionable spa, where the musical tastes, like the buildings, were basically nineteenth century. During rehearsal, the string players resented making the effort to master the quarter tones, sneering audibly amongst themselves over my 'strange' ideas; and they clearly manifested their disdain even in the concert performance. The audience seemed confused, if not downright disappointed, and the applause sounded like damp linen flapping on a clothes line. The only favourable response came from the British critic, Desmond Shawe-Taylor. Perhaps he sensed that the work was conceived in his own capital.

On my return to Poland, I learnt that I had been appointed a member of the Polish Committee of the Defence of Peace. This high-sounding organisation was a creation of the Government. Leading personalities from every walk of life — art, literature, science, engineering — had been co-opted. The conductor Fitelberg and the singer Bandrowska-Turska were my fellow-

1. Published in England as *Hommage à Chopin*.

musicians. Had we objected to being hi-jacked into partici-
pating, the authorities would have only smiled sweetly or
sourly, and asked: 'Are you not against war? After all the
sufferings in Warsaw don't you want a lasting peace?'

I had never grudged the hours spent as Union Vice-
President fighting for the rights of my fellow composers, but I
was beginning to resent deeply the precious composition time
stolen from me through being forcibly paraded as a political
pawn on public platforms.

I had not only to accept membership of the Committee, but
also to take part in the International Congress in Defence of
Peace, which was scheduled to take place in August 1948 in
the city of Wrocław.

Distinguished left-wing intellectuals had been invited from
all over the world, no doubt to emphasise the importance of the
enterprise. A very small man with a very large title, the Director of the Committee for Cultural Relations with other Countries, delegated me to act as official host to Pablo Picasso.

Not trusting my French, I carefully prepared some official
words of welcome, and was ready in attendance at the airport
when Picasso's plane touched down. As soon as it had halted, I
hurried across the runway, accompanied by a swarm of international journalists and cameramen.

Among the passengers I caught sight of Picasso, a simian
figure with wild penetrating eyes. I pushed my way towards
him, and delivered my well-rehearsed sentences of welcome. To
my surprise, as soon as I had finished, he asked me to come
closer and repeat my words, slower and louder for the press
and radio. Clearly he wanted to be well documented. We
shook hands also for an extended period for the sake of the
photographers.

At the dinner in Picasso's honour, the Party officials appeared in dark suits and silver ties, more bourgeois than the
'bourgeois'. Picasso seemed ill at ease in this excessively formal
gathering. To my delight, he shattered the stuffy atmosphere
by removing his shirt and finished his dinner half naked. The
shocked officials had to smile in artificial appreciation so as not
to offend their main propaganda asset.

His general intentions were friendly. He had even brought

with him some of his exquisitely decorated ceramic dishes which he asked me to present on his behalf to the National Museum in Warsaw. When I handed them over to the Ministry of Culture, I was told that they were 'decadent Western art', and were not suitable to be shown to the general public. I wondered if Picasso even began to understand how cynically he was being exploited as a political ally while his art was condemned to a dark cupboard.

I wondered if he knew also what the Eastern bloc Communists meant by 'peace'. For me (and probably for him too), peace meant peace with the universe, with nature, with all living things, and within oneself.

But this was not what the conference organisers had in mind. I recognised the noxious truth behind the flag-draped façade of the International Congress in Defence of Peace. The organisational directives plainly came from Moscow. The word 'peace' was no more than a pretext. Used by the Soviets it could only mean an imposed, hypocritical peace, based on terror. Since the 1917 Revolution, in the name of 'justice' and 'equality', the Russians had already killed and imprisoned millions; they would find no difficulty in sacrificing millions more under the slogan of 'the Struggle for Peace'. Most of the speeches seemed to be inciting a burning hatred of the West, manufacturing artificial fears that the 'capitalist' countries, particularly the 'bloodthirsty United States of America', were avidly preparing for another war.

Amongst the delegates were many eminent visitors who one might have hoped would not tolerate such flagrant propagandising, including the nuclear scientists, Frédéric Joliot and Irène Joliot-Curie (daughter of the great Polish chemist Maria Skłodowska-Curie who discovered radium); also French Marxists such as the poet Paul Eluard, the painter Ferdinand Léger and Jean-Paul Sartre himself. It was painful for us besieged Poles to see such distinguished creative and academic personalities strutting about exuding a sense of their political importance whereas in fact they were the merest camouflage for the hidden Soviet offensive.

The British historian A.J.P. Taylor, as I recall, was the only person at the Congress to stand up and object to the nonsense about American Fascism that was being bandied around. He said that it was the business of intellectuals to refute inaccurate assertions of this kind – just as it was the business of intellectuals in the West to reject a view too frequently advanced, that the dictatorships of the Soviet Union and Nazi Germany were now indistinguishable. Instead he pleaded for intellectual honesty, tolerance and love. His frankness and integrity made a deep impression on me. But the Conference organisers had arranged that we Poles were given no opportunities to make friends with our guests from the West – I suppose in case we let slip what life was like in Poland.

Once or twice, in momentary lulls in the proceedings, I did find myself in conversation with visitors. One of them, thinking to please me, remarked wistfully how very lucky I was to be living in a 'true Communist country'. The other – from a neutral state so he had not experienced the reality – used up a lot of energy trying to convince *me* that war was evil. Of course I had to keep a diplomatic silence.

I also once found myself with the Soviet writer, Ilya Ehrenburg. He wanted me to tell him about the state of the housing problem in Poland. Knowing of his closeness to Stalin, I was careful not to blame the political system for neglecting this basic human need. Guardedly I said that we Poles were still devastated by the recent war, and for this reason the situation was extremely difficult. I could then admit that our houses were dreadfully overcrowded, so that large families often had to live in one small room.

Ehrenburg responded with an ironic smile and said, 'Moscow wasn't even damaged by war, but we have a housing problem too.' He told me about a young couple, friends of his, with a one-room flat in Moscow. They divorced, the husband having fallen in love with another girl. The new girlfriend had no flat, no allocation was forthcoming from the authorities, so the couple moved in with the first wife. The first wife then fell in love with another man. Again no further accommodation was available, so they ended up living as two 'happy' couples in one tiny room.

Was I expected to be indignant, or merely to take the story as a joke? What was Ehrenburg's purpose in telling it? Was it just a piece of gratuitous cynicism or was it intended as a kind of consolation to us Poles in our dismal economic situation? I never discovered. Ehrenburg and I, trapped by uncertainty and political constraint, side-stepped round each other and could never really communicate.

Quite shortly after the International Congress for Peace, I was dragooned into another sinister official congress: a General Assembly of Polish Composers, held in Warsaw. The climax was a speech by the Polish Deputy Minister of Culture and Art, Włodzimierz Sokorski. It was a very long speech, and our chairs were hard; but harder still was the message we heard. We were not unprepared for it. Early in 1948, reports had reached us from Moscow about a speech by Commissar Zhdanov, one of Stalin's closest cronies. Zhdanov had exhorted Soviet composers to write music more like Glinka or Tchaikovsky; he had said that contemporary Western 'bourgeois' tendencies were to be totally eliminated, and henceforth 'cultural products must serve politico-economic ends'.

Then, in June the same year, Zosia had attended an International Conference of Composers and Music Critics in Prague, where most if not all the presidium were dedicated Communists, including Alan Bush from England and Hanns Eisler from Austria. Though the venue had been Czechoslovakia, the proceedings had been directed by the Russians, with Khrennikov (General Secretary of the Soviet Composers' Union) at the head, his friends the musicologist Yarustovsky and the composer-teacher Shaporin dancing in unison.

The main subject of the conference had been the universal 'crisis' in modern music, caused by the 'extreme subjectivism' of composers and their failure to understand 'progressive' ideas and 'the feelings of the masses'. Khrennikov had fiercely condemned contemporary composers for neglecting the melodic element, if not entirely at least in effect; their music he said lacked clearly-defined, 'easily recognisable contours', resulting in an 'artificial complexity'.

Apparently the composers were not to blame for this deficiency: it was the result of 'an unsound social structure' − a non-Marxist political system. Zosia, her eyes alight with zeal, had told us that the delegates had unanimously agreed that all 'progressive' composers henceforth had a 'sacred' (!) duty to take part in the realisation of the great 'historic' tasks awaited by 'all mankind'.

When I heard Zosia's report, what had worried me most had been the embracing suggestion that *all* composers were to comply: could this mean that in the future we Poles might find ourselves under the same constraints as our Russian colleagues? Might we also be prevented from writing music according to our own creative consciences? I could see a distinct danger that we too might find ourselves being 'mobilised' to produce music in the spirit of Marxist ideology, permeated with the 'struggle for Communism', and be forced to praise the greatness of Soviet leaders past and present so as to join their 'historic task' of 'building a better tomorrow'. Momentarily, this new jargon had sounded so ridiculous that I had failed to hide my amusement from Zosia. But then I had been overcome with a gloomy foreboding that music for music's sake could soon be a luxury of the past. Now my worst fears were to be realised.

Minister Sokorski had a dangerously disarming sense of humour and we all had to tread warily with him, knowing that he was yet another of those Polish wartime refugees to Moscow who had been trained to carry out Russian commands. At this General Assembly I realised that he had also picked up the Soviet weakness for interminable speeches. He began by paying some compliments to us composers, congratulating us on our successes abroad. After these few flattering words he went straight into the attack. He said that most of us worked in a state of reprehensible isolation from our society, especially from the 'broad masses', and that this state of affairs created a tragic division between the composer and the listener. The only solution to this problem, he asserted, was to reject the music of the 'decadent' capitalist epoch, which was already showing clear signs of 'formalistic degeneration', and to search for a new artistic expression as regards thematic subject and form.

Quoting chunks of Lenin and Zhdanov as infallible authorities, Sokorski then ordered us to create music for our 'socialist epoch'; music which would reflect the aesthetic and psychological experiences of the 'new man'. He repeated himself constantly, but considering that he was not a musician himself, he seemed to be sailing so skilfully in an unknown sea I felt sure that Zosia had primed him in his use of words.

At the end of his oration, he gave us a final assurance that all our artistic organisations were to be united in a policy 'based on the experiences of the Soviet Union and the ideological achievements of the Marxist-Leninist Party of the Polish proletariat'! Although the Deputy Minister had the look of a priest speaking from his pulpit, this last sentence rang in my ears like blasphemy.

My gloom was shared by everyone around me. Picking ourselves up wearily from the hard wooden chairs, we knew that the comparative cultural freedom of the past four years was finished. From now on we would be expected to subordinate every note we wrote to the interests of the 'Polish Workers' Party'[1]. Our music was now to be 'national in form and socialist in content', 'depicting socialist reality' in a way that would be 'simple and understandable to the broad masses', 'deeply ideological' and 'worthy of the great Socialist epoch'.

It was not long before we received our first directive to put the new theories into action. The Union was ordered to organise a competition: the composition of a *Song of the United Party*.

Although the Composers' Union numbered roughly a hundred, we had only one Party member. The lyric we were supposed to set was sheer jargon, and no one wanted anything to do with it; but all of us were ordered to take part. I tried to extricate myself, insisting that I was not a good song writer, that the specialists in popular music would produce much better entries. Zosia refused to let me back out, eventually threatening that, if I failed to produce an entry, our whole Union would lose the financial support of the state.

I contemplated the awful title for days in a state of anguish,

---

1. (The 'Workers' Party was so-called because care was always taken to avoid open use of the word 'Communist' which had a repulsive sound to all but a small minority of Poles; the repulsion was due not only to present difficulties, but also to the general unpopularity of the pre-war Communist Party).

knowing that I could not let down my fellow composers who, though sharing my political views, felt that I must enter. Then I found what I thought was a cunning solution. I would produce some sort of concoction so that the authorities would note my participation, but it would be so bad that it could not possibly win. I took a piece of manuscript paper and composed a song 'on my knee', literally in a few minutes, setting the ridiculous text to the first jumble of notes which came into my head. It was rubbish, and I smiled to myself as I sent it off to the adjudicators.

To my great surprise, the jury was chaired by Bolesław Woytowicz, who had always scrupulously avoided any kind of political involvement on the excuse that he had serious heart trouble, so serious that he might not live more than a few weeks, or even days. (He lived for at least thirty years after the competition.) I respected him as a talented composer, excellent pianist and skilled teacher, and thought of him as a good friend – until I heard his verdict. He awarded me the first prize!

It could only be a political rather than a musical decision. I found no comfort in reminding myself of the necessity to save the Union finances, despite the friendship and approval of my colleagues. I deeply regretted that I had allowed myself to be cornered into betraying my self-imposed artistic standards. Over and over again, I asked myself whether my sacrifice had been necessary. Did I really have to be a tool of the political system?

In the spring of 1949, I received an official letter from the Committee for Cultural Relations Abroad, informing me that 'The citizen has been delegated to Palermo for the International Festival of Contemporary Music.' (Party members were always addressed as 'comrade', non-Party members as 'citizen'.) The date of my departure was already fixed a few days hence. It was not an invitation, it was an order. The thought of escaping for a whole week was, in my present downcast mood, stronger than my resentment at being once more used as a pawn.

The main purpose of my visit was to report for the Polish musical magazine, *Ruch Muzyczny*, on the performance of *King*

Roger, Szymanowski's opera based on Sicilian history. The Sicilian production looked magnificent, but unfortunately I did not hear a single note. My keepers had arranged that I should arrive only one hour before the curtain rose. They had booked me via Prague on a Czech plane and the cabin was not pressurised. I then had to take another small noisy plane from Rome to Palermo, and arrived not only exhausted but also virtually deaf. My report for *Ruch Muzyczny* had to be based on information from the other delegates.

I recovered in a day or so and was able to appreciate the rest of the concerts in the Festival. The Italian organisers hospitably arranged a number of outings, and I was thoroughly enjoying the beautiful Sicilian spring when suddenly I was cornered by four highly-committed comrades from the Czech delegation who might have been there for their political beliefs rather than for their musical talents. Because of my international standing as a composer, they insisted that I should be their mouthpiece at a meeting of all the composers, with a resolution which made my heart sink to the soles of my ill-made Polish shoes.

It was a typical concoction that took in vain the real meaning of peace and called on the humanitarian aspirations of the composers of the Festival. Though carefully veiled in harmless-sounding language, it was in fact in direct contravention of the International Society for Contemporary Music's stated intention to avoid politics. It had been translated by the English composer, Benjamin Frankel, who, I was informed, was very far to the Left, but apparently did not wish publicly to commit himself by reading his own transcript to the assembled delegates.

I told the Czechs that, having written their resolution, they should present it. First aggressively, then changing their tone to 'friendly' persuasion, they gradually trapped me into co-operation. As a Pole from recently annihilated Warsaw, they answered that I had greater authority than anyone present to speak out against war. The danger which finally won me over was that one of the group, called Urban, an extremely charming man but a Stalinist zealot, made sure that I knew that he was on his way to a diplomatic posting in Moscow. If he reported my intransigence, he indicated, the Russians would

have a good excuse to clamp down on Polish composers travelling abroad for future music festivals. The significance of this
threat was clear to me. Not only would we miss valuable opportunities to get our music played, but we would also find ourselves cut off from the Western contemporary music scene; a
damaging blow to us, but an advantage to the Soviets who
were eager to isolate Polish culture and curtail our natural
affinity with the West in order to force us more closely into
their own sphere of influence.

With this threat in mind, I finally capitulated. After I had
read out the statement, an embarrassed silence hung over the
body of the hall. But Edward Clark – the husband of Elizabeth Lutyens whose music was performed in the Festival – was
chairing the meeting: by reputation a fellow-traveller, he
nodded his approval, with the ultra-British comment, 'Oh, very
interesting!' However, other less enthusiastic voices were then
raised, protesting in quiet but unmistakable anger that politics
must not be allowed to enter this purely musical scene. The
Czechs loudly defended their resolution, arguing that composers in the past had not been ashamed to express their love
for humanity, citing Beethoven and his Ninth Symphony as a
precedent.

Although there was no major disturbance, I felt disgusted
that I had once more been manoeuvred into a false position.
Perhaps the Czechs had exaggerated the threat to my fellow
composers or perhaps not. In any case I was being drawn into
a propaganda machine that opened and shut my mouth for me,
while gnawing away at my dwindling reserves of independence
and objectivity.

My dream of a carefree visit to Italy evaporated. Just before
I left for home, I received a telegram from Warsaw telling me
that my *Sinfonia Rustica* had won first prize in the Chopin
Competition. I should have been delighted at the news but no
longer could distinguish whether the honour was political or
purely musical. I was anyway too depressed to care.

About three months after my visit to Palermo, all Polish composers and musicologists were summoned to the small provincial town of Łagów for yet another crucial conference on

the future direction of music. The Poznań Philharmonic Orchestra had been engaged to perform some of our orchestral works in order to refresh our memories and enable us to 'ventilate the burning question of formalism and realism' in composition. My *Nocturne* was amongst the programmed works, and I was expected to be present to express my views 'frankly and freely' in an open, 'friendly' conversation.

Anticipating that this event was unlikely to be enjoyable, I managed to construct a pressing excuse to stay in Warsaw. Afterwards I heard that almost none of the participants had got away unscathed. In the course of the 'friendly' discussions, my *Nocturne* had drawn more fire than any other work, being declared 'unsuitable for the broad masses', failing adequately to express the 'joyful life under socialism'! If I had been there, it seemed, I would have been forced into self-criticism, even into solemn promises in front of my colleagues that I would not 'escape from the reality of life' in my future compositions.

As I had feared, this event, despite its lightweight appearance, had crushingly confirmed the new policy; that music now had to be of political significance. It had further hammered home the final tin-tack in the coffin of music for music's sake.

The new rules really were intended to bite now, far more deeply than we had imagined on the basis of the previous rather woolly statements. Minister Sokorski, in a closing speech, had attacked anyone still composing the 'anti-humanistic' abstract music of the 'decadent period of imperialism' instead of 'inspiring the masses' with the 'humanistic, ideologically conceived, emotionally charged new music of the Socialist epoch'. He had written off all abstract, experimental, even faintly dissonant music as the 'dying convulsions of the capitalist system', the final 'stagger' of collapsing aesthetic concepts in all the arts. He had poured scorn on composers who displayed a 'characteristic helplessness' when faced with 'the objective truth of a new epoch'.

Now we were to create 'strictly according to the principles of Socialist Realism'; an awkward task since the precise meaning of this ominous phrase, sweeping over us amidst a cascade of incomprehensible slogans, remained hidden and obscure. None of us could quite make out what was expected of us. We only knew that Socialist Realism would henceforth be the 'sole valid foundation for artistic endeavour' because 'certain changes cannot be reversed', because of the 'historic mission of creative artists', because of the 'struggle for peace', because of a 'better tomorrow', because, because, because — the outpouring of catch-phrases seemed inexhaustible.

An equally destructive political offensive was launched at the other arts too, with the intention of channelling all creative output into the service of the propaganda machine. Painters, sculptors and graphic artists were to become like photographers, to provide not only images of the current 'socialist reality', but also stirring reminders of the history of the revolution. Poets were expected to become reporters-in-rhyme of political events. Novelists had to tailor their work to carry suitably optimistic messages, and to write with bland simplicity for 'the broad masses'.

Musicologists, art historians and literary critics were also harnessed to the machine and expected to extol the virtues of Socialist Realism. Still unable to clarify the ill-defined differences between 'formalism' and 'realism', some Marxist writers produced such subtly clever and complex dissertations that they accidentally succeeded in blurring the issue even further. Warsaw humour humped up above the quagmire: the word went about that Socialist Realism was like a mosquito — everybody knew it had a prick but no one had seen it!

It was clear that the attack on formalism and 'decadent' Western art was part of a campaign of Russification of all aspects of our life, specifically cutting us off from the West. Before the First World War my father's generation could be sent to Siberia for the crime of speaking Polish. The Russification we experienced was more of a cultural and spiritual nature. Every day it grew more insistent — in radio programmes, in the repertoires of concert halls, in the books published, the plays performed, and, above all, in the cinema. I had only to pick up a newspaper or magazine to see how successfully Russia had penetrated every area of our lives. Each day we were bludgeoned by hymns of praise for the Russian nation, and for the Soviet 'supermen' who were set up as our examples of perfection, leading the world in science, literature and all the arts.

I saw Communism emerging as a new kind of idolatrous religion which had as its icons the portraits of Marx, Lenin and Stalin. They were the new divinities, their images plastered everywhere on the most absurd pretexts.

Even at a Warsaw exhibition commemorating the centenary of Chopin's death, the largest portrait, dominating the whole area, was not that of Chopin but of Karl Marx, whose colossally enlarged features dwarfed the interesting documents, manuscripts and photographs illuminating the composer's life. A musicologist friend of mind with 'progressive' views, Stefan Jarociński, had mounted the exhibition, and I innocently asked him what Marx had to do with Chopin. 'Oh, a very great deal,' Stefan assured me, blinking earnestly. 'The portrait shows us the epoch in which Chopin lived!' Shamelessly the press proclaimed that for the first time in the history of Poland the great genius of Chopin was finally recognised and acknowledged, thanks to our Socialist government.

The reigning deity was of course Stalin (*Słoneczko*, 'the little sun', to his most passionate fanatics). The Teatr Polski staged a mammoth play about him. In one scene lasting an eternity, no words were spoken at all. Stalin was seated at his desk, reading silently to himself. Slowly he rose to his feet, took a few deliberate steps, lit his pipe, returned to sit again at his desk, took up a pencil to make some notes, laid his pipe in the ashtray, then again got to his feet very slowly, walking a few steps and standing motionless as though in deep meditation, then went to the desk again.

The Poles never took to the Stalin cult. A typical Warsaw joke described the result of a competition for a memorial sculpture to Pushkin. After considering several hundred entries, the jury's decision was unanimous. The prize-winning monument was a gigantic, seated figure of Stalin holding a tiny book, on the cover of which were printed in miniscule letters just two words: 'Pushkin – *Poems*'.

As the Stalinist policies invaded every corner of our lives, I found myself quite unable to compose. In the early part of 1949 I had managed to carry on with my bread-and-butter work of music for the film unit, including two short films,

Earth Our Planet about nineteenth century Polish painters, and *Children's Hands at Play and Work*, for which I used some traditional children's songs interwoven into a score for small chamber orchestra.

However, since the dictates of Socialist Realism had been thrust upon us, I had found it impossible even to dream of tackling new, seriously creative compositions. During the war, the Nazis had occupied our country but not our minds: however much we had suffered, at least we could maintain a thread of hope for the future so that we might continue to 'write for the drawer'. But faith in the future now drained from me altogether. I was faced with an insoluble dilemma: how could I reject the method of Socialist Realism which the state imposed on me and, at the same time, remain a loyal subject of my native country?

I felt that it would be artistically and morally dishonest to accept the basic principle that music was to be 'national in form and socialist in content'. My musical imagination turned somersaults at the thought of reflecting the 'struggle of the people victoriously marching towards socialism'; and I hardly found myself burning with eagerness to write music celebrating the 'eternal and unshaken Polish-Soviet friendship'! Ghastly propaganda titles apart, I was simply not willing to write in the musical language of the nineteenth century, which was supposed to appeal to the ears of the vast majority of uneducated listeners.

However, if I rejected Socialist Realism, and persevered in composing abstract music, searching independently for my own spiritual and poetic inspiration, with my own ideas on structure and means of expression, I would be accused of 'writing for the élite', of 'striving desperately for originality' (as if this were such a terrible sin). I would be branded as a 'formalist', castigated as an 'enemy of the people', and probably accused of 'professing the art of the rotten West', or even, 'serving the end of American imperialism'.

After lengthy thought, at last I worked out a way to avoid either confrontation or capitulation. Following the example of our architects who at that time were most inspiringly reconstructing whole sections of old Warsaw, I decided to get myself to work as a restorer of sixteenth- and seventeenth-century Polish music, which was not so much a victim of the recent war as of successive centuries of foreign invasions. I directed my interest towards early composers whose incomplete and unknown works were no more than fragments mouldering in dusty libraries. Thus I could help to reconstruct a small part of our missing inheritance, working more as a scholar than as a composer.

My *Old Polish Suite* for strings seemed unexceptionable to the stewards of the new order. I conducted its first performance at the beginning of 1950 with the Warsaw Philharmonic Orchestra and even the most accomplished experts in dialectic sloganry had difficulty in finding any derogatory labels to apply. I had genuinely enjoyed my new departure, finding it not only a musically opportune but also a pleasurable and absorbing way of escaping suffocation from political pressure.

If some of us were looking to the past, not everyone was ignoring the new stylistic impositions. The parallel in architecture with Socialist Realism in music was exemplified hideously by the Palace of Culture, a wedding-cake-shape skyscraper, Stalin's gift, a 'little sister' to the University of Moscow, designed by the same appalling architect. This monster dominated our capital, inescapably visible from all sides and hated by everyone. The pile of Warsaw jokes about it soon grew as tall as the palace itself. For example, a Pole approaches the Housing Ministry to exchange his three-room luxury flat for a single room in the Palace of Culture. 'Why?' the official asks in amazement. 'Because then I would not be able to see the Palace from my window!'

My loathing for this excrescence almost outstripped my resentment of the second-rate anonymity of the rest of the new building in Warsaw. Our 'progressive' architects, were remorselessly rebuilding the remains of our once beautiful and characterful city in the drab spirit of Socialist Realism.

'Poor Man's Moscow' we were dubbed by travellers. The Moscow greyness was in everything – even the paintwork of our few, elderly taxis. The shops were a grey nightmare. We could not have imagined a walk through a supermarket tempted by brightly coloured goods. In our shops there was no food in sight at all, and often none worth having even when you did queue. Butter was a rare treat, coffee and meat other than chicken was unobtainable.

In order to buy anything, it was necessary to stand in a long queue to give an order, then to join a second queue to reach the cashier, then to stand for an age in a third queue actually to pick up the packaged goods — a system carefully copied from the Moscow model.

The visitors from the West never saw these miserable emporiums. Special shops existed for those who could show foreign passports — bringers of much-needed foreign currency — with oceans of vodka, lashings of sausage, fur coats, amber jewels and carvings.

One of the jobs landed on me, because of my position at the Composers' Union, was to entertain official foreign guests. With a few delightful exceptions, most of them were avowed Communists, spewing out flattery in the mistaken impression that it would please me, yet surprisingly avoiding ideological discussions on matters requiring intelligence like culture and the arts. They always seemed to be thirsty (for vodka) and hungry (for good Polish food from the restaurants unaffordable by resident Poles). The question which usually interested them most was how they could change their money to best advantage on the black market, and where they could most profitably shop (usually for jewellery and art). To talk to them freely was out of the question. If I had been able to tell them how we longed for democracy — how millions of my fellow countrymen had fought bravely in the war, at home and abroad, many of them losing their lives, for a free and independent Poland, *not* for a Moscow-controlled Poland — they would most probably have pretended that they could not hear me, or shrugged their shoulders, and taken me for an *agent provocateur* employed by the Polish or Russian secret service.

In February 1950 I was sent off to be a visitor myself, to Budapest, to make recordings for the Hungarian Radio of my *Old Polish Suite* and *Sinfonia Rustica*.

I stayed in a hotel reserved for foreign visitors only. The only guest in a huge restaurant, I was obsequiously served and observed by a dozen over-attentive waiters. This was the nearest I came to being alone, except when I could retire to my room.

Otherwise I had two constant companions: a young Hungarian man and an attractive red-haired girl who had been officially delegated to 'look after' me. They were so friendly that they took care never to let me go out by myself or talk to strangers. They accompanied me everywhere, even to the Radio building, seated either side of me in the back of a car.

I enjoyed working with the Hungarian Radio Orchestra. They were patient and co-operative and their playing was of a high standard. I was irritated, however, by restrictions within the Radio building. The door of the sound engineer's room, two floors above the orchestral hall, was guarded by a sentry with a rifle. (Did the authorities perhaps fear the enemies of the state could burst in and broadcast messages of defiance?) Each time I climbed the stairs to listen to a playback, the soldier insisted on seeing my identity card. After this had happened four or five times in one recording session, I lost patience, and demanded (in German) if he couldn't try to remember my face. He appeared not to hear me and checked my card just as seriously – on every like occasion.

During this short stay in Budapest, I was eager to see Zoltán Kodály again. At first my 'guardian angels' seemed unwilling to arrange a visit, but I insisted until they finally obtained consent from above. As they drove me to his home in the outskirts of Budapest, quite a distance from the hotel, I was struck by the unrelieved drabness on every side. Strangely few people were in sight, scurrying about their business, looking poor, sad, even frightened, like animals constantly wary in case a hunter was after them. How different from the lively, colourful pre-war Budapest that I remembered, and what a lamentable testimony to the Rákosi régime.

The house where I had visited Kodály twelve years before was unchanged. He greeted me most warmly, but conversation was difficult, not because of the language barrier – we both spoke fluent German – but because the two guardian angels hovered closeby. Just in a brief moment when they left the house to call the driver I quickly whispered to Zoltán, 'How is it with you, truly? How do you feel? What are you working on at the moment?' He replied in a soft voice that was close to breaking, 'I am not composing at the moment. I cannot find the peace of mind I need. It is terrible here. Terrible!' As he spoke there were tears in his eyes.

In 1950 I was elected Vice-President of the Music Council of UNESCO together with Arthur Honneger. Though the Ministry of Culture delightedly accepted the honour for Poland, I was never allowed a passport to take up any invitations to attend conferences or visit the headquarters in Paris.

I carried on with my administrative work at the Composers' Union, but always avoided ideological discussions. Never did I let myself be drawn to comment on speeches delivered by 'our Zosia' or by the Minister of Culture or by any visitor from a 'friendly' country.

Once our guest of honour was the General Secretary of the Soviet Composers' Union, a protégé of Stalin, Tikhon Khrennikov, a stocky young man with thick fair hair and a pale complexion. He listened intently to a debate on recent works by Polish composers, in the course of which one of our music critics, a Party member, attacked *Sinfonia Rustica* as a 'formalistic composition'. To my great surprise, one of my colleagues, the Chairman of the jury which had awarded the symphony first prize in the Chopin Competition the previous year, supported this accusation, declaring that its content was 'alien to the Socialist era'. Under the eyes of our powerful and alarming visitor none of my friends, whatever they really felt, could safely utter a word in protest. Minister Sokorski, having listened attentively to the political condemnation of this patently innocent piece, announced his verdict in sonorous tones: '*Sinfonia Rustica* has ceased to exist!'

I observed the satisfied expression of our Russian guest Khrennikov. As to myself, I did not utter one word. My face remained as expressionless as a wooden mask, as though I had heard nothing. Nothing at all.

17

PUBLIC AND PRIVATE DRAMAS

The authorities now assumed a stick-and-carrot technique in dealing with me. While declaring my symphony extinct, they awarded me the highest honour in the land, the Standard of Labour First Class!

This carrot was worth more than the gilded and red-ribboned medal that came with it. It entitled me to the special facilities enjoyed by our top politicians and Party members, including improved medical care and the right to obtain foreign medicine, otherwise unavailable.

I decided to try to re-apply for an apartment. My father, always longing to return to Warsaw, urgently needed to be rescued from the unlovable cousins. The Kraków flat was my only proper home, though I stayed most of the time in the Union house in order to carry out my Warsaw duties. With the political pressures, composition was receding out of my life yet again; my creative imagination had gone numb. I wondered whether, with reasonable privacy and quiet working conditions, I might still, without betraying my aesthetic principles, find some musical solution even within the constrictions of Socialist Realism. Part of me had become cynical about having to eat and breathe the system, but another part remained patriotic, needing — indeed, wanting profoundly — to remain a Polish composer able to function creatively in my own environment.

Only a matter of weeks after my application to the Housing Minister, I was informed that a two-room flat was at my disposal, by chance in a district of Mokotów, on land which had formerly belonged to my great-grandfather Szuster. My father was overjoyed. In a hired lorry, I transported him with his violins and the little furniture we possessed to Warsaw. Climbing to the first floor of the small, modern block, I took the key from my pocket and opened the front door, drawing back to watch the happiness in his face at the sight of his new home; but his features crumpled in anger and disgust.

'Do you call that a flat?' he asked me reproachfully. 'It's a doll's house!' He was quite unable to appreciate the miracle that we had anything at all: two small, bare, square rooms, a kitchen one could hardly turn round in and a bathroom like a cupboard. Soon, however, with the violins crowding my father's room and my piano filling mine, the place seemed more reassuringly our own. We even found a comparatively honest woman to cook and clean for us; good fortune in circumstances where the whole population had become so demoralised by corrupt officialdom that petty theft was an accepted norm.

Our new peace lasted for a fortnight and then we had an unexpected visit from the Housing Commission. Two severely frowning, middle-aged inspectors measured the modest rooms, then announced: 'Your flat is too large for only two people. Your father must move in with you. We are putting a stamped label on his room. From now on you must keep it empty until your co-tenants arrive.'

I replied angrily: 'Look at my room! It already contains my bed, and my piano and desk which I need for my work. There is not one inch for anything else. Am I supposed to put my father's bed under the piano or on top of it?'

'That's your problem, Citizen!' the inspector replied coolly.

Fortunately Deputy Minister Sokorski was still feeling conciliatory after stifling my symphony. With his influence, the label was eventually removed, and we were left to ourselves.

I could not help liking Sokorski. At our frequent meetings to hammer out Union members' problems, he would skilfully exercise his vivid sense of humour and persuasive charm. I often left his office, still smiling at some seemingly kind concession on his part, only to realise later that I had won less ground than I had intended for my colleagues. He was wily, very sharp indeed, and a much more experienced negotiator than I; though little by little I learnt how to stand up to him — quite a different art from knowing how to arrange notes on paper.

A return to putting notes on paper remained a distant hope. After a few weeks in our new flat, I received an order from the Ministry of Culture: 'The Citizen is delegated to Moscow, Leningrad and Kiev in order to study Soviet methods of teaching.'

Although I had no choice about going or staying, I was curious to discover more about the mysterious Soviet Union and to fill in the bare outlines of my distant impressions, which were partly based on the Communist writings that had attracted me before the war, and partly on my uncomfortable experiences since our Polish 'Independence' of 1945.

On the day of departure, I found myself on a train to Russia with about twenty leading representatives of art, music, theatre and film, and, no doubt, the Secret Police. We were led by the omnipresent Sokorski who, at about that time, had been promoted to become the Minister of Culture.

After a night in quite comfortable sleepers, we stopped for breakfast at Brest, just over the Polish border. The restaurant was full of Russian officers, eating steak and onions and downing glass after glass of vodka. Some were already very drunk, falling about, shouting, even vomiting. The smell of cigarettes, burnt onion, cabbage and alcohol hung heavy on the morning air.

After breakfast we were taken to an empty waiting-room reserved for foreigners. In contrast to the restaurant it was clean, furnished with old-fashioned velveteen chairs and a garish assortment of pictures on the walls, including, of course, one of Stalin. We sat waiting for the Moscow train for many hours; nobody told us when it was due. I wandered out on to the platform into the May sunshine, to stretch my legs and breathe some fresh air. Suddenly a woman's voice announced over the loudspeaker: 'The train to Paris is leaving in five minutes.' I stared at the assembled passengers on the opposie platform, intrigued to discover what sort of Soviet citizens would be setting out to France. Without exception they were army officers, presumably heading for East Germany. But 'the train to Paris' must have rung gloriously in the ears of the local population, who probably would not guess the truth.

Still without any hint of when we might continue our journey, the day dragged on; our train did not come in until after dark.

Arriving next day in Moscow we were taken to our luxurious hotel, the National, by four Soviet officials, who were to watch over us throughout the three weeks of our stay. Obviously from the NKVD – the future KGB – they purported to be representatives of 'The Office for Collaboration with Foreign Countries' (or something of the sort).

That first evening we were bidden for dinner at our hotel with a high-ranking Soviet official, who categorised us as 'film workers', 'art workers', 'music workers' or 'theatre workers'. As the meal finished, we were of course required to drink to Stalin's health.

The programme drawn up for our stay was so arranged that we had not even a minute free to explore on our own. We were constantly moved about in groups, accompanied by our 'guardian angels', only meeting carefully selected professional people, in my case music professors and students, performers, composers. No chance was afforded to hold a private conversation with anyone; no question arose of visiting our hosts at home. Everyone I met seemed charming, modest, genuinely friendly, but our exchange of polite smiles, warm handshakes and formal details about teaching methods in no way satisfied my desire to learn about the real life of the Russians, about their day-to-day work, living conditions and family life. Above all I was longing to attempt a fair assessment of how Communism succeeded in its home base as compared to the exported version which was throttling Poland. However, it was clear as under the sun that our Russians would show us only what they wanted us to see, and would not risk us looking behind a single door. The aim of their operation was to impress us with the quality of their music, art, theatre and film schools, and in this I have to admit that they were successful.

The Conservatoires I visited were all of the highest standard, all unstintingly well financed by the Soviet Government. I could see nothing new or unusual about the actual teaching methods; on the contrary, they were fairly traditional. However, the professors were fiercely demanding, and the discipline and dedication of the pupils extraordinary. And since Russia without doubt is one of the world's most musically endowed nations, with a population of over 200 million from which to select the most talented pupils, I was hardly surprised to find that the results were consistently superb.

Performance quality in any of the arts was never in doubt: the dancers in the ballet companies were technically brilliant, the opera singers admirable, the orchestras not bad at all, the theatre superb and sometimes quite moving (especially when the highly-strung actors cried real tears!).

But everything we saw was permeated to a greater or lesser degree with propaganda. At the famous Moscow circus, for example, the wire-boned acrobats, the horses, the bears riding motor-bikes and the clowns — a marvel of training and humour — all performed under a gigantic painting of Stalin. At one point a pig appeared with the name 'Churchill' painted on its flanks; the audience laughed, hissed and whistled.

In Leningrad I enjoyed the beautiful architecture and the pictures in the Hermitage Museum (though I was not aware that their supreme collection of French Impressionists was imprisoned in the cellar, too subversively Western and decadent for our eyes). In Kiev I was enchanted by the picturesque hillside setting and struck by the chauvinism of the Ukrainians, who considered themselves in every respect superior to mere Russians.

I was never alone except at night. Even then I had to go to bed and wake up when told. I had to eat on order, usually rich, indigestible food and often late at night, which kept me awake. I was constantly short of sleep — our hectic programme started early in the morning and continued sometimes till after midnight — but I was never allowed to miss one scheduled meeting, even a concert or a play. On occasions, like a small schoolboy, I even had to ask my 'protectors' for permission to go to the lavatory.

Back in Moscow, as a 'music worker', I was a guest at the Soviet Composers' Union, where I witnessed a discussion of some new compositions which had just been performed. Khrennikov was no less awesome on his native ground than in Poland. Entitled to praise or condemn the work of his own composers too, he seemed – in front of foreign visitors – to be indicating that all was perfection.

But what was the reality of the Soviet musical output? My personal impression was that, out of the 1,200 Composers' Union members, just a handful produced music of quality: Prokofiev, who had composed much of his best work as an emigré in the West, and whom alas I was never allowed to meet despite my frequent requests; Shostakovitch (half Polish), Khachaturian (Armenian) and perhaps Kabalevsky. The scores I saw, the music I heard, was mediocre, grey and dismally boring. The prospect of a similar state-organised music in our own country was not enthralling.

It was too much to hope that I could keep out of hot water for the entire three weeks of my stay in Russia. I enjoyed meeting up again with Shostakovitch with whom I had made friends on previous occasions at international congresses and in Berlin. I also was pleased to see Khachaturian. Neither of them made any difficulties for me, but we never had a chance to talk frankly. My main problem came at a reception when a number of the lesser Soviet composers clustered around me, questioning me on the activities of our Polish Composers' Union. They also quizzed me on what my colleagues were composing and what I would be writing next. Realising that candour would be counter-productive, I tried desperately to divert their suspicions that we might be 'reactionaries'. Carried away by my efforts, I heard myself say that I hoped to begin a new symphony, probably a *Symphony of Peace*. No sooner had I uttered those words than I bitterly regretted them. But my Russian colleagues sighed audibly with relief: at last someone in Poland was taking up an ideologically important subject!

Before leaving the Soviet Union, each member of our delegation had to give a radio or press interview. I was with a tough journalist from the popular weekly magazine *Ogoniok*, who immediately asked me about my *Symphony of Peace*.

'The *Symphony of Peace* has not been written yet – it's still just an idea,' I said, trying to dismiss the subject.

He insisted, 'That doesn't matter. We can talk about this

idea. We can talk about the World Congress for the Defence of Peace, which you attended in Wrocław. We can talk about peace generally. And of course your impressions of our country . . .'

It was a long conversation and I felt like a prisoner under interrogation. I hoped that I had skated successfully over the very thin ice, and comforted myself that I was unlikely ever to see his article.

Our delegation returned to Warsaw in the second half of June. As we separated at the airport, Minister Sokorski instructed me to attend the annual general assembly of the Polish Composers' Union next morning.

'Comrade Khrennikov will be there!' he announced happily. 'You are to deliver a speech on your experiences in the Soviet Union.'

I answered in a weak voice that not only was there too little time to prepare a talk but also I was feeling ill with exhaustion after our hectic tour of Russia.

'You feel ill?' The Minister repeated my words with an ironic smile. Then in a firm voice he said, 'Even if you die, your dead body will be taken to the Union meeting tomorrow.'

Genuinely worn out I staggered home, with much to think about. If I was neither to upset our 'honoured guest' nor to grovel, I would have to choose my words very carefully.

Next morning I tottered into the Union headquarters after a sleepless night. Almost all our members had been assembled in the small hall. I was soon called to speak, and made my way to the podium, to play the double rôle of diplomat and actor. Khrennikov was in the front row, a Polish woman interpreting my words for him as I spoke.

In my short speech, I used the phrase 'if I am honest' to introduce some critical remarks about performances of Bach, Mozart and Beethoven by the Russian conductors. I then lavishly praised the Moscow Metro as the best in Europe: I said how impressed I was with the magnificent subway stations, which were clean and almost as grand as palaces with their marble sculptures, mosaics and huge chandeliers.

I did not hear what Khrennikov thought about my report on

his country, but my colleagues were delighted. The only person to attack my speech was a Party representative who was upset by my use of the words 'if I am honest' in connection with my remarks on classical interpretation, and feared that Comrade Khrennikov would suspect that I was insincere about the underground stations!

A few weeks later, my interview with the *Ogoniok* journalist suddenly turned up in our music magazine, *Ruch Muzyczny*. As I read how he had distorted my words, my eyes almost fell out of their sockets.

Not only had half of my comments been omitted but they had been replaced by a string of outrageous fabrications. The article 'quoted' me as saying: 'The people of the new, true democratic Poland . . . are united in their contempt for the imperialistic beasts of prey, the warmongers . . .' I was also supposed to have indulged in a number of self-criticisms, to have admitted that my *Tragic Overture* was 'permeated with pessimism', that I had used 'complex language inaccessible to the broad masses', going on to declare that, in recent years, 'life has forced me to revise my artistic stance'!

One real pearl shone amongst the Soviet journalist's impudent invented quotes: 'There could not be a more wonderful source of inspiration for a man who wishes to sing the praises of peace than to see the life of the Soviet land and the work of this great nation in building Communism.' And the final comment attributed to me was, 'We join with you, Soviet friends, in creating a beautiful new life, and in the struggle for the peace and happiness of all nations!'

My colleagues were comfortingly quick to recognise the 'poetic licence' of the journalist, but I was nauseated.

I was not allowed to forget my inadvertent conception of a *Symphony of Peace*. Those in power around me developed a new concern lest my frequent attendance to Union matters might impinge on my creative output. By the autumn there was still no sign of the awaited symphony. So eager were they to assure its emergence that I was 'awarded the privilege' of a stay in the Government Rest House at Obory near Warsaw, previously the home of an aristocratic family, now used for artists and writers as a retreat, to work or to convalesce from illness.

Lodged in an enchanting small mansion, surrounded by glorious countryside, undisturbed by the other guests working quietly in their rooms, peace for my piece for peace was suddenly mine.

My whole being was longing to compose again, though I felt weak and empty. Channelling my mind into another symphony seemed the only possible way of becoming a complete human being again. If only I could write according to my own instincts! Wandering day after day through the autumn-tinted woods and fields, I agonised about the jargon of the title to which I was inescapably committed.

For a while my innate need to be writing music seemed to be outweighing the outside pressures. I managed to persuade myself that, while using the officially-blessed title, I could write a work dedicated to real peace, my sort of peace, the peace the world really wanted. On my walks through the gentle cornfields and woodlands, I set my mind to planning my new work: its design, emotional content and its musical language. In a few days, already my first general ideas were crystallising. I could see clearly now a symphony in three contrasting movements. The first, *Lamentoso* for chorus and orchestra, would be a kind of elegiac song without words, an expression of my sorrow for the victims of the recent war. The second, *Drammatico*, for orchestra only, would be my protest against war — any war. The third, *Solenne*, using the words of a recently published poem by my friend Jarosław Iwaszkiewicz, would have a hymn-like character, emphasising the poem's power of invocation in the cause of peace.

After the initial surge of excitement and ideas, inhibitions took over. It was impossible to clear my head completely of the political directives of the Party. I would think that I had found a way to walk the tight-rope of honesty above the chasm of conflicting pressures, but whenever I put myself in front of the beckoning sheets of manuscript, my mind kept returning involuntarily to the slogans and events of the previous two years — Zosia Lissa, Sokorski, Khrennikov, Prague, Palermo, Wrocław, Moscow. They had all left their mark.

Struggling to compose a *Symphony of Peace*, I had no peace within myself. Then, after a few weeks in which I felt I was just beginning to win through, something happened which was to shatter my peace altogether.

One morning a new visitor appeared at our Rest House, an exquisitely beautiful girl with long, dark auburn hair, light grey eyes, and a milk-white complexion. She was wearing a white dress of fine, clinging fabric which accentuated her very attractive figure. My reaction was instant – I lost my head.

She was of Irish parentage, born in London, called Marie Elizabeth O'Mahoney, though everyone knew her as Scarlett, because of her striking resemblance, both in character and physique, to the heroine of the film, *Gone with the Wind*. Still in her early twenties, she was on her honeymoon with a leading novelist called Marian Rudnicki, her third marriage in the four years she had been in Poland.

I could not keep my eyes or my mind off her for a moment. I could not help noticing that she was also casting her hypnotic eyes in my direction; that, despite the presence of her new husband, she seemed to reciprocate my feelings.

We somehow found ourselves together each day, and soon each night as well. The explosion between us was so intense that I don't even know what happened to her unfortunate third husband. My head having flown away from me, all thought of my symphony went with it, as well as any grain of common sense. Never in my thirty-six years previously had I fallen utterly in love and now that it hit me I was more foolish than a teenager.

After a few weeks of our burning affair, I discovered that from time to time Scarlett suffered attacks of epilepsy. When she felt an attack coming on, she would quickly lie down on a bed or sofa. It was frightening to see her. She would become unable to speak or answer my questions and would lose consciousness completely for several minutes, her body growing stiff, her hands jerking, while strange muscular spasms caused her face and body to twitch all over. Then she would suddenly relax and return to normal, remembering nothing.

I hid from her my alarm about these attacks, but insisted on seeking medical help when we returned together to Warsaw. With the help of influential friends, I was able to arrange that she underwent the fullest physical and neurological examinations. The electrical encephalograph machine, tracing the activity of her brain, produced jumpy, irregular wave patterns which the doctor showed me, confirming the diagnosis of epilepsy. I asked what could be done, and was told that no special medication was needed, but a tranquil life was essential. Pregnancy would be especially beneficial, the doctor added: her symptoms would diminish and her children, he assured me, would not be affected by her state of health.

I felt that these words were addressed to me personally, and I took them seriously to heart. On top of her health problems, Scarlett also needed protection, part of her nervous state resulting from constant cruel and frightening shadowing by the security forces on the suspicion that she was a Western spy, which had periodically reduced her to a state of terror ever since her arrival in Warsaw. I felt that at least I could offer her some sort of protection. After a few days and nights in restless contemplation, wondering how matrimony would fit in with my still mainly unrequited love for composition, I took the insanest risk of my life: I asked her to marry me.

Before our wedding, I had to finish my *Symphony of Peace*. Its first performance was scheduled to take place in Warsaw in the spring of 1951. With enormous difficulty, I managed to deliver the full score to the PWM at Easter so that the orchestral material could be ready in time.

I conducted the première myself with the Warsaw Philharmonic Orchestra at the end of May. When the performance was over, the audience applauded with tremendous warmth – but the official response was frigid. Though the emotional content was unarguably directed straight towards the listeners, and despite the simplicity of the musical language – undeniably comprehensible to the 'broad masses', the authorities damned the symphony on the grounds that my style was 'weak in ideological eloquence', accusing me of an even worse crime, that I was 'praying' for peace instead of 'fighting' for it!

My father, to his great disappointment, was too ill to attend that concert. His health was deteriorating rapidly and he was virtually bedridden. It was difficult to arrange any medical attention at home. Once, after my desperate pleas, a doctor finally arrived – he rushed in without even removing his coat, and did not so much as ask my father how he felt, let alone examine him. Demanding the last prescription given by another physician, he scribbled a repeat of it and dropped it casually on the bed. As he brushed past me making hastily for the stairs, I begged him to tell me what was wrong with my father.

'Old age,' he said curtly.

'But why is he in such pain? You haven't even bothered to try to find the cause,' I exclaimed.

The doctor looked at me coldly, said that he was a state employee and that he had a huge list of people to visit. If he did not get to see each of them, he could be accused of 'sabotage', and I wouldn't want that to happen to him, would I? Had no one told him that in Socialist Poland, the old and the sick received 'better care than ever before'.

Eventually, because the director of the nearby hospital happened to like my music, he worked a miracle, bringing my father into his crowded wards for a thorough examination. After a week, though the old man was still terribly ill, I had to collect him. The X-rays had shown serious damage to his lungs, and though nobody actually told me he had cancer, he was in his own words a 'murderously' heavy smoker. It was difficult to nurse such a very sick man day and night; and I could not really see that my frail Scarlett would manage much better after our marriage. I was lucky enough to find a friendly old lady who cared for him with great warmth, though we could only make sleeping arrangements for her in the minute kitchen.

Our wedding was approaching fast – too fast. I had never imagined myself married, recognising the conflict between the artist's total dedication to work and the duties of a husband. As I came to know Scarlett better, I was rather shaken to discover the extent of her need for constant attention. She could not be ignored even for a moment, by her future husband, his friends, even strangers. She could never resist exerting her colossal charm. Her Polish was excellent, but sometimes for effect with newcomers she would flirtatiously exaggerate her accent and use wrong words. There were few foreigners living in Warsaw at the time, and my exotically lovely fiancée thoroughly appreciated the worship of every man who saw her. They all fell like flies before her.

Her extraordinary beauty still mesmerised me, but I was unnerved to discover that she was too demanding even to allow me to look dreamily out of a window at a tree; nor could she tolerate my silences if I momentarily forgot her presence and started to think about my music. I was in serious doubt about how this marriage could work. Yet I felt I could not let her down, mainly because of her health, but also because her slightly dangerous political situation would be ameliorated once she was the wife of someone of my official standing. Anyway, she was growing very impatient, perhaps sensing my fears. I took courage and agreed a day.

On 13 July 1951, after a simple registry office ceremony, we set out for our honeymoon on the Baltic coast, in a noisy, overcrowded Government Rest House, the only possibility since passports abroad were unobtainable. At least we had a room to ourselves and could spend the days on the beach refreshed by the chilly Baltic Sea.

After two weeks, we had to return to Warsaw. I did not try to compose anything serious, but just carried on working for the Film Unit to earn our living, and, of course, continued my unpaid attendance to Union matters.

Our circumstances for establishing a new marriage were not too romantic or auspicious. The flat was very crowded: the nurse-housekeeper slept on a mattress in the tiny kitchen and my room was the only day and night space for Scarlett and myself, my piano doubling as a dressing-table, pots of face cream turning up amongst the manuscript paper.

Scarlett looked upon my dying father as a tiresome rival for my attention. However, I firmly spent as much time as I could with him, watching over him as he coughed agonisingly and panted for breath, pale and restless and in terrible pain. One afternoon as I was quietly holding his hand in mine, he suddenly sat up in bed, looked at me as if he were going to say something of immense importance, then fell back, motionless.

His life was over. I stayed with him for an hour or more, contemplating his fanatical devotion to his beloved violins, his ardent patriotism, his failures and his achievements. He was buried beside my mother and brother in the family tomb. I found later, when clearing his room, three volumes of his hand-written diary. The final sentences moved me to tears: 'Andrzej always takes care of me and surrounds me with solicitude. Good and beloved son. May God reward him for all his good-ness!' Through these words I found some little comfort even though now all my closest relatives except little Ewa had gone.

I visited Ewa in Silesia as often as possible, as well as con-tinuing to support her financially. Now in her early teens, still with straight flaxen pigtails and huge blue eyes, she always greeted me with captivating affection. She was doing well in school and already showing signs of artistic ability in drawing and pottery. She had settled down contentedly with her rela-tives and, though sometimes I longed to look after her more myself, I knew Scarlett would resent sharing my attention with her, and anyway I felt that it would be selfish to uproot her from her country security into the difficult atmosphere of Warsaw.

I can imagine that for Scarlett herself I was not all that easy a person to live with at that time. I found it difficult to work and difficult not to work! The attacks on my *Symphony of Peace* had extinguished any remaining desire to search for new musi-cal ideas. However, my compositional instincts were not alto-gether quenched. I was once more haunted by the echoes of my unfinished *Heroic Overture* of 1939. The theme and the har-monic and rhythmic elements came drifting back, reminding me that this overture had been intended as an expression of my confidence in my fellow countrymen to survive as an indepen-dent nation in the face of the Nazi invasion. This time the nature of our invasion was more psychological than physical, but the need to assert defiance and faith in our future was greater than ever.

Telling no one its true meaning, I entered the newly com-pleted *Overture* for a pre-Olympic competition. The jury of composers (apolitical for a change) awarded me first prize, which to my pleasure resulted in a trip to Helsinki for the Olympic Games of 1952 – a completely novel experience for me. I conducted the *Overture* with the Finnish Radio Orchestra in front of an enthusiastic international audience.

The *Heroic Overture* belonged to the category of goods suitable for export: abroad, the West had to be shown that Polish composers were 'free to write as they wanted'. However, home consumption was another matter. Even after its success in Helsinki, the *Overture* had to be examined by the political assessors to decide whether it was safe to unleash on the Polish public.

Its audition – or trial by jury – took place in Katowice, performed by the Polish Radio Orchestra under the baton of their director, Witold Rowicki. The judges included the conductor Fitelberg, plus a miscellaneous group of musicians and Party faithful.

Almost before the last note had sounded, two players (both Party members) leapt to their feet and loudly condemned my music as 'formalistic' and 'decadent'. The oboist, Comrade Smyk (an easy name to remember since it means violin-bow in Polish), then announced that he 'and a number of his colleagues' regretted that they had failed to do me the favour of burning this perverse piece of music – the score and the orchestral parts – before I had even arrived in Katowice! It was obvious that these 'spontaneous' reactions had been carefully set up in advance. No doubt the politically 'trusty' members of the jury also had noticed that the triumphal trumpets at the beginning did not come in from the Communist battle line. My *Heroic Overture* was torn to shreds and banned as unfit for performance for Polish audiences.

The composers and musicologists on the panel were silent witnesses of the verdict. They could not risk arguing with the Party zealots. Privately, after the audition, Fitelberg whispered in my ear how shocked he was by their attack on me, adding that he admired my overture and was pained by his inability to defend me.

After the Katowice farce, I knew that if I wrote music true to myself it would only be banned again. I was warned that, unless I conformed, I might be excluded from all my professional activities, including film music. The threat of losing my one source of income was alarming especially because in January 1952 Scarlett had joyously told me that she was expecting a baby. For the sake of my unborn child, I had now to obey every command, which included politely shepherding ardent left-wing musicians from abroad without blinking at their praise of our Stalinist heaven. I had to suffer further hypocritical peace conferences, and carry on the only work that remained worthwhile, battling with bureaucracy for the rights of my Union colleagues.

Within our ranks, my colleagues were bowing to control in different ways. The sensible Witold Lutosławski quietly continued his work for the radio, and I had no idea whether he was working seriously or not in the privacy of his home. He rarely appeared at Union meetings, except at the compulsory annual general assembly. Of the younger generation, Serocki, Baird and Krenz founded the Group 49, momentarily playing the Party Game, writing according to the slogans of Socialist Realism. Zygmunt Mycielski did not compose at all, but turned to his other great talent, writing words instead of music. Everyone to a greater or lesser degree had either to shut up or to compromise. I think my situation was worse than the others: it felt as if, each time I appeared in action, the searchlights focused on me so that I could more easily be gunned down.

Once I asked Zosia if she could momentarily forget her duties as a member of the Party and talk to me as a musicologist and a friend. She agreed to a private off-the-record conversation. I told her that I was deeply worried that the political impositions on composers were killing the true creative force in each of us. I felt that such interference would totally crush the possibility of any successful development of Polish music.

I said that I understood her genuine commitment to her political cause. But, since she was so musically literate and perceptive, how could she reconcile her natural good taste with the stylistic anachronisms she was dictating to us?

She answered that her situation was similar to being part of an artillery brigade where a general orders a colonel to fire ten shots, upon which he orders the lieutenant to fire twenty, and the lieutenant orders his men to fire forty. She saw herself in the position of the men ordered to fire the forty shots to be sure that the general (Moscow) was satisfied with results.

My work for the Film Unit, though not profoundly creative in musical terms, gave me a welcome artistic outlet. I was asked to compose music for a short film about the magnificent altarpiece of the Marian Church in Kraków created by Wit Stwosz, one of the greatest European sculptors of the fifteenth and sixteenth centuries.

Determined for the time being to avoid further conflict with the authorities, I turned again to the restoration of fragments of early Polish music, attempting to produce a work which, if not strictly in period, was at least trying to echo the innocent humanity of these sculptures. The orchestration was for trumpet solo with a small string orchestra, harp and timpani. Though initially written in short sections to fit in with the photography of the film, the music which emerged seemed also suitable for concert performance. Because I had successfully side-stepped the problem of formalism and Socialist Realism, the score[1] was published by the PWM and not only was I able to conduct it with the Warsaw Philharmonic, but further performances were unrestricted by auditions or censorship.

Though I was still privately considered by my colleagues as the most advanced Polish composer, my reconstructed old Polish music was almost the only music of mine which could be heard. Officialdom applauded both the music and the visual content of the Wit Stwosz film. The Polish Government sent it abroad to festivals as evidence that People's Poland preserved and valued the great artistic achievements of the past — even those of religious character. (At home they were trying to cramp the activities of the Church, though the general public were attending church services in greater numbers than ever before, not just out of religious feeling, but also to demonstrate *en masse* the only way they could.)

On 14 September 1952 we rushed to the Polish Army hospital near our home thinking the baby was about to be born. But Scarlett remained in labour for two whole days; it was a terri-

---

1. Published by PWM as *Koncert Gotycki* (Gothic Concerto) and later in London as *Concerto in Modo Antico*.

ble experience; the Russian doctor who attended her (wearing the uniform of a Polish colonel), refused her any sort of sedation despite her pleas.

At last a red and wrinkled baby girl was born, healthy and strong. We gave her the Irish name of Oonagh and were overwhelmingly proud of her. She instantly changed the atmosphere of our home. I spent hours just staring at her; she was so small and perfect, every day growing more beautiful. After a while I noticed how my professional and political problems receded in importance, while this tiny creature's smiles, or cries, could make my emotions soar up, or down, in an instant. Her domination of our small flat made it even more impossible to compose. My dream of continuing the search for my own musical expression had vanished possibly for ever. Yet the enchanting little Oonagh, also in part my creation, seemed to compensate for all that was lost.

18

MOUNTING STALINIST PRESSURES

In the spring of 1953 I was urgently summoned to Minister Sokorski's office. His unctuous greeting alerted me to the fact that an important announcement was imminent, and that I was once again going to be used, even though my compositions were still being regarded with suspicion.

'Citizen Panufnik, in order to deepen the friendship between Poland and China, we are sending a cultural mission to the Republic of the People's China without delay, of about 200 Polish performers, including not only the Chamber Orchestra of the Warsaw Philharmonic, but also the Mazowsze Song and Dance Company. The tour will last two months, and you, Citizen Panufnik, will lead this delegation.'

I was appalled. I insisted that I could not afford to interrupt my work as a composer, and that it was impossible for me to leave my seven-month-old baby and my wife who was far from well. Sokorski cut me short, making it clear that I had no choice but to shoulder with pride the rôle cast upon me by the Ministry of Culture. 'You cannot refuse!' he snapped, as I continued my pleas. 'The Party needs you!'

'But I am not a member of the Party,' I replied, trying to match his determination.

'The Polish Government makes it your patriotic duty to go!' he insisted, by now quite angry. I was unable to find a quick enough answer. Sokorski carried on as though I had agreed to do as I was told.

As a musician, I was to be in charge of the artistic delegation, with another musician, Sokorski's own brother-in-law, as my second-in-command, telling me what to do. A youngish woman of Russian origin, of political rather than artistic authority, had been appointed as director of the Mazowsze Company, supported by two members of the ZMP (the Communist Youth Organization) who were to 'take care of the political education' of the Mazowsze performers. We would also have with us two conductors, two choreographers (a married couple who had together helped to create the magnificent Mazowsze Ensemble), a doctor fully equipped with medical supplies and a travel specialist from the Government agency Orbis to look after timetables and arrangements.

Still not allowing me to get in a further word of protest, Sokorski shook my hand warmly, adding that without doubt we would have a great artistic success and that I would find the whole trip a rewarding and fascinating experience.

Scarlett well understood that I had no choice but to obey, but was desolate at the thought of having to manage without me for so long. I imagined that her admirers would not allow her to be too lonely, but I worried about leaving her with Oonagh, even though her epilepsy seemed to have disappeared as her doctor had predicted, and a nanny came in daily to help her. Kindly neighbours from within our building promised to keep a watchful eye on her and close friends assured me that they would call frequently. But two months seemed a long time to be leaving them both.

The moment of my departure at the Warsaw railway station was distressing. Poor Scarlett was on the platform, trying forlornly to say a last goodbye through the train window. But the arrogant envoy from the ZMP kept elbowing me aside so that he could chat with some young friends outside. Though I was 'Leader of the Cultural Delegation', this political puppy clearly intended to demonstrate from the start where the power really lay.

In Moscow we changed to our own comfortable train for the Trans-Siberian journey of almost two weeks. Since the terms 'first class' and 'second class' were contrary to the Marxist ethics, the distinction made was between 'soft' and 'hard'. As Head of the Delegation, I was travelling 'soft', with a spacious compartment which was clean and comfortable; almost a room by day, converting into a sleeper at night. I shared it with my deputy, Sokorski's brother-in-law.

I amused myself at first with the private game of 'spot the undercover policemen'. The Russian domestic attendants for each sleeping car obviously came from the police department, but my bet was also on Polish Comrade Berman (officially the Orbis representative) and Soviet Comrade Rapaport (officially in charge of the restaurant car). Every evening as I fulfilled my duty to inspect the entire train, I would find this pair in the restaurant car tucking into large portions of caviar and tipping back glasses of Armenian brandy. If they were not secretly our political bosses, then for whom was that wonderful-looking caviar intended? Regrettably not for the accredited Head of the Delegation.

To kill the boredom and monotony of our long, uninterrupted journey, I organised a few activities as well as rehearsals for the musicians and exercises for the dancers. I had to keep everyone busy and ensure that we arrived in good shape for the performances ahead. We talked a lot about music; I coached some of the instrumentalists in interpretation; and I gave composition lessons to a talented enthusiast from the Mazowsze.

Our political guides, meanwhile, the boy and the girl from the ZMP, set about organising lectures on Marxist-Leninism, exuding confidence as representatives of the Party. However, after about three days, these young zealots came to me to complain that no one was interested in their lectures and that their audience was undisciplined, even disruptive. Would I please as leader use my influence to strengthen their authority?

Not without pleasure I reminded them that, though Head of the Delegation, I was answerable only for its musical and artistic success. I was not a Party member; it was up to them to make their lectures irresistibly interesting, if they could. From then on, they behaved towards me with extraordinary politeness, perhaps frightened that their failure to establish political authority might result in loss of face on return home, or even get them into serious trouble with the ZMP.

The Mazowsze Ensemble had been created just after the war in imitation of the Soviet state companies devoted to folk song and dance. Our government trumpeted its claim that the company was developing the potential of boys and girls of peasant origin; however, in reality, most of the Mazowsze performers were children of the intelligentsia and came from the cities. They were supposed to be 'cultivating the original folk art' of our country alongside the genuine regional music, but were forced also to perform political 'mass songs' by contemporary composers. Performances usually ended with the whole cast joining and raising their hands together to sing the *Hymn to the World's Youth*, an invocation to the Marxist deities comparable in impact to the *Internationale*.

Despite the compulsory political content of their programmes, I had always greatly admired the company; they had an apparent spontaneity, as if their performances were improvised at some country festivity, and their exuberant, skilful dancing and singing was embellished by brilliantly colourful traditional costumes. On stage they always looked fresh and full of enthusiasm, and I was saddened as I got to know many of them during the journey to find that, despite their extreme youth, they were worn down by over-frequent appearances in unchanging programmes and by too much travelling. They complained that with the endless repetition of repertoire they could not properly develop their talents, and, as soon as they lost their first brightness of youth, they were replaced by younger performers; their only options then were to become teachers or leave their chosen profession.

The monotony of our journey across the limitless undulating green landscape of the Steppes was at one point interrupted by the failure of our water system. With everyone complaining, I insisted that we should halt at the next station so that we could all take baths.

At some remote small town in Siberia, an infinity away from civilisation, we were led to a huge hall with hundreds of showers (presumably belonging to the Army). The ladies had their turn, then the men took over. I was standing stark naked under a stream of water relishing the cleansing heat when suddenly I was approached by a young amazon in a sleeveless overall, brandishing a loofah, offering to scrub my back. She was an alarmingly tough-looking specimen of Soviet youth, with impressive biceps and the expression of a determined wolf-hound. I hastily replied, 'Thank you, no!' in my very clearest Russian.

Before we reached the Chinese border, the constant movement and enclosure in small spaces so deeply affected one member of the orchestra that he went mad, smashing objects, striking out at his colleagues, screaming in rage and claustrophobic panic. Our doctor described his symptoms as 'train madness', though we could not tell if other personal pressures had contributed to the unfortunate man's breakdown. My first act in China was to ask the Chinese Government officials to get him to a psychiatric hospital for some help, but I was informed that no one needed such hospitals in People's China, and therefore none existed! I had to arrange for him to be flown home under heavy sedation.

We now set out for the northern part of China in another equally comfortable but smaller train with low ceilings. From our first stop, it was apparent that our visit had been excellently organised by our hosts and that we could expect to be received wherever we went with genuine friendliness and warm enthusiasm.

We realised also that we would need to exert not only colossal artistic effort but considerable endurance. We were travelling immense distances, so great that it was almost impossible to take in the continually changing landscapes despite their breath-taking beauty and variety. I still have imprinted on my mind cascades of terraced rice fields descending steep mountain-sides; and the Yellow River, which was not yellow but light-brown, like milky coffee, as it tumbled fiercely over its rocky bed. The images could be no more than picture-postcard impressions. Our schedule included Peking, Shanghai and Canton. We performed before a total of more than half a million enthusiastic people, with several millions more listening to our music over the radio. With thirty performances in as many days, as well as official receptions, exhaustion was inevitable.

I was not inconsolable, however, about the glorious duty of having to consume a number of banquets of the divine food of China. During these dinners with high-ranking officials, we were willingly seduced by a symphony of tastes; rare dishes prepared by chefs of genius, using local meats, fishes and an infinite variety of exotic vegetables. Sometimes we would encounter as many as thirty tiny courses in succession, each one a masterpiece, rocking the senses with exquisite aromas, arranged to please the eye almost as much as the palate.

The Chinese officials also proudly showed us the other great arts of China, including magnificent painting and sculpture in their museums; and I was particularly stunned by their ancient tradition of classic opera, which combined subtle acting, singing and dancing with acrobatics of such staggering contortion that the performers seemed to have no bones. I noticed, however, that they were more restrained about their more recent artistic creations manufactured under the influence of the Soviet method of Socialist Realism. Literature was not discussed. I saw little modern painting.

In contrast, their music was inescapable: everywhere we went, blaring out at us from hoarse loudspeakers, we were assailed by mass songs with titles like *We are Members of the Youth Corps of Tomorrow*, *March Forward Shoulder to Shoulder*, *Bloody Blows* and the unforgettable *Let Us Together Repulse the Attack of the Bourgeoisie*. In a great country with a wonderful and wise people, I found the superficial slogans and showmanship ugly, disturbing and not convincingly heart-felt.

At this epoch the Soviet-Chinese friendship was still officially 'unshaken' and 'eternal'. Indeed, the political members of our delegation were under orders to include frequent reference in their speeches to 'our mutual struggle for peace with the Soviet Union at the helm'. However, in spite of publicly demonstrated unity, the growing rift between the Eastern powers was evident wherever we went in China. Sometimes, thinking we were Soviet citizens, people were cold towards us; but when they discovered our true nationality, their faces instantly crinkled into friendly smiles. Individually they often criticised the Russians, nicknaming them 'the long-nosed ones'.

One episode confirmed my impression of unease between the two allies. One evening I had a quiet dinner with my Chinese interpreter. After a few drinks of the potent rice spirit, tears fell from my companion's eyes and he told me that as soon as we left he would be out of a job; his mother was

Chinese but his father was Russian, which meant that he was no longer trusted by the authorities.

I noticed further signs of the impending rift with the Soviet Union when I met a group of Chinese composers. They were agog that I had conducted my works in London, Paris and Berlin, and eagerly interrogated me about the contemporary music of Western Europe, evincing not an atom of interest in the music of Soviet composers or in the principle of Socialist Realism, even in front of their political bosses.

I was not surprised that the Chinese people, even the dedicated Marxists amongst them, while rejecting the idea of being controlled by the Russians, still leaned towards pure and all-embracing socialism. With the problems of feeding such a vast population, as well as guiding an immense and diversified country to greater prosperity, a united national effort perhaps needed to be controlled by a single political group, at least for the moment. Since the Chinese had suffered centuries of Japanese and Western imperialism, I sympathised (coming from a similarly oppressed country) with any bitterness over the past. I was shown in Canton a restaurant sign preserved from the days of British rule saying: 'CHINESE AND DOGS NOT ADMITTED.' Why should the Chinese, having freed themselves of British domination, then allow the Russians to meddle in their internal affairs? They preferred to search for their own way to Communism without aping their 'long-nosed' neighbours.

Yet, despite this deep-running feeling, the Soviets were still officially 'at the helm', and Mao Tse Tung ranked second to Stalin. When I received instructions for our special performance in Peking for Mao himself, I was ordered to precede our normal Mazowsze programme not with a special piece in honour of the Chinese leader but with a performance of Khachaturian's *Poem to Stalin*. Though I tried hard to wriggle out of this duty, the Peking organisers insisted that the Head of the Polish Delegation should take the baton for the gala occasion. Not only was I an internationally known conductor, but anyway, they added with charming smiles, my name was already printed in the programmes. There was no escape. The spider's web was beginning to reveal itself in China too.

We arrived in Peking in time to witness the colourful and joyous May Day parade, which was a brilliant contrast to the gloom and greyness of the same event in Moscow or Warsaw.

I spent a fascinating evening at dinner with the foreign minister, Chou En Lai, who spoke fluent German. His manner was dignified, and though he exuded confidence and a consciousness of his undoubted power, he seemed accessible, even friendly most of the time, only at moments suddenly turning icy if something momentarily displeased him. I was astonished by his extensive knowledge of our European arts and I felt ashamed that I knew so little of China's great cultural traditions. He had heard about my enthusiasm for the classic opera, so he had summoned some of the most eminent Chinese artists to perform for us between the myriad exquisite courses of our lengthy dinner. Sharing with him his enthusiasm for this extraordinary art-form, I was enthralled by his accounts of the deep symbolism within the sparkling acts.

I longed to tackle him also about Socialist Realism, which I could see already gaining a hold on centuries-old rich and magnificent Chinese traditions in painting, theatre and music. However, the conversation was kept strictly on non-political rails.

Shortly before the gala concert for Mao Tse Tung, I received a curt telegram from Warsaw, which, without explanation, wished me 'deepest sympathy'. With a shock I realised that somebody close to me must have died. Scarlett? Oonagh? Ewa? I was frozen with dread.

I begged my constant guardian, a Chinese general in civilian clothes, to arrange a telephone call to a family friend, Krystyna, who had promised to visit our home frequently in my absence. However, due to 'technical difficulties', despite my frantic pleas, I had to wait three unbearable days before I heard any news at all. Then, just a few hours before I was due to meet Mao Tse Tung and to conduct the nauseating *Poem to Stalin*, the call to Warsaw came through.

The kindly Krystyna's distant and nervous voice came over the whirring line, growing alternately loud then soft with the distortions of the telephone system. Hurrying her words, through fear that the connection would be broken, she told me of a tragic accident. On 5 May, on our nanny's day off, Scarlett, thinking herself well enough to break her usual rule, had decided to risk bathing the baby herself. As she began, however, she had been overwhelmed by an epileptic attack, regaining consciousness to discover that our beloved eight-month-old Oonagh was drowning. Despite help from neighbours and attempts at resuscitation at the hospital, our adorable little girl's heart had stopped beating for ever. Oonagh was dead.

I could only think of getting back to be with Scarlett. I decided that nothing would induce me to stay on as Head of the Delegation.

While expressing a humane concern for my personal tragedy, and a willingness that I should depart 'as soon as a flight could be arranged', the authorities would not release me from performing at the gala concert that night. This appearance, which I had tried so hard to avoid, in the end bothered me not at all, as my mind was elsewhere. I thought to myself, reeling in agony of spirit, that it would be all the same to me whether I was conducting the *Hallelujah* Chorus, a song in praise of Mao Tse Tung or even a cantata to the Devil himself.

After the concert I underwent the privilege of meeting the famous Mao, a bear-like figure who shook my hand for a long time and looked at me with his penetrating eyes as if he wanted to tell me something very important. I never discovered what it was as he could have spoken to me only through two interpreters, and he elected not to do so. (Perhaps he was silently expressing his sympathy?)

A seat on the infrequent flights between Peking and Moscow was difficult to obtain in the days of small propeller planes. Though the officials had nodded their agreement to my 'immediate' departure, it was four days before I received confirmation that a seat had been reserved for me, and I do not remember how many more protracted days crept by before I actually flew. Each hour of waiting seemed to go on for ever.

At last, I found myself ready to depart at Peking airport, not realising that I still had three exhausting days of travel ahead of me.

Our first stop out from Peking for refuelling was in the middle of the Gobi desert. The view as we landed was astonishing; an undulating yellow ocean of sand stretching endlessly in all directions. I experienced for the first time on the tiny landing strip the strange silence of the desert, a silence broken only by the airport mechanics. There were no fences, no limits to the airport, just the imprisoning sand on every side.

At Irkutsk by Lake Baikal, our second stop, we spent the night in the airport hotel which consisted of a single large hall like a hospital ward with a dozen or more beds down each side.

The following night in Moscow I hardly slept. A Russian girl kept telephoning me, insisting in an artificially sweet and giggly voice that she must come to my room. Assuming that she was a fake prostitute, soliciting me on the orders of the Soviet Secret Police to glean my impressions of People's China and the Chinese leaders, I eventually left the telephone ringing. All I needed on this interminable journey was a Russian spy.

As I flew from Moscow, the recurring images of my little daughter were almost more than I could stand. I was longing to be with Scarlett yet dreading being in our flat with an ever-present absence..

I arrived at last in Warsaw, in no state to meet anyone let alone comfort Scarlett, but reality forced me to start coping with life again. There was no car to meet me at the airport: I was no longer an ambassador of People's Poland, but an exhausted human being who had to climb with a heavy suitcase full of scores and dress suits on to an overcrowded bus heading for the city centre. I then had to hunt for a taxi — it took an hour to find one willing to take me to the part of the city where we lived.

When at last I reached the house, I went up to the first floor and knocked softly. Scarlett, who had been listening for hours and recognised my step on the stairs, opened the door immediately. Her face was white as paper, her eyes swollen and red. We sat down on the sofa, hand in hand, for a long, long time in silence.

Life had to continue, but as a composer I felt empty, finished, defunct. I had no strength left to tilt against the system nor to dream of composition for composition's sake.

I had to carry on, behaving like a squirrel, somehow gathering enough money for our daily bread (without butter). Though short of money, I still officially was Composer Number One, and the authorities still needed me on my pedestal as a symbol of musical respectability in Poland and abroad. But I was just a stuffed dummy of a composer now.

A year or so went by. Then suddenly the grey atmosphere of pervading gloom was lightened by the news of Stalin's death. (The great composer Prokofiev died on the same day, which was unfortunate as the newspapers could not find space properly to eulogise him).

Amongst our trusted friends we discussed with a breath of hope whether the death of the tyrant could bring changes in Poland. A series of rumours started to trickle through to us from unknown sources that a relaxation in the political climate might be expected.

Quite soon, in the spring of 1954, leading writers, architects, painters, musicians, actors and film directors in Warsaw were summoned to a session of the Council of Culture and the Arts, where Minister Sokorski was to deliver a speech on cultural policy. For once we did not moan at the chore of attending yet another official function: we all arrived eagerly anticipating news of change. As we gathered in the hall, the excitement in the air seemed to affect Sokorski himself who, with his own hands, helped us to arrange the chairs, expressing his concern that we should all be sitting comfortably, that we could easily see him (and he could observe our faces too).

Sokorski took the floor almost immediately. We hung upon his every syllable, waiting for hints of a softening of artistic policy as he launched into a characteristically prolonged discourse. I felt that we were being led up a mountain of hope – the higher he took us the more the cloud was obscuring the clarity of our view of our future. Were we really going to find sunlight and a clear perspective at the peak?

Suddenly Sokorski's tone indicated that we were reaching the summit of his monologue and he started to ask searching questions (to be answered by himself of course!).

'Was the turn towards Socialist Realism in 1949 CORRECT?' A few seconds of silence followed as we held our breath in anticipation of good news. However, the minister continued with another pivotal question: 'Was it right to pose the problem of creating a new art, socialist in content and national in form?' The tension in the hall was as electrical as a thunderstorm, but then the verdict came like lightning striking right between our eyes: 'Undoubtedly, Y E S!' Sokorski asserted fiercely.

Bemused and appalled, we were then subjected to a further hour or so of the familiar slogans, Sokorski acidly insisting that the *method* of Socialist Realism was sound, but that we Polish composers had failed to take to our hearts the 'unavoidable application' of the new aesthetics. We had been oversimplifying and 'vitiating' them, merely managing to produce a distortion of a great ideal!

Sokorski's speech was followed by another of those 'frank discussions' during which no one dared say an honest word. We all realised that those rumours of 'liberalisation' had been a subtle trap laid by the authorities in the hope of spotting the 'reactionaries' amongst us: as if we were in a hot and stuffy room, and the latch of a window had been lifted in order to discover which of us inmates would run forward to catch a breath of fresh air. (None of us did).

Our tormentors continued to keep the 'liberalisation' theory in play. A few weeks later at the General Assembly of our Union, we were forced to discuss contemporary Western music, to debate the 'ideological significance' of Stravinsky, Schoenberg, Webern, Hindemith, Roussel and Messiaen without listening to examples of their works beforehand. Our younger members had never heard the music of these composers, for obviously our orchestras would never have been allowed to perform any of their works.

Writers were likewise forced to discuss Orwell's *Nineteen Eighty-Four* without being allowed to read it (except the few who had got hold of illicit copies, but they could not of course admit to this). In all the arts, the subject of Socialist Realism was fast turning into Socialist Surrealism.

The increasing hypocrisy and nastiness did not stop there. After a particularly grim marathon lecture by Zosia on Polish music over the last ten years, to my deep displeasure, the subsequent 'discussion' was dominated by another ardent Party member. I remembered this character, Dr Mieczysław Drobner from just after the war, when he came to the office of the PWM in Kraków, demanding that we should publish his *March for Orchestra*. Though wearing the uniform of a Polish officer, the title of the work and his name were lovingly inscribed upon his score in Russian characters.

Drobner, in a voice filled with venom, described Polish composers as 'ideologically and artistically immature', and recommended that we should be 'led' into more correct ways.

His words rankled so deeply that I could not restrain myself from writing an answer which somehow got past the censor and was printed in full in a newspaper. I praised Polish musicians for the prominence and respect that they had achieved in Europe despite 'a cultural policy not lacking in faulty directives, which have created enormous difficulties in our work'. Drobner's accusations of ideological and artistic immaturity were, I suggested, an attempt to discredit and block off our search for any individual means of expression. I ended by remarking that this tactless judgement phrased in such brash and peremptory language had emanated from a man who had contributed nothing of value to Poland's musical culture.

My statement caused considerable pleasure amongst my colleagues. Because of the way in which I had praised our own composers, Sokorski was hamstrung.

So far as I knew, only one of my colleagues, Alfred Gradstein, was actually a Party member. To underline his allegiance, he had quite recently composed a *Stalin Cantata*, which was musically quite skilfully put together, though the praise received from the press obviously was for the wrong reason. However, just as poor Gradstein was enjoying the first real success in his life, Stalin died; the personality cult disappeared – the *Cantata* too!

I liked Gradstein. While superficially an opportunist, he actually showed more courage questioning the system than many composers who remained outside it. One afternoon,

finding ourselves in Sokorski's office without any outside witnesses, Gradstein and I started to corner him, trying to draw
him into providing intellectually viable justifications for 'the
struggle towards socialist art' which he had been inflicting on
us at his masters' bidding for five miserable years. We chal-
lenged him to explain precisely how 'formalism' could be harm-
ful. In a voice tinged with deep concern, Gradstein bravely
added: 'Comrade Minister, please tell us frankly . . . Perhaps
you consider at this stage in our country's development we do
not NEED a genuine creative art as we composers understand
it?'

Sokorski suddenly looked very sad, bowing his head and
remaining silent for some time, eventually replying with a hint
of defeat in his voice: 'I cannot answer this question.' So our
two officially-committed Marxists both were privately admitting a crisis in faith: for me, Sokorski's failure to answer *was* his
answer.

Despite this encouraging though brief flash of private honesty, I was now feeling the pressures tightening on me every
minute. A ballot was held for a new President of the Composers' Union; the result was a tie between the distinguished
musicologist, Professor Doctor the Reverend Hieronim Feicht,
and myself. Neither of us wanted to accept.

While I was pleased at the confidence shown in me by my
fellow composers, the idea of the presidency appalled me. To
my dismay, at a meeting with several of my colleagues in
Sokorski's office, I found myself being strongly persuaded to
take on the job, especially by the two outstanding younger
composers, Serocki and Baird. If Poland's leading composer
did not accept the nomination, they said, the Union would lose
status in the eyes of the authorities, resulting in a weakening of
bargaining power. If I let my colleagues down and refused the
post, the privileges, subsidies and all the other facilities which I
had fought for over the years would most probably be re-
tracted, and the Union might end up as no more than an
administrative front.

But I had had enough of the official limelight, of constant
negotiation and unavoidable compromises. I could feel my
nerves were on the verge of cracking. I pointed out that for ten

whole years — years of youthful maturity which might have been totally dedicated to my composition — I had spent a large part of my time and energy on the welfare of my colleagues. I felt it was time for someone else to make a contribution. I referred both to my professional and my personal upheavals, pleading that I was mentally and spiritually exhausted, and needed at least a year's respite.

It was Sokorski rather than my colleagues who helped me off the hook. I was allowed to refuse the presidency of the Union, which went instead to my teacher of composition, Sikorski. But still I had no peace. Shortly after that meeting, I was urgently summoned to the office of Comrade Ostap-Dłuski, a senior official in the Department of Foreign Affairs at the Party headquarters.

I remembered Dłuski with displeasure from one of the International Peace congresses, where he had acted like a puppeteer, manoeuvering my friend, the poet Jarosław Iwaszkiewicz, who, in his rôle as Chairman of the Polish Committee for the Defence of Peace, was about to make a major speech. Right up to the moment that poor Jarosław actually walked to the podium, Dłuski kept grabbing the text from his hands, making alterations, additions and cuts, — 'improvements' in answer to the speeches of the other delegates to which he was listening carefully through earphones. Each time Dłuski snatched the pages away, Iwaszkiewicz reacted with growing annoyance at this public demonstration that his text needed the added 'political maturity' of a senior Party member.

Knowing Dłuski's penchant for manipulation, I walked warily into his office. Though it was some years since I had last met him, he greeted me like his oldest friend. 'I was very much on edge, but controlling myself with extreme effort, I sat silently across from his desk.

He began hesitantly. 'As you probably know, the activities of our Committee for the Defence of Peace are intensifying from day to day. I want you to help me with a new idea.' After a slight pause during which I remained silent, he continued, unctuously flattering me about my professional successes in western Europe, my 'world-wide' reputation, my Vice-Chairmanship of UNESCO. He pointed out that this gave me access to the entire international musical fraternity. Now he was coming to the point: 'Therefore I wonder' – he shuffled in his chair – 'I wonder - er - I think it would be a splendid idea for you to write a personal letter to all the leading musical figures in the West, in which you could, amongst other matters, in a subtle way emphasise the importance and significance of the noble cause to which the World Congress for Peace is dedicated, and persuade them to give their active support.'

Then, smiling artificially, he repeated, 'I wonder . . .' Trying to avoid discussion, I replied that I would think it over. The sweet expression melted rapidly. 'This is an urgent matter!' he countered swiftly. When I said nothing more, his brow furrowed deeply. 'It is a request, my direct request to you. You *must* do this for me.'

He elaborated his plan as if I had agreed, ending his instructions with the request that I should send him copies of the final letter and that he would let me see the replies. It was all very casual, as though he were proposing something completely natural, simple and logical.

I went home in a fury, and repeated the whole conversation to Scarlett. She could not see why I was so indignant, and seemed inclined to gloss over the whole incident. I had to explain to her the full enormity of Dłuski's demands; that he was trying to force me to deceive my friends and colleagues abroad by writing them letters of a personal and private character with the purpose of spreading Communist propaganda for the bogus Polish 'Peace Movement'. Western musicians receiving such letters might not guess the true purpose behind them. Still less could they know that their replies would be scrutinised by the Polish Communist Party, and in some cases, where relevant, passed on to the Polish and Soviet Secret Police. In other words, without disclosing his real intentions, Dłuski was wanting to find out whose sympathies or vanities might best be exploited, just as in the past they had exploited Picasso, Eluard, Sartre and many others. In short, he was forcing me indirectly to spy for Moscow.

'I've had enough!' I shouted at Scarlett! 'I must get out – I MUST LEAVE POLAND!'

19

ESCAPE

'I MUST leave Poland!'

Scarlett stared at me in disbelief and alarm. She did not at first take me seriously.

After a night without one blink of sleep, I reaffirmed my intention; a further twenty-four hours passed and my resolution had become even more firmly fixed, despite my awareness of gargantuan obstacles ahead. My escape from Poland would be extremely perilous; but this was not the only danger I was facing. I had no idea if I would be able to build a career elsewhere: I might neither be accepted into the musical life of any other country, nor, tearing my roots from my native soil, find myself able to develop further as composer. However I could not compose at home either. I felt not one ounce of hesitation about throwing away my exalted but empty position in Poland in exchange for the unknown. The succession of final straws had beaten me into a state of absolute determination to leap into any void rather than submit to the absurd pressures for an instant longer. And, as I went, I planned to make enough clatter to ensure that the whole world would hear about the hell experienced by creative artists in the countries of the Eastern bloc.

Poor Scarlett had not the slightest desire to leave. Companionship counted much more for her than politics or even music. She seemed to feel that she belonged now more to Poland than to her native Ireland. She had made many friends in Warsaw — and they were now perhaps her only friends after eight years away from home. She thrived on the waves of adulation emanating from the gallant Poles, who know better than anyone else in the world how to show admiration for attractive women. In Warsaw her pale skin and glinting auburn hair were exotic, almost unique. It was asking a lot to expect her to give up her reign as a great beauty as well as her privileged social standing in Poland as my wife. However, if she were to remain in Warsaw, it could only be without me.

She gradually understood as I told her that my nerves would crack totally if I stayed on; that I was on the point of mental breakdown; that I had to burst out of our prison, whatever dangers lay outside, because otherwise inside I would suffocate, explode. I explained that I not only needed peace and freedom for myself in order to compose, but that it was vital that some-one should alert the Western world to the sufferings of the Poles. I could achieve nothing more in Warsaw, in my own work or for my fellow-composers; but perhaps by escaping and making a noise in the outside world I might be of service to my colleagues, describing our plight to the free press, possibly bringing outside pressure to help those still in the trap.

I felt brutal, uprooting Scarlett and throwing her into uncertainty. But she soon realised that for me no tolerable alternative existed. She bravely agreed, not only that I should go, but that she would help me in my escape.

I had a plan ready: the first part was quite sensibly thought through, the second part risky, depending on Scarlett's success in finding help in the West without anyone betraying us. There was no hope that we would both be permitted to travel abroad at the same time. We would have to take flight in two stages. Scarlett's father happened to be seriously ill in London. On compassionate grounds, she was likely to be allowed to leave the country without the usual difficulties. I suggested that on her arrival, she should try to contact my Conservatoire friend, the distinguished pianist, Witold Małcużyński, who had stayed in the West since the 1930s and never returned to Poland, and also my wartime friend, Konstanty Regamey, whom I had seen comparatively recently in Zürich. Of course it would be dangerous to trust anybody, even people I felt in my bones were good friends; but I thought that these two would be as safe and sensible as anyone I could imagine. I asked Scarlett to try to arrange with them that I should receive an offer as soon as possible to conduct some contemporary Polish music in a Western European country; the kind of invitation that the authorities in Poland would want me to accept for propaganda reasons. In order to avoid any suspicion, Scarlett would have to keep in constant touch with the Polish Embassy in London, putting in an appearance there regularly, accepting all their invitations to receptions and parties, taking care to create the impression that her presence in London was only of temporary nature, that she was eager to rejoin me in Warsaw as soon as her father's health had improved.

Scarlett accepted this suggestion and agreed to our temporary separation until she could arrange our *rendezvous* in the 'rotten West' (in the language of Comrade Dłuski). Having made up her mind to help me, with her liking for drama she was becoming quite excited over the idea of an escape.

The first stage went smoothly. She obtained a passport in record time, the British Embassy instantly gave her a visa, and she bought a return air ticket in order to avoid suspicion.

As our taxi approached the airport, I noticed a sudden change in Scarlett's mood. She seemed to be losing confidence, becoming nervous and worried, especially as she looked at my happy face which reflected my pleasure that our plan was going so well. For a moment she misunderstood my cheerfulness, remarking with tears in her huge grey eyes that I was glad to be getting rid of her. It was an uneasy moment for us both. Fortunately I was allowed to accompany her to the steps of the aeroplane, and managed to reassure her. By the time she disappeared into the cabin, she looked calm and optimistic, giving me a smile which clearly meant 'See you soon!'

Now I had not only to worry about Scarlett, lonely and insecure without my presence and support, but also myself. I had to survive an indefinite period of uncertainty, with my nerves alight and crackling like fireworks at the slightest provocation.

Though the authorities could not yet have guessed my plans for escape, they seemed to have sensed my resentment at the culmination of recent events. Evincing a sudden new concern for my welfare, they suddenly allocated me a large, luxurious apartment right in the centre of Warsaw. I was reluctant to spend precious time and energy preparing a new home which I was not going to need, but, to avoid suspicion, I forced myself to appear delighted with this gift from our political gods, sparing no effort or expense, buying the best available furniture, curtains and carpets, fastidiously arranging the lighting.

It soon became obvious why our bountiful authorities had set me up with such a handsome home: official visitors from the West (kept away from ordinary situations where whole families subsisted in single rooms) were brought to my flat by the Committee for Cultural Relations Abroad to witness the standard of living of composers in Warsaw. I smiled behind closed lips, accepting any such hypocritical demonstration which they chose to impose upon me, putting up nonchalantly with a succession of ghastly sycophantic Western Communists, wondering how they would react if we were to meet perhaps only weeks or months later in the West. Fortunately not all my official guests were politically involved. One evening the brilliant and beautiful French pianist, Monique Haas, was brought to dine with me by her 'minder' from the Committee for Cultural Relations Abroad: I made a mental note that I would later in Paris greatly enjoy calling on her and the composer Mihalovici, her emigré Romanian husband.

Meanwhile I admitted my intention to no one and planned to say no goodbyes; I did not want to put anyone into danger should they find themselves questioned by the Secret Police after my departure. The worst wrench would be leaving Ewa. Now eighteen years old, a promising student at the Academy of Art in Wrocław, she was settled and secure with her mother's brother and his wife, so I was not worried about her future. However, she was my only close living relative, the only person I would deeply miss, and I lost a great deal of sleep wondering when or how I would ever see her again.

For weeks (which seemed like months) after Scarlett's departure I knew nothing of her progress on my behalf. Although she occasionally telephoned me, she was so careful not to let slip any hint to the 'ears' which monitored all foreign calls that she gave *me* no clues either. Since letters were censored too, she had no safe means of communicating anything important to me. I swung between faith and despair, aching for at least a slight indication that something was being achieved.

Then quite suddenly I received a note from the Director of the Committee for Cultural Relations Abroad, ordering me to see him on an urgent matter. I had no way of guessing whether I was just going to be ordered to entertain more appalling foreign guests, or whether my plans had been discovered. I went to his office, my heart clattering with fear, my mind circling on how to warn Scarlett, if necessary, to keep away from the Polish Embassy in London, while trying to invent ways to talk myself out of danger should the Director appear suspicious.

With my years of training in hiding my emotions, I gave no outward sign at all, neither of fear, nor of pleasure when he told me: 'You have been invited to Switzerland to conduct some contemporary Polish music with the Zürich Radio Symphony Orchestra. The only snag is' – the Director interrupted himself with a cough, while I choked back my gasp of nervous anticipation – 'that the date for recording is in two weeks' time: 7 or 8 July.' He was confident that I would jump at such an opportunity – most people welcomed the chance of a few days' break from Poland. However, still fearing a trap, or that my plans had been leaked, I maintained a wooden face and lugubriously expressed my regrets that it would not be possible. 'I can't accept this invitation. There is not enough time to study the scores properly, and besides, I have just begun to compose a new work. It would be disastrous to interrupt my train of thought at this early stage.'

'But this is a splendid opportunity to promote contemporary Polish music,' the Director insisted anxiously. 'And, after all, they specifically requested you as conductor.'

'It really would be very difficult for me to get away at this moment. Perhaps' – here I paused and took a deep breath – 'Perhaps you could send somebody else to Zürich?'

'No!' he snapped decisively. 'You are the right person to represent our music, especially as you are requested to conduct your own work. It is only a matter of two or three days in Zürich. Kindly do not refuse the invitation!'

I then submitted gracefully, at last agreeing to fly out from

Poland to Switzerland to make the recording.

With just two weeks to survive before my departure, the idea of leaving Poland for ever suddenly seemed like setting out for another planet. I had not realised until this moment how deeply my lungs required the oxygen of my native land.

As I felt time running out, the days seemed very short, the nights unbearably long. Through dark sleepless hours, I was haunted by vivid recurring images of my past life, which flickered through my mind as they do with a drowning man.

At last it was time to pack. Since officially I was going for no more than three days, I took only a small suitcase containing my conductor's baton, three shirts, some underwear, three pairs of socks, a toothbrush and a razor — a modest trousseau on which to begin my new existence. The rest of the space was filled with the pathetically few musical scores of my first thirty-nine years of life.

Just for one moment, I was almost overwhelmed by the temptation to pack one of my father's violins. I had rescued them twice — for my father, not for myself. Regretfully I left them — his own beautifully constructed instruments along with a Stradivarius, a Guarneri and an Amati — hoping that they would be handed over to a museum, or better still used by talented students in need of good instruments.

I paused for a moment before shutting the door behind me for the last time. Once my defection was known, the flat would undoubtedly be raided by the UB (Polish Secret Police). I decided that they deserved a pleasant sight to greet their eyes as they broke in, so I opened the flap of my desk, and carefully arranged on it all the medals awarded to me by the Government of People's Poland: my two State Laureate medallions, and the highest decoration of the land, the Standard of Labour, First Class. Playing with them for a few moments, I tried to find the most effective triangular pattern to delight the future intruders. The sun seemed to reflect my defiance: a shaft of light set the medals aglow just as I turned away.

Wasting hardly a glance at my pictures, my collection of books, the material luxuries I might never possess again, I strode out with my small suitcase of worldly possessions, and closed the front door without turning the key in the second lock, so that the Secret Police could reach my medals without too much struggle.

All went well at the airport. The plane took off precisely on time. We climbed steeply and very fast; definitely much, much too fast for me, as I pressed my face to the window, and watched the diminishing meadows, fields and woods till the clouds covered them completely. This short but painful moment was my farewell to Poland.

I landed at Zürich Airport on the afternoon of 9 July 1954. Waiting eagerly to greet me, standing between two officials of the Polish Legation, was the Director of Music of the Zürich Radio, the Swiss composer, Rolf Liebermann. I had never met him before but his friendly welcome instantly gave me extra courage.

After much heavy and serious hand-shaking, one of the Polish men said he would drive me to my hotel. However, Liebermann said that I must come with him to the Radio building: it was essential for me to meet the sound engineers before the next day's rehearsals to discuss the rather complicated symmetrical orchestral lay-out for *Sinfonia Rustica*. The Poles reluctantly handed me the pittance of Swiss francs I was allotted for my stay. I smiled my thanks and managed another convincingly friendly handshake. Fortunately, away from Eastern Europe, they were unable to impose themselves on me as constant 'guardian angels', though they stuck to us like glue as we went to find Liebermann's car. I tried to walk slowly and calmly. As soon as we slammed the car doors, leaving them behind, Liebermann said excitedly, 'We've done it! We've managed it!'

I was almost overwhelmed by the enthusiasm of this total stranger who had been urged into helping me by Regamey. But it was too soon to feel safe. 'I'd like to think so,' I said. 'But the problems are not yet over. Moscow's arm is very long . . .' (I only wished that I could fly out immediately to London but I had to fulfil my commitment first to Zürich Radio. And I wanted to ask for political asylum in Britain rather than Switzerland.)

After a brief meeting with the radio engineers, Liebermann

left me at the hotel booked for me by the Polish Legation. I hardly imagined that my masters would leave me unwatched, so I set about the game of 'spot the shadow'. After filling in my registration card, I walked swiftly to the lift, and turned sharply to see who, in the lobby, had his eyes on me. I caught the glance of a nondescript looking man in nondescript-looking grey clothes. I walked to the main exit, turned sharply again. His eyes were still latched on to me. I was well practised in the Eastern European habit of quickly memorising a shadowy face.

I had planned to telephone Scarlett immediately, but the presence of the grey shadow made me cautious. It would be wiser to make my first contact with her from a telephone outside the hotel, without an operator who could unknowingly give me away. I decided to wait.

My first rehearsal at the Radio was not till the following afternoon. The grey shadow was in the lobby when I came down in the morning. Pretending not to notice him, I led him on a long refreshing walk through the town, giving him plenty of opportunity to share my enjoyment of the shop windows as well as viewing a few statues of some worthy Zürich burghers. Eventually I took him to a rather expensive restaurant. He sat at a table not too near and not too far from mine. I had a talk with the waiter, and discussed a few promising items on the menu, saying I would wait for a friend before ordering. I was delighted meanwhile to see the shadow order himself a good meal. I then casually strolled out towards the lavatory, speedily left the restaurant by a side entrance, and took a taxi to the nearest post office.

I got through to Scarlett in London without difficulty. She was so overwhelmed to hear me that at first she could hardly speak; she said she could scarcely believe that in two or three days I would be by her side. She was in contact with the British Foreign Office about my impending defection, and everything seemed straightforward, but the unspoken feeling drifted between us that the danger would not be over till my feet were safely on British soil.

As planned, Scarlett had been in such constant touch with the Polish Embassy that she had almost been living there! She had visited the Ambassador and his wife in their Hampstead home, and her passport had been extended so that she could make a speech to foreign diplomats invited to celebrate National Independence Day, about how she enjoyed life in a Communist country! She had conscientiously acted the part of the homesick wife, to whom the Polish Embassy was a lifeline, while her duty to her sick father kept her in London. Her play-acting had amused but also terrified her.

I hated putting her through so much strain, and was tempted to tell her to go at once to the Home Office to request their protection. But normal appearances had to be maintained for just a little longer. 'I'm sorry,' I said, 'But please go to the Embassy tomorrow as if nothing has happened. Pretend you still think I am in Warsaw. If anyone mentions that I'm in Zürich, you must appear to be amazed.' Scarlett bravely agreed to carry on, though she felt that the Embassy officials would be much more vigilant now we were both in the West.

My personal dramas had to be pushed from my head that afternoon, and all my energies poured into working with the orchestra. To my joy, my dear friend Konstanty Regamey was waiting for me in the recording studio. Surrounded by engineers, producers and musicians, no mention could be made of our secret plan, but I could read in his smiling face that everything was going well. The rehearsal went smoothly, and I returned to my hotel feeling optimistic.

Next morning, as I was about to leave for another rehearsal, the telephone rang. It was the Polish Legation. A polite voice asked me to come to their office to fix my return flight to Warsaw. I suddenly felt that my legs were made of straw. At all costs I must avoid entering the doors of the Legation in case they had become suspicious. Taking a deep breath, hoping my voice was steady, I replied that I still did not know whether the recording would take two or three more days, so it was impossible yet to fix the flight. I added that I had a meeting with a couple of music producers after my rehearsals: I had brought scores by Serocki and Baird and I had to make sure that they also received performances in Zürich. 'It is extremely important at this stage to do everything possible for the promotion of contemporary Polish music; to make known our great achievements since the war.'

I carried on with a lecture on the duties of Polish artists to help each other, which, for the time being, silenced the polite voice. But I found myself in a cold sweat as I replaced the receiver. Already I had slipped my shadow, as well as twice avoiding contact with Legation staff. From the tension in the voice of the polite official, I feared that they were already starting to ask questions among themselves. I quickly telephoned Regamey and Liebermann. They both thought my fears exaggerated, but to be safe, they decided to speed up the rehearsals, attempting *Rustica* only, not any other works, and to record next morning, then get me quickly to London, where I could more easily disappear into the crowd.

My rehearsals with the excellent, cooperative orchestra went smoothly, and I was confident that the recording would go well the next day. On the way back to my hotel again I telephoned Scarlett from a post office, desperate to know how she had got on at the Embassy, suddenly afraid that they might have found some excuse to detain her.

She was safely back at her lodgings, but she almost cried with relief on hearing me. Her efforts at keeping calm under the scrutiny of the Embassy officials had been almost too much for her. Without doubt, they were suspicious.

'What happened?' I asked.

'It was most uncomfortable,' Scarlett replied. 'When I arrived, the Ambassador and First Councillor were both out, but they'd left a message for me to wait until they returned. I was scared to death and had to control myself from trembling. I said I wasn't well, and must go home to lie down; and suggested that the Ambassador should ring me later if there was anything urgent. However, an attaché suddenly appeared and prevented me from leaving. I tried to look calm, and waited to hear what he would say. He stood eyeing me quite sharply for some moments; then said he had to discuss the speech I was to make to the foreign diplomats on National Independence Day. I replied that I would greatly appreciate his help with my speech, but another time as I was feeling faint. He seemed to believe me, more or less.'

It was unbearable to think of Scarlett frightened and alone. I reminded her that the very next day we would be together again. We decided that she should keep up her pretence of feeling ill, whatever 'friendly help' the Polish officials might try to inflict on her. I promised that our Zürich friends would contact her as soon as possible, though they could not yet risk booking my flight in case information was leaked.

As I was dressing next morning, the telephone rang. I answered in case it was Regamey or Liebermann, but to my dismay it was the Polish voice again, this time sounding much less polite. I was ordered to come 'straight away' to the Polish Legation to discuss a 'most urgent' matter.

'Certainly I'll come,' I replied subserviently. 'I'll come as soon as I've finished my recordings which are due to start in an hour's time.'

As I paused, I overhead a woman quietly giving orders *in Russian*, which meant that he had an 'adviser', and that they almost certainly knew about my escape, through guesswork or perhaps even a leak. The official said sharply, in a voice bristling with irritation, 'I repeat, come NOW! At once. We will not detain you for more than a few minutes. Take a taxi here and you will not be late for your recording session.'

Trembling from head to foot, I answered in the steadiest tones that I could manage, 'I'm so sorry, but I have to be in the studio for a last-minute discussion with the sound engineers at least fifteen minutes before the recording. I'll come to the Legation as soon as we've finished the session.'

My promise seemed to calm them for the time being, but I had not the slightest intention of going anywhere near them. Once I entered the Legation, I would be on Polish territory, and they could do with me what they wished; cross-questioning or worse.

I set about recording *Sinfonia Rustica* – the symphony condemned within Poland as 'alien to the great socialist era' yet deemed suitable for export. It was fortunate that the music was my own and I could conduct it almost without thinking, because my mind was elsewhere, wondering if one of Scarlett's secret contacts amongst the Polish emigrés in London had committed an indiscretion over a drink, or if the KGB had a mole in the section of the Home Office dealing with my defection.

At last the recording was perfected, and the engineers declared themselves satisfied. I slipped quietly out of the Radio building, into a taxi, and directed the driver straight to my hotel, asking him to wait while I collected my case and paid my bill. I spent the minimum time possible in my room fearing, more than another summonary telephone call, a visit by some comrades wishing in their great kindness to take good care of me. With no time to check for shadows, I paid the bill and rushed back into my taxi, asking the driver to take me to another hotel at a distant part of the city, an address given me by Regamey the previous night.

As we set off, I sat back in relief, but looking round, I saw a car close behind us, driven by a grim-faced man with three equally unattractive passengers.

I was about to shout to the stolid taxi-driver that we were being followed by the Communist Secret Police. But I stopped short, realising that, after witnessing my frantic dash into the hotel and out again with a suitcase, he would probably assume I was a thief chased by local plain-clothes detectives!

So I leant over and told him in an urgent voice, that I had just noticed the time; that I had to meet a friend at the hotel and catch a train; that we were professional musicians and if we missed our connection we would be late for our concert. I offered him double rates and begged him to go at double speed.

The driver, encouraged by the idea of a reward, took my request to heart. For some time the black car held on to our tail like a limpet. I could not quite imagine what my pursuers planned to do — probably wait until I left the taxi, then drag me into their car, take me to the Legation, and pump some drug into me so that they could fly me back to Poland as a stretcher case.

'Can you not go even faster?' I asked the driver despairingly. Now his pride was at stake. He screeched round corners like a stunt man, rattled along tiny, narrow back-streets, dodging pedestrians and parked cars like a good Swiss slalom skier. I was soon more frightened by our speed than by the car still tagging along behind. Then suddenly, as a traffic light changed, we shot through it on red and left the Legation car standing. I never saw it again. On reaching my destination, I gratefully gave the driver almost every franc that I had left.

I went straight to my room and rang Regamey. It was a tremendous relief to hear his reassuring voice. He had managed to arrange for me to fly to London late that night. He would come and collect me at the last moment and drive me to the airport. Meanwhile he thought it would be safest for me to stay hidden in my room.

It was still only mid-afternoon. During those long hours of waiting, I struggled to concentrate my thoughts on my future in England. I felt excited and impatient to begin my new life in the country where I had met such kindness and enthusiasm for both my composition and conducting. But at the same time I had to face once again the implications of the final, irrevocable step I was about to take. My departure from Switzerland would close the doors of my native country against me for ever. I reflected that such a situation was almost unimaginable to people in the West who are free to keep their passports and not hand them in every time they return from abroad, and who can leave their countries and go anywhere in the certain knowledge that they can return when they wish.

As I sat huddled on the bed fearing I know not what, I lost all sense of time. Suddenly there was a loud knock on the door. My heart stopped beating. I waited silently.

Then I heard Regamey's voice telling me to hurry. In no time at all we had reached the airport. Even if anyone from the Legation had been watching my departure, under the eyes of the airport police they would have been powerless. I was struck more than anything by the almost surrealistic normality of procedures as I checked my ticket and passport and went through to the plane. A couple of hours later I was in London.

20

FROM NUMBER ONE
TO NO ONE

I arrived at Heathrow airport early in the morning of 14 July 1954. Waiting for me was Scarlett in the company of two representatives of the British Foreign Office Special Branch, ready to receive my instant request for political asylum. They took us to a hiding place up-river on the Thames, the unpretentious home of a charming middle-aged couple who treated us more like prodigal children than official guests. As the Foreign Office already knew all about me from Scarlett, and probably from undercover enquiries through their contacts in Poland, I was never interrogated, only treated with the utmost courtesy, kindness and discretion.

My escape was reported dramatically in the newspapers of the free world. A press conference, for which I briefly left my country retreat, allowed me to give my precise reasons for leaving my native country as well as the opportunity I had longed for to speak out about Poland's enslavement by Soviet Russia, about the misery of our people and the frustration of intellectuals, scientists, writers and all creative artists. I prepared a full statement, which was printed and broadcast all over the free world, ended with the words, 'I hope very much that my protest will help my fellow composers still living in Poland with their struggle towards liberation from the rigid political control imposed upon them . . .'

The Government of People's Poland, already furious over my escape, was clearly even angrier about my statement. I was condemned in the Polish press as a 'traitor to the Polish nation'. In addition to a bitter charge that I was 'running away from the task of creating a new style in Polish music' and 'avoiding the duties of creative patriotism', I was subjected to the customary methods of character-assassination. I was said to have 'stolen' the small sum of money handed to me on arrival in Zürich, which I had quite legally used to pay for my meals while still recording and promoting Polish music. My 'cynical desertion' of my native land they said was for financial gain – and added that I had illegally smuggled out of Poland musical instruments inherited from my father. A political zealot called Jerzy Broszkiewicz published an article saying that the evidence of all my 'criminal activity' could be found in my musical scores! And they then crowned their inventions by denouncing me as a spy! (I wonder what classified information a composer could betray?)

As anticipated, all my possessions in my Warsaw flat (including the string instruments which I was supposed to have smuggled out of the country) were confiscated. My printed compositions were destroyed, my music was banned and my name was not allowed to be printed in any future publications, books or magazines.

Just before I became a non-person, and officially ceased to have ever existed, the Polish Composers' Union published a sort of obituary:

> In July of this year, Andrzej Panufnik broke the bond which attached him to the Polish nation, remaining abroad and renouncing his Polish citizenship. In this way he has betrayed his own country and nation, as well as the cause for which all artists and Polish composers are fighting.

It was 'unanimously' resolved that my name should be removed from the list of members of the Union, and this example of 'free speech' in Communist Poland was signed by the Praesidium of the Union as well as their President, my poor old teacher, Kazimierz Sikorski, on behalf of all my friends and colleagues for whom I had battled over the years, but who could no longer utter a word in my defence.

The notion that I had defected 'for money' or 'with money' was in sharp contrast to the reality of my life with empty pockets in London. Although I was penniless, I was unwilling to capitalise on the publicity which had accompanied my arrival and I agreed only to give a couple of broadcast interviews with the BBC and Radio Free Europe, and to write two serious articles for *The Times*. To my bewilderment I was asked to make cuts in the latter because they were 'too anti-Communist'! – censorship in the West?

Before my escape, I had been so preoccupied that I had failed to consider how Scarlett and I would survive in our new environment. I had presumed that, with my existing reputation as both composer and conductor, I would be able at least to make a modest living. I was not looking for adulation or fame; only privacy, peace and freedom in which to compose as I wanted, with the opportunity to earn my living decently in my profession. The welcomes I had received when an official guest from Poland had convinced me that I was reasonably known and respected within the musical fraternity in Britain. I hoped that my presence would even be welcomed in my new country, chosen without hesitation not only for Scarlett's sake but also because of my mother's English origins, and because I admired the British tolerance and respect for privacy.

However, the privacy was all that I received. The musical fraternity which had welcomed me as a visitor was much less friendly now that I had come to stay. For instance I was disconcerted by a chance meeting with the distinguished composer, Sir Arthur Bliss, who had generously invited me to dinner at his home in 1948, and written a most flattering dedication on the score of his Piano Concerto (which he wanted me to conduct in Warsaw). He did not recognize me, so I reminded him of our earlier meetings; but he said firmly, 'No, I don't know you. I don't remember,' and walked on, his eyes averted.

In spite of the huge world-wide publicity which followed my escape, no one invited me anywhere near an orchestra nor showed the slightest sign of commissioning a new work.

Nor did the hundred-thousand strong Polish community in England make any move to help. Despite their 'Government in Exile', a President and Ministers, and their enormous 'Fund for National Culture', they did nothing other than request me to

1a. Henryka Thonnes, my adored grandmother (Warsaw, end of the nineteenth century).

1b. My parents on honeymoon in Siberia (Samara, 1908).

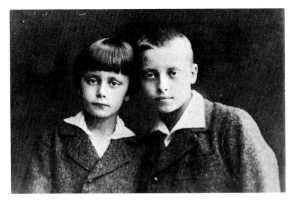

2a. Myself at seven, with my brother Mirek aged twelve.

2b. Myself aged twelve, after my failure as a pianist at the Warsaw Conservatoire.

2c. At seventeen, when I re-entered the Conservatoire as a full-time student of percussion, and then composition.

2d. Myself as an officer cadet doing National Service (1936).

3a. With my friend, composer-conductor Hisatada Otaka, in front of the house where Beethoven composed his Ninth Symphony (Baden, 1938).

3b. My great teacher, Felix Weingartner, with his kind words of dedication (Vienna, 1938).

4a. Rehearsing my *Tragic Overture* for its première at a wartime charity concert (Warsaw Conservatoire, 1943).

4b. My post-war identity card showing me as Director of the Warsaw Philharmonic Orchestra (a piece of history later deleted from the Orchestra's records when I 'ceased to exist' after my escape to the West in 1954).

5a. The cover of the programme for my concerts in Berlin (1948).

**BERLINER
PHILHARMONISCHES
ORCHESTER**

5b. Receiving first prize for *Sinfonia Rustica* in the Chopin Competition. From the left, composers Artur Malawski and Grażyna Bacewicz, the Minister of Culture, myself and my great friend, composer and writer, Zygmunt Mycielski (Warsaw, 1949).

6a. Meeting Shostakovitch for the first time in Warsaw
(1950).

6b. Conference in Prague. From left, Prof. Dr Zofia Lissa ('our Zosia'), myself, a Czech
musicologist and Witold Lutosławski (1950).

7a. At a concert. From the right, my 'controller' Minister Sokorski, the Soviet Vice-Minister of Culture Bespalov and his wife, and myself (Moscow, 1950).

7b. Meeting Khatchaturian, who poured me five vodkas while drinking none, but who, unlike most other Soviet composers, did not try to drown me in political dogma (Moscow, 1950).

7c. On the famous ship *Aurora*, from which the first shot of the Bolshevik Revolution was symbolically fired. Myself, fourth from left; in the middle, facing the camera, ever on watch, Minister Sokorski (Leningrad, 1950).

8a. A concert in the presence of Mao Tse Tung, with myself as Head of the Polish Cultural Delegation forced to precede the music with a speech (Peking, 1953).

8b. Meeting Chairman Mao and Premier Chou En Lai. From left: the Polish Ambassador, myself, my deputy, the acting director of the Mazowsze Song and Dance Company, their chief choreographer and their leading dancer (Peking, 1953).

conduct a charity concert without any fee later in the year.

After about two months, I thought that Scarlett and I would probably soon be discovering that our main freedom was the freedom to starve. I had leapt from my Polish position of No. One to No One at All in England. But then things started to look up. The first person to take an interest in my financial problems was Sir Steuart Wilson, whom I had met briefly some years before in Paris. Formerly a distinguished singer, he had founded his own choir with a particular interest in the madrigal, making this glorious English heritage known throughout the world. By the time I arrived in London he was in his sixties and had become Deputy General Administrator of the Royal Opera House, Covent Garden. He seemed to me the personification of an English gentleman, with his exquisite pronunciation, his face both noble and kind, his manner modest and direct. He always dressed immaculately in a Savile Row suit, with a rather over-large white stiff collar attached to his shirt and a ring under the knot of his tie. He was witty, imaginative and generous, and when he (belatedly) heard about my escape, he tracked me down and invited me to be frank about my situation. I admitted the urgency of my problem and he reacted swiftly, raising a guarantee for a bank overdraft of up to £400 (a tidy sum in those days).

Ralph Vaughan Williams most generously backed him up together with Arthur Benjamin and a few other British composers; a gesture of professional solidarity which meant even more to me than the actual money and gave me renewed courage. Other people whom he made aware of my difficulties were very kind in other ways: Lord Norwich, for example, generously invited me to work in his home until I was able to obtain my own workplace, going so far as to give me a key to his house and access to his excellent piano, for which I was deeply grateful. Steuart's next step was to put me in touch with the concert agency, Harold Holt Ltd, who were soon able to arrange a London appearance for me. I was invited to conduct the splendid Philharmonia Orchestra at the Royal Festival Hall on 4 October 1954. The concert had been planned to give fullest possible exposure to a young pianist, Colin Horsley, who was to perform both Beethoven's Piano Concerto No. 4

and Rachmaninoff's Piano Concerto No. 2 both in one evening. I had the impression that the soloist's sponsor and agent engaged me at the last moment for the benefit of the box office as my escape from Poland was still newsworthy. I did not object to this commercial gambit – I was only too delighted to be able to earn some money and cheer poor Scarlett up.

I started the concert with Beethoven's Symphony No. 4, and concluded it with my *Nocturne*. It was a long programme, but the audience, filling the hall to capacity, at the end of the concert gave me a tremendous standing ovation and the press was excellent.

At last, I thought, my London career had started. A few days later I went to Harold Holt Ltd to collect my fee, the grand sum of fifty guineas. To my dismay, one of the the directors handed me a cheque for just £6 10s. When I protested, I was told that, for the performance of my *Nocturne*, some extra players had been engaged, and to pay them, £46 had been deducted from my fee!

Anger and financial desperation rendering me speechless, I took my miserable cheque and stalked from the room, shutting the door behind me more loudly than British good manners would require.

When I told Scarlett about the disaster, it turned out that, fearing that I might lose an opportunity to conduct my own works, she had capitulated on my behalf to the concert agent's outrageous demand that I should cover the cost of the extra instrumentalists. Later, however, friends chastised me for my highly-strung behaviour at the Harold Holt agency. Apparently I should politely have thanked them and begged for another appearance: as it was, despite the success of my concert, I never heard from Harold Holt Ltd again.

My unpaid charity concert took place at the Albert Hall less than a week after my Festival Hall appearance. It was in aid of Polish children, and my friend Witold Małcużyński came over from his Swiss home to play the Chopin Piano Concerto No. 2. I decided to perform my own *Tragic Overture*, and, since the concert was for Polish emigrés, I chose a work I had arranged myself by a third Polish composer, also in his day an exile, Felix Janiewicz.

Janiewicz had been a pupil of Haydn's, staying in England till his death in 1848, and was a founder member of the Royal Philharmonic Society. (He partially anglicised his name, spelling Janiewicz with a 'Y' in the hope that it would be correctly pronounced. I momentarily thought of following his example and changing my first name to Anjay!)

Musically the concert was a very happy occasion. Witold's performance of the Chopin was inspired, and the London Symphony Orchestra played for me with great spirit and precision. But in other respects it was a near disaster. The Polish community, thinking themselves self-sufficient, did not advertise the event in the English press; the hall was depressingly empty. The organisers told me that they had not actually lost money, but the poor Polish children got nothing at all. Afterwards, a journalist covering the event for the London *Polish Daily* lambasted his fellow exiles for their lack of interest in music and their failure to support their own charity. He said there were so few people in the hall that individual handclaps could be heard.

Although my name was already banned in Poland (officially I had never been born) the Warsaw press saw fit to break the rule. The words of this journalist were eagerly quoted, my name included, to prove that, by leaving Poland, I had now ceased to be of interest to anyone. The implication was clear as daylight: 'Serves him right!' (The quality of the music of course was not mentioned, nor my excellently received concert the week before.)

Witold Małcużyński was not only a great pianist: he was also a very good friend to me. After the concert he asked me about my financial situation, and took my difficulties to heart. He approached an Argentinian of Polish origin, a Madame Rosa Berenbau, who was a generous sponsor of the arts. She happened to be visiting London, and personally presented me with a handsome cheque 'to help me start to compose again'. I promised to dedicate my next major work to her and in the circumstances decided that it should be a piano concerto for Witold, though, with his hectic international concert schedule, I was not at all sure that he would ever have time to study it. Time, I realised, was also going to be a problem for me. Even with Madame Berenbau's cheque I could see that over the next few years I would probably have to earn our crusts through conducting, and I was unlikely yet to be able to fulfil my dream of concentrating entirely on composition, let alone tackling full-scale orchestral works. Witold, though he was excited about the idea of a new concerto, was understanding about my fears and made no demands at all, except that there should eventually be a work dedicated to Madame Berenbau.

Now at last Scarlett and I began to feel more secure financially. We stopped worrying about finding money for food and for the rent of our tiny two-room flat near Sloane Square. I even started looking for an upright piano for my work.

The world suddenly looked brighter, especially after an invitation to conduct l'Orchestre National de Belgique for four concerts. To my joy the soloist was to be the great Joseph Szigeti, whom I had long admired from gramophone records. He would be playing Mendelssohn's Violin Concerto in Ghent, then, in the three Brussels appearances, a concerto by the Swiss composer, Frank Martin. I had minor reservations about the time it would take me to study this work, which was completely unknown to me – time again taken away from my composition – but was greatly relieved to find myself back on the international circuit.

Working with Szigeti was an intense pleasure because of his great musicianship and friendly cooperation. I enjoyed conducting Martin's beautiful concerto, and I finished the concert with my *Tragic Overture*. As I was leaving the podium after an ovation from the orchestra as well as the audience, I was informed that Queen Elisabeth of the Belgians was waiting to see me in the Royal Box. I had previously met the dowager Queen as a visiting adjudicator for her composition prize and had been greatly impressed by her charm, her intelligence and personality, and her love of music. In her palace I had seen her own work as a sculptor, and her beautiful old Italian violin.

After congratulating me on the concert, the Queen cross-examined me intently about my reasons for leaving Poland. I was not surprised. People sometimes nicknamed her the 'Red Queen'. The Russians, quick to take advantage of her apparent sympathy, had been trying to win her over, sending her some of their best and most famous string players, including David

Oistrakh, to make chamber music with her (she not only owned a beautiful violin, she played it too). Quite why the Russians needed to indoctrinate royalty I never could quite imagine. I tried gently to counteract the propaganda she had been receiving by explaining the difficulties of creative artists under the system.

On my return to London, I learnt from Scarlett that she had begun to write a book, on a commission from Hodder and Stoughton, describing my conflicts with the Polish authorities and telling the story of my escape. Although she had no previous experience of writing professionally, she attacked her task with great speed and panache.

In order to produce a book that would be attractive and accessible to a wide readership, she wrote freely and directly from her own point of view — the experiences of a young Irish girl going to live in a strange and distant country. My artistic and political dilemmas were sketched in almost as background to her personal dramas, with a strong emphasis only on the sensational aspects of my escape and her significant rôle in it.

The publishers had in fact approached me initially, but I had refused on the grounds that I would rather write music than words; that I found Westerners little concerned with the artistic and ideological problems of life in Eastern Europe; and that I myself had had enough of those problems.

So I rashly allowed Scarlett to write this book without even a glance from myself. It was published in 1956 under the title *Out of the City of Fear*. It caused me considerable distress as it was peppered with minor inaccuracies, particularly about my days in Zürich before my flight to England, which she had not even asked me about, but had probably pieced together on the basis of vague comments by friends. More seriously, it seemed to describe my difficulties in Poland but failed to convey their extreme gravity to any outsider.

The New Year of 1955 started well with the news that Leopold Stokowski would be conducting my *Symphony of Peace* in Detroit in mid-February. My advisers in England strongly recommended that I should attend the performance and try to make contact with musical life in America. I wanted particularly to meet Stokowski, knowing him only from his sensational recordings and his reputation for caring deeply about contemporary composers. He had already conducted my *Tragic Overture* in 1949 with the New York Philharmonic Orchestra.

However, when I went to the American Embassy to obtain my visa, the Consul seemed not at all impressed by my wish to visit his country, nor by the fact that my symphony was to be conducted by Stokowski. On the contrary, he cast a suspicious glance at me, and handed me a quantity of forms, to be returned to him the following week. On my next visit the Consul scathingly corrected some 'wrong information': under the heading of race I had described myself as white instead of Caucasian. He then sent me away again saying that he had to write to Frankfurt and Washington for further instructions.

For a moment I was amused at how terribly dangerous I was to the Government of the United States of America, but I was also annoyed with their bureaucracy. How could they be so obtuse and unfriendly in the face of the political stance I had taken?

By the time I arrived for my third appointment at the American Consulate, I was not in the best of tempers. But this time the Consul was more polite: Washington had decided they dared to let me in. But first I had to fill in more forms, then follow him through the winding corridors of the huge building as I was led to a small sinister room to be fingerprinted like a criminal. As the ink was transferred with my prints into their records, I asked myself, 'Is this freedom?'

After a long flight, I was confronted by an American customs officer asking me yet again whether I had been a member of the Polish Communist Party. I said, not without irritation, that I had already supplied this answer a dozen times at the American Consulate in London. Fortunately on the other side of the barrier were the friendly faces of some representatives of the Polish-American choir taking part in my *Symphony of Peace*.

Stokowski's choice of venue for the performance obviously was not accidental since, after the war, more Poles lived in Detroit than in the whole of Warsaw! There were – and still are – Polish churches, shops selling Polish food, Polish newspapers. (Perfect Polish continued to be spoken by whole generations born in America, and, in order to earn a living, even a few black Americans have found it essential to learn Polish too!)

My American-born Polish hosts were touchingly warm and friendly, and excited to have read an article in the press describing my arrival as 'the greatest event since the last visit of Ignacy Paderewski'. The same paper quoted Stokowski as saying that my symphony was 'great and beautiful'.

My eyes were wide on my first drive through an American city, trying to take in all the new sights and impressions. The snow-covered streets were full of cars, but the pavements were empty: it seemed that everyone was moving on wheels. I regretted that I was too tired to explore further that night, but planned to walk miles the following day.

Next morning I was awakened early by a telephone call. A voice said, 'Is that Maestro Panufnik speaking?'

'It is,' I said hesitantly, wondering who on earth could be addressing me as 'maestro'.

'This is Leopold Stokowski,' the shy voice continued. 'I wonder if I could see you now?' He spoke slowly, pronouncing his words with careful deliberation.

'Yes, of course – I shall be very honoured!' I replied, moved by the unexpected modesty in his request. I asked where he was staying.

He was in the same hotel, and within moments was at my door.

I had seen many photographs of him, and the famous Disney film of *Fantasia*, from which I had gained the impression of a tall man, with a proud head carriage and the face of a dreamer, romantic and at the same time rather arrogant. The man who walked into my hotel room was of less than medium height with a slightly stooping posture, his head bowed forward, a mild expression on his face. He was dressed in tweed like an English country gentleman. His voice was not fierce or loud as I had imagined, but soft, gentle, and almost exaggeratedly polite.

He did not want to discuss the score of my symphony, just wished to greet me as a friend and express his enthusiasm about my composition. He invited me to the rehearsal next day.

The rehearsal in the huge Masonic Hall was a nightmare for non-musical reasons. As I sat hoping to concentrate on the proceedings, more than a dozen American Poles approached me in turn, as if I were present for no other purpose than to meet and talk with them. Since they were all delightfully friendly, I could not turn them away. I had to apologise to each one, explaining that it was not the right place and time for a conversation, and that we must not disturb Stokowski in his work. I spent about half an hour repeating this request — almost exactly the time it took the orchestra to play through my symphony. I had hardly heard a note of it.

At the concert, I was deeply impressed by Stokowski's direct and powerful interpretation. It was true, as I had always heard, that Stokowski could conjure a special sound of his own from an orchestra. When the symphony was over, I was called to the platform three times by the 5,000 applauding listeners.

In spite of this magnificent performance and reception, and the praise of the maestro, I was not happy with my composition. I felt that the emotional content dominated the form in such a way that the balance was disturbed and that the musical language was not fastidious enough. Above all, I found the work too long (how much easier it is to write with great density at great length than it is to use discipline and economy to produce something short but good!). The symphony had been written in a hurry and under duress from the Polish authorities. Its flaws were all too apparent to me. Despite Stokowski's protest, I decided to withdraw my *Symphony of Peace* for the peace of my artistic conscience.

I stopped in New York in order to try to enlarge my contacts with America's musical world. Thanks to Boosey & Hawkes, the London music publishers (with whom I had signed a contract just before leaving for the USA), I met Arthur Judson, the leading American concert agent. I had been warned many times over by British friends that American agents were seldom trustworthy. However Judson was very honest. He promised me nothing.

On my return to Britain in the early spring of 1955, I found a letter from Richard Howgill, the Music Controller of the

BBC, confirming his earlier suggestion that I should conduct my *Sinfonia Rustica* at a Promenade Concert at the Albert Hall in July. This was a most encouraging prospect: I settled down to think about a new composition.

I was longing to forget both political and material problems, and submerge myself in this new work. But again my plans were frustrated, now because of an urgent request from Boosey & Hawkes, who to my great joy were planning to add all my works to their catalogue which already included the music of such composers as Stravinsky, Richard Strauss, Bartók and Prokofiev. PWM, the Polish State publishers (whom I had helped to found), had presumably been ordered to destroy all existing copies now my music was banned but Dr Roth, the publishing director of Boosey & Hawkes, was worried about copyright if he printed the works precisely as in their first editions. He had written to PWM, asking them to confirm in writing that my contract with them was dissolved and that I had no further obligations to them, but they did not answer his letters.

So I was asked to make small changes in each work, sometimes altering their names. Dr Roth was perhaps being over-cautious, but because I needed all my works in print and available for performance as quickly as possible, I went to work obediently; comforting myself with the fact that, since perfection is an ever-elusive goal, some of the works might benefit from the scrutiny of my more mature, more critical eye.

It was therefore the slightly revised version of my *Sinfonia Rustica* that I conducted with the splendid BBC Symphony Orchestra at the Proms on the unforgettable 27 July 1955.

Sir Malcolm Sargent (with the inevitable white carnation in the lapel of his beautifully cut tail coat) began the concert with Tchaikovsky, and handed over to me a well-warmed orchestra which gave me of its very best. The reception was wildly enthusiastic, and after the concert I was besieged by a large crowd of fans and autograph hunters so that eventually it was a relief to be swept to my taxi by some waiting policemen. (I wondered if their presence was arranged in advance as a precaution, as it was still only a year since I had come to the West.)

The Prom made a cheering break from the drudgery of revising my music. This task was at last completed in the early
autumn – shortly before Dr Roth received a belated reply from
the PWM, saying, 'We inform you that we do not intend to
publish the works of Andrzej Panufnik and regard our contract
with him as dissolved.' This gave Boosey & Hawkes a free
hand to publish all my music, even without revisions. Much
precious time had been wasted.

I decided not to begin a totally new work until I had set my
mind at rest over my *Symphony of Peace*. Looking objectively at
the score, I still judged that the original work was too long and
too much of an outburst of raw feeling. If I could express the
same musical thoughts more economically, the emotional and
dramatic aspects would surely emerge more forcibly. I decided
to rebuild a new symphony out of the first two movements of
the *Symphony of Peace*, putting aside the choral section for the
time being, and discarding the word 'peace' which to my ears
had been perverted and corrupted by Soviet misuse. I chose instead the title, *Sinfonia Elegiaca*, and dedicated the work to the
victims of the Second World War.

The new version of the symphony was to be in one continuous movement, built in three parts, symmetrically arranged
like a vast triptych. It did not have any literary programme,
only allusions to contrasting aspects of war. The central section
('molto allegro') would be a dramatic protest against inhuma-
nity, madness, blood-lust and violence. The two outer sections
(both 'molto andante') would be lamentations for the dead and
for the bereaved, with added grief that their agonies and sacrifices had failed to bring peace to the world, or full freedom to
countries such as my native Poland.

I was able to complete this work quite quickly. I then took a
deep breath, and poised my pencil for some real new work. I
tentatively started some sketches for my Piano Concerto, with
Witold Małcużyński's unique virtuosity and inborn facility for
con bravura playing vividly in my mind while I wrote.

However, yet another interruption got in the way of my
composition. In December 1955, the French magazine *Preuves*,
together with *Kultura*, a monthly literary and political magazine published by Polish emigrés in Paris, held an open discus-

sion on 'The Artist and Creativity in Poland today', which was attended by about 200 leading French intellectuals from literature and the arts as well as politics and philosophy. Much as I disliked any recourse to words rather than music, I felt impelled to share my first-hand experiences with interested Westerners. Once more I had to put my manuscript paper in a drawer.

The Chairman of the discussion was the French writer and critic, Jean Cassou, Director of the Musée de l'Art Moderne.

The other speakers were Czesław Miłosz, contrasting the experiences of writers under Stalin and in the West, and Józef Czapski, the painter, describing his experiences in Russian concentration camps.

In my awful French, I explained the dilemmas affecting Polish composers working under the rigid control of the Communist authorities.[1] My friend Konstanty Regamey then summed up with his enviably sharp intellect and perfect French. Judging by the discussion afterwards, the evening had been well spent and had made a strong impression among French intellectuals, including some Marxist sympathisers who were overtly shaken by the evidence of what happened when their precious doctrine was actually applied.

I returned in time for Christmas which coincided happily with our celebrations of being able to move into a new home.

Looking for a quiet place to live, I had found a flat in the house of a retired diplomat in The Boltons in South Kensington. With my advance royalties from the kind and helpful Boosey & Hawkes, I had been able to buy a seven-year lease, an investment (I hoped) for my work and our private life, giving us both a solid base, and myself a chance to work intensively on my composition in reasonable peace.

Peace unfortunately continued to elude me. The windows of our flat on the second floor looked out on to a fashionable little church where the frequent weddings and funerals were accompanied by the slamming of car doors and the revving of expensive engines. Our tree-lined crescent was not the backwater I had imagined, but carried a stream of traffic day and night. And for a neighbour I had the famous and very hospitable

---

1 Published in *Kultura*, *Preuves*, and *Encounter*.

Douglas Fairbanks Jr, who organised many late parties with happy, jolly guests, who shouted and sang as they left his house in the small hours of the morning. It was hardly the setting for the sort of concentration and deep contemplation required to write music.

An even more serious problem had to be faced in my personal life as it became clear to me that my marriage was not going to last much longer. Maybe Scarlett had become resentful of the lonely times in London during my short trips to France, Belgium and America, when I could not afford to take her with me. She may also have been influenced by friends who encouraged her to grumble about my musical ambition and my single-minded dedication to long silent hours of work. Our companionship could never have been described as a true meeting of spirit or mind, but we had muddled along somehow, through extremely difficult times. Now the rift between us was widening with every week, almost every day, that passed.

Scarlett was driven by a craving for excitement and glamour; a lifestyle with one social adventure following another. She expected me to accompany her for lunches, dinners and parties. She even adored night-clubs, which I found unbearable. The thought of spending a peaceful evening at home filled her with horror. Her need for me to join her expeditions far outweighed any serious thoughts in her mind about what would happen to us financially if I became a social animal and abandoned my work. Being still young and very beautiful, and the wife of a composer who had made headlines, she wanted to enjoy the attention and curiosity which we still aroused. But I loathed the din of overcrowded parties, the pointless chatter, the juggling with people, plates, and wineglasses. I longed only for solitude and peace.

My search for a defence strategy was just driving me to distraction when I was asked by the BBC to compose a work for the tenth anniversary of the Third Programme. With a date for completion hanging over my head, I had the perfect excuse, at least for part of each day, to shut the door on social life. In those precious hours which I could steal for total involvement I began at last to feel sane again. It was pure happiness, like breathing again after having almost drowned, to find myself absorbed in the first new music I had written for about four years.

An idea came to me right away. The title would be *Rhapsody*, and it would be designed to reveal the virtuosity of the players of the orchestra both individually and as an ensemble. The work would have a symmetrical, ternary structure. The first section, in slow tempo, rather lyrical in character, would give the impression almost of an improvisation, each instrument of the orchestra introducing itself in a brief solo passage – one after the other, with the exception of the double bass (I could imagine the disappointed expression on the face of the leader of the double-bass section as he read the work for the first time). The central section, a very fast and vigorous tutti, would resemble a Polish folk dance, but with a hybrid rhythm invented by myself, the binary metre of the *Krakowiak* dance superimposed on to the ternary metre of the *Mazurek*, which should achieve an unsettling and evocative effect. The third section would use the same thematic material as the first, reflecting its steady crescendo with a matching diminuendo, brought about partly by the gradual reduction of instruments, down to the end of the piece, when the double bass – not forgotten after all – would have the final word.

The musical ideas were clear in my head long before I was able to get them all down on paper. It was a struggle in the midst of Scarlett's daily merry-go-round, but somehow I finished on time, and the work was first performed and recorded in the BBC studio at Maida Vale (a converted skating rink with a curious echo) in the New Year of 1957.

On 22 January, out of the blue, I received a telegram from Houston, Texas:

TONIGHT WE PERFORMED YOUR POWERFUL AND PROFOUNDLY MOVING SINFONIA ELEGIACA AUDIENCE'S AND ORCHESTRA'S REACTION DEEPLY EMOTIONAL AND ENTHUSIASTIC SHALL REPEAT TOMORROW

THANK YOU FOR UNFORGETTABLE MUSICAL EXPERIENCE – LEOPOLD STOKOWSKI

This is a complete surprise to me. It seemed that, without telling me, Boosey & Hawkes had packed off the score of my new symphony to Stokowski, at that time Musical Director of the Houston Symphony Orchestra. He had reacted promptly, enthusiastically slipping it into a programme without delay. Soon afterwards Stokowski wrote more extremely warm words, and sent the programme, which read:

> Panufnik's *Sinfonia Elegiaca* expresses in musical terms exactly what the title suggests – a symphonic lamentation. Its introductory section is sung plaintively by the muted strings – a song of mourning. The main body of this one-movement work shows the strength of character and the heroic concept of that which is being lamented in its brilliant Allegro. The sombreness of the beginning elegiac theme returns in the Epilogue.

Very nice, flattering words, but why 'the heroic concept of that which is being lamented'? Why were they afraid to say what the symphony was about, to mention World War Two and my lament for the lack of freedom in my own and other Communist-dominated countries? Would the West not allow music to have a theme? Did we all have to be abstract, polite, antiseptically detached from issues of importance? Was art to touch only upon the pretty sides of life and have no relevance to issues which affected huge slabs of humanity? Was I after all so conditioned by Socialist Realism that I wanted to speak through my music even if along another line of thought?

But it was no use intellectualising about the pros and cons of abstract art. The unabstract fact in my life was an acute shortage of money. I had no further commissions in hand. With our home expenses at that time steadily increasing, I recognised that circumstances were again forcing me back towards conducting and away from my true vocation as a composer. I would have to accept that my original plan, to finance my composition by intermittent conducting dates would be difficult if not impossible to achieve. I began to keep half an eye open for a permanent appointment as a conductor.

Meanwhile great changes were taking place in Poland as a result of the so-called 'Bloodless Revolution' of 1956.

After the demise of Stalin, through sustained and courageous protest, composers (and some other intellectuals) had at last succeeded in creating enough political upheaval to gain for themselves greater freedom of expression. The concepts of formalism and Socialist Realism had been forced aside, written off as belonging to a 'past epoch'. The younger generation, starved by years of isolation from the West, had seized greedily upon all that was most interesting in twentieth-century music, which, till that moment, had been totally withheld from their eyes or ears.

The authorities had averted their gaze, seeing the new freedom in composition and the other arts as a kind of safety valve, preferring this dialectic aberration to the risk of further protests or escapes to the West! The Composers' Union was even permitted by the new Government to organise a festival of contemporary music, and to include works which in Stalinist times had been designated as 'alien to the great Socialist era'.

Arnold Schoenberg was no longer a proscribed composer: his Piano Concerto was performed with enormous success. My old friend Konstanty Regamey had attended this concert, and described how, as the last notes died away, a young Pole next to him had burst out clapping and shouting in the wildest fashion. Konstanty, though influenced by Schoenberg for many years, was startled by quite so strong an emotional reaction. He had turned to the young enthusiast, and said, 'So you really like this concerto?'

'No, I did not!' the young man replied.

'But then, why did you applaud it so violently?' Konstanty asked.

'Because this music is so DIFFERENT!' his neighbour unhesitatingly replied.

This 'difference' came as a revelation to many composers, who were too excited to notice that they were jumping out of one stylistic straightjacket into another. Not only did the young Polish composers (most using the serial method as a springboard) plunge head first into the inviting experimental pool, but old ones also – like Bolesław Szabelski, who, after fifty years of writing tonal music, became an atonalist over-night.

The key to this universal passion for experiment was re-vealed to my by a composer friend who, in the freer atmo-sphere of the moment, had managed on some professional pre-text to get a passport and visit the West. He confessed to me in greatest confidence that he hated Schoenberg, Webern and all their myriad disciples, but felt that he had to employ their ad-vanced methods in his own composition as a patriotic duty — otherwise his colleagues would accuse him of toadying to the Russians who still, at home, were insisting on the tonal idiom.

Of course the truly inspired amongst my fellow-countrymen managed brilliantly to transcend the restrictions of the fashion-able idiom, and some extremely exciting music started to emerge. The fervent application of the Warsaw composers' high-spirited creativity and flair to an already slightly tried compositional convention filled the Western critics with awed delight. But in the eyes of many participants, this flowering of the Polish avant garde was a political demonstration as well as an artistic revelation, though no one could risk letting Western visitors into the secret. Experimental music was an ideal language for the expression of anti-Soviet feeling which it was still dangerous to put into words.

Such ways of demonstrating against the Soviets were seized upon eagerly by my besieged compatriots, religion for example presenting another avenue for veiled protest. Prohibited from gathering in large groups, people throughout the land regularly manifested their dislike of the imposition of the Marxist doc-trine by crowding into the churches every Sunday (then and now), probably in greater numbers and worshipping with greater intensity than in pre-war times when Catholicism was the approved religion.

It was with mingled amusement and admiration, that I watched from afar the dazzling avant garde acrobatics of my colleagues. The finest somersaults of all were turned by the party officials, who consigned their millions of words in praise of Socialist Realism to the dustbins where they belonged, glos-sing over the harm caused for seven agonising years by their boot-licking enforcement of ruthless policy. The blame for their previous rigidity was placed on Stalin, not on the system which 'was and always will be perfect'.

In due course the news filtered through to me that the most fanatical proponent of the method of Socialist Realism, the former Minister of Culture, Sokorski, in his new job as Chairman of the Polish Radio, was promoting such 'degenerate formalists' as Boulez, Cage, Stockhausen and Xenakis. He even presided over an experimental studio which was equipped with the latest electronic facilities. The Polish composers, who for years had been coerced by him into moving towards turgidly bland tonality, were now encouraged to come and play with these exciting new gadgets.

Despite apparent greater freedom, no one in Poland was able publicly to admit that my protest two years earlier had been just. The printed word was still subject to censorship by our Soviet masters. My name was still not allowed to be published, my music was still banned. I was moved to learn that a couple of my colleagues had daringly tried (unsuccessfully) to side-step this ban by mentioning me casually in magazine articles. Yet I was not dissatisfied that my name was still too seditious even to be printable in a magazine dedicated entirely to music.

Other than that, I had little cause for satisfaction. Looking back over my first two and a half years in the West, I realised that, in my passion to find peace to compose, I had perhaps failed to chase after some opportunities that had arisen. On the other hand, too much public attention would also have stood in the way of the quiet and calm essential for my creative work. I needed only a minimum of paid commissions plus occasional concerts to enable me to write music every hour of every day and make up for my lost years.

I had only achieved one completely new piece of music since arriving in the West, the *Rhapsody* for orchestra. Although I was by no means displeased with it, I did not count it as a major work, and had not dedicated it to the generous Madame Berenbau since I felt she deserved something more substantial.

Of course there was a lighter side. One day, when I rang the ever friendly Dr Roth at Boosey & Hawkes, my own publishers

the horrified telephonist to ask me to repeat my name twice
and then to spell it out . . .

'P-A-N-U-F-N-I-K,' I enunciated each letter slowly and
clearly.

'Oh, yes, of course,' she said with obvious relief. 'Dr
Bronowitz . . . If you'll just hold on a minute, I'll put you
through.'

21

SCENES FROM PROVINCIAL LIFE

Realising that I could no longer leave my financial survival to fate, and persuaded by my good friend, John Denison, of the Arts Council, I allowed my name to be put forward for the post of Music Director and Conductor of the City of Birmingham Symphony Orchestra (CBSO). After an enjoyable and very well received trial concert I was offered the job. It was a daunting prospect: fifty concerts a year, a huge number of rehearsals, much travelling around the countryside for out-of-town performances, heavy administrative duties including the engagement of soloists and orchestral players, and social appearances as well. To take on this catalogue of responsibilities I would again have to say goodbye to my manuscript paper. A London orchestra would have been less demanding and the London Symphony Orchestra had indeed made tentative enquiries, but this was too remote a prospect. If I could not soon show myself solvent, I might fail to qualify for British naturalisation.

My eventual acceptance of the Birmingham offer resolved my pecuniary problems, but was the death knell for my marriage. Scarlett, after her glamorous life in London, was repelled by the idea of living in what she described as a 'dull provincial Midland city'. She refused to come to Birmingham with me, even for a single concert. Grateful as I was for Scarlett's courageous participation in my escape, she had contributed to many of the problems which were keeping me away from composition and had never outgrown her hunger for admiring words and constant attention. Her desire for my success did not arise from any belief in what I was trying to do, but because it would provide the social position she felt she needed to shine at her brightest. If she was an unsuitable sort of wife for a tunnel-visioned, dedicated composer, I was equally the most ill-fitted sort of husband to assist her in her social ambitions. Even if I would be lonely, it would be a major relief to escape from our endless quarrels.

The Management of the CBSO wanted me to sign a contract for three years, but I explained to them how little I had been able to compose since I had come to Britain, and they most mercifully agreed to two years with an option to renew.

It was a condition of my contract that I should live in Birmingham. Just before moving, I conducted my *Rhapsody* with the Royal Philharmonic Orchestra at the Proms, and again was delighted by the uniquely appreciative and enthusiastic young audience. Richard Howgill, now in his last months at the BBC, gave me another commission, which I accepted with some trepidation, wondering how I would find time to complete it.

My mind was now almost entirely on my new job. Channelling my thoughts as far away as possible from the crisis in my personal life and the seductive image of blank manuscript paper, I took up my new responsibilities with optimism and faith, trusting that I could help improve the artistic standards of the CBSO.

Birmingham's Town Hall, sometimes known as 'Hansom's Cavern', was designed by the man who achieved even greater renown through the development of the hansom cab, the horse-drawn ancestor of the London taxi. Other great names connected with the Town Hall made deeper impressions on me: Mendelssohn, Gounod, Dvořák and Sibelius had all performed there. The most illustrious child of the orchestra, the young Edward Elgar, had spent some years in the first violin section and returned to conduct the première of his *Dream of Gerontius*: the hall was redolent with great tradition.

In drawing up the programme for my first season (1957-8), I felt obliged to base the orchestra's repertoire on the music of the great classical and romantic composers, according to the expectations of the orchestra's regular public. At the same time, I hoped to introduce some lesser known works, both ancient and modern. I particularly wanted to share with my new audience my discoveries from before the war of then almost unperformed early English composers such as Arne, Avison, Boyce, Byrd and Stanley.

When it came to twentieth-century music, I was disappointed not to be allowed to programme more music by living British composers, though I managed to slide in several works by Vaughan Williams in celebration of his eighty-fifth birthday, plus four or five more British works in addition to Rubbra's Symphony No. 7, the orchestra's annual commission through the Feeney Trust. Feeling that I must show solidarity with the composers of my chosen country, I did not therefore include any of my own works, despite the kindly pleas of the Management Committee. Elgar was of course wholly acceptable and I could not resist his symphonic prelude, *Polonia* – (composed for a charity concert for destitute Poles shortly after the First World War, it had not been played since so far as I could discover). I also performed some Stravinsky to celebrate his seventy-fifth birthday year. *The Rite of Spring*, which I had always longed to conduct, was ruled out because of the need for a dozen or so extra players, which proved too costly for the burghers of that rich city to contemplate. Roussel and Ravel passed muster in deference to the twentieth anniversaries of their deaths, and I smuggled in a few more modern foreigners: Copland, Nielsen, Skalkottas, Janáček and Hindemith; also Arthur Honegger, whose *Rugby* I programmed in the knowledge that I was booked for a concert at Rugby School, the birthplace of the game portrayed in the music. But the school authorities did not allow their sensitive young charges to be exposed to such dangerous modern stuff – foreign at that!

The season started off auspiciously enough. There were murmurs of disapproval from the Committee that Scarlett was not in evidence even at my opening concert, but our separation was still unofficial and I did not feel like making any announcement. Otherwise everything went off splendidly. The local press were enthusiastic, the public attentive and warm. My early inhibitions dropped away and I started to enjoy my new situation.

Only one cloud frowned over the horizon. The Committee had suggested that my first task would be to improve standards of playing in Birmingham. The string sections especially lacked precision and produced a poor sound quality. Spoilt perhaps by my experiences with great orchestras such as the Berlin Philharmonic, l'Orchestre National in Paris, the LSO, RPO and Philharmonia in London, I was determined to make use of the considerable potential Birmingham talent and concentrate on bringing the playing up to the international standards of which they were fully capable. In this urgent task, I naturally hoped to rely on the cooperation of the orchestra's experienced leader, Norris Stanley.

Despite my diplomatic approach, Mr Stanley became defensive and argumentative during rehearsals. He then set about turning the rest of the orchestra against me. He suggested that I was going to replace some of the violinists with Hungarian refugees who had arrived after the 1956 Budapest Uprising, and he also played on the fears of less confident musicians in other sections of the orchestra, with fabrications about my supposed plans to get rid of dead wood.

The atmosphere during rehearsals became unbearable and I was often frustrated in my struggle to improve the quality of our performances. Fortunately most of the musicians remained loyal to me and appreciated my efforts to improve standards. Through this friendly element of players, I discovered that the leader had some extra-musical prejudices against me. He was both anti-Semitic and anti-Communist, and had the mistaken impression that I was a Jew and a committed Marxist, if not actually a Soviet spy!

Since Stanley refused to carry out the normal duties of an orchestral leader, I started to rely on the assistance of the principal of the viola section, Samuel Spinak, an outstanding musician with an imagination for solving technical problems which Stanley totally lacked. Spinak's clever and useful suggestions irritated Stanley hugely for two reasons: he was always right; and he was a Jew, speaking out authoritatively in a strong East London Jewish accent. As Spinak's and my friendly cooperation developed, Norris Stanley involved the Management Committee in his attacks on me but fortunately the audience knew nothing of the backstage backbiting.

The soloists each brought their individual and interesting personal touches to the concerts.

At one of my first appearances, Janos Starker and I crossed swords over our interpretations of Elgar's Cello Concerto. I found his rubato somewhat excessive, and the general effect sentimental. He said he agreed that the music was too great to need this kind of exaggeration, but added: 'The English people prefer it this way.' How odd that a Polish conductor should argue with a Hungarian soloist on the interpretation of an ultra-British masterpiece! On the other hand there was no clash with Claudio Arrau, who gave an extraordinarily poetic interpretation of Chopin's Piano Concerto No. 2. It was a privilege to work with Arrau; pure, pleasurable music-making.

My memory of Dennis Matthews's excellent interpretation of Mozart's Piano Concerto No. 27 is somewhat coloured by the succession of extremely funny and scabrous stories he told me on the way to the concert platform. Mozart himself no doubt would have appreciated them; I was still shaking with laughter as I lifted the baton, and I am not sure how this affected the spirituality of the performance. Daniel Barenboim, a slightly chubby *Wunderkind*, looking much younger than his fifteen years, turned up escorted by a rather fierce father, and, with calm professionalism, gave a touching rendering of Mozart's Piano Concerto No. 9. Ralph Holmes, a great talent never properly recognised in his native country, amazed me not only with the glorious musicality of his playing. Seemingly a very shy and sensitive man, he showed great sang-froid when one of his strings snapped at the beginning of the Mendelssohn Violin Concerto; without pause, he turned round, removed the violin from under the chin of the startled Norris Stanley and completed the concerto with the utmost virtuosity.

Halfway through the season, I decided that I could no longer tolerate the banal arrangement of the National Anthem which I was required to conduct at the start of each concert. I therefore asked Anthony Lewis, then a professor at Birmingham University, to produce a fresh version based on the early origins rather than the Victorian distortion of the traditional tune. He prepared two excellent, scholarly restorations for me, one for strings, another for brass. For some reason, Mr Stanley had missed the final rehearsal. As I came on to the platform for the concert, I observed that his nose was even redder than usual. He was obviously not seeing his part too clearly for it seemed that he thought the new arrangement of the National Anthem was my work. In a loud stage whisper quite audible to the audience he hissed, 'Go back to Siberia!'

Stanley was not the only person to object to the innovation. Furious letters appeared in the newspapers, protesting that this 'foreign composer' had distorted the National Anthem. The management committee enjoyed replying that the new arrangement was by Professor Anthony Lewis.

Anthony Lewis was the only musician on the Management Committee. But several of the non-musicians were most encouraging and polite to me, especially the Chairman, Alderman Stephen Lloyd, a distinguished, extremely upright man, married to Neville Chamberlain's daughter Dorothy who was also on the committee. The Lloyds remain my good friends to this day. Others kept themselves apart, judges and jury, intent on extracting maximum value for money. I came to know many of the orchestra's benefactors, including one dear old man who, though he had made millions in the shoe or leather industry, could never have strayed far beyond the confines of his native city. One day, puzzled by my accent, he asked where I was born.

'Warsaw,' I replied.

'Walsall, Walsall, well that's not far away –' he muttered, looking even more confused. Probably for him, a suburb nine miles outside Birmingham was indeed far enough away for foreign accents to be normal.

There was not much to laugh about that first year in Birmingham. Though I made diplomatic overtures to Stanley many times, I realised as my first season drew to a close, that it would never be possible to counter his jingoistic hatred. He was still mobilising members of the orchestra against me, including an unlikely new ally in the first horn player, a member of the British Communist Party and powerful Chairman of the Players' Committee.

Stanley, eventually realising that he had driven me to the

point where either he or I would have to go, built himself a defence dossier, collecting letters of support and praise from various conductors, including Sir Adrian Boult. When I proposed to the Management Committee that he should be dismissed, I was asked, 'If Mr Stanley is good enough for Sir Adrian, why isn't he good enough for you?'

I replied that this question was irrelevant. If he was not replaced by a much better musician I would not continue in my work for another season as my contract required. The Committee dismissed Mr Stanley – giving him generous financial compensation to dry his tears – and I was able to engage a brilliant young Australian violinist, Wilfred Lehmann, as the CBSO's new leader for the coming concert season of 1958-9.

That summer I took a brief, solitary holiday on the French Côte d'Azur, then returned to London to my flat in The Boltons, which I had decided to maintain as a bolthole for composition. It was time to tackle my new commission for the BBC. I hesitated momentarily because Richard Howgill had specifically asked me to compose (for his Light Music Festival) a set of Polish dances to go alongside the much-loved twentieth-century orchestral repertoire of Hungarian and other Eastern European dance music. Although I was longing to write a more serious work, I comforted myself that I would be joining some of my more illustrious predecessors – Bartók, Kodály, Vaughan Williams to name but three – in celebrating the joy of the dance.

It was not easy to start those spirited dances at a time of great loneliness, when my hopes of being able to compose to my fullest ability or capacity seemed even more remote than they had been in the East. For a while I could not start. But then I started to think about Elgar's sombre and noble *Polonia*, a work most evocatively echoing both the heroic and tragic elements of Poland's history. I decided to use the same title but to adopt a completely different approach, so that the two works together might provide a full spectrum of the Polish spirit and colour. Elgar made use of Polish patriotic songs but also took some of Chopin's melodies, ending powerfully with the Polish National Anthem. In contrast I based my new-born *Polonia* on folk melodies and the vigorous, full-blooded rhythms of peasant dances.

The first movement, *Highlanders' March* was based on a melody I had heard in the Tatra Mountains played by a band of three violins and one cello. During the procession, the cello hung from the player's neck, bouncing about on the cushion of his enormous paunch as he struggled to play and march at the same time. The buffeting caused the strings to go exceedingly flat, so I decided to re-create this comedy by composing the double bass part a minor second lower than required for conventional harmony.

The second movement, *Mazurek*, I wrote cantabile, using a much slower tempo than normal for a mazurka, in order to emphasise the lyrical aspects of the dance. Next, in *Krakowiak*, I underlined, sometimes even caricatured, the syncopated rhythms of the Kraków region. *Song of the Vistula* I conceived as a sort of interlude between the dances. Trying to portray the Vistula river as it rises high in Tatra and winds its way right across Poland to the Baltic, I set long melodic sequences against a flowing ostinato background which carried through to the very end, then disappeared gradually like a river being swallowed into the sea. The last movement was based on the *Oberek*, a hectic dance not dissimilar thematically to the slower, more graceful mazurka which also hails from central Poland. In the happier past, the *Oberek* used to be drunkenly and joyously performed as the sun rose after a night of inebriation and revelry.

It was hard to climb back from this nostalgic journey to the new season in Birmingham, although, with the presence of a new leader, I was looking forward to a far happier year. I had not been able to get my way altogether over programming, but I anticipated some considerable pleasures ahead. With my passion for the classical composers, I had been able to include several Mozart works, and, as a special feature, a six-fold series of programmes dedicated to Bach, Beethoven and Brahms. (My general manager, Blyth Major, shaking his head at my lack of sophistication in English, refused to let me call the series 'The Three Bs'.) The Management Committee firmly insisted that this time I should feature a few of my own works, saying in their brochure:

> Andrzej Panufnik . . . is also conducting four works from his own pen, these latter at the express wish and, in fact, instructions of the Management Committee as he himself was most diffident about their inclusion. It was felt that his *Sinfonia Elegiaca* which recently received its first performance in America conducted by Stokowski and was acclaimed by the American musical public, should be a 'must' in Birmingham where we have the composer himself to direct the performance, particularly *Sinfonia Elegiaca* in view of its warm reception in America. (sic)

The presence of four of my own pieces was embarrassing, especially because the selection committee had criticised me for performing too many contemporary works the previous year and had set a severe limitation on the amount of music I could introduce which was not already comfortably familiar to the average concert-goer. I regretted that I was still unable to programme much modern British repertoire, though I was happy to conduct Lennox Berkeley's splendid Symphony No. 2, and we also had a new piece from Anthony Lewis, *Homage to Purcell* (I had to pretend not to hear when the orchestra insisted amongst themselves calling it 'Insult to Purcell').

Amongst my soloists, I was highly delighted to welcome Yehudi Menuhin, whom I had not seen since my trip to Paris just after the war, and I will never forget his inspired interpretation of the Beethoven Violin Concerto, especially in the slow movement.

I also wanted the Committee to invite Szigeti, with whom I had so much enjoyed playing in Belgium. But his name was new to them, and his desire to work with me led him to suggest an absurdly low fee. I was not able to attend the crucial selection committee meeting, but to my chagrin later heard (in a characteristically hilarious send-up from Blyth Major), how a businessman on the Committee, comparing Szigeti's modest request to the other soloists' fees, had decided that Szigeti 'could not be any good', and had insisted that they turn him down.

The friendly cooperation of the orchestra's new leader, Wilfred Lehmann, transformed the atmosphere at rehearsals.

My work with the orchestra now became easier, and much more rewarding artistically. I soon found myself really enjoying our performances of classical music — once we had overcome, by sheer hard work, some bad habits that seemed to have crept in during the post-war period.

I had to take on the rôle of a teacher, encouraging not merely a general sense of style, but fastidiousness over rhythmic precision and dynamic contrast, as well as discernment and taste in musical phrasing, particularly vital in Mozart and Beethoven. Especially with the string players, I worked hard to achieve a singing quality with some human warmth and incisive attack in place of the somewhat weak and 'woolly' sound that had been previously tolerated.

My approach to the classics, strongly influenced by my great Viennese master Felix Weingartner and by performances I had attended under great conductors, above all Wilhelm Furtwängler, must have seemed 'foreign' (in a negative sense) to most players in the CBSO. I went at them relentlessly in rehearsals, with attention even to the smallest details and I realised that they thought me pernickety. However, when it came to the concert, I trusted them to remember all the finer points so that I might turn my full attention to the musical content — the spiritual and poetic elements which lay behind the notes — doing everything in my power to give the performance vitality, while never allowing any of the players to lapse into gliding along on autopilot. I conducted almost all the classical symphonies from memory; not to impress the audience but because knowing the music by heart helped me to get inside it and be part of its magic, and enabled me to use my eyes as well as my hands to control the orchestra.

The Birmingham audience was generally appreciative, especially the younger listeners. There was one complaint that I recall with particular amusement. Having timed a concert with a stop-watch, someone wrote in to object that they had not had their money's worth: we had provided seven minutes less music than usual. It was another object lesson in the Birmingham philosophy of value for money!

As the end of the second concert season was approaching, the Management Committee and most of the the players urged me to prolong my stay. Their request was supported by the general manager, Blyth Major, who painted a picture for me of my great and happy future ahead with the CBSO, culminating in an inevitable knighthood in twenty years' time! But, having hoarded every possible penny of my Birmingham salary for the future, my urge to return to composing was so strong that, much as I now hated leaving them, I could not contemplate reversing my decision.

At the end of the season I was presented with some beautiful farewell presents from the office staff and the orchestra. But what touched me most was a second gift from the players: a sheet of unused manuscript paper with their sincere good wishes for my continuing success as a composer.

After two years in Birmingham, I was at last free to return to London, to my first love, composing. The Management Committee of the CBSO had some difficulty in finding my successor. The press finally announced that the post of Conductor had been taken over for one year by Sir Adrian Boult, aged seventy, from Mr Andrzej Panufnik, aged forty-five, who had retired!

22

AUTUMN MUSIC

Not long after my return to London, I was moved to learn that the loyal and caring Stephen Lloyd had arranged that I should receive the Feeney Trust Commission for the following year, and it was agreed that I could use it to complete the Piano Concerto for which I had made sketches three years previously.

Before I could return fully to composition, I had to fulfil one more conducting date at the Proms. With the BBC Symphony Orchestra, I again shared an evening with Sir Malcolm Sargent, finishing the concert with my *Polonia*.

It was loudly acclaimed, and I was called back to the platform several times, little knowing that it was to be my last appearance at the Promenade concerts for many, many years to come. Though my *Polonia* pleased the orchestra and the public, it evidently did not please the new Music Controller at the BBC – for when I asked to hear the tape afterwards I was told that it had been destroyed.

I still had not fully realised the significance of the retirement of Richard Howgill, nor the full implications for my future of the new régime at the BBC. Longing to fly freely as a composer, I had leapt from the financial security and respected position of Musical Director in Birmingham without noticing that a new fashion was about to grip all the modern music outlets, not only in Britain but throughout the Western world, and that, as an independent Pole with an independent compositional style and a considerable obstinacy about allowing anyone to dictate to him, I would, once more, have to write with little hope of performance for a matter of many years before at last my musical voice could again be allowed to filter through.

Meanwhile I was feeling unusually optimistic about my private as well as my professional life. In the early autumn of 1959, I was introduced to Winsome Ward, a most attractive woman of my own age, with a pale, delicate complexion and light reddish-brown hair. She was a specially English type: as a girl she must have been the ultimate 'English rose'. She had a broad, attractive smile which could illuminate a whole room like a shaft of sunlight. Yet there was a sadness in her eyes, a melancholy that was part of her spell.

She lived in a strikingly original Chelsea studio, decorated with beautiful paintings and sculptures left over from when she had run it as an art gallery some years before. With a tiny bathroom and a cupboard of a kitchen adjoining, it consisted of one huge room with a glass roof, divided asymetrically into four different shapes, one sector a sitting-room with a sofa, another a bedroom with a large couch, the third a dining-room with table and chairs, the fourth an 'office' with a writing desk.

Both of us were lonely. She had lost her fiancé some years ago in a tragic accident, while I was solitary after my divorce. With time, our friendship intensified to love of a kind I had never experienced nor even imagined possible. Within our close relationship we respected one another's independence, she fully understanding my firm determination never to marry again. We always met with the same joy, without any fear of the jealousy, reproaches or demands which, up to that moment, I had thought inevitable in any involvement with a woman. We never made plans for the future, spontaneously enjoying our moments together and looking forward to seeing one another again whenever it was mutually convenient. In retrospect I realise that she was being exceptionally generous in giving me her friendship and her love without expecting any commitment or matrimonial promises in return. The haven of content and calmness which she brought into my life at last seemed to be leading me into the peace of mind that I needed for my work.

Still not feeling ready to tackle a major work such as a piano concerto in that beautiful autumn of 1959, as the leaves changed colour, I began in the happiest frame of mind to compose my *Autumn Music*, intending quite simply to give poetic expression to the season. I could not tell that, after we had drifted from glowing autumn into the darkness of winter, another more sombre theme was destined to invade our lives and my music.

When I was quite well advanced on my new work, I was interrupted with an invitation to conduct a charity concert at the Royal Festival Hall with a rather curious two-fold dedication: simultaneously in aid of World Refugee Year and a commemoration of the 150th Anniversary of Chopin's birth! As a refugee and a Pole, I could hardly have refused.

The soloist was to be Fou Ts'ong, whom I remembered well from Poland. Shortly after he arrived from China to complete his studies in Warsaw, he had come to ask my opinion about the interpretation of Chopin. I had been impressed by his sensitive playing and unusual feeling for the spirit of Chopin's music, so I greatly looked forward to working with him on the two Chopin piano concertos, both of which he was to perform on this unusual occasion.

Unlike most conductors who, with some justice, grumble that Chopin did not know how to write for orchestra, I love these two concertos, and will always gladly direct an appropriately modest accompaniment to such inspiringly conceived writing for piano. Another complaint of conductors is the inclination of pianists to over-romanticise these concertos by indecent excesses of rubato playing. (I remember telling Fou Ts'ong the experience of a conductor friend of mine working with a famous pianist, who, rehearsing on the day of their concert, indulged in frequent and unpredictable changes of tempo. The poor conductor became quite frantic trying to keep the orchestra within the same bar as the soloist, to prevent the whole performance from falling apart. After the rehearsal, seeing my unlucky friend tearing his hair and making quick marks in his score to remind himself of the details of this erratic interpretation, the soloist practically gave my friend a heart attack by saying, 'Please don't worry. Tonight will be *completely* different!').

There was no such danger with Fou Ts'ong. His good taste and musical discipline were exemplary and the concert went just as we would have wished.

With Chopin's music still in my head, I returned to my *Autumn Music*, not realising that I would be prevented from finishing it as quickly as I had imagined by two unforeseen events; one of them a worrying call from Winsome saying that she had to go into hospital for some tests.

Before the full implications of the tests were clear, I unexpectedly received a cabled summons to conduct three concerts in Buenos Aires. In a typically South American manner, this invitation was not for a year or two years ahead but in just a matter of weeks. I was asked to include works by Argentinian composers and some of my own music. It was an exciting invitation from the musical point of view, as well as a chance to see a part of the world which was new to me. Since my Birmingham savings were not going to last as long as I had hoped, it was financially imperative that I again interrupt my newfound freedom to compose.

I enjoyed every minute of my stay in Buenos Aires, not just for the warmth and friendly hospitality of the people there, but because I was intrigued by the Latin character of the city, which gave an impression of being built by the French, and inhabited by Italians who spoke Spanish. Unlike London, concerts were still a special event for which people dressed up, anticipating each one with considerable excitement. With only one orchestral performance a week, unlike London, I had plenty of rehearsals. The orchestra combined high standards with an enthusiastic response both to my compositions and my conducting, and I reciprocated their warmth. I did not notice in the intensity of rehearsing that I spoke several languages in rapid succession: my record apparently was five in one sentence, since there were Argentinians of Polish, French, Spanish, Italian and English origin and I was in a hurry to be understood. I carried away the happiest memories, marvellous press reviews and the pleas of the orchestra to stay on with them for ever!

I returned from a wintry June in Buenos Aires to a warm and sunny London, feeling cheerful and confident of my musical abilities. But Winsome was still in hospital, looking alarmingly pale and much thinner than when I went away. Her sister told me in confidence that the doctors had diagnosed advanced cancer.

It was a horrifying blow. I returned to my *Autumn Music*, its theme of seasonal decline now cruelly apt alongside my heart-broken consciousness of a most precious human life in a different sort of decline — which would not be renewed by the coming of another spring.

Beside my almost demented grief for Winsome herself, I could not thrust away the notion that I was doomed never to experience the warmth and calm of a permanent relationship and love.

At this point though, which was one of the darkest of my life, developments quite unknown to me were afoot, which before long would transform my whole existence.

During my first, tempestuous season with the City of Birmingham Symphony Orchestra, I was unaware of the existence of an English girl of twenty who, almost without money, was working her way alone around America, determined, after a comfortable childhood, to see the world and prove that she could look after herself. She worked as a temporary secretary in New York, Princeton, Washington, New Orleans and then Dallas, eventually reaching California. San Francisco proved very much to her taste, and she settled for a while into an unusual and challenging post as executive secretary to the telephone workers' union (the Communication Workers of America) her twenty-sixth job in her sixth city. She did not intend to stay in America for ever, but was in no hurry to move on. Her parents, however, were desperate to persuade her to come home, and offered all manner of temptations, to no avail.

Then one evening she was taken to see *A Midsummer Night's Dream*. Hearing her beloved Shakespeare in a Californian drawl suddenly made her yearn to experience it again in the pure English rhythm. By coincidence a letter arrived from her mother the very next day, mentioning that they had tickets for *Othello* at Stratford-on-Avon in eight weeks' time. It was irresistible. She decided to go home. Without Shakespeare's help,

we never would have met. However, many coincidences had to
occur before we finally came face to face.

Camilla's parents, waiting at the Southampton dockside,
were momentarily shattered as she greeted them from the deck
with a tiny baby in her arms, which she had borrowed from
fellow-passengers as a joke to shock them. Though their reunion was extremely happy, she soon became bored in an
Oxfordshire village after the pace of her life in San Francisco.
Fate interceded again with the announcement of a general elec-
tion. She volunteered, and, because of her secretarial skills, was
made personal assistant to the candidate, Neil Marten, the
Foreign Office man who had looked after my defection. He
and his wife Joan had become close friends of mine. Another
strand of destiny was tugging us — very slowly — towards each
other.

After Neil was elected to Parliament, Camilla went off to
work for Oxfam and the Committee for Algerian Refugees on
the Morocco-Algerian border. Months later, home again in
England, she heard about me from the Martens who were
worrying about my excessively low spirits. Since Camilla
adored music and had many friends in the musical world, they
asked her to make contact with me and try to arrange some
introductions and performances.

The first I knew of this was on a beautiful day in the late
summer of 1960, when I received a telephone call from an unknown girl, who explained that she had been asked by Neil
Marten to contact me. Though somewhat sceptical about the
ability of such a young-sounding person being able to help me
in my dire professional straits, I was intrigued and charmed by
her sensitive approach and by her warm, quiet personality
which I sensed even over the telephone. I suggested that she
should visit me that very day at my flat in The Boltons.

When I saw her standing at my door, not only was my
impression from our telephone conversation confirmed — I was
completely conquered by her beauty, unique charm and sense of
inner calm which was combined with a strong aura of spirituality I found most surprising in a girl of her age. She was not
much more than twenty. Her figure was slender, even fragile,

but very shapely in the pleated tartan skirt and simple dark shirt that she wore with a typically English string of pearls round her neck. She had short, dark hair, a small nose and intriguingly arched eyebrows. Her eyes seemed to change colour with the light and the expression on her face altered constantly.

The purpose of her visit, she told me, was to interview me and find out my plans before arranging introductions to musician friends. As she sat on the floor, listening quietly to everything I said, I found myself more and more intrigued by her, and stopped talking about my problems in order to ask her questions. She was far less conventional than she looked. The daughter of a retired naval commander, she was quite a rebel, having taken very little notice of her education and systematically broken every rule at a conventional girls' public school. When she was sixteen, her father was seconded to teach higher strategy to young officers of the Indian Navy just after their Independence. Though Camilla had a scholarship and should have gone on to university, he took her with him, saying that he did not like 'blue-stocking' women, and that living in an Indian community for an extended period would be a far better education than finishing her ordinary studies. She adored India and her Indian friends, and, for a while afterwards, she contentedly pursued her father's theories on education, travelling round America before dashing off to Morocco, where she witnessed terrible deprivation and famine which made her determined to dedicate her future work to children in need. In North Africa she had become frustrated by her lack of fluent French; she decided to live in Paris for a year and make some amends for her missing education by studying French literature at the Sorbonne.

She remained sitting at my feet for more than three hours as we in turn talked about our lives. Afterwards I wished that I had asked her to stay longer. As she was about to leave for France, and I had already bought a ticket to try to redeem my fortunes in the United States, it seemed as if we had met for the first and last time.

I had decided only a few days before Camilla's visit to make another trip to New York, hoping that this time I might be more successful and return with a commission for a new piece of music, or at least some conducting engagements. I even considered the possibility of settling in America, as its musical life seemed more dynamic and adventurous than Britain's. I had become discouraged living in England by the general sameness and 'safeness' of concert programmes, and the falling artistic standards of the orchestras, partly due to their constant economic difficulties.

I had also become depressed by the radical change that had taken place in the contemporary music policy of the BBC. The new Controller, William Glock, with his articulate and persuasive Viennese friend, Hans Keller, were now almost exclusively promoting the 'Second Viennese School', Schoenberg, Webern and Berg and their new generation of followers, allowing only a few exceptions, mostly senior non-dodecaphonic British composers (combined rather oddly with Gershwin). Obviously I was by no means the only composer to fail to fit into this new mould. Many of my British colleagues of independent enough nature to withstand the trend towards dodecaphony were also experiencing crushing rebuttals from the Selection Committee of the BBC Music Department. It was admirable that more radio time was to be given to contemporary music. However, I had always been in favour of *all* schools of thought being allowed to be heard. I remain fanatically against fanatics, whether in the arts or in politics.

So I set out to explore musical possibilities across the Atlantic. I had enough money for my fare to America because, by good fortune, my landlord at The Boltons wanted to sell his whole house and bought back the last two years of my lease. I had no regrets about abandoning my unhappy London home. After another protracted bout of discussions trying to obtain a visa from the hostile American consulate, I left my few possessions in the care of friends, and enjoyed a storm-tossed crossing on the *Queen Elizabeth* to New York.

On my arrival I telephoned Leopold Stokowski, the only friendly soul that I knew in the city. In his gentle voice he invited me next day to lunch at his home, which was a tree-top-level flat with a beautiful view over Central Park. He greeted me warmly and immediately led me to the table, where he was busy over a huge wooden bowl putting the finishing touches to the mixed salad he had made for me himself. Sprinkling a few chopped walnuts over it, he declared that I should always eat this kind of food for lunch if I wanted a long and healthy life.

Turning from culinary delights to orchestral, Stokowski remarked that it was high time that I was invited to conduct one of the top American orchestras. I asked his advice about agents, but he deplored them all. His own affairs were handled by Wendy Hanson, his very attractive English personal assistant whom I had met just before lunch. Wanting to help me, Leopold most generously undertook to write some letters on my behalf. I saw Wendy send off these catalogues of praise about me to at least a dozen managers of leading American orchestras. But in spite of Stokowski's eminence, not a single one of these letters was answered. At first it seemed like apathy and bad manners, but, after I had been in America a while, I started to wonder. Perhaps this lack of reaction *was* an answer? In the musical world, the fashion for everything Russian was apparent, with the names of Soviet artists topping a large proportion of the concert programmes. Perhaps as an anti-Communist Pole I was actually an embarrassment? The US Government policy at the end of the '50s was to 'build bridges' with the Soviet Union. Hearing people talking politics at social gatherings, I was struck by a complete indifference to the fate of Moscow's satellite countries. Many Americans I met seemed to regard the division of this planet between the USA and the Soviet Union as a logical conclusion to World War Two, and it seemed quite acceptable to them that geographically Poland had fallen for ever into Russian territory.

I found this political climate profoundly depressing, especially as I thought about my fellow countrymen back in Poland with their great faith in America's professed dedication to justice, liberty and full democracy; and the persistent hope of the Poles that the greatest power in the Western world would one day come to their aid and free them from the Soviets, or at least give them some moral support in their pursuit of independence and freedom under the shared banner of Western civilisation. This passionate longing of my countrymen was obviously not understood by Americans, who did not seem to me to have any concept that Polish people had a need for democracy as great as theirs.

Perhaps it was my wish to do something positive about this situation that led me to an idea for a new symphony. Poland's Millennium Year, 1966, was fast approaching: I would compose a work which, through its emotional impact, would forcefully remind the Western world, especially the Russophile Americans, of Poland's thousand years of history as a country with its own rich culture and identity deeply rooted in the Christian tradition.

Unfortunately if I were just to sit down and write the symphony without any sponsorship I would probably starve before it was finished. After a few enquiries, I found my way to the Kościuszko Foundation, a Polish-American organisation which had no ties with the Government of People's Poland. The President of the Foundation, Professor Stephen Mizwa, was a remarkable doughty character of peasant stock who had arrived in the States totally penniless as a very young boy. Thanks to his intelligence and determination, he had risen through American academic life to create this prestigious institution, whose purpose was to bypass politics and cultivate closer intellectual and cultural relations between Poles and Polish-Americans, mainly through academic exchanges on both professorial and student levels.

By constantly reminding (some say by bullying!) rich Polish Americans to endow the Foundation in their wills, Professor Mizwa had collected a huge amount of money for his cause; enough, after the war, to obtain an impressive mansion off Fifth Avenue, convert part of it as a lecture studio and art gallery, and to decorate it with magnificent pictures by Polish artists. When I visited him one morning, Professor Mizwa showed me round his creation with tremendous pride, but, when I mentioned my desire for sponsorship, he became noticeably less expansive. It was torture for me to overcome my reticence, not to feel humiliated in having to ask for money, but being stateless and having no agent to speak for me, I had no choice but to persevere. After all, his declared purpose was to encourage Polish culture.

I outlined my plan for a 'Millennium' symphony, based on the first hymn in the Polish language, the *Bogurodzica* – the inspiring Gregorian chant which the Polish knights used to sing on the battlefields. The Professor quickly saw that my idea could bring credit to his Foundation. Almost before I could finish outlining my musical ideas, he was starting to plan a prestigious première, to which leading figures in the American cultural, artistic and political firmaments, even the President himself, could be invited. He warned me that he would have first to win approval from the board of trustees before any commission or fellowship could be confirmed – but I left America with some hope at least.

I arrived back in England just after the Christmas of 1960. Since I had sold my lease, I was homeless and had nowhere to work – a situation from which I was rescued by the faithful Martens. They arranged that I should rent a room from friends who lived near their home in an old grey stone farmhouse in the small Oxfordshire village of Adderbury.

I travelled to London every few days to see Winsome, my heart nearly cracking to watch her wasting away. I could not make myself think about my new symphony. I plunged fervently back into my *Autumn Music*, which was taking on more and more of a dirge-like character, reflecting my sense of doom: I composed the whole central section of the work against an ostinato pattern on the piano, a single repeated note in the lowest register. This sombre, deep note, regular as a striking clock, seemed to suggest in my imagination the ruthless passing of time, the cruel foreshortening of a human life, and, at the same time, the relentless progression of nature in autumn, the season of decline.

Before long I heard from Professor Mizwa that the Trustees had approved my fellowship. I was sent an agreement form, offering me a sum of money to be paid in ten monthly instalments: but, in signing, I was expected to agree not only to their suggestions over the title of the symphony but to defer to their instructions over the style, and even the content of the music I was to write! I suddenly felt as if I were back in Poland with another Sokorski breathing down my neck as I read with amazement:

> It is mutually understood that the proposed symphony will be based on Polish musical tradition, revealing the spirit of historical Poland rather than be an experiment in contemporary medium, and will contain accents of Polish religious or patriotic elements, preferably the latter — such as *Bogurodzica, Boże Coś Polskę, Rota Konopnickiej* or the Polish National Anthem — but that it will be a solid piece of work and not a medley . . .'

I was also sent some anonymous comments by a trustee from Miami which momentarily left me gasping:

> I think . . . that the proposed name, *Sinfonia Sacra*, has undesirable overtones, certainly if it is to commemorate Poland's Millennium. With that name as a sort of *Leitmotif* the composer is apt to go off on a tangent and create something that might be more aptly called *Sinfonia Catolica* or *Vaticana*. Do we want that sort of thing? That sort of music can be an awful bore as consider, for instance, Bloch's *Jewish Symphonies* based on Jewish sacred music. . . .
>
> The music should be dramatic enough to stir the hearts of men and not merely lull them to sleep with otherworldliness. Not knowing the composer makes it difficult to predict what will come of this assignment. Good modern symphonies are exceedingly rare; most of them are of the 'once-played' variety. I hope this one will be an exception to that rule.

As I read these instructions and comments, I began to notice a familiar sensation of utter defiance creeping over me. Controlling my anger, I wrote back diplomatically to Professor Mizwa agreeing to wait as they requested over finally deciding the title, but reserving my 'full rights and freedom in the choice of musical language and all artistic mediums'. I expressed my understanding that they required 'a work of international significance and of lasting value' — which was precisely what I hoped to write anyway. And I asked him to wait to announce the commission until I was well advanced in my work.

Professor Mizwa understood my anxiety at finding myself in a situation where the style of my work could again be 'dictated' to me, as it had been in Poland. He wrote back a reasonable and reassuring letter.

It was by then February of 1961. I was in for a shock. I received a letter from Stephen Lloyd, asking how my Piano Concerto was progressing, and requesting me to contact the Manager of the CBSO to fix the date of the première! I was overwhelmed with embarrassment. I had spent all my time absorbed in *Autumn Music* which had become an expression of my despair about Winsome. My inability to help her against her inexorable mortal disease had pushed everything else from my mind except the music I was writing for her. When *Autumn Music* was completed, trying to keep myself sane and think positively, I then had been so carried away by my future plans to bring Poland's plight to public consciousness through my Millennium symphony that my commitment to the Piano Concerto had gone quite out of my mind. Now I was in a frightening predicament, owing not only colossal debts of gratitude but even more colossal quantities of hefty orchestral music to the two Stephens on either side of the Atlantic.

Since there was no question of letting Stephen Lloyd down or postponing the Birmingham première, I rashly fixed the date for January 1962, leaving myself merely a few months in which to write not only the full score but also a piano reduction from which the soloist was to work.

While I was battling away with some excitement as well as urgency I received a nudge from Professor Mizwa: 'Now half a year is over . . . how are you getting along and what results are you accomplishing . . .?' I did not want to tell him that I had not written a note of his symphony, since it would be discouraging after all his kind help in obtaining the commission. Yet his impatience was unreasonable: I had not the slightest intention of letting him down. Meanwhile, to my shame, I fobbed him off with a white lie, comforting myself that many a composer before me had protected himself similarly from importunate prince or patron. To salve my conscience slightly, I made some slight sketches for the symphony, but emergencies had to come first, with a première rocketing towards me and publishers muttering about having the score in time to write the orchestral parts.

I was unaware all this time that Camilla's parents also lived in the village of Adderbury and were close friends of my host. The Fates, perhaps perceiving I had experienced almost more grief than a man can survive, were still struggling away to bring us together, but not effectively as yet. I had by no means forgotten the dark-haired, rather mysterious girl, but I had no idea, as my frequent long lonely promenades took me past a mellow sixteenth-century manor house, that I was walking right by her home. Anyway she was still in Paris, and I, when momentarily lifting my head from my concerto, thought only of my poor Winsome.

The farmhouse at Adderbury did not turn out to be an ideal setting for the intensity of work required, especially since the piano in the living room was often unavailable – a fairly harrowing disadvantage while composing a piano concerto. All the same I finished the concerto just about in time, and had to turn to my new symphony before the ink was even dry. I decided I must find somewhere more isolated for my work, and was lucky enough to rent cheaply a small secluded cottage just outside Dockenfield, a tiny Surrey village near Farnham. It had a magnificent open view of fields and woods.

Sinfonia Sacra was on the writing desk as soon as I had moved in – my first priority. I engaged all my willpower to make some progress with it – but a great deal of my time and attention was taken up with visiting Winsome.

Just before Christmas 1961, the papers for my British citizenship came through the letter-box, including a form which had to be signed by an established pillar-of-society who knew me well, such as a doctor or MP. Neil Marten was the obvious choice. He invited me to bring the papers and have tea with him at the House of Commons. By coincidence, Camilla Jessel was there too. Back from Paris, though still working freelance as a secretary, she was trying to establish herself as a photographer, and the helpful Neil used to invite her along to immortalise, on the steps of Westminster, visiting worthies from his Banbury constituency, for publication in their local paper. The three of us had tea together, during which Neil, guessing how I neglected my professional affairs, suggested that Camilla should look after my secretarial work.

At this point our conversation was interrupted by a division bell, and Neil had to rush off to vote. Camilla and I went on exchanging our news, admitting that we had both quite often thought about each other since we had last met. I told her of my anguish over my beloved Winsome, about my problems with the BBC, and, more cheeringly, of my new rustic home in Surrey. She told me of her photographic work for the Save the Children Fund, and her efforts at writing. By the time Neil rejoined us Camilla had agreed (without much difficulty I think) to tackle my correspondence. As I had to take the train back to Dockenfield, she offered me a lift to the station. She said her car was outside.

It was still there – in spite of being illegally parked right opposite Parliament – but when she pushed the starter button, the motor coughed coldly: the petrol tank was empty. (I could not guess that this would be only the first of innumerable times I would be landed in this situation by my absent-minded Camilla.)

Chaotic as she might have been about her treatment of her bolt-upright little car with its souped-up engine, she was extremely efficient with my correspondence. In no time at all she had dealt with an enormous pile of unanswered mail. Gently she rebuked me for drifting into pessimism about my prospects when I had left unacknowledged an invitation to conduct my music on a German radio station, a request about a commission, and various other useful approaches. I had failed to answer these letters not only because of my inborn aversion to writing but also because I had nobody to help me with my English grammar, or my spelling (which reduced Camilla from time to time to helpless laughter). Deftly, she mended old bridges and built new ones -- her diplomatic skills were invaluable to me. However, my intuition told me nothing about her future rôle in my life: uppermost in my mind at this time was my all-consuming despair as Winsome slipped away from me.

In the midst of these devastating last weeks of Winsome's life, I had to go to Birmingham to conduct the world première of my Piano Concerto, which I had faithfully dedicated to Rosa Berenbau, who had helped me out of my financial difficulties some years before. Unfortunately Małcużyński, as I had guessed, had been unable to find time to study the work, though I was privileged to have in his place a superb, much under-estimated British pianist, Kendall Taylor. The critics were generally enthusiastic about the concerto, but as usual I was tormented by my perfectionism, and knew, in my heart of hearts, that at some point I must come back to this work and improve on it.

We gave a second performance of the whole concert in Cheltenham, and were booked to record the programme in Birmingham for the BBC. However, when I arrived for the session to record the concerto, there was no piano. Eventually one was trundled in, and, although the delay had cost us much valuable time, we managed to get a satisfactory recording of the concerto. But for reasons known only to the BBC it was never broadcast; eventually I was told that the tape had been 'lost'.

I returned to Dockenfield, trying to concentrate on my *Sinfonia Sacra*, frequently visiting St Thomas's Hospital. All too soon a telephone call from the hospital brought me the news I had been dreading: Winsome was dead. As her family showed no sign of taking further action, I went to London to arrange the funeral, choosing a place for her at the Gunners-bury Cemetery. I had the first few notes of my *Autumn Music* (which I had dedicated to her memory) engraved onto a beauti-ful headstone, and arranged for a funeral service to be held at St Luke's Church in Chelsea, near where she lived. The fine Oromonte String Trio played Beethoven and Mozart during the service. As I listened bleakly to the notes reverberating around the cold stones of the church, I realised that the curtains had closed on another chapter of my life.

23

TO WED OR NOT TO WED

In the peaceful surroundings of my Dockenfield cottage, *Sinfonia Sacra* was making steady progress. Meanwhile I evolved an excellent system of working with Camilla. She would drive down to Dockenfield for a day and prepare a tasty lunch for us (she was already a promising cook). Then we would go for a long walk through the pine forest behind my house, after which the serious work would begin: I would take a block of my headed writing paper, scrawl my signature at various levels on the page and hand the signed blanks over to Camilla, plus any letters that needed answering. She would stay on to cook supper, eventually returning to London. Thereafter, whenever I needed a letter written I would telephone her, and she would type in whatever was required above my signature and post it off without my ever having to bother with detail.

In the summer of 1962, I stopped seeing Camilla. It was a hard decision, but after my unhappy marriage and my very recent, sad involvement I was determined to steer clear of any serious relationship. I had mentioned to her many times my intention never to marry again, and she had nodded quietly and understandingly. However, not only was my attachment to her growing apace, but she, despite her heroic attempts to avoid impinging on my independence, was bad at hiding her feelings. Her eyes spoke emotion that she would never have voiced. I decided it was unfair to allow such a young person to become remotely dependent for happiness on me, and I attempted to end our affair.

But it was too late – for both of us. We needed each other.

Soon we were spending more and more time together, though we both had to be strong-willed not to allow our longing to be together to interfere with the symphony.

Time was flying very fast, and it was clear by November that I would have to accelerate my efforts on my *Sinfonia Sacra*. I urgently needed those magical American dollars! As the weather deteriorated, I remembered the iciness of the previous winter in my uninsulated, underheated cottage. I suddenly resolved to take off for southern Spain and work full-tilt on the symphony, to have it ready as promised by March.

When I told Camilla my plan she looked at me as if I were a murderer, and promptly arranged to set out in the New Year on a courageous lone photographic mission for the Save the Children Fund in East Africa.

Though it was painful parting from Camilla, I soon felt myself lucky to be in sunny Spain, especially as I turned out to be missing the hardest winter in living memory — apparently my Dockenfield cottage was buried under the snow. I found myself a shabby, virtually empty hotel in the village of Calpe, beneath an extraordinary vast, phallic rock with sea on three sides. The hotel was fortunately empty for the whole winter, and even more fortunately, it had a separate annex with a tin-can, out-of-tune, upright piano, where I could work all day without interruption.

I was not strong-willed for more than two weeks: I telephoned Camilla in London and asked her to join me before leaving for Africa, for Christmas and New Year. To my great joy, she arrived almost instantly, looking so pale and fragile that I feared for her setting off on her arduous solo journey through Africa. *Sinfonia Sacra* was cast aside while we explored the curious Spanish landscape together and attended Midnight Mass on Christmas Eve at a tiny chapel in the hills.

After Camilla left I returned to my symphony with renewed energy, and my work progressed at speed. But I worried about her as she travelled alone, at first through the wild country of Somalia, photographing polio victims, children of nomadic families who had been left behind because of their sickness to die in the desert and who had been rescued by the Save the Children Fund. From Somalia she went on to Kenya, where she was working in child care centres, then on to famine areas and leper colonies in remote corners of Uganda.

Every day I walked two or three miles to the post office in hope of finding letters from her. My constant visits and anxiety were noticed by the sympathetic young post office clerk, whose name I was enchanted to discover was Jesus. When I arrived he would leave his post and join me for a coffee, telling me in his broken English about his own sweetheart.

My work went so well that *Sinfonia Sacra* was almost finished by early March (1963). So I felt free to write and ask Camilla if she could switch her air ticket, and return from her African mission via Madrid.

We had a wonderful few days together, spending a great deal of time at the Prado Museum gazing at the Goyas when we were not gazing at each other.

Then we flew on to Paris to meet a close friend of mine who had managed to get out of Poland for a short time. I was eager to have recent and accurate news from him of life in Poland and our mutual friends there. He told me that I was still black-listed and that my name was totally censored from books, periodicals and newspapers. I had officially ceased to exist. For my friends, he told me over a *café filtre*, it felt as if I had died.

After a few days Camilla had to fly back to London with her photographs, which the Save the Children Fund wanted urgently to tie in with their publicity for World Hunger Week. When her plane landed at Heathrow she was still weeping, she told me, at having left me behind in Paris. She was amazed to discover that her publicity-minded employers had organised a press reception to greet their glamorous young photographer. She had a tricky moment avoiding any explanation to the waiting pressmen why, returning from her intrepid trip through Africa, she was stepping off a plane from Paris with her eyes streaming with tears.

I knew now that I was likely to break my resolution and ask Camilla to marry me. I was not really worried about her answer, but I was profoundly worried about something else; that the remaining fee for *Sinfonia Sacra* would only just pay off my debts. I was, as the Poles say, naked as a Turkish saint; contemplating marriage on an empty pocket. I had no further commissions in view and no conducting engagements either. I felt it was impossible to enter the married state in these circumstances, even though Camilla was working and was plainly undeterred by my financial disabilities. However, Polish pride and some sense of responsibility prevented me from being led astray by her comforting reminders of how many composers, even my revered Mozart, had been in constant financial trouble. I went away as far as I could manage, accepting free accommodation from a French aristocrat who lent rooms in her château to indigent artists.

It was no use: I could not compose at all. I was waiting, just in case a miracle could save us. Fortunately sometimes miracles do happen.

While in Paris, I had heard about a competition run by the Principality of Monaco, offering a substantial prize for the best orchestral work, to be chosen by a highly distinguished international jury of composers. Much as I hated competitions, my need for money was so imperative that I decided to risk entering; at least the compositions were submitted anonymously, so no one would know if *Sinfonia Sacra* were to fail.

The weeks of waiting seemed like years. I felt as if my whole future depended on this judgement, not just for a good financial outcome; professionally at my lowest ebb, I also needed the approval of that eminent international jury to tell me that it was worth carrying on composing despite my entrenched and lonely position in the musical world.

I grew more and more pessimistic. (Camilla, not being allowed to know what was going on in my mind, became so desperate to see me that she posted me express a cashmere sweater to 'warm my cold heart'.) Then suddenly I received the joyful news that my symphony had been awarded first prize, chosen out of 133 entries from 38 different countries. With the announcement came an urgent summons to Monaco to receive the prize in person from Prince Rainier.

I telephoned Camilla to come and join me. This time she was less quick to rush to my side. With cool professionalism, she decided to make sure that my publishers were aware of my success, and to work with their publicity department to spread the news that I had won first prize for Great Britain. Then, very quickly, she and her small, prim, blue car made their way south for a rapturous reunion.

Though the money from Monaco was hardly enough to keep us for years, it paid for a blissful month together in a primitive hotel at Pramousquier on the coast of the Alpes-Maritimes. We wrote off proudly to Professor Mizwa telling him that his symphony had already won an award, and with considerable magnanimity, he forgave the fact that the world première would have to take place in Monaco.

It was midsummer, and time, I felt, to return to England. I settled into another dreary cottage, also near Farnham, but not with any sense of permanence. Camilla and I knew that we were going to get married.

I had not quite found the courage to commit myself in words. But one day, about a month after my return, we were driving through Richmond Park, and we stopped for a moment under a magnificent oak. Suddenly, perhaps under some mysterious influence emanating from the tree, I said quite formally, 'Will you marry me?'

Without hesitation, Camilla said 'Yes.' While we were sealing our pledge with a more-than-traditional kiss, we were brought back to earth by a distortedly loud voice angrily shouting 'Move on! Move on!' Turning our heads, we saw a police car, the driver not only assailing us through his loudspeaker, but gesticulating furiously to indicate that we had stopped illegally in the middle of the park. We laughed and laughed as we resumed our journey.

Soon afterwards, Camilla took me to visit her parents at their home in Adderbury, the village where I had spent those lonely months only two years previously. I immediately recognised the house I had passed so many times on my dismal walks, an unpretentious but rambling house of golden Cotswold stone surrounded by a well-tended flowery garden. Inside, the old English furniture glowed with constant polishing and the walls and windows were decorated in modest but perfect taste. It was a warm, welcoming atmosphere.

I had suffered a certain amount of nervous anticipation at the thought of encountering Camilla's father, Dick Jessel, a war hero who had won many medals commanding destroyers in the

Mediterranean and Atlantic. A typically brave action involved taking his destroyer by night into a Norwegian fjord at the height of the German Occupation to rescue a group of cornered Resistance fighters. He was descended from a distinguished family of lawyers, including the famous nineteenth-century Sir George Jessel, who made legal history as the only Master of the Rolls even to this day never to have had a judgement reversed. My future father-in-law was not musical: he was tone deaf, Camilla had warned me, hardly able to recognise Mozart from the Beatles. What was he going to think of a penniless composer from a foreign country, twenty-three years older than his adored youngest daughter?

With his smile-creases round his twinkling eyes, and his broad, friendly smile, he certainly did not appear too terrifying, so I immediately put to him my formal request: 'Please may I have your daughter's hand in marriage?' He looked absolutely amazed, replying, 'Is that all you want?'

Camilla's quiet, gentle mother, Winnie, with her fair hair and still beautiful skin and elegant clothes, I had met once before, when she came with Camilla to hear my Piano Concerto in Cheltenham. In many ways she reminded me of my own mother. She was deeply musical, and enjoyed singing in an amateur chorus. At first she was rather shy, though extremely kind and concerned that everything should be just right for me. I was given an enthusiastic welcome into the family.

I suppose that, having wound down to the lowest depth of the vortex after Birmingham, either I would have had to disappear totally under the stormy waters, or, by the law of perpetual motion, I was bound gradually to start to spiral up again. The surge upwards now seemed constant: another miracle came our way. As we racked our brains about where we should live, Winnie remembered a beautiful town house which had been willed the previous year to the people of Twickenham by Camilla's philanthropic grandmother. Though the land and the historic building next door were to be used by the public, the will had stated that the house should be used as a private dwelling place. A rapid telephone call established that the council had just decided to let the house on a long lease; that they had particularly wanted a member of the family to move in, but since none had come forward, they were about to advertise. We were in time by just a week. The Town Clerk, who had had great respect for Camilla's remarkable grand-mother, was eager to make things easy for us, pronouncing in his witty, ironic manner that I was also a particularly suitable tenant, having been a 'council employee' in Birmingham. Winnie and Dick decided that they would like to buy us the lease as a wedding present, and we found ourselves as Council tenants, at a peppercorn rent of £200 a year, of a glorious Georgian house overlooking the Thames. Its numerous damp shabby rooms, without curtains or furniture, needed an alarming amount of repair and refurbishment. Yet even in its neglected, empty state, the house had a friendly atmosphere, as if Camilla's grandmother was welcoming us in.

We wanted to get married the next day, but my seemingly diffident future mother-in-law insisted on doing things properly and said she needed a couple of months to organise the wed-ding. On 27 November 1963 we were married at Caxton Hall, the drab registry office made unusually resplendent by Winnie with a mass of white flowers. Camilla and I were festively garbed too: she wore a long white dress and I wore my conductor's morning suit, but without a top hat as this had never been required on the podium and I saw no sense in ob-taining one specially. Just before the ceremony, I panicked for a moment, recalling my vow never to marry again, and dear Dick, noticing the disturbed state I was in during my last few minutes of freedom before signing a life contract, consoled me in his quiet, reassuring voice, 'Don't worry, everything will be all right!' The ceremony itself, very simple and to the point, I found deeply moving. Camilla could hardly speak the crucial words; she just stood there, her eyes shining. Afterwards Winnie had arranged a magnificent reception, not only for friends: suddenly, after years of having no family of my own, I found myself part of a vast clan as Camilla introduced me to yet another aunt, a dozen more cousins, fifty-three second cousins, umpteen uncles, swarms of nephews and nieces, all enthusiastically clamouring to make the acquaintance of their new relative.

The moment came for us to cut the wedding cake, a huge

ornamental structure which looked to me alarmingly like the Palace of Culture in Warsaw. We seized the knife together and tried to perform the ritual of plunging it in. But our efforts were in vain: the blade of the knife wobbled, bent and almost broke, but made not the slightest impression on Stalin's architectural gem. We heard around us whispers, giggles and a hiss of tension as if this might be a terrible omen. Then we realised that the central section of the cake which we were attacking was in fact a hidden wooden platform beneath the icing, there to take the weight of the higher tiers. Triumphantly we attacked the outside edge of the Palace. It fell to our sword amidst laughter and applause.

Soon we escaped from the sisters, the cousins and the aunts, friendly and enthusiastic as they were, and were rushed off to London airport, for our planned four-day honeymoon in Dublin, but a blanket of November fog forced us to spend the first night of our marriage at an airport hotel. The manager, somehow hearing of our situation, sent up a bottle of champagne. I drew the cork immediately and we drank a toast, not to ourselves, since we knew that our marriage would be a complete success – but to Shakespeare, who had made it possible.

24

NEW HOME, NEW FAMILY, NEW MUSIC

Our honeymoon was hasty, not for lack of romance, but because we were both longing to start our new life in our new home. It mattered not a jot to us that we would be camping for months in a tiny, damp cottage in the grounds, while Camilla struggled with roof repairers, builders and acres of sticky wallpaper.

Her first priority was the conversion of the old stable and carriage house at the end of the garden into a warm, pine-panelled studio for my use. Meanwhile, as I had an urgent commission for a choral piece, I was able to work just along the river in St Mary's, a beautiful small eighteenth-century parish church with an eleventh-century tower, the burial place of the great poet, Alexander Pope. (Our corner of Twickenham was potent with its history of interesting inhabitants.)

Though only twenty minutes by car from central London, our surroundings were almost rural, with trees and greenery running down to the River Thames. When the moon was full and the tides high, the river would rise above its borders and fill the little lane past our house, surging up our drive, often preventing us from leaving. (Sometimes it made us embarrassingly late for crucial appointments; we could only give the unlikely-sounding excuse that we had been cut off by the tide in Twickenham.) Gratifying my lifelong passion for trees, I now had as my companions in my own garden towering ancient chestnuts, a gigantic plane, and, on our river frontage, three whispering willows which acknowledged the coming of spring before any other plant: in early March they turned golden, soon to become daubed, like an Impressionist painting, with tiny specks of exquisite pale green as the myriad leaves budded along the delicate wind-swung umbrella-like branches.

Every day I would walk a mile or so along the towpath to Richmond with our yellow Labrador puppy, past Orleans House, the home of Louis-Philippe of France when in exile, with its extraordinary Gibbs Octagon Room; past the magnificent Palladian Marble Hill House, the residence of King George II's mistress, the Countess of Suffolk, stopping often to admire an ancient rare black walnut tree, planted in her grounds in the early eighteenth century; past ducks, swans, more willows, more boats, following the river's curve to Richmond Bridge, and, if I cared to walk further, to Kew Gardens.

Our house was so well proportioned that it was beautiful even in its unfurnished and undecorated state, with damp pouring in from ceilings, rising from the foundations and assailing the walls from every drainpipe and gutter. The benign spirit of Camilla's grandmother seemed to be watching over us. Camilla had been very close to this remarkable old lady in the last years of her life, spending three weeks a year with her when her private secretary was on holiday, dealing with her vast daily correspondence about her charity concerns and her *sorties* into the salerooms. (She had been a famous collector of Chinese porcelain, Meissen, Battersea enamels and pictures, most of which she left to museums; notably she bequeathed to the borough of Richmond a huge collection of paintings, drawings and prints of Twickenham and Richmond, as well as Riverside House, our home, Orleans House and the surrounding parks.) She was one of the first people in Britain actively to start worrying about conservation, and she had bought our house, Orleans House and the surrounding riverside lands to prevent the whole area, including the Gibbs Octagon, from being turned into gravel quarries, which would have not only ruined Twickenham but also the famous view from Richmond Hill which, to this day, remains entirely green and unspoilt. She also grew prize-winning orchids and freesias, bred and showed champion Hackney ponies, champion Jersey cows and the internationally famous Vulcan strain of huge poodles, who used to be driven to dog shows in a Rolls Royce (an old hearse), while she went about in a much more modest car.

Feeling her presence, I regretted I had never met her – she had died a few months before our engagement. She loved all the arts, and had many brilliant and interesting friends, including Queen Mary, for whom she sometimes acted as lady-in-waiting, and who, in her lifetime, often visited our house.

One of our first visitors was Arthur Hedley, the British expert on Chopin who had learnt to read and speak perfect Polish to complete his researches. I was enthralled when he showed me a letter indicating that Chopin had visited King Louis-Philippe next door to us at Orleans House in 1848. Since our house had also been part of the French king's estate, Chopin might even have strolled into our garden! I knew there were good ghosts around us, wanting us to live and work there.

Suddenly I was in a kind of ideal existence I had only imagined, never experienced before in my life. I never had to answer the telephone, hardly even open any letter. Delicious meals were put before me three times a day without my having to spare even a thought in advance unless I cared to dream up some gastronomic treat. A wedding gift of a Polish recipe book meant that I was re-introduced to my favourite soups, but Camilla also excelled in French and other continental cooking, as well as old-fashioned English fare (though she never served over-boiled vegetables!).

Wanting to know what else besides food drew nostalgic memories from me, Camilla asked, 'What do you miss most about Poland?'

'Mostly the Polish forests,' I said. So, outside my studio she planted several green pines, which have grown now into quite a respectable mini-forest. Also, learning that my family crest was three roses, we ceremonially planted three climbing roses, symbolising putting down our new roots in the Twickenham soil.

I was soon made to feel even more at home: through the interest of the editor of our local paper, Reg Ward, a local committee was formed, the English Chamber Orchestra was hired, and a 'Panufnik Celebration Concert' was held in St Mary's Church to welcome me into my new community. I was asked to become president of the local concert society, and found myself described as 'our local composer'.

After years without having any close family, I became aware that I suddenly had acquired a blue-eyed, blonde-haired sister, Peggy, married to a brilliant solicitor, John Walford; not to mention two brothers: Toby, as yet unmarried; and Oliver, with his wife Gloria, all of whom seemed to accept me most warmly as one of the clan. Oliver, the eldest, was a tycoonish company director. Since I knew nothing about high finance, and Oliver was so tone deaf that music actually brought him physical pain, at first I wondered what we could talk about together; but our mutual passion for good food and fine wine quickly brought us together. Camilla's second brother, Toby, a talented pianist, had dreamed of taking up music professionally but instead had gone into politics. At the time of our marriage he was fighting a hopeless seat in South London, but later he became MP for our own constituency, Twickenham. He has always been the member of the family who took the most active interest in my work. Together with Camilla's ever-supportive parents, he enthusiastically flew to Monaco in the first summer of our marriage to join us for the performance of my prize-winning *Sinfonia Sacra* at a picturesque outdoor concert in the courtyard of Prince Rainier's palace.

Sinfonia Sacra was already rapidly establishing itself as my most performed work. The Monaco Orchestra featured it again shortly afterwards in Paris at a United Nations concert; then, with Prince Rainier's patronage, I recorded it in Monte Carlo for the French branch of EMI. Leopold Stokowski enthusiastically agreed to direct the American première at the Polish Millenium Concert; Hans Schmidt-Isserstedt performed it in Hamburg and later with the Berlin Philharmonic; Daniel Chabrun's splendid rendering with the l'Orchestre Philharmonique du RTF in Paris was televised; Constantin Silvestri won a standing ovation with his magnificent London première, as did Colman Pearce in Dublin, and I conducted it with my old orchestra in Birmingham, in Lisbon and Brussels, and on my tour of South America in 1965.

Thereafter the performances multiplied too fast to keep track of, though some events, such as Sir Georg Solti's dazzling performances with the Chicago Symphony Orchestra, remain etched in my memory.

Camilla and I were travelling together quite a lot, as I still could not avoid conducting altogether until I could increase my earnings as a composer. One tour was to South America, starting with three concerts in Buenos Aires. These concerts were a particular pleasure, especially because of the number of rehearsals. To my momentary annoyance, a souvenir-hunter absconded with my baton in the interval of the first concert. Since then I have almost always conducted without a baton. Journeys like these provided an excuse for glorious extra honeymoons together, and gave Camilla as well as myself extremely interesting work opportunities. For example, in Buenos Aires, while I rehearsed my three concerts, Camilla was collecting material for a freelance article for the *Times Educational Supplement* on adult literacy schemes, taking pictures for the British Council of a visiting exhibition of Henry Moore sculptures, and obtaining fund-raising pictures for a British charity in a grim shanty town, which had one water tap for several hundred desperately deprived families who had arrived from country districts hoping (in vain) to make a living in the city.

Irresponsibly but most pleasantly using up my Argentinian earnings, we travelled on round South America together to Chile, where Camilla photographed earthquake victims. In Santiago I admired the splendid centre for contemporary composers where all their works were printed, performed and recorded on tape. In Lima, beside the magnificent ceramics and exotic churches, our only (inescapable) cultural experience was a concert conducted by the Peruvian President's nephew.

Then we set out for the Andes in an elderly unpressurized propeller plane, inhaling our oxygen from primitive hosepipe outlets, flying up valleys with rows of peaks towering above us until we bumped down at the hidden city of Cuzco. Breathless from the height we took a tiny train which chugged over sky-level passes to Machu-Picchu. For enchanted days we wandered amongst the immaculately preserved temples and terraces of the Inca city, which tumbles over a vast slope between pointed mountain tops and the hairpin bends of the Urubamba River. Throughout the magical sunset and twilight we joyfully found ourselves alone in the ruins: the other guests in the small hotel (a group of professorial Americans), having travelled thousands of miles to visit one of the great sights of the world, had to sit indoors for a lecture on the economy of Patagonia.

We returned home via Brazil. Camilla, aghast at the poverty in Rio, remarked that her camera seemed an inadequate weapon against such injustice.

As to musical life there, I received a warm welcome from the Brazilian composers: one of them tried at once to lay on a symphony concert so that I could acquaint them with my music. However, the concert hall was already booked that week by a dance company. 'What a pity,' my Brazilian friend said. 'Last week the hall and the orchestra were free, but we never got round to deciding what to perform.'

We travelled quite widely in Europe too for musical purposes. Apart from our trips abroad, we lived very quietly at Riverside House, concentrating almost entirely on our work, just from time to time seeing close friends and entertaining some very interesting guests.

Leopold Stokowski became a frequent visitor. At the time of our marriage he wrote enthusiastically to congratulate me, and urgently asking, though he was in his late seventies, if Camilla had a little sister. Thereafter, whenever he came over to England for recordings or concerts, he would book himself into his Twickenham hide-out for two or three days, and not tell anyone where he was going, exercising both his love of the mysterious and his desire not to be disturbed. He considered our spare bedroom his own, and ordered us *never* to allow another conductor to sleep in his bed.

He adored Camilla and always referred to me as her 'boy-friend', refusing to accord me my full rank as husband. He also loved animals and used to address affectionate and funny letters to our labrador, Kasia, and to our talking mynah bird, Daumier, when he wanted to let us know he was coming.

He liked to preside in the kitchen while Camilla prepared us sumptuous meals. He would sit on our old Welsh farmhouse pine pew, peeling vegetables, or giving gastronomic advice. He also enjoyed working in our garden; he had a fervent mission to remove dead twigs from even the smallest trees and bushes –

which rather reflected his attitude to musicians he no longer wanted in his orchestra. He loved plants, and he looked upon the cutting of flowers for vases as the unscrupulous murder of living beings. (Once, after a concert, an admirer arrived with a vast arrangement of exquisite roses, a new strain which had been named after him; indignantly he sent the poor man away with ears as red as the spurned blossoms.)

Stokowski longed for the simple life; he hated hotels, loathed social events. He appeared to care nothing for acclaim or success, but spoke with the utmost intensity about the beauty of nature, about peace and the brotherhood of man. He also was concerned to make music accessible to everybody, especially to young people.

He was always extremely courteous, though he confessed to us one occasion when he had been impolite: 'When my wife [Gloria Vanderbilt] kicked me out, I forgot to say thank you.'

We often talked about contemporary music, which I found especially fascinating since he had been responsible for introducing to American audiences three generations of contemporary composers, with styles as widely differing as Rachmaninov and Schoenberg (with whom he had played tennis when they were both in Hollywood during the war). Only once I regretted chiding him, having mentioned how Bartók went hungry in New York: Leopold's face suddenly became tragic as he said, 'We all make a few unforgivable mistakes in our lives. I failed at the time to recognise his greatness.'

He was censorious of the musical trends of the moment, attacking a number of fashionable composers, who, he complained, used 'highly complicated technical devices involving excessive numbers of notes to create very poor musical substance if not total emptiness'. He added, 'Look at the beginning of Schubert's 'Unfinished' Symphony: cello and double basses starting with octaves, then violins with semi-quavers, then a simple tune in the woodwinds. On paper this looks uninteresting, even dull — but what divine music it is!' It was an example of the *magic* of music, he added, possessed only by great composers.

I was reminded of my conclusions so many years previously in Vienna, that true charisma only emanated from very few great composers or performers; Stokowski himself certainly possessed this rare power.

At his rehearsals he always created a highly charged atmosphere, almost a sense of suspense. He had a colossal insight into the minds of orchestral players. As well as lucidly transmitting to them his required interpretation, he never hesitated to use either barbed criticism or devastating wit, or — more shattering still — an attack of excessive politeness.

I recall one of his rehearsals with the New Philharmonia Orchestra in Croydon; he suddenly waved everyone to silence, pointed his long bony finger at a player at the back of the second violins, and said, with a dangerously quiet voice, 'What are you eating?'

'I'm chewing gum — it stops me smoking.'

'Take it out!' said Stokowski.

A deathly silence ensued. The player, a real orchestral tough, sat unmoved. One could almost hear him determinedly continuing to chew. The tension in the orchestra was alarming.

'Take it out!' Stokowski repeated softly but clearly. 'You are not chewing in time with your bowing!'

All the players roared with laughter, and the gum-chewer slunk from the platform.

He often used his wit to release tension between himself and whichever orchestra he was conducting. Another time, rehearsing at the Festival Hall, one of the harpists earned a fierce rebuke from him over some notes he had wanted accentuated. The player defensively replied, 'It's not printed like that in the score,' to which Stokowski replied in his slow, deliberate manner, 'I have been married several times, and I have learned that there is much to be performed in a marriage which is not printed in the licence.'

He was often accused of exaggerating or distorting scores for effect. However, I usually found him incredibly modest, with sincere determination to interpret my music exactly as I wanted it. I remember once explaining how I wanted a passage performed in one of my works, then questioned whether it was technically a reasonable demand to make of the players; he gently replied, 'Everything is possible — tell us what you want and we shall do it.'

It was true, as people complained, that he sometimes took liberties with tempo or dynamics in the music of both past and present composers. Prior to his thrilling New York première of my *Sinfonia Sacra* at Carnegie Hall, he carefully consulted me about his dramatic idea to place two of the four trumpeters for the opening fanfare high on the balconies of Carnegie Hall, which produced a remarkable effect, sounding like twelve rather than four players. However, he omitted to ask my consent to speed up the last movement. If he had discussed his idea with me first I would have objected strongly. As it was, during the performance, I had to confess to being at least temporarily convinced, because of the spontaneity and excitement he achieved.

Nadia Boulanger was another frequent visitor to our home. She had been a staunch supporter of my music since she first heard it in post-war Paris, and would give me tremendous encouragement with her faith in me. I often wondered if she liked me all the better just because I had never been one of her pupils.

Despite her puritanical appearance, she also was extremely fond of good food, like so many of the naturally sensuous breed of my fellow-musicians, and Camilla would go to great lengths to please her. Being used to giving orders in her own home, she would imperiously state what she required: 'Nothing complicated this evening, my dear,' she once said, 'Just a little cheese soufflé.' Camilla had to rush to her favourite cookery book, and somehow master this difficult art at her first attempt. (That was nothing! I heard from an ex-pupil of Nadia's about her visit to Warsaw, when, as usual, the shops were almost bare. He started to explain to her that meat was unavailable and she said, 'It's perfectly all right — we'll just have a little smoked salmon.')

Nadia, though over eighty, would take me out for long vigorous walks, during which she would maintain an animated monologue in her incredibly strong French accent, often about the work of 'M'ssieur Straveenskee,' whom she continued to admire unswervingly despite his drastic stylistic changes of direction, through his neo-classicism even to his post-Webernist phase.

The ardent promotion of post-Webernist and post-Schoen-

bergian composers remained severely damaging to my prospects for the moment. One had to be glad that more contemporary music was being broadcast than ever before, and to
respect William Glock, in that he was a man with strong views
who was not afraid to carry them through. Unfortunately,
however, much of the music he promoted with the power of
radio was so grimly and drily static and 'intellectual' that a
large part of the previously open-minded musical public were
put off the concept of new music altogether, often resulting in
empty seats at contemporary music concerts.

More than seven years had passed since any work of mine
had been broadcast. I was of course not at all alone in experiencing difficulties with Glock and with Keller, who had special
responsibility for contemporary music broadcasts. The Composers' Guild of Great Britain was up in arms against their
régime, and I have to confess that I smiled to see them depicted
in the satirical *Private Eye* as 'Block and Killer,' because this
was such a strikingly accurate description of the effect they
were having on my career.

Sinfonia Sacra had been rejected by the BBC selection committee, written-off according to one of their administrators as
'unsuitable for broadcasting on any wave-length', even though
it had won first prize for Great Britain in Monaco. So
thoroughly were the British audience to be protected from its
seditious influence that the Monaco concert containing the
première of the work *and* the United Nations' Concert from
Paris were both relayed in Britain by the BBC shorn of my
symphony! Somehow it appealed to my sense of irony to find
myself banned both in Poland and on the BBC.

However, nothing that becomes a trend remains one for
ever. At last, towards the end of 1966, at least on my behalf, a
faint crack appeared in the armour of the BBC third programme. One day, I received a telephone call from a young
BBC producer, Martin Dalby, saying he wanted to bring
about a programme on my music in his series, 'The Composer's
Portrait.' Camilla thought this must be a practical joke, and
rang Barrie Hall, the BBC's publicity officer who had befriended me during the happier BBC days when my works
were frequently broadcast.

The call indeed was genuine. The ban at last seemed cracked if not broken. Martin Dalby, a charming man and gifted composer, came down to discuss his programme, after which we blessed our meeting with a considerable intake of Polish vodka. He then invited us back to seal the union, presenting to us a vast array of his native drink; at least twenty varieties of Scotch whisky of varying colours, flavours and vintages, all of which we sampled, until we were hardly capable of leaving his house. Despite this, the programme was successfully achieved.

Martin's bosses remained intransigent, but at least he and John Amis, and later Antony Hopkins, found some loopholes in the inexplicable embargo. Meanwhile the dearth of broadcasts and the shortage of new music emerging from my pen were grist to the propaganda mill of the Polish Embassy in London, which put it about that I was finished as a composer and was only able to rework old compositions.

I did indeed produce only one new piece in the mid-1960s, the *Katyń Epitaph*, premièred in New York in 1968 by Stokowski. It was dedicated to the 15,000 Polish officers slaughtered in Katyń Forest. All Poles had always known who the murderers were, but Stalin had cunningly shifted the blame on to Hitler's shoulders; a few years after I composed this work, however, indisputable evidence was unearthed showing that the Russians were responsible for the massacre. Because of the Soviet guilt, no one in Poland could openly write music or pay any poetic tribute to these victims, so I felt, in my new freedom, that it was my privilege to be able to do this.

Otherwise I wrote nothing new for four whole years. Camilla never expressed aloud any concern at the slowness of my musical output despite the perfect conditions which she was creating for me; she always reiterated her faith in the theory that a period of calm and rediscovery was essential, as convalescence, she said, from a quarter of a century of adversity. She stood guard and quietly waited, while I learnt how to be a complete person again, and found life could indeed begin at fifty.

Only gradually did my energy, my inner creative urge, begin to function again. This was a period of gestation, as my new

After My Escape

9a. and b. Delivering statements for both Radio Free Europe and the BBC, explaining my reasons for leaving Poland (London, July 1954).

9c. Immediately after my first appearance at the Royal Festival Hall with the Philharmonia Orchestra. Musically successful, financially disastrous (London, 1954).

9d. After my second London concert, at the Royal Albert Hall with the London Symphony Orchestra, also musically successful, but with no financial profit, as it was a charity concert for Polish children in England. From left, the soloist, Witold Małcużyński, Artur Rodziński, ex-director of the New York Philharmonic, and myself (London, 1954).

10. At last, relief from successive disappointments and disasters: celebrating my engagement to Camilla Jessel (London, summer 1963).

11a. After our wedding at Caxton Hall (London, 27 November 1963).

11b. Slicing the Warsaw Palace of Culture (see p. 296-97) at our reception at the Dorchester Hotel (London, 27 November 1963).

11c. Decorating our crumbling eighteenth-century council house with the help of our labrador, Kasia (Twickenham, 1964).

11d. Nadia Boulanger in my studio, just converted from the ancient stable buildings (Twickenham, 1965).

12a. Holding his god-daughter, Roxanna (1968).

12b. Pruning dead wood from our fruit trees (1965).

12c. Midnight recording of my *Universal Prayer* at Westminster Cathedral (London, 1970).

13a. Rehearsing *Sinfonia di Sfere* with the London
Symphony Orchestra for the televised Promenade Concert at
the Royal Albert Hall (London, 1977).

13b. Rehearsing our children at home for the recording of *Thames Pageant*. From left:
Roxanna – flute; Camilla – appreciative audience; myself – orchestra (piano); and
Jeremy – treble (Twickenham, 1979).

14a. Rehearsing my Violin Concerto with Yehudi Menuhin at the Goldsmiths Hall for its première during the City of London Festival (1972).

14b. LSO Chairman Anthony Camden and Leader Michael Davis jointly rehearsing *Concerto Festivo*, which I composed without conductor as a Gala piece for the orchestra's seventy-fifth anniversary (1979).

14c. Discussing my *Concertino* with André Previn for the première with the LSO (London, 1981).

15a. Rehearsals for the première of *Sinfonia Votiva*. Seiji Ozawa insisted on having me at his right hand, in the midst of the Boston Symphony Orchestra (Boston, 1982).

15b. With Sir Georg Solti between his rehearsals of *Sinfonia Sacra* with the Chicago Symphony Orchestra (Chicago, 1982).

16a. Recording *Metasinfonia* with the ever-friendly LSO at the Royal Albert Hall (London, 1985).

16b. After my seventieth birthday concert with the London Symphony Orchestra at the Barbican Hall, with my most beloved trio: Camilla as ever in support, and, on my right Roxanna, a promising composer, and Jeremy, a gifted artist (London, 24 September 1984).

roots were slowly working their way into the Thames-side soil. At last released from the fight for sheer survival, it seemed vital to stand back for a while and assess what I had achieved in my existing music, then to seek out the directions I might want to explore in the future.

In the very first weeks after our marriage I had composed my *Song to the Virgin Mary* to a beautiful mediaeval Polish Latin text, '*Tu luna pulchrior, Tu stellis purior, Tu sole clarior, Maria!*' The first of numerous works dedicated to Camilla, this *a cappella* choral prayer, which emerged from a memory of ardent Polish peasants at worship in a country church, was written in a tonal language similar to my earlier *Five Polish Peasant Songs*.

Now, inevitably, my ties with my native country were becoming less binding. I realised that even if I wished I would no longer be able to continue producing works like my *Polonia Suite, Rhapsody, Sinfonia Sacra* or *Katyń Epitaph*. Though written since my escape, they had still been dominated in their musical content by my innate Polishness. While in no way rejecting my past heritage, nor the works I had composed under its influence, I knew also that if I continued to rely on similar musical material, still drawing on the haunting echoes of Polish folk music, the result would be artistic stagnation. I felt a yearning to step even further beyond the humdrum realities of our everyday world and reach out for a more universal spirituality. I was searching too for a new dimension in musical grammar and language, because I felt that somewhere within my imagination lay something different, undiscovered, a future source for fresh creative endeavours.

I resolved, however long it would take me, to persevere relentlessly until I could discover a new way of expressing myself, influenced neither by my native culture nor by the language of any other existing composer or musical school of thought. Almost every day, not for weeks, nor for months, but for three, almost four years, I spent hour after hour in my converted stable at the end of the garden, reflecting how to tackle my new task. Sitting at my desk I would search on the staves of my manuscript paper, scribbling down endless different ideas, then trying them at the piano, until at last one day I realised that my ear, together with my intuition, was beginning to win over intellectual speculation: I suddenly found a group of three notes which, as I manipulated them within the stave and on the piano, I perceived had some evocative and strangely expandable qualities – even, it felt to me, some magical power.

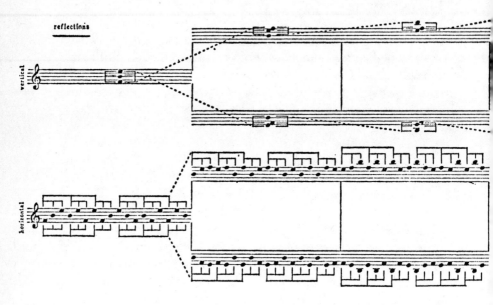

Echoing Archimedes, I wished to shout 'Eureka!' But instead, in tremendous suspense and elation, I repeatedly sang and played the three crucial notes of my three-note cell: F-B-E, (fa-si-mi) adding in subconsciously its two reflections, B-E-F (si-mi-fa) and E-F-B (mi-fa-si). I then tried various transpositions of these cells on the piano, using them both horizontally (melodically) and vertically (harmonically), which seemed to produce an extraordinary sense of organic unity. At the same time, as I played on, I heard to my amazement new harmonies, new expressions, new sound colours. I knew within minutes that this three-note cell would be the material out of which I could build both small- and large-scale musical structures; that it had as much potential for poetic and human expression as it did for intellectual fastidiousness; that it was the ultimate basis from which all my future compositions could grow.

I was not the only person in the household in a creative, expect-
ant state.

The spring of 1968 saw the completion of the first of my
new line of compositional progeny, the piano piece, *Reflections*,
within days of the birth of our exquisite, tiny, gentle Roxanna.
Somehow I do not think that their arrival together was entirely
coincidental.

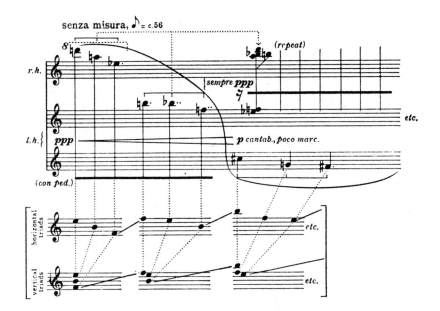

25

MUSIC POURING FROM MY PEN

With the birth of my new language and the beginning of our parenthood, we stopped rushing round the world for concerts, and settled down into an even quieter life in Twickenham. While Camilla contentedly absorbed herself in caring for our baby, I was plunging into a much larger-scale composition, again built out of my three-note cell.

For some time, I had wanted to compose a work with a spiritual message, intended to unite the feelings of all people of all races and religions, attempting to bridge the tragic divisions within our disturbed and ugly world. I was searching for a concept less corruptible than the great ideal of 'peace', which had been so distorted and misused by the Soviets and their sycophants. To my joy, I discovered amongst the poetry of Alexander Pope, who had lived only a few hundred yards up the Thames from my home, the magnificent *Universal Prayer* to the 'Father of All, by every race and every creed ador'd', a visionary concept for anyone brought up within the confines of eighteenth-century religion, yet so close to my heart that it might have been written not 250 years ago, but especially for me today.

I took the first words, 'Father of All', as an invocation to be sung by the chorus throughout the cantata, imagining as I composed, a vast assembly of performers incorporating men and women of every imaginable colour, race, opinion and belief. The four soloists, I dreamt, would also be each of different race, with a multi-racial chorus too. For musical instruments, however, I decided to use simply an organ and three harps.

The construction of the cantata was imposed on me by the classical form of the poem. Alexander Pope himself had written that 'Order is Heav'n's first law', a remark which brought me tremendous satisfaction, echoing as it did my own sentiment regarding any viable work of art.

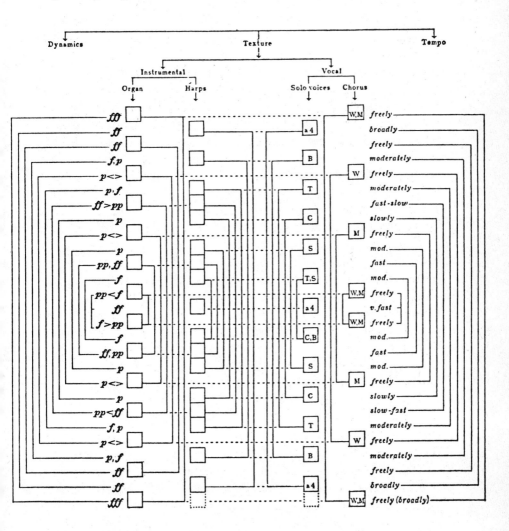

Keeping these words in mind, I created a huge symmetrical framework, and within this structure, my three-note cell with its perpetual transpositions and reflections served me for the

313

whole extended work. It was a stern self-discipline, almost an extreme in economy and simplicity of sound organisation, yet I found it aesthetically most satisfying. Somehow, at the same time, the dramatic aspects of the poem being of paramount importance, I felt I was able to keep the technical side subservient to the all-important spiritual and emotional content.

I showed the sketches of the *Universal Prayer* to Leopold Stokowski when he visited us again that summer, and he immediately ordered that no one else was to see the score, insisting that he would give the world première in New York.

Meanwhile, agreeing to take on the rôle of godfather to our two-month-old Roxanna, he pronounced that it was time she was initiated into the world of serious music, and ordered us to bring her to his next rehearsal at the Royal Festival Hall. The attendant at the Artists' Entrance looked rather startled as we wandered in with our tiny bundle in a large white shawl. Roxanna slept blissfully throughout the whole of the Scriabin *Poème d'Extase,* including its huge fortissimo in the last bars, but woke up and screamed loudly as, at the end of the play-through, an unwelcome silence assailed her ears. Leopold insisted that this was her appreciation and that she must be extremely musical since she did not want the orchestra to stop.

It was in fact a couple of years before the première of the *Universal Prayer* could take place. I have no less than twelve letters about Leopold's attempts to overcome the apparent fear of both the Catholic and Protestant hierarchies of the effect of the eighteenth-century words sung in their cathedrals! (It was before the ecumenical movement had come into fashion.)

On 3 December 1968, he wrote to me for several copies of the poem to show to the authorities, 'so that they will be sure there is nothing in Pope's philosophy or religion contrary to their ideas (or prejudices)!' On 17 February 1969 he wrote:

> I have the impression that the top minds are not sure about *Universal Prayer's* effect on the religious dogmas they have inherited from the past. Both in the Catholic and Protestant atmosphere in the United States there is much disturbance. Some are wishing to face the changes of life today and others standing for the ancient dogma. All this causes great delay regarding *Universal Prayer.* I cannot receive a definite No or Yes!

Though he preferred St Patrick's, the Catholic cathedral, because it was more central and had better acoustics, eventually he settled for a première at the Protestant Cathedral of St John the Divine where he had met with marginally more tolerance. Even then he fretted about the delays, and wrote that he was trying to advance the date of the performance. 'I have so much difficulty with these priests! We plan our time – priests dream of Eternity!'

An astounding crowd of 5,000 people attended his New York première on 15 May 1970 in St John's with its thunderous organ and excitingly reverberant acoustics. He performed the cantata twice with just a brief organ solo in between performances. The work seemed to have enormous significance for him personally and the commitment of his interpretation was extraordinary.

Finally, a few months later, he won his running campaign with the Catholic authorities. A triumphant letter arrived, 'We shall perform your *Universal Prayer* in St Patrick's cathedral on Sunday evening, 29 November 1970 . . .' The solo voices, the three harpists and the organist were to be Caucasian Americans, but, 'The chorus will be composed of Catholics, Protestants, Jews, Arabs, Hindus, and Buddhists, and *all other* religious groups that we can reach.' At last there was to be a 'universal' performance almost as I had dreamt.

Leopold also battled to make a record of the *Universal Prayer* in America, but, he wrote, 'All recording companies are thinking about *money* and we are thinking about *music*.' England turned out to be a more fertile field. He recorded the work in 1971 – without fee – for Unicorn Records, at the age of eighty-three; working determinedly through the night because Westminster Cathedral could not be closed to the public during the day.

Some months later, wanting to pay tribute to the author of the words, he performed the cantata, again without a fee, in the tiny parish church in Twickenham where Alexander Pope was buried, even though it seemed that the concert could only be experienced by a congregation of 300 people. Happily the arts department of television's BBC 2 (then under the Controllership of David Attenborough and completely independent from

BBC Radio) relayed the event so that Leopold's wonderful gesture was made available to a vast audience. I was fortunate to have such a venerable and ardent champion of my music.

Meanwhile, my newly established Twickenham roots led me into another composition, not significant in my creative development, but important to me because I wanted to help encourage children towards music, as well as to express my appreciation of my new environment. In 1969, I was asked to write a cantata for young singers and instrumentalists from all the schools in our locality. Though I was longing to continue my experiments with my three-note cells, I accepted this commission and decided to base the cantata on the River Thames which runs right through the centre of the Borough. The only problem was where to find words suitable for children. Most conveniently I was able to turn to my wife, who took a historical rather than a geographical view of the river, and wrote a set of lively lyrics, starting with Julius Caesar fording the Thames, and going right through to modern days, ending with a vivid account of the University Boat Race, with half the choir supporting Oxford and the other half Cambridge.

People kept warning us how risky it was to work as a husband-and-wife team, but all went well until at the last moment I decided I wanted one more dramatic item right in the centre of the cantata. Camilla, increasingly pregnant with our second child, suddenly became less fertile in her imagination: the words absolutely would not emerge. I did not want to put pressure on her, nor to turn away from the cantata to start a more serious, complex composition, and have to come back later to my simplified, direct language for children. Fortunately, after an alarming delay, she made a last (gigantic) effort and I was able to finish the cantata on time.

Though not excessively polished, I found the performance of *Thames Pageant* an extremely moving event. The energetic Music Education Officer of the borough had brought together four hundred children who had struggled for weeks with my rather heavy demands upon their skills. Disaster almost struck at the first performance: the crucial side-drum player, aged eleven, lost his nerve and failed to turn up. Fortunately one of the great professionals of the percussion world was in the audience – James Blades, who was passionately interested in music for young people. Jimmy took over at an instant's notice, and sat on the stage amongst the children, elfin-like, not much larger than his neighbours. Afterwards, when I was thanking Jimmy for this incredibly generous act, he said he would have played much better if he had brought his glasses and been able to see the notes clearly . . .

I was moved to discover that it was Jimmy Blades who had recorded on the timpani the famous wartime signal for the BBC's 'London Calling' broadcasts to German-occupied territories, which I had heard hundreds of times listening to our illicit radio in our Warsaw cellar.

Once Camilla and I were safely delivered of our cantata, *Thames Pageant*, we had to await the delivery of our second baby. Camilla developed an unusual quirk of pregnancy. Instead of manifesting the customary passion for some special or exotic food like most women, she kept on requiring to go to the theatre or to the opera. She almost went into labour a month in advance when she insisted on attending one of the longest operas, the five-hour *Die Meistersinger*, at Covent Garden – a superb performance, dynamically conducted by Georg Solti. By chance, our seats, bought at the last moment, were in the front row, right on top of the orchestra. As the opera progressed, Camilla whispered that the unborn baby, wildly affected by the music, seemed to be turning somersaults inside her. By Act III she suspected that we might have to make a dramatic dash to the hospital. However, some glorious choral singing seemed to lull the baby to rest again.

He stayed in place long enough for another almost disastrous theatrical event the following week. This time she persuaded me to go with her to a matinée performance at Richmond Theatre.

She had been trying to learn Polish with the idealistic intention of bringing our children up bilingually, but I had been no help because I wanted to speak English with her to improve my fluency, and because anyway it was boring to tailor our conversation to her limited vocabulary. However, on this occasion I regrettably did speak to her in Polish. Someone came and sat down beside me in the almost empty theatre, and I said, gasping for breath, 'We must move: the hag next to me stinks like a dead fish.' Camilla did not understand what I said, but my neighbour instantly got up and moved away. I never spoke Polish to Camilla again.

Our little Jeremy arrived soon and in a great hurry. Fortunately it was four o'clock in the morning as I had to ignore the traffic lights in order to get Camilla to the hospital in time.

Our two children were just thirteen months apart in age. The privilege of working for them put all my difficulties into perspective. With a future generation to inherit my music, the past sank even further into oblivion and present problems paled.

At about this time, one of my father's violins reached England. Lilian Hochhauser, the wife of the impresario who then represented all leading Soviet artists in London, had heard through a mutual friend that I had left all my father's instruments in Poland. She also heard that one Panufnik violin had been won before the war in the Wieniawski Competition by David Oistrakh. Visiting Russia on her husband's business, Mrs Hochhauser had asked Oistrakh about the instrument, and he warmheartedly had insisted that it should come to me. With colossal courage, she smuggled it out of Russia in her suitcase; a considerable risk taken for a total stranger! I was greatly touched by this amazing act, and moved also to find on the much-played instrument worn strings and fresh rosin, which showed that the great Oistrakh had not exclusively been using his famous Stradivarius all these years and that my father's instrument had not merely been sitting in a cupboard. I wanted to thank Oistrakh personally the next time he came to play in London, but I was afraid to approach him in case the security men from his Embassy would find out about his generosity to a dissident Pole and make serious trouble for him.

Not long after this event, I had cause to think again of violins. Yehudi Menuhin commissioned me to write a concerto. He wanted it quickly, for performance only a few months hence. I accepted the commission gladly, but murmured some doubts about finishing on time. 'Start with the last movement!' said Yehudi with a brisk smile.

Hurriedly sitting down to plan my new work, I found myself delayed by an internal debate; whether or not I should stick rigidly to my new three-note cell language. My primary consideration, I concluded, must be to display the violin as a warm expressive instrument. I decided that I could afford to employ my new self-imposed rules with flexibility, expanding or contracting them according to the requirements of each new commission, never permitting myself to become a slave of my own invention. Writing for the violin I suppose I felt the pull of my childhood memories — the smell of wood as my father constructed his instruments, and my mother's constant playing — so that the work became a sort of pilgrimage into my past and inevitably emerged somewhat Polish in atmosphere.

The language meanwhile was not without discipline. The first movement was based on a three-note cell with three intervals, though a different combination to that of the *Universal Prayer*. In the second and third movements, I limited myself to an even greater economy, with only two intervals (major and minor thirds) as my basis for melodic structures. This discipline served to exploit to the utmost Yehudi's rare powers of spirituality in his interpretation, and gave him every opportunity to maximise the singing quality of the instrument. Throughout the concerto, I consciously avoided the temptation of including purple passages of virtuoso 'pyrotechnics' (so beloved to technically adept but less profound violinists). I was composing a piece to expose the soul of the performer rather than to transform the fingerboard of the violin into a gymnasium for bouncing fingers. Yehudi momentarily questioned my asceticism, warning me that audiences enjoyed the showing-off aspects of concerto performances, but he did not try to persuade me to alter a note for the sake of popularity.

Such were the feelings I invested in my Violin Concerto that I found it essential to dedicate it to Camilla. For her part, she insisted that it should be dedicated to Yehudi. I wrote to Yehudi about my dilemma, and he replied with the utmost grace that of course it should be for Camilla, and that he would dedicate his performance to her too!

I was moved to find that Yehudi had taken the trouble to memorise the whole work. Though our original intention had been that he should direct the concerto from the violin, the cross-rhythms of the fast last movement turned out to be too tricky and dangerous to risk without a conductor's baton, so in the end he asked me to conduct the first performance, which took place under very happy circumstances at the magnificent Goldsmiths Hall during the City of London Festival.

Some time afterwards, Yehudi arranged with EMI to record the concerto together with my *Sinfonia Concertante* for flute, harp and strings, which I composed as a tenth wedding anniversary present for Camilla. With three gramophone records already made by the path-setting Louisville Orchestra in America, I now had a considerable amount of my output on commercial records. As comparatively little contemporary music is available in this way, I have been exceptionally fortunate to have a number of recording companies interested in my compositions.

Unicorn Records especially has given me the fullest support over many years. Their founder John Goldsmith became committed to my music after experiencing the memorable London première of my *Sinfonia Sacra*, when Constantin Silvestri and his Bournemouth Orchestra gave such a sensational performance of my symphony that they brought the whole Festival Hall audience cheering to their feet.

John, six-and-a-half feet tall with a mop of red hair, had started his working life as a policeman on the beat, but his main interest was always gramophone records. Frustrated at being unable to find the more unusual items he wanted for his collection, he first started his own shop and then began making his own records to fill unforgiveable gaps of repertoire in the catalogues. He also recorded some distinguished artists whose work was unavailable on disc because they were not part of the musical mafia of the moment. One great conductor he rescued from unjust neglect was Jascha Horenstein, who recorded for him Nielsen's Symphony No. 5, Mahler's Nos. 1 and 3 (well ahead of the Mahler boom), and some Bruckner (also ahead of the current fashion).

Before long, he discovered that Horenstein shared his own enthusiasm for my music, and in 1970, with the London Symphony Orchestra, they recorded four of my orchestral pieces,

Nocturne, Tragic Overture, Heroic Overture and *Autumn Music*. This triggered off not only a number of records over the years with Unicorn, but also my long friendship with the LSO, who have so warmly taken my music to their hearts from that day to this.

Also during the 1970s, John Goldsmith licensed my *Sacra* and *Rustica* recordings from EMI, reissuing them on the Unicorn label. He then recorded Stokowski conducting *Universal Prayer*, followed by several more of my works. Decca made a record of two of my symphonies, and other companies followed suit in the Eighties. These discs were of course enormously important, not just because they were the best way of reaching the people who cared about my music (difficulties with the BBC were not yet over), but also because they served to bring it to the attention of conductors, performers, choreographers and even film producers.

The film producer who *almost* commissioned some music from me was Ken Russell. Both Camilla and I tremendously admired his early films and we were both more than excited when we heard that he was eager to meet me. Although I had sworn I would write no more film music after I left Poland, Ken was after all a major artist. We were both greatly looking forward to his visit. However, before he and his wife were due to come to dinner (brought by John Goldsmith), we thought we ought to see his latest film, *The Devils*. Camilla knew the novel (*The Devils of Loudun*) and warned me that the film might be gruelling. However, neither of us were quite prepared for the full impact, laced with the additional brilliant and shattering Russell imagery, and although we survived the masturbating, sex-crazed nuns we slid out squeamishly as the priest-hero was about to undergo torture.

Camilla was so busy domestically that somehow we omitted to discuss our reactions to this experience. On the night of the dinner party, she was hardly to be seen, trying to get the babies fed and to bed before our famous visitor arrived, as well as rustling together some sumptuous food. Conversation over our meal was very cordial – and very general. Then Ken's wife Shirley came firmly to the point, asking me if I was interested in writing film music, adding that they were about to put into production a film about the half-Polish sculptor, Henri Gaudier-Brzeska.

Running through my mind, as I sat silent a moment, were not only the sensationalist images from *The Devils*, but also my memories of working with film directors in Poland; the need to churn out fragmented chunks of music subservient to visual takes; never being allowed to think about composing in a complete architectural structure in the way which had now become essential to my being. Of course we desperately needed the marvellous film industry money, as Camilla was too wrapped up in her babies to work and we had immense extra expenses. But I could only blindly think, in a totally impractical way, that at last in my life I had time and space to compose seriously; that I must not at this point lose my independence or have to write according to anyone else's orders.

'Are you interested in writing film music?' Shirley asked again, when I did not reply.

'No,' I said. Camilla's face for a moment was quite a picture, but of course she understood perfectly. She only said later that she wished I might have decided before she took quite so much trouble over the dinner.

I think that the Russells did not understand. They left rather quickly which I shall always regret.

Another direct result of my gramophone records was that several leading choreographers discovered my music. It came to me as a most flattering surprise that my works apparently kindled ideas for these masters of the ballet. The first was Gerald Arpino at the New York City Centre Joffrey Ballet, who created his *Elegy* to my *Sinfonia Elegiaca*. Soon afterwards, I heard that Kenneth MacMillan was planning to use my *Sinfonia Sacra* with his Deutsche Oper Company in Berlin. Camilla and I attended the première of his *Kain und Abel* and found it magnificent, despite feeling distinctly uncomfortable about sitting almost behind enemy lines close to the Berlin Wall. Just for a moment, I also felt uncomfortable experiencing, for the first time, my own very familiar music transformed into a different concept by a choreographer. But I was quickly convinced and conquered by the emotional impact of MacMillan's poetic yet almost violent interpretation, and was only too happy to work with him the following year to produce an extended score – partly new, partly existing music – for his staging of *Miss Julie*, this time with John Cranko's Stuttgart Company, the great Marcia Haydée dancing the part of Miss Julie.

A year or so later, John Cranko invited himself to stay with us, to discuss a new three-act ballet score, *Othello*. Again I had to turn down a prestigious commission because it did not seem right for me at the moment. In an optimistic mood, wanting to reach out towards spiritually uplifting ideas, I found that I could not face writing a whole evening's music describing the depressing concepts of jealousy, malice and racism. Also I recognised from within myself that I did not adequately 'feel the stage' (I had already turned down opportunities for opera). So while the charming John Cranko continued his advocacy of *Othello*, I tried to tempt him into collaborating on something more philosophically positive. We separated, planning to meet again and dream up a scheme that would suit us both, but within a few months he had met his tragic early death.

Later in the 1970s, Kenneth MacMillan approached me with another tremendous balletic temptation, a fascinating three-act dance-drama. I was overjoyed at the idea of a further collaboration with Kenneth but was then devastated to find in myself a mental block about writing music according to even the most promising story-line. Part of the problem was, I think, that to do full justice to the existing highly-coloured scenario, I would have to work in short sections rather than allow musical form to dominate; so that I would not be able to build my work according to my need – my self-imposed aesthetic rule first to create a total structure. I regretted desperately turning down this great opportunity to work again with Kenneth, whom I continue always to admire enormously and who is godfather to our son, Jeremy. Sometimes I feel my tunnel vision regarding my direction as a composer interferes maddeningly with projects which might otherwise have been most exciting or artistically valuable.

Another dazzlingly talented young Royal Ballet choreographer has since taken up my music. David Bintley has produced no less than three wonderfully sensitive and musically conceived one-act ballets, including his choregraphic début at Covent Garden, when he used my Violin Concerto for his *Adieu* (which, I discovered at the dress rehearsal, was based on my own life and my personal 'Adieu' to Poland).

The New Zealander, Grey Veredon, with the Ballet de l'Opéra de Lyons, then used my *Sinfonia Sacra* for *Bogurodzica*, his emotional choreographic tribute to the suffering of the Poles under Martial Law.

Then the legendary Martha Graham, already in her eighties, discovered my music, using my *Nocturne* for her ballet, *Dances of the Golden Hall*. I shall never cease to regret that I was unable to witness this reportedly splendid event. When any of my works are used for ballet it remains a tremendous fascination, and an interesting lesson, to see how my feelings have been transferred into dance through a choreographer's poetic visualisation of my music.

Fortunately, meanwhile, other commissions were now rolling in so that I could choose what I would do next. Still BBC Radio were dragging their feet about my music, although (presumably by some oversight) *Sinfonia Sacra* was broadcast in a relay from the Edinburgh Festival.

The world of television was more liberal, ignoring this apparent prejudice – the producers independent from the dictates of the radio. BBC TV invited me to compose a piece with my own visualisation, with the idea that a new art form, music especially created for the television audience, should occasionally be offered as an alternative to the conventional documentary filming of orchestral performances.

The idea of a new art form was exciting. I decided to produce a work based on the mystical Indian Tantrik philosophy and art, which I had just discovered at a London exhibition. Using the title *Triangles*, in reference to the two triangles which depict the basic concept of the Tantrik philosophy, I chose as my theme the fundamental dualism between the static male force, macrocosm – which represents the world of pure spirit, symbolised by a triangle with the apex upwards – and the active female force, microcosm – which represents the world of pure matter, also symbolised by a triangle but with the apex pointing down. In Tantrik diagrams, these triangles appear either separately or interpenetrating, together forming a diagram called a Yantra, symbolising the union of opposites, the amalgamation of the spiritual and the erotic elements.

We filmed the performance from above. Two vast triangles were painted on to the floor; the three male cellists, dressed in white, were at the corners of the white (male) upward-pointing triangle; the three rather stunning female flautists, dressed in orange gowns were at the corners of the red, downward-pointing triangle. By cinematic trickery the Tantrik images were made to emerge and dissolve through the triangular frameworks – ending with Yantra, two superimposed triangles.

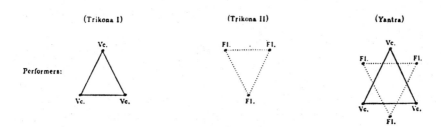

Musically, I was trying in the first movement to convey a sense of philosophic and contemplative calm, expressed visually through colourful geometric Tantrik patterns, followed in contrast by the rhythmic life force emanating from the dancing goddess sculptures. In the finale, I then tried to reflect the dualism by combining the contemplative and dance-like music, illustrated by vivid yet mystical erotic Tantrik paintings of sexual union.

Though my *Triangles*, composed in 1973, was intended purely for television rather than concert performance, and at the time did not seem of particular importance in my musical output, it engendered the vital next step in my discoveries as a composer. The idea of a musical work being contained and shaped by the perfect order of a geometric form was soon to emerge as a driving force which would permeate almost everything I wrote.

Refreshed after my enjoyable excursion into the ancient traditions of the East, I then had to turn speedily to my next commission: an inescapably Western choral work for a Christmas concert. I turned in despair to my home-based lyricist, complaining that there could not possibly remain a single new idea about such a traditional event; I swore that nothing would induce me to write yet another carol.

Camilla pointed out that dualism did not only appear in oriental philosophy, but that it was also a fundamental part of the origins of Western beliefs; and that the Christmas traditions of Jesus in the stable and the supposed date of His birth had grown out of the pagan winter solstice ceremonies, when a new baby was always brought in at the darkest point in the year as a symbol that life on earth would soon be born again.

She disappeared for days into two gigantic volumes of *The Golden Bough* and the sermons of St Augustine, a Christian convert who had powerfully battled with the pagan beliefs which had surrounded his upbringing. She emerged from her searches suggesting that we should have two soloists, a soprano taking the goddess rôle of the Earth Mother, and a baritone, St Augustine, exhorting the pagans to accept conversion.

The work started with a cheerful mistletoe carol, with the Christian chorus of women enthusiastically singing about the evergreen aspects of Christmas while the pagan men simultaneously extolled the mistletoe as the healer of all ills and the symbol of fertility. Then followed a self-glorifying aria by the Earth Mother. For the central section, in deference to my passion for symmetry, Camilla wrote virtually symmetrical words using the coincidental pun between the sun and the Son, so that the two choruses could sing the same words with different meanings. Then came a moving 'sermon' from the baritone St Augustine, quoting his own words, 'Worship not the sun but Him who made the sun'; and it ended with a unifying hymn for the New Year, in which the Christians and the pagans could share their aspirations, their seasonal joy and their wish to celebrate.

For the rest of the 1970s, after *Winter Solstice*, I became deeply bound up in my explorations of the potential use of geometry within my compositions. Whether in science, mysticism, religion or works of art of any period, geometric configurations, both coincidental and intentional, had always hypnotically appealed to my eyes. I had, for instance, been deeply drawn to the mysterious designs on pre-Columbian ceramics in Peru, and had read with fascination about the complex patterns of lines and angles which the people of various early civilisations used to draw in the sand or paint on to the walls of their caves to help contemplation, or sometimes to induce a heightened mental state. Equally important to me were the striking forms to be found in Nature, evolved without assistance from mankind: the perfect pentagon of the five-petalled rose, the logarithmic spiral in the centre of a sunflower, the arch of the rainbow, the parabola of a waterfall, hexagonal snow-crystals.

I felt that geometric shapes could provide my compositions with an unseen skeleton within which my harmonic, melodic and rhythmic concepts could be bound together as a cohesive whole; an organised framework out of which both spiritual and poetic expression could freely flow.

Accepting the definition of music as 'unfrozen architecture', it seemed suddenly obvious that a composer, like an architect, might draw on the inspiration of geometric form. I could imagine that the works of Bach and Mozart would exhibit most wonderful geometric structures and patterns if a means could be found to visualise them. As I planned my next compositions, it became clear to me that each of them would have to grow organically out of its own individual geometric base.

My next three symphonies – *Sinfonia di Sfere, Sinfonia Mistica* and *Metasinfonia* – were all expressions of my desire to explore to the extreme the concept of a substantial piece of music being built up out of its own geometric core.

In the first, my *Sinfonia di Sfere* (Symphony of Spheres), I was attempting to create a large-scale musical structure permeated by a sense of geometrical pattern and order. Through the title I hoped that I was suggesting to listeners a kind of journey in space experienced inwardly and outwardly. (I was not referring directly to astronomy, astrology, cosmology, nor the mystical philosophy of Pythagoras and his 'music of the spheres'.)

I conceived the work structurally as a framework of spheres, but also clearly patterned into definable spheres of harmony, spheres of rhythm, of melody, of dynamics and of tempo.

As I composed, I maintained an image of the listener's perception as a circular disc, journeying upwards from nothingness through the first, lower hemisphere of Sphere I; through Sphere II, still partly influenced by Sphere I; continuing its ascent through the upper hemisphere of Sphere I; progressing, with expanding awareness, through the rest of the spheres of contemplation, experiencing their symmetrical re-arrivals back into previous areas of contemplation, as happens to any thinker whose ideas flow into fresh spheres then return again to earlier thoughts.

Perhaps rather naïvely, I carried the circular concept through even to the choice of instruments, hoping to provide visual stimulae during the performance, as well as musical excitement and drama for the listener. Drums, having been used

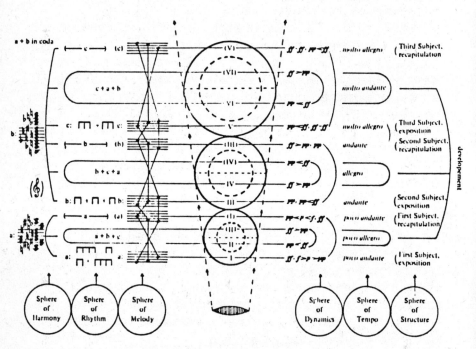

Listener's perception – starting point.

since pre-history to convey messages over distances, being also circular in form, seemed ideal as the dominant force in the instrumental make-up of the orchestra. Three percussionists, each with four drums, were placed around the outside of the platform, arranged so that the sound would constantly orbit the orchestra, clockwise or anti-clockwise. Four brass soloists, their instruments of course with circular bells, were to stand as soloists at the centre front of the platform. When the work was televised from the (circular) Royal Albert Hall in the 1978 Promenade season, the Television Director, Peter Butler, made brilliant use of every circular or spherical symbol he could find within the auditorium.

Circles were again the key to my next, sixth symphony, *Sinfonia Mistica*, where I drew upon the phenomenon that it takes six circles precisely equal in size to encircle a seventh circle of the same size:

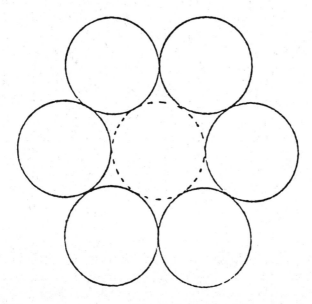

Probably some quite earthy mathematical formula would explain what to me seemed a sheer visual miracle. I was unendingly intrigued by the apparently mystical significance of these circles, which struck me as a potent symbol of inner harmony.

Perhaps in this work (commissioned by the Northern Sinfonia for Christopher Seaman), I allowed my fascination with geometric coincidence to dominate my intention to communicate with the performers and the listeners: I felt when I heard the first performance that I might have gone too far in allowing intellect to outstrip intuition. I noted to myself that I should never, under any circumstance, allow the technical side of composition to become an end in itself, but that I should always humbly seek to find the truest possible balance between feeling and intellect, heart and brain.

I think that I came nearer to achieving this balance in *Metasinfonia*, my seventh symphony, composed a year later for the Manchester International Organ Festival for Geraint Jones (who had also commissioned my *Song to the Virgin Mary*). Scoring the work as a rather dramatic duo between the solo organ and the timpani with string orchestra, in my imagination I was using a double helix as a ground plan, the first half of the symphony spiralling towards the centre, the second concentrically and symmetrically working its way outward again.

About then, I also wrote, for Peter and Meriel Dickinson, my *Dreamscape*, using Meriel's rich, warm voice predominantly as a musical instrument, with no words. In composing this work, I was trying to express the unconscious 'language of the soul', the mystery of dreams. Searching for different musical textures and seeking the extremes of emotional and poetic elements, I made use of quarter tones combined with my three-note cells.

In 1979, to my greatest delight, I was asked to compose a special piece for the London Symphony Orchestra's seventy-fifth Birthday Gala Concert 'at the wish of the players'. Orchestral players are famously hard to please, so I took this commission as the greatest compliment and decided to pay them a compliment in return, by composing them a special work which they could play without the dictatorship of a conductor. In recognition of their virtuosity, I intended not to make the task too easy for them.

Surprisingly, the rehearsals were more unnerving and tense than the actual performance, when the hundred-strong band played together with the brilliance and precision of the finest string quartet. The concert was attended by a glittering and appreciative audience including the Prince of Wales.

Afterwards at the orchestra's party, the ex-Prime Minister, Edward Heath, who had ambitions as a conductor, saltily complained in his speech that it was becoming even harder for him to get his hands on the baton when soloists such as Vladimir Ashkenazy (who played that night) were taking over the rostrum, and worse still, composers were writing music which needed no conductor at all.

Prince Charles also remarked upon my conductorless music, saying that he appreciated it as a pleasing symbol of democracy in Britain!

This event was a climax to a very happy and satisfying decade. Never in my life before had I been able to write so much music. The domestic front was calm and satisfying, seeing our two babies growing into adorable small people, manifesting not only great warmth, but a strong sense of humour and marked creativity.

Roxanna, initiated into music by Leopold Stokowski, appeared to have responded to his influence. Aged three, watching television, she witnessed our old friend, Ida Haendel, playing the Brahms Violin Concerto, and came rushing to her mother, crying, 'I want a violin with a stick to make it sing!' We found her a one-eighth size Japanese violin and discovered a teacher of the Suzuki method long before it had caught on in England. But Roxanna refused to follow Suzuki and learn the essential *Twinkle, twinkle little star*. She wanted to play the Brahms Concerto with an orchestra. Nothing else would do for her. She was too young to conceive that first things had to come first, and would rush to the radio, fiddling with the knob till she found an orchestra at full tilt; then she would pick up the tiny violin, with a beatific expression on her face and try to play her approximation of the Brahms Concerto (on open strings). Her first music lessons were a total failure.

Jeremy's talent from an extremely early age was unmistakably in drawing, with an alarmingly accurate eye for detail. In his first term at school, the teacher told all the children to draw pictures of their mothers. While all the other four-year-olds produced the normal infantile concept — a huge face and stick-like arms – Jeremy drew a quirky but convincing frontal nude, greatly embarrassing the kindergarten teacher.

Though we never forced music on the children, Roxanna was always improvising her own harmonies on the piano and later took up the flute, showing rapid promise; and Jeremy, with his touching treble voice (and perfect pitch) joined his school choir, performing semi-professionally in choral concerts at the Albert Hall and elsewhere. In due course, his choir-master, Michael Stuckey, recorded *Thames Pageant* for young singers and players on the Unicorn label, with the two dedicatees of the cantata taking active parts in the recording; Roxanna on the flute and Jeremy in the choir.

Despite domestic responsibilities and continuing to write all my letters, Camilla somehow carried on with her books, several of them designed to overcome children's fears or worries. Amongst others, she wrote a story about a child's stay in hospital, using photographs of real children in a hospital ward to help prevent fears of the unknown. Then she received an academic research grant from the Nuffield Foundation to produce a book that would help ordinary children to understand how it felt to be handicapped, and that handicapped children also could identify with and enjoy. Later, with Kenneth MacMillan's encouragement, she produced a book, *Life at the Royal Ballet School*, illustrating the toughness and challenge of the life of emerging dancers, published in Japanese as well as other languages. When our dog had puppies she photographed the birth and subsequent developments for an educational book, which was published in seven countries.

She was frequently almost overwhelmed by paperwork, which seemed to grow mountainously as a result of her administrative committee work for the Save the Children Fund, while in a voluntary capacity she continued to take photographs for them and for numerous smaller children's charities. Her only fault so far as I could see was that, with my correspondence, her books and everything else she was doing, every inch of her office, especially the floor, was covered in such a quantity of paper that it always made me giddy to see it. It seemed a miracle to me how she seemed to run a successful career without stinting on care for myself or the children; also cooking;

making clothes; digging the garden; growing marvellous fresh fruit and vegetables and keeping highly productive hens.

Absorbed in my work and my family, I was not aware of a marginal easing of censorship in Poland. However, in 1977, an employee of the Polish censorship office made his escape to Sweden, smuggling out some official documents which were published in the West. On the printed list of proscribed and almost proscribed non-people which was a required reference for all editors of Polish newspapers and journals, my name featured with eleven others including Czesław Miłosz (later a Nobel Prize winner), showing that a slight relaxation was now to be permitted from the total ban on printing our names. We could still only be discussed mainly in professional journals: '. . . in scientific and specialist publications it is permitted to mention the name and the creative activity. . . .It is not allowed to over-praise the creativity of these persons or to represent them in too favourable a light.' Outside the specialist press, editors of organs for the general public had to be even more careful: '. . . One must eliminate the name or titles of their works from articles in the daily press, radio or television, unless accom-panied by critical information.'!

It was against this almost impossible background that a group of composers and musicologists, mostly of the younger generation and therefore strangers to me, started their coura-geous struggle to get my music performed once more in my native land. Finally, after being banned for 23 years, my musical voice was heard again in Poland with a performance of my *Universal Prayer* in the Warsaw Autumn Festival of 1977. I was deeply touched by the efforts of my colleagues who had fought on my behalf. The following year, Józef Patkowski, the new Festival director, requested that the visiting Scottish National Orchestra perform my *Sinfonia Sacra* which, ac-cording to reports, was received with tremendous emotion. For a while, public hearings of my music were permitted only at the Warsaw Autumn, an international event, which was advanta-geous for the authorities in that people stopped asking them awkward questions about banned composers. Then gradually enthusiastic and friendly performers managed also to slip my compositions into programmes of provincial Polish orchestras.

Every year since 1977 at least one work of mine has been included in the Festival, and now many of my younger compatriots afford me great pleasure by visiting our home when they can get to London on musical business.

At the end of the 1970s, however, I was deeply wrapped up in my geometrical experiments, with another commission from the London Symphony Orchestra urgently awaiting my attention; Poland still seemed very remote. It was not until the the following decade that I found myself once more turning musically back towards my native land and feeling again the pull of my origins.

26

ACCELERANDO

The 1980s began auspiciously with a telephone call across the Atlantic from the Boston Symphony Orchestra, requesting that I should compose a work for their Centennial celebrations. Unable to imagine any greater stimulus than to compose for this magnificent American orchestra, I immediately agreed.

Before I could start, I had already on my plate some interesting commitments. Accepting a new commission is always a euphoric experience and I spend happy moments after signing an agreement dreaming of how I can make the most of each particular opportunity. However, I always resist the temptation of tackling the fresh project until any current undertaking is safely completed. I do not like to involve myself with several compositions at once.

So for a long time the promised piece remains a pleasurable future challenge. Then suddenly an alarming moment arrives, when I come face to face with blank manuscript paper, often with a deadline roaring towards me.

That early stage in the creation of a new work is for me the hardest. Everything has to be imagined and worked out in my head before a single note is put on to paper. Here my geometry is a great help, providing as it can an unseen framework around which I can organise my notes, my thoughts and feelings. Sometimes an idea comes at once; sometimes this chrysalis stage takes weeks, even months. I just think and plan, keeping to my daily discipline, going to my studio from nine in the morning till seven in the evening, either sitting silently, or experimenting with new harmonies and new sound combinations at the piano. Most days I continue my efforts as I go for walks along the River Thames, my mind totally abstracted in my search for a new musical architecture and climate, which I try to make different for each successive work. At these times, I am so absorbed in my patterns of emerging sound that, apparently, I stride straight past and stare right through my Twickenham friends and neighbours, who by now understand and do not take offence.

Once the structure of a new work is clear to me – once I know where I am going – I roughly sketch the whole outline in pencil and the first important stage of creative work is over. Every note, every sound-combination, whether for symphony orchestra or small ensemble, is safely in my head. Now follows the hard manual labour – literally hard: when I come into the house in the evening my wrist is aching.

Even when I am composing for a large symphony orchestra – say twenty instrumental parts – because the whole work is clearly mapped out in my imagination I write the full score immediately as the composition will sound, unlike many composers who write a kind of piano reduction and orchestrate later; and perhaps this gives me the advantage that from the very beginning I conceive the music symphonically.

People often sympathise with creative artists about being subjected to deadlines; I find them stimulating. All my first four commissions in the 1980s were composed against deadlines.

The first was *Concertino* for timpani, percussion and strings, a test piece for the Shell-LSO competition for percussion players, a pleasing commission not only because I always enjoy working for young performers, but because percussion has been important to me since my year of study at the Warsaw Conservatoire at the age of seventeen. The *Concertino* had to be for two soloists, one on timpani only, the second playing all the other pitched and unpitched instruments. To make it a true test of musical interpretation as well as rhythmic precision, I took a fresh look at the potential of the wide range of instruments involved, emphasising, especially in the timpani part, the expressive, even singing qualities wherever possible, as well as the drama and excitement that only percussion can provide.

Coincidentally, just as I had started to write this *Concertino*, André Previn asked me to write a percussion concerto for the brilliant timpanist in his USA Pittsburgh Orchestra, and I regretfully had to refuse because I did not feel able to write two percussion concertos in rapid succession. Previn forgave me, not only superbly conducting the world première of the *Concertino* with the London Symphony Orchestra and the two young winners of the competition, but also performing the work shortly afterwards in Pittsburgh with his percussion soloists.

Since then, the *Concertino* has been performed not only by students but by leading percussion players both sides of the Atlantic. It was used again for the Shell-LSO competition in 1984, producing as outright winner the talented Evelyn Glennie, who gave a faultless and thrilling interpretation of the percussion part despite being totally deaf, a phenomenon of which I was completely unaware until after I conducted the finalists' performances with the LSO, and had voted for her as the best performer!

Next I plunged into writing a string quartet for the North Wales Festival. It was commissioned at least a year in advance, but my start was delayed, and I found I had an unnervingly short time in which to complete the piece. This urgency was all the more apparent to me because, when commissioning the work, William Matthias warned me of the shortage of accommodation in the cathedral city of St Asaph where the Festival was based, and advised me to make my reservation immediately. It is the only time in my life I have booked a hotel room for a first performance before even putting a note on paper – several months before . . .

Whereas in the *Concertino*, I had looked back to my experiences of studying percussion at the Warsaw Conservatoire, now, in my new quartet, I caught myself delving even deeper back into my childhood, to when I was on holiday in the country at the age of seven or eight, and made the enthralling discovery that, putting my ear to the wooden telephone poles, I could hear curious, magical sounds made by the wires vibrating in the wind. It seemed to me then that I was listening to real music; it was my earliest experience of the creative process, the

337

first time I made use of my musical imagination.

I decided now to draw upon those childhood fantasies, allowing them to suggest to me both the design and musical material of the quartet. I gave the work a sub-title 'Messages', and created a musical language almost like a secret code, as if perhaps the messages were written not with words, but with squares (four-note cells) and triangles (three-note cells). The quartet began from total silence just as when my ear was placed against the apparently lifeless wood, through to a hardly audible chord, gradually transforming into melodic lines, which wove throughout the work with various shades of expression, conveying to the listener, I hope, some of the mysterious messages which I used to overhear. The première took place in the small wood-lined cathedral of St Asaph with its perfect acoustics, splendidly executed by the Gabrieli Quartet who gave many more performances afterwards.

My third work that year, *Paean for the Eightieth Birthday of Queen Elizabeth, the Queen Mother*, was distinguished by having the longest title but being the shortest work that I had ever written. This was not for lack of respect for the Queen Mother, for whose warm and beautiful smile I would gladly have written an entire symphony, but because I was under orders from the organisers of the Royal Concert to be brief and to the point. The *Paean* was performed from the heights of the Royal Albert Hall by the brightly uniformed brass players of the Royal Military School of Music, with gaudy banners hanging down from their trumpets. It was a resplendent and cheerful occasion presided over by Princess Alexandra. A private performance took place a few days later at the Royal College of Music in the presence of Her Majesty, so that I was privileged to be introduced to her and to experience myself that wonderful smile.

At last in August 1980, my desk was clear of my previous commitments and I could start to think about my symphony for Boston. It was quite an awesome prospect to be following in the footsteps of Stravinsky and Bartók.

Just as I started to plan my work, dramatic events were taking place in Poland. The shipyard workers in Gdańsk courageously broke the law against strikes, demonstrating, in defiance of the Security Police, in the cause of justice and human dignity. I was moved by their outcry as well as appreciating the irony that the labourers themselves had risen against the so-called 'United Workers' Party'.

As the strikers marched they painted on their banners and wore in their lapels the image of the famous Black Madonna of Częstochowa, who has always been the sacred symbol of independent Poland. Through the centuries, Poles have prayed to the ancient icon of the Madonna and taken to her a great wealth of votive offerings, especially in times of national crisis when their country was threatened by foreign invasion. Artists, poets and painters too have contributed their work as votive offerings. With a surge of optimism I thought that, through the will of my oppressed countrymen, change might at last be achieved in Poland: I decided to write the new symphony as my own votive offering to the Black Madonna, joining my voice to the strikers' by invoking her aid on their behalf.

The ikon of Our Lady of Częstochowa has always been reputed to have supernatural protective powers; according to tradition it was painted by St Luke on a piece of cypress wood used as a table top by the holy family in Nazareth. It was brought to Poland some 600 years ago by way of Byzantium, and is still preserved at the Monastery of Jasna Góra (where my parents were married). Throughout my childhood, a large reproduction of the ikon hung in our home in Warsaw. Wherever I stood in the room, the Black Madonna always seemed to be looking straight at me – my home was very much in my mind while I was composing *Sinfonia Votiva*.

Another moving event took place that year which helped to bring me much closer to my native land again. During the time that the Solidarity supporters were successfully putting the Polish Government under pressure, ordinary Polish people momentarily enjoyed greater freedom and it suddenly became easier to obtain a passport to travel abroad. At last, in an extremely exciting reunion, I was able to see my niece, Ewa again, and to meet her husband, the talented sculptor Jacek Dworski. With their son, Mateusz, almost exactly the same age as our Jeremy, they came for Christmas, and we merged happily as a family as if we had always been close together. Ewa by then was a very successful ceramic artist. She instantly got on with Camilla. We did not realise as we waved goodbye at the end of an extraordinarily happy visit that within the year martial law would be imposed and that their new-won comparative freedom would be curtailed.

In the twelve months which I took to compose *Sinfonia Votiva*, Poland remained in an explosive state, and, as I completed the symphony the following August, the men, women and children of the Polish cities were beginning a series of determined hunger marches. Though I could not walk shoulder to shoulder with my compatriots, I felt at least I could join with them through my music.

The symphony was intended as a prayer, a votive offering, containing no literary reference to the events. Once more I used a geometric device to hold the work in unity: circles again, since they were so characteristically a compositional element in the early Byzantine icons. As it was my eighth symphony, I also divided the work into eight sections: four 'circles' of sound in the first movement, four in the second.

After the Boston première, many people approached me saying how they themselves interpreted my intentions. They read a variety of ideas into the music which certainly had not been consciously intended, but which quite possibly could have emerged through my subconscious, just as had happened almost forty years before with *Tragic Overture*. For example, some listeners found the sound of tubular bells like a distant echo of bells from the monastery where the icon is preserved. Others found the use of powerful unpitched metal percussion like an echo of the clanging and clattering of metal pressing at the shipyard in Gdańsk. Neither idea had occurred to me while working, because for me the work was abstract rather than pictorial, but I am always content if different people find their own personal interpretations of my music.

It was also suggested that my *Sinfonia Votiva* was 'prophetic' because, though it builds up at the end into a ferocious climax, it does not finish triumphantly with the conventional resolution of the musical medium into a major chord, but rather ends on a kind of musical question mark, highly dissonant and disturbing in the last bars.

However, I am no political prophet or pundit. I completed the symphony in August 1981, about four months before the imposition of martial law in Poland, still dreaming of new-found liberty for my native land. Possibly I unconsciously fore-saw the disastrous outcome, the tragic destruction of all the wishes and hopes of the people and the crushing of the Soli-darity movement, but my *conscious* intention was to create a kind of desperate supplication for Poland's lasting freedom, built up out of the growing urgency of my ardent petition to the Black Madonna. The meaning of the dissonant last chord in the symphony and its extremely extended reverberation, emanating from the metal percussion instruments, I intended as a shout of sheer protest which I imagined reverberating into the future until Poland finds her independence. Deeply inbuilt into my symphony is my faith that, one day, all prayer and all the votive offerings to the Black Madonna will at last be fully answered and that Poland will become free.

The Boston première in January 1982 was a great event for me. The orchestra was superlative, finer even than I had dared to imagine, the string sound magnificent, and all the instru-mental sections supreme. I was struck by Seiji Ozawa's genuine modesty and his will to perform the work as I required: no other conductor has invited me up from the auditorium to stay beside him on the platform throughout rehearsals. He gave three marvellous performances of the work, then recorded it for the enterprising Hyperion Record Company, together with another Boston Centenary commission, the Concerto for orchestra by the distinguished American master, Roger Sessions. Boston remains a most happy memory in spite of the freezing January weather and the frustrations of not having enough time to visit all the amazingly rich museums.

In the same year, I was privileged to hear another truly great American orchestra, Chicago, under the baton of Sir Georg Solti, in three thrilling performances of *Sinfonia Sacra*. Solti's performances were so exhilarating that they earned a standing ovation: my charming elderly neighbour became very excited, assuring me that in Chicago this was a most unusual response to a contemporary work.

Since Stokowski's retirement in the mid '70s, the American

scene had been rather quiet for me; but the Chicago and Boston performances drew attention again to my work and my next commission was an 'award' from the Koussevitsky Foundation. After the substantial *Sinfonia Votiva*, I did not feel ready immediately to approach another heavily scored composition, so I decided to write a large-scale work for just twelve solo string players, which could also perhaps be performed by the full string section of the orchestra – and I used an evocative idea which had been planting itself in my imagination for some time.

My *Arbor Cosmica* (Cosmic Tree) was a work which brought me great happiness and contentment during the many months I was absorbed in its composition. It grew organically out of my passion for trees, dating back from my childhood expeditions to the Warsaw park with my beloved grandmother. Still today I am entranced and comforted by the individual beauty of each tree; by the endless variety of shapes and colours. Always I find delight in watching the dance-like rocking branches in the wind, in listening to the song-like groaning and sighing, or the leaves rustling and whispering their mysterious secrets. Beauty, harmony, strength and order are the aesthetic qualities which seem to me dictated by the form and the life of trees: but they also communicate to me something much more than sheer physical presence. Beyond the aesthetic pleasure and sensual delights of appearance, touch or smell, trees seem to me to exude some mysterious power through their moods, and through their souls.

In transferring these thoughts and deep feelings into music, first I had to think of a structure for my work. Though my music, coming as it did from an earthbound, human conception, would have its roots in the ground, my mind kept coming back to the curious symbolic image of the cosmic tree, which in art and literature is often depicted upside-down with its foliage running into the earth, its roots stretching up towards heaven.

Again I used my own language based on cells, emerging from the notes C-D-E♭, which (see opposite) I imagined as the roots of the tree, out of which I caused to grow a further chain of cells (the same ones that I used in my previous works) which constituted the musical trunk of the tree, holding in unity and

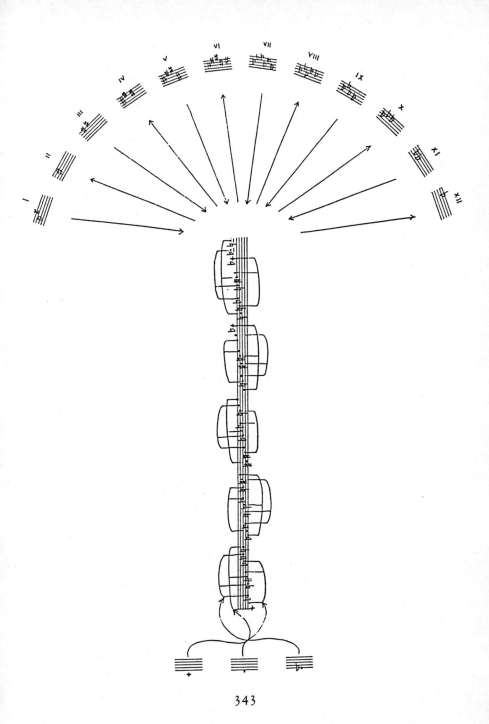

nourishing each of the twelve movements which I conceived as twelve branches.

The vivid first performance was conducted in New York to my utmost satisfaction by the rising American star, Gerard Schwarz, with the fine very young players of his Music Today Ensemble. Following straight on the US accolade, I returned to London, thrusting aside my jet-lag instantly to start rehearsing the same piece with our own splendid Ensemble of the Academy of St Martin's-in-the-Field for the British première at the Queen Elizabeth Hall, preceded by a BBC recording.

I gather from friends that the Polish première of *Arbor Cosmica* at the 1985 Warsaw Autumn Festival by Jerzy Maksymiuk and the Polish Chamber Orchestra was another extremely exciting event. Maksymiuk received the Festival's annual Orpheus Award from the Polish critics 'for his interpretation of several Polish works, especially Panufnik's *Arbor Cosmica*'. The prize, by glorious coincidence, was a sculpture by my niece Ewa's husband, Jacek Dworski!

I regret only that I could not be there to hear this prize-winning interpretation. After the performance, I was told that Maksymiuk lifted my score and held it up as a symbol of my presence, and apparently the audience responded with great emotion.

My presence in Poland meanwhile can sadly still be only in voice, through my music. Although I would love to walk again through the city of my birth, to see my ageing relatives before they die and meet again with dear old friends, my physical presence in Poland is hardly essential. It matters to me infinitely more that my musical voice is occasionally allowed to be raised in my native land. In what I compose, I stand right by my countrymen with all my heart.

Therefore perhaps it is not surprising that my Bassoon Concerto commissioned for Professor Robert Thompson by the Polish Community of Milwaukee, is dedicated to the memory of the recent Polish martyr, the young and fiery priest, Father Jerzy Popiełuszko, slaughtered by the Polish Security Police for his outspoken and defiant sermons on truth and justice by non-violent means; he preached not just humility and pure love, but that 'we should be free from fear, intimidation, but above all from the desire for revenge or violence'. Just as my Boston commission coincided with the birth of Solidarity, I found my-self by chance accepting this commission just at the moment of Popiełuszko's horrifying murder.

Apart from my deep emotional involvement with my subject matter, I was also particularly interested in the challenge of tackling a work for the bassoon. Wanting to maximise its evo-cative, rather modest voice, I decided on a small orchestra, pre-ponderantly strings, with just a flute and two clarinets, leaving the lower woodwind register to the soloist. I pushed aside any thought about previous compositions for this sometimes un-gainly instrument, which has been treated too often in a grotesque or comical manner as the 'clown of the orchestra'. In my own ears I heard its sounds as deep brown, velvet black. I imagined it singing dramatically, almost operatically.

Although the concerto was basically an abstract work with-out any literary programme, listeners, especially those with some knowledge of Father Popiełuszko's dedicated religious life and savage death, might recognise in my music just an echo perhaps of the priest's patriotic sermon, his humble prayer, or even his last, fatal interrogation by the Secret Police before his tortured body was thrown into the reservoir by the Vistula river.

As in my *Arbor Cosmica*, again I experimented with the use of tonal melodic lines in combination with a disciplined basis of three-note cells, with a hidden geometric structure as a back-bone to provide cohesive form. In the fourth section, the Aria, a kind of elegy, I composed a long melodic line in the spirit and character of Polish rustic music, perhaps evoking Father Popiełuszko's peasant origins. At first I thought of finishing the work on this sorrowful lament for the dead priest, but in dramatic terms this would have meant a pessimistic conclusion, of passivity and resignation. I decided therefore to add a spirited assertion in order to express musically the symbolic significance of the martyrdom, to assert positively my faith that, though his earthly frame had been destroyed, his spirit would live on indefinitely; it would unquenchably continue to influence the Polish people in their heroic struggle for truth and basic human rights.

In a moment of brief quiet between the American assignments (though due to lack of time, I was turning down a number of tempting commissions), one request for a short orchestral piece was irresistible. 1984 was declared Peace Year by the Greater London Council. Much criticised at that time for their extreme left-wing politics, they still saw fit to approach a composer who was anti-extreme-left-wing – in fact anti-extreme anything after a lifetime's experience of various forms of extremism. Their Arts Department suggested that they would like a work composed in the name of peace by someone who actually knew what war was about. I was touched by this proposal, and succeeded in putting behind me the pervasive Soviet misinterpretation of a great ideal, composing my *Procession for Peace* with the dedication: 'To peace-loving people of every race and religion, of every political and philosophical creed.'

I conducted the first performance of this work with the Royal Philharmonic Orchestra in front of an audience of 13,000 people, on a glorious August evening at a GLC outdoor concert by Kenwood Lake; and a rather damper second performance in the rain with the Philharmonia Orchestra, also by a lake, in the park of the Crystal Palace in South London a few weeks later.

In the same month, I also conducted my *Sinfonia Votiva* with the BBC Symphony Orchestra at the Promenade Concerts at the Royal Albert Hall, much to my delight, because I always particularly enjoy that young and enthusiastic audience.

One minor penance for the privilege of having contemporary music performances at the Proms is the custom for the composer, backstage in a small hall, to give an introductory explanation of his composition before he leaps on to the rostrum. No doubt these talks are of real help to the more searching members of the audience, and many composers genuinely enjoy holding forth about their intentions. But regretfully not me! Being rather shy and reserved, though I can cope with the still unnerving ordeal of standing up in front of an audience in order to conduct an orchestra, to make any sort of a speech is torture. I have gradually grown used to writing about my music for programme notes, and, according to my editor's wishes, have made the greatest efforts to expose in this book some indication of how I work. However, I still find myself battling against a deeply held conviction, that what I compose, and how I compose it, really belongs to my intimate, private musical kitchen. For all my efforts, it also worries me that anything I put into mere words must inevitably be incomplete. Art, literature, composition are the end-products only partially of rational or explicable craftsmanship; the essential core, the truly creative factors, rely on the elusive and inexplicable materialising of the artist's intuition, a process which defies verbal definition.

When someone asked Beethoven what he meant in one of his compositions, he simply sat at the piano and played the composition a second time. I long also to say, 'Don't ask me how this music materialised. Just listen to it, share the experience of my creativity through instinctive response rather than intellectual analysis.'

Professionally it harms me as a composer that I cannot find it within myself to lecture in universities, to teach, to hold forth on every imaginable occasion. Nowadays those activities are part of the essential activity that surrounds my most highly successful colleagues.

The sight of a microphone with an interviewer behind it paralyses me with recollections of being held at pistol point, or of Stalinist times when any word we spoke before visible or invisible microphones could be taken down on tape and twisted when used in evidence against us.

In New York and Boston, before the première of my *Sinfonia Votiva*, I underwent seventeen press, radio and television interviews, which was important in terms of publicity, but in human terms I found agonising. I also visited various universities, but there I was saved by my good friend Bernard Jacobson, who lectures for me with consummate skill and who has a great feeling for what my music is about.

People also often want to know what I think about the other living composers; but this, as my old friend Nadia Boulanger used to say, is the territory of gossip, which I do not personally enjoy, especially where I cannot with true honesty speak positively: I dislike beyond anything to write or talk unfavourably about others.

For example, I recently encountered a violinist from a London orchestra who had just come from rehearsing a contemporary work by a leading avant garde composer. This work, he told me, consisted of thousands if not millions of notes. The composer gave numerous written instructions in the orchestral parts: when to perform, what and how to perform, whether to hit the instrument or actually to play it. During the rehearsal the players became extremely irritated and frustrated by the complexity and contra-musicality of their instructions. So they turned their boredom into making fun of the piece: during the rehearsal some instrumentalists played completely different notes to those written in their parts, some omitted whole passages, and others carried on playing where they should have been silent. Neither the distinguished conductor, a specialist in contemporary music, nor the famous composer, who was present in the auditorium, noticed the mistakes or even sensed the orchestra's rebellion.

In the eyes of experienced orchestral players, the emperor is easily naked. The violinist asked me, 'Now tell me, Maestro, you should know, is this music?' I disappointed my orchestral friend with a diplomatic non-committal answer, not wanting personally to criticise my colleague.

We need a rich and varied musical repertoire and every school of compositional thought has its virtues and intellectual justifications. For myself, I continue my quest for clarity and transparency in my scores. I never was tempted by the trend to construct music of such density and intellectual complexity that even the finest musical ear cannot discern inaccuracies in performance. And just as I bypassed the now eclipsed fashion for dodecaphony, I also felt no urge to leap on to the bandwagon of aleatoric music: the element of chance is contrary to my passion for order which in my eyes is the intrinsic core of a viable work of art. For me, economy of means and my responsibility over each and every note I put on paper is crucial.

While maintaining my absolute independence, however, I try also to keep myself aware of where my more interesting colleagues are looking. Of late, I have been afforded an excellent opportunity to keep myself up to date on the works of many leading composers as a Jury Member of an international award, the Prix Prince Pierre de Monaco. In 1983, the Prince Pierre Music Foundation altered the formula of their annual music award. Instead of selecting individual works from younger composers, they decided to choose their Laureate from amongst the senior composers of the world, assessed for their entire output. I was co-opted on to the jury after finding myself the first Laureate of this new prize, which was very pleasurable, falling as it did precisely twenty years after I had won a previous Monaco prize with my *Sinfonia Sacra*.

Though some of the gimmicks encountered in scores and in tapes I have found painfully tedious, it has otherwise been interesting to study in depth and to appreciate the splendid intellects of some of my distinguished international colleagues. In the first year that I was involved in this judging, I found particular pleasure in pressing the cause of Sir Michael Tippett, and I was more than happy when he became the subsequent Laureate of the Monaco prize.

In 1984 I was privileged to experience gestures by two British orchestras who decided to celebrate musically my seventieth birthday: the Birmingham Symphony Orchestra most warmly invited me back for two enjoyable performances of my *Sinfonia Sacra*, while the exact date of my seventieth birthday had been booked up four years in advance by the ever-friendly London Symphony Orchestra, for a magnificent concert at their Barbican Hall where I conducted my Piano Concerto and *Sinfonia Votiva*; it was an immensely festive and heart-warming musical occasion which I value almost as much as any other in my life.

My highly supportive publishers, Boosey & Hawkes gave me a splendid party afterwards. A monumental birthday cake was produced with the first notes of the fanfare of *Sinfonia Sacra* as decoration on the icing, and I cut the cake standing there with my beautiful smiling wife and two extremely handsome, proud-looking teenage children. Just for a moment my mind swung back to my earlier loneliness, and all that I had undergone; then I looked round and saw not just my family but my friends from the orchestra, from my publishers and from throughout the musical world – even from the BBC! It was a warm and marvellous sensation. It had taken me perhaps until that moment to find that at last I was no longer an exile.

The following year I was honoured by another compelling commission. The Royal Philharmonic Society requested me to write a Symphony No. 9. Asking me to complete this work for their 175th Anniversary Season (1986-7), the members of this prestigious organisation rather alarmingly pointed out to me that their Society had also commissioned Beethoven's Ninth. They even suggested that I should write a choral symphony. However, though I decided that the symphony should have some uplifting message, perhaps expressing my faith and hope for humanity, with homage to Beethoven's ideal of the brotherhood of man, I could not (perhaps would not) find an ideal text to set to music: maybe my tenth symphony will be choral.

Meanwhile the urgent challenge of a ninth symphony has forced me to compose myself yet again. Because the date of the first performance surges all too fast towards me, I have to plunge back into my lifelong search, in music rather than words, and must now put a double bar line to these notes upon my life.

CHRONOLOGICAL LIST OF WORKS
PUBLISHED BY BOOSEY & HAWKES LTD, LONDON

Date	Title	Commissioned by	Dedicated to	Premièred	Recorded by
1934	PIANO TRIO reconstructed 1945		To the memory of composer's mother	1935 Warsaw	
1940	5 POLISH PEASANT SONGS reconstructed 1945			1945 Kraków	
1942	TRAGIC OVERTURE reconstructed 1945		To the memory of composer's brother	1943 Warsaw	Unicorn RHS 306
1947	12 MINIATURE STUDIES (piano solo)			1948 Kraków	
	NOCTURNE			1948 Paris	Columbia LOU 654 Unicorn RHS 306
	LULLABY (29 strings & 2 harps)			1948 Kraków	
	DIVERTIMENTO (on trios by Janiewicz – strings)			1948 Kraków	
1948	SINFONIA RUSTICA (Symphony No. 1)			1949 Kraków	Unicorn UNS 257
1949	HOMMAGE À CHOPIN (soprano & piano)	UNESCO		1949 Paris	
1950	OLD POLISH SUITE (strings)			1951 Warsaw	

Date	Title	Commissioned by	Dedicated to	Premièred	Recorded by
1951	CONCERTO IN MODO ANTICO (trumpet)			1951 Kraków	
1952	HEROIC OVERTURE			1952 Helsinki	Unicorn RHS 306
1956	RHAPSODY (orchestra)	BBC		1957 London	Columbia LOU 671
1957	SINFONIA ELEGIACA (Symphony No. 2)		To the victims of World War II	1957 Houston	Columbia LOU 624
1959	POLONIA (orchestra)	BBC		1959 London	
1962	PIANO CONCERTO	Feeney Trust	Rosa Berenbau	1962 Birmingham	
	LANDSCAPE (strings)			1965 Twickenham	Unicorn-Kanchana DKP 9016
	AUTUMN MUSIC (orchestra)		To the memory of Winsome Ward	1968 Paris	Unicorn RHS 306
1963	TWO LYRIC PIECES	Farnham Festival	To the memory of composer's mother	1963 Farnham	
	SINFONIA SACRA (Symphony No. 3)	Kościuszko Foundation	Tribute to Poland's Millennium	1964 Monaco	Unicorn UNS 257
1964	SONG TO THE VIRGIN MARY	Lake District Festival	Composer's wife	1964 London	
1966	HOMMAGE À CHOPIN (arr. flute & strings)			1966 London	HMV ASD 3633

Date	Title	Commissioned by	Dedicated to	Premièred	Recorded by
1966	JAGIELLONIAN TRIPTYCH (strings)			1966 London	
1967	KATYŃ EPITAPH (orchestra)		To the memory of 15,000 defenceless Polish prisoners-of-war murdered in Russia	1968 New York	Unicorn-Kanchana DKP 9016
1968	REFLECTIONS (piano solo)		Composer's wife	1972 London	
1969	UNIVERSAL PRAYER (cantata)		Composer's wife	1970 New York	Unicorn-Kanchana DKP 9049
	THAMES PAGEANT (cantata)	Richmond Borough	Composer's children	1970 Twickenham	Unicorn UNS 264
1971	VIOLIN CONCERTO (string orchestra)	Yehudi Menuhin	Composer's wife	1972 London	EMI-EMD 5525
1972	TRIANGLES (3 flutes 3 cellos)	BBC-TV	Composer's wife	1972 BBC 2	
	WINTER SOLSTICE (cantata)	Thames Chamber Choir & Orchestra	Composer's children	1972 Kingston-upon-Thames	
	INVOCATION FOR PEACE	Southampton Youth Choir & Orchestra	Composer's children	1972 Southampton	Unicorn UNS 264
1973	SINFONIA CONCERTANTE (Symphony No. 4)	Redcliffe Concert Society	Composer's wife	1974 London	EMI-EMD 5525

Date	Title	Commissioned by	Dedicated to	Premièred	Recorded by
1975	SINFONIA DI SFERE (Symphony No. 5)		Composer's wife	1976 London	Decca HEAD 22
1976	STRING QUARTET NO. 1		Composer's wife	1977 London	
1977	DREAMSCAPE (Mezzo-soprano & piano)	Meriel & Peter Dickinson	Composer's wife	1977 London	Unicorn UNS 268
	SINFONIA MISTICA (Symphony No. 6)	Northern Sinfonia	Composer's wife	1978 Middlesbrough	Decca HEAD 22
1978	METASINFONIA (Symphony No. 7)	Manchester International Organ Festival	Composer's wife	1978 Manchester	Unicorn-Kanchana DKP 9049
1979	CONCERTO FESTIVO (orchestra)	London Symphony Orchestra	Composer's wife	1979 London	Unicorn-Kanchana DKP 9016
1980	CONCERTINO (timpani, percussion, strings)	Shell-LSO	Composer's wife	1981 London	Unicorn-Kanchana DKP 9016
	STRING QUARTET NO. 2 'MESSAGES'	North Wales Music Festival	Composer's wife	1980 St Asaph	
	PAEAN		For the 80th Birthday of Her Majesty Queen Elizabeth, The Queen Mother	1980 London	

Date	Title	Commissioned by	Dedicated to	Premièred	Recorded by
1981	SINFONIA VOTIVA (Symphony No. 8)	Boston Symphony Orchestra	The Black Madonna	1982 Boston	Hyperion A 66050
1983	A PROCESSION FOR PEACE (Orchestra)	Greater London Council	To peace-loving people of every race and religion, of every political and philosophical creed	1983 London	
1983	ARBOR COSMICA (strings)	Koussevitzky Music Foundation	To the memory of Serge and Natalie Koussevitzky	1984 New York	
1984	PENTASONATA (piano solo)		Composer's wife		
1985	BASSOON CONCERTO (string orchestra)	Polanki of Milwaukee	To the memory of the Polish martyr, Father Jerzy Popiełuszko	1986 Milwaukee	
1986	SYMPHONY No. 9	Royal Philharmonic Society	Composer's wife	1987 London	

INDEX

Berkeley, Lennox, 271
  Symphony No. 2, 271
Berlin, 168–71, 322
  Polish Military Mission, 169, 170
Berlin Philharmonic Orchestra,
  166–67, 170–71, 266, 301
Bierdiajeff, Walerian, 39–40, 52
Bintley, David, 323–4
  Adieu (ballet), 324
Birmingham, 352
  Town Hall ('Hansom's Cavern'),
    264
  see also City of Birmingham
    Symphony Orchestra
Black Madonna, *see* Częstochowa
Blades, James, 317
Bliss, Sir Arthur, 244
  Piano Concerto, 244
Bloch, Ernest, 284
  Jewish symphonies, 284
Bogurodzica, 59–60, 284, 285
Bohdziewicz, Antoni, 144
Boosey & Hawkes, 252, 253, 254,
  255, 258, 261–62, 349, 351–55
Bordeaux, France, 177
Borodin, Alexander, 177
  Polovtsian Dances, 177
Boston, 340, 341, 347, 355
Boston Symphony Orchestra, 335, 355
Boulanger, Nadia, 54, 55, 156–57,
  160, 306, 347
Boulez, Pierre, 261
Boult, Sir Adrian, 269, 273
Bournemouth Orchestra, 320
Boyce, William, 90, 265
Boże Coś Polskę, 284
Brahms, Johannes, 54, 67, 71, 113,
  147, 270
  concertos, 8
  Symphony No. 2, 70–1
  Symphony No. 3, 170
  Violin Concerto, 29, 331
  waltzes, 114
Brazil, 303
  Rio de Janeiro, 303
Brighton, England, 165–66
British composers, 265
Bruckner, Anton, 68, 80, 320
Brussels, Belgium, 248, 301
Budapest, Hungary, 76–7, 192–94
  Hungarian Radio, 192–93
  Liszt Academy, 77
Buenos Aires, Argentina, 277, 302
Bush Alan, 181
Butler, Peter, 329
Byrd, William, 265

Cage, John, 261
Cannes, France, 88, 124
Carnegie Hall, 306
Cassou, Jean, 255
Cękalski, Eugeniusz (Polish film
  director), 61–2, 81
censorship, 149, 151, 242–43, 261,
  291, 306–8, 333
Chabrun, Daniel, 301
Chicago Symphony Orchestra, 302,
  341
Children's Hands at Play and Work
  (film; AP's music for), 190
Chile, 302
  Santiago, 302
China, 213–22
Chopin, Fryderyk, 43, 49, 85, 112,
  113, 147, 176, 189, 269, 276, 300
  Ballade in F minor, 149
  Etude in C minor 'Revolutionary', 62
  Etude in C sharp minor, 15
  Etude in F major, 62
  *Etude in G flat major 'On the Black
    Keys'*, 62
  Piano Concerto No. 1, 276
  Piano Concerto No. 2, 246, 247, 276
  piano studies, 62
Chou En Lai, 220
Chrapowicki, Wiktor, 19, 20–1, 50
Churchill, Winston:
  joke about, 124
  Soviet circus pig, 199
*Circle of Fifths, see Twelve Miniature
  Studies*
City of London Festival, 320
City of Birmingham Symphony
  Orchestra (CBSO), 263–69,
  270–73, 286, 301, 349
Clark, Edward, 186
Classical Suite, 35–6
Columbia Records. 351–52
Committee for Cultural Relations
  Abroad, Polish, 184
Committee for the Defence of Peace,
  Polish, 177–80, 227–28
  International Congress in Defence of
    Peace, Wrocław, 178–81
Committee of Verification, Polish
  ('Committee of Fools'), 146–47
Communist Party/Communism, 44, 84,
  94, 123, 144, 147, 172, 175–76,
  179, 183n, 184, 188, 198, 209,
  225, 228, 250, 268
Communist Youth Organisation, *see*
  ZMP
Composers' Guild of Great Britain, 307

Poland – *continued*
  Socialist Realism and architecture,
    190–91
  Russification, 188
  corrupt officialdom, 196
  health care, 206
  'psychological invasion' of, 208
  attendance at church/religion, 211,
    260
  enslavement by Soviet Russia, 242,
    282–83
  'Bloodless Revolution', 259–61
  avant garde music expressing 'anti-
    Soviet feeling', 260
  US indifference to, 282
  Millenium Year, 1966, 283–85,
    286
  National Anthem, 284
  AP's music performed again, 333
  Solidarity, 338–39, 340–41
  United Workers Party, 147, 339
  martial law, 340
Polignac, Princesse de, 157
Polish Army Film Unit, 144–46, 149,
  149–51, 155, 156, 159, 161, 164,
  189–90, 207, 211
Polish Chamber Orchestra, 344
Polish Daily (newspaper), 247
Polish Embassy, London, 233,
  236–37, 238, 308
Polish Radio Orchestra, 209
Polish Underground, 115; *see also* AK
  and AL
Polish Workers' Party, 183
Polonia, 269–70, 274, 309, 352
Pope, Alexander, 298, 312–13, 314,
  315
Popiełuszko, Father Jerzy, 344–45, 355
Poulenc, Francis, 85
Poznań Philharmonic Orchestra, 187
Prawin (or Levin), General, 169, 171
Preiss, Jerzy, 65
Preuves (magazine), 254
Previn, André, 337
Private Eye (magazine), 306
Procession for Peace, A, 346, 355
Prokofiev, Sergei, 36, 200, 223, 253
  piano concertos, 41
propaganda, 161, 179
Psalm, 51, 143
Pushkin, Alexander:
  and joke about Stalin, 189
PWM (Polskie Wydawnictwo
  Muzyczne – Polish State Music
  Publisher), 49, 154–55, 156, 205,
  211, 225, 253, 254

Queen's Hall, London, 91

Rachmaninov, Sergei, 304
  Piano Concerto No. 2, 246
Radio Free Europe, 244
RAF pilots, Polish, 132
Rainier III of Monaco, Prince, 293,
  301
Ravel, Maurice, 41, 82, 113, 158, 265
Redcliffe Concert Society, 353
Reflections, 311, 353
Regamey, Konstanty, 160, 230, 235,
  237–38, 239, 240, 241, 255, 259
Respighi, Ottorino, 41
RGO (Rada Główna Opiekuńcza –
  Central Council for Care) concerts,
  124–26, 133, 134
Rhapsody, 257, 261, 264, 309, 352
Ribbentrop, Joachim von, 94
Richmond Theatre, 317–18
Rimsky-Korsakov, Nikolay, 50
Riverside House, Twickenham,
  295–96, 298–99, 300, 303, 306
Roosevelt, President Theodore, 172
Rosé, Arnold, 78
Rota Konopnickiej, 285
Roth, Dr (Director of Boosey &
  Hawkes), 253, 254, 261–62
Roussel, Albert, 158, 265
Rowicki, Witold, 209
Royal Albert Hall, London, 246–47,
  332, 338; *see also* London:
  Promenade concerts
Royal College of Music, London, 338
Royal Festival Hall, London, 245–46,
  276, 305, 314, 320
Royal Military School of Music, 338
Royal Opera House, London, 91, 245,
  317, 324
Royal Philharmonic Orchestra (RPO),
  264, 266, 346
Royal Philharmonic Society, 247, 350,
  355
Rubbra, Edmund:
  Symphony No. 7, 265
Rubinstein, Artur, 39
Ruch Muzyczny (magazine), 184–85,
  202
Rudnicki, Marian, 204
Russell, Ken, 321–22
Russell, Shirley, 321–22
Rydz-Śmigły, Marshal, 94
Rytel, Piotr, 39, 46, 52, 161